CASTLE OF WOLFENBACH

Gothic Classics

CASTLE OF WOLFENBACH

A GERMAN STORY

Eliza Parsons

Edited with a new introduction by
Diane Long Hoeveler

Kansas City:
VALANCOURT BOOKS
2007

Castle of Wolfenbach by Eliza Parsons
First published in 1793 by William Lane
First Valancourt Books edition, November 2006
Second (revised) edition, July 2007

Introduction © 2006 Diane Long Hoeveler
This edition © 2006 Valancourt Books

ISBN 0-9777841-6-9

Published by Valancourt Books
Kansas City, Missouri
http://www.valancourtbooks.com

Parsons, Mrs. (Eliza), d. 1811.
 Castle of Wolfenbach: a German story / by Eliza Parsons ; edited
with a new introduction by Diane Long Hoeveler. -- 1st Valancourt
Books ed.
    p. cm. -- (Gothic classics)
 Includes bibliographical references.
 ISBN 0-9777841-6-9
 1. Germany--Fiction. 2. Kidnapping--Fiction. I. Hoeveler, Diane
Long. II. Title. III. Series.
 PR5127.P15 C3 2006
 823'.6

Set in Dante MT

Printed in the United States of America

CONTENTS

INTRODUCTION

Castle of Wolfenbach was published in 1793 and is an interesting example of what I would call an ideologically bifurcated female gothic, part liberal and cosmopolitan in its endorsement of liberty, equality, and fraternity, and part conservative in its sympathy for the rights of the patriarch (even the most egregiously violent, murderous, and abusive ones) and the native superiority of the British people. Its author, Eliza Parsons (1748-1811), is remembered today, if she is remembered at all, as the author of two of the books that Isabella Thorpe and Catherine Morland discuss as being "all horrid" in Jane Austen's *Northanger Abbey*. As Michael Sadleir pointed out in 1927, early critics of Austen assumed that the titles were fictitious until gradually all of them were discovered, some in only one surviving copy. This is indeed ironic, as in their day they were immensely popular and widely available, but printed on such poor quality paper that they literally disintegrated with over-use. All of the titles are now being reprinted by Valancourt Books with the intention that they should be rediscovered and taught along with Austen's *Northanger Abbey*, thereby setting the Austen title in its fullest gothic context.

The Author

What we know about Parsons has been summarized by Devendra Varma in his introduction to her other Northanger novel, *The Mysterious Warning* (1796). Born in 1748 to a prosperous Plymouth wine merchant, Mr. Phelp, Eliza was an only daughter and adequately educated for her day. She married a turpentine distiller named Parsons and moved to Stonehouse. The advent of the American Revolution brought financial ruin to Mr. Parsons, then working as a government contractor for the British navy, when two of his ships were seized by the colonists. The family sold their home in Stonehouse and regrouped in the London suburbs, building warehouses and storage facilities for the turpentine trade. In 1782 a fire destroyed the whole property, also wiping out goods that were due to be shipped imminently to America. This time the devastation was complete, and the husband and father of eight suffered a paralytic stroke and died three years later.

During this three year period their eldest son died while in military service in Jamaica, and Eliza Parsons was left as the sole support of her family. Like Charlotte Smith before her, she picked up her pen, and like Smith, lived to witness the early deaths of a number of her other children: another son in service off St. Domingo, a daughter who died in 1803, and her only surviving son in 1804, while commanding a gun boat at sea. From 1790 until her death in 1811, Parsons published over 20 novels (comprising more than 60 volumes), some less than mediocre (Varma, xv) and some "respectable performances" (Summers, 117). She was certainly popular in her own day, although the critics of her time castigated her grammatical errors (particularly her tendency to use "neither . . . or") and the lack of organization in her novels. As Varma notes, "the principal narrative is often splintered into different stories, and although the various strings of tales and sub-plots are entertaining and the attention is seldom permitted to flag, the reader's mind can at times experience *ennui*" (xi). In addition, given the speed with which she churned out works, there had to be and there were a number of errors in her writing, and in this particular novel, the ending seems to me less interesting and much more unnecessarily drawn out than the earlier sections. Given the desperate personal and financial situation she was facing at home, it is difficult to condemn her works. As Varma notes, "few female writers have had a sadder biography. Haunted by misfortune, and broken by a struggling career," Parsons died at the age of 63.

During her lifetime, Parsons was a deeply religious Protestant with a simple, child-like faith in the benevolent ways of an all-seeing Providence. As Sadleir notes, "no novelist was ever more pugnaciously Protestant" (22). In Parsons's religious scheme, the good are rewarded and the wicked are punished in this life. She also held conservative views on marriage, stating, "I have rarely observed through life that any union, contracted to a parent's disapprobation, has been fortunate or happy" (qtd. Varma, ix). Although she clearly did not support arranged marriages motivated simply by the desire to acquire title or property (as witnessed by the catastrophic events in *Castle of Wolfenbach*), she did support a father's right to make decisions for his children, and Matilda's defiance of her uncle is not an act that Parsons would have condoned (and indeed Matilda does pay a price for her rebellion). We would say now that Parsons was an advocate of companionate marriage, a union of two people who love and esteem each other, and have chosen to marry each other (rather than have their parents arrange the marriage to consolidate property). The evolving nature of the increasingly popular companionate marriage, as well as the rights of women, is certainly at issue here. As Stone has noted,

> in France [and England] in the second half of the eighteenth century there was some intensive propaganda, both in writing and in art, in favour of the affective family type, free marriage choice, marital love, sexual fulfillment within marriage—the alliance of Cupid and Hymen—and close parent-child bonding. [...] Despite this, however, there is strong evidence that the practice of marriage arranged by parents for material advantages was reinforced by the legal code of both the *Ancien Régime* and Napoleon's Code Civil. (390)

Whenever a culture is changing the nature of its basic unit of kinship (marriage and family), there is bound to be a tremendous amount of anxiety about the new arrangement, not to mention angst about displacing a system that had persisted for centuries. This anxiety results in what I initially called ideological bifurcation. On one hand, Parsons endorses the "old" ways, while on the other hand she is clearly sympathetic to reform and goes to great lengths in this novel to depict the abuses that can occur when fathers select completely unsuitable husbands for their completely dependent daughters.

We can make some other assumptions about Parsons's personal beliefs on the basis of her novel. In addition to her religious agenda and conservative ideologies about the sanctity of the patriarchal family, she was also blatantly nationalistic in her celebration of British superiority. For her, the British people had been blessed with a Constitution that was ratified by the 1688 Glorious Revolution, and this Constitution insured their rights and freedom under the legal and court systems. She further presents the bourgeois agenda in a number of statements throughout the novel that condemn gambling, over-dressed and gossiping aristocratic women, and lecherous and violently jealous aristocratic men. She goes so far to say in this novel that middle-class people are more attractive than aristocrats because they do not stay out late at night partying, drinking, and losing their looks. As Varma points out, she was strongest in depicting characters in the lower and middle classes of society rather than in describing aristocrats (xi), while her heroines are always young, innocent, and naturally elegant and her villains are "morose, savage, sneering, revengeful, jealous, and cruel. In their psychological make-up passion lies dormant, but once roused into action, it blazes forth in uncontrolled fury" (x). In short, Parsons was engaged in writing to the gothic formula that had been established already: part sentimental virtue in distress, part novel of manners, part melodramatic confrontation between good and evil. Although Parsons was no "feminist" in the line of Mary Wollstonecraft, she does share a number of what I have labeled elsewhere gothically feminist traits: heroines who manipulate their way into inheritances, all the while proclaiming their incompetence or vulnerability.

The Novel and its Contexts

Castle of Wolfenbach has been analyzed by Sadleir and other critics as an imitation German gothic novel, complete with a supposed German heroine and at times a setting in Germany ("supposed" because she turns out to be Italian). Styling itself as a translation of a work originally written in German, the book is of course completely British, but it reveals the vogue for all things Germanic in the 1790s. As Tompkins points out, "Germany soon rivalled Italy as the land of romance; by 1792 a heroine's accomplishments include German, and a year later the Minerva Press had discovered Central Europe" (290). Varma claims that the novel is most likely inspired by the adventure of the Duchess de C. in the French novel Theodore and Adelaide by Madame de Genlis (xii), originally published in 1782, and translated into English in 1783. Genlis stated in her footnotes that the story of a jealous husband who imprisoned his wife for nine years in a subterranean cavern without light was true and that she, in fact, had met the lady in question (Tompkins 273). Virtually everyone who has talked about Castle of Wolfenbach also claims that Radcliffe's novels A Sicilian Romance and The Romance of the Forest are also definite influences on Wolfenbach, and I would agree. One of the earliest discussions of the novel, Sadleir's, criticizes Parsons for being "too occupied with 'terror' and with Gothistic décor to allow herself much realism. Here and there she betrays personal pre-occupations or prejudice" (13), and by that I think he is referring to her rabid pro-British statements. More tellingly, Sadleir criticizes Parsons for what he calls her "coldly violent scenes of almost sadistic cruelty" and her "habit of giving deliberately trivial interpretations for pseudo-ghostly phenomena" (13). He places her in the school of Matthew Lewis, the school of horror rather than terror (contradicting his earlier statement, quoted above), and certainly there are a series of extremely bloody and shocking murders in this and her later novels that rival anything Lewis presented in *The Monk* (1796).

In approaching a female gothic text, the first order of business is to analyze the nature and characteristics of the heroine. Matilda Weimar is very much in the mold of other gothic heroines, particularly those of Radcliffe's early novels (cited above). She is beautiful, pursued by a lecherous uncle who intends to rape and then marry her, and she is of unknown or mysterious parentage. Her challenge in the novel is to discover the secret of her birth, find her parents, and inherit her rightful property. Much like Radcliffe's heroines, she must save a woman trapped in a "haunted" castle, she must find protectors and mentors, and she must negotiate to get a rival out of the way so that she can marry the man she loves, the Count De Bouville. Although she loves the Count, she cannot admit her feelings until her status as an aristocrat is ensured, and so her reserve and native modesty are continually tested, and because she is a heroine, she constantly behaves in an impeccable manner. Mellor has claimed that "women writers [of this period], denouncing sexual passion, urge their readers to embrace reason, virtue, and caution" (60), and such would be an exact description of the character of Parsons's heroine Matilda. She is the soul of reason in discovering the Countess of Wolfenbach, while virtue and caution mark her every move while she flees her uncle's embrace and finally marries the man of her choice.

The other characters in the novel are all stock types. The Count and Countess of Wolfenbach form one of the inset narratives here, the story of a disastrous arranged marriage that ends in murder and mayhem. The story is, of course, fantastic and quite implausible, but the "willing suspension of disbelief" necessary in reading fiction requires us to believe that such a situation (the eighteen year imprisonment of a wife by her husband) could, in fact, take place. The other inset narratives are equally extreme. Mother Magdelene's story is one of unrelieved tragedy and betrayal, and again serves to warn women that men are interested in only thing: their money. We also have the central narrative, the story of Matilda, her uncle, her parents, and the Count De Bouville, but this story splinters into the stories of Matilda's protectors, the Marquis and Marchioness de Melfort, and De Bouville's female suitors, Mademoiselle De Fontelle and Mrs. Courtney. In short, these narratives spin in and out of contact with one another and at one point we hear Victoria Wolfenbach's story told from three different points of view.

In addition to character and plot, Parsons's novel is interesting for its engagement with some of the major ideological issues of its time, the early 1790s. With the French Revolution raging and the guillotining of King Louis XVI in 1793, the situation in France was very much in the forefront of British consciousness. Many Britons were initially sympathetic to the overthrow of the King and his excessively extravagant wife, Queen Marie Antoinette. As the Revolution proceeded, however, its violence and horrors shocked the British and they turned against not only revolution, but even the notion of reform. Parsons is writing at precisely this moment. She is, in fact, caught between an attraction to France (as represented by the devoted hero De Bouville and the chivalrous mentor-father substitute the Marquis De Melfort) and a repulsion for its excesses (as represented by the odious liar and gossip monger Mlle De Fontelle). It is perhaps most accurate to see Parsons as part of a trend that Adriana Craciun has recently charted: cosmopolitanism.

As Craciun points out, many women writers in Britain subscribed to the principles of the French Revolution but filtered them through a celebration of the British constitution as it had been ratified following the 1688 Glorious Revolution. Craciun points out that these women writers "cultivated a radicalized cosmopolitanism through their engagement with French revolutionary politics" (1). The cosmopolitan ideal was ushered in as a result of the French Revolution, and it spoke to the need to promote a reform agenda in the face of counterrevolutionary, reactionary politics. To be a citizen of the world was to believe in the universalism of the Rights of Man, "Liberté, Égalité, Fraternité"—Liberty, Equality, Fraternity. But achieving such an ideal, nay utopian, goal is inextricably bound up with the features of an aristocratic tradition: primogeniture, a rigid class system, and inherent gender inequalities in the legal and political systems. As Parsons makes clear, for a woman like Matilda to be free, she would need to acquire autonomy, sexual agency, and economic independence in her own right. These she eventually does acquire, but only through the confession of her uncle, who ultimately holds all power over her life.

Although critics have tended to see *Castle of Wolfenbach* as a "sham" German gothic in the tradition of *Schauerromantiker* (German-horror-romanticism), most of the action takes place in Bath, scene of so much intrigue in *Northanger Abbey*. In addition to Bath, numerous scenes take place in Germany, Vienna, the French countryside, Paris, London, Nice, and Tunis. The characters are in fact constantly on the move, by horse, runaway carriage, or boat attacked by pirates. Despite the international nature of the varied settings, however, no one could doubt that the novel was written by an English woman of the middle class. A clear British nationalistic agenda suffuses the scenes set in England. The British are praised for their complexions, their court and legal systems, and their freedom from the notorious *lettre de cachet*. Gerald Newman notes that in addition to the pervasive cosmopolitanism that characterized Europe in the eighteenth century, the decades leading up to the French Revolution "also witnessed an awakening of national pride, a proliferation of national cultural institutions, and myriad attempts to excavate the foundations and define the type of the national self" (50). This "national self" for Parsons was characterized by honesty, sincerity, transparency, and virtuous self-possession. In contrast to the French, British citizens were praised for their rationality, their adherence and respect for the law, and their deeply religious practices.

Wollstonecraft was not above distinguishing British women from French women, noting that the latter were given to a lack of "personal reserve, and sacred respect for cleanliness and delicacy in domestic life, which French women almost despise" (70). Further, she notes that "in France the very essence of sensuality has been extracted to regale the voluptuary, and a kind of sentimental lust has prevailed" (70). The very negative portrait that Parsons draws of French women shows that, although she embraces some of the ideals of cosmopolitanism, she eschews the "French influence" which could be found in depictions of sexual license, excessive gossiping and rumor mongering, overblown displays of sensibility, and social disorder. Although cosmopolitanism had a natural affinity with French culture, in the final analysis it was largely an aristocratic phenomenon (witness Mary Robinson's poem celebrating Queen Marie Antoinette, "Monody to the Memory of the Late Queen of France"). Francophilia contested mightily with Francophobia in the hearts and minds of the British, and as the Revolution went on and the violent excesses piled up, British sympathizers with the Revolution became more and more scarce (and quiet).

Castle of Wolfenbach deserves to be more than a footnote to literary history, read and remembered only because its title is mocked in *North-*

anger Abbey. It can tell us much about the middle-class project in Britain during the early 1790s and it can tell us much about how the gothic novel evolved. I would not claim that it is a great novel. Instead, I see it as a historical document that speaks to us about the fears, beliefs, and prejudices of its era. As such it is an interesting text to study in relation to other gothic, sentimental, and melodramatic works of the 1790s. In a decade that saw the fall of a King and the rise of the Emperor Napoleon, this novel spoke about the attraction and allure of France and the French people to the British bourgeois imaginary. Unpacking that allure even today is an engaging exercise in literary archaeology.

DIANE LONG HOEVELER
August 9, 2006

ABOUT THE EDITOR

Diane Long Hoeveler is Professor of English and Coordinator of the Women's Studies program at Marquette University. She specializes in late eighteenth and early nineteenth century British literature and teaches courses in Romanticism and Gothic literature. She is the author of *Romantic Androgyny: The Women Within* (1990) and *Gothic Feminism: The Professionalization of Gender from Charlotte Smith to the Brontës* (1997). She is currently working on a forthcoming project, *Genre Riffs: Sentimental, Gothic, and Melodramatic as Cultural Discourse Systems, 1750-1850.*

WORKS CITED

Craciun, Adriana. *British Women Writers and the French Revolution: Citizens of the World*. Basingstoke: Palgrave Macmillan, 2005.

Hoeveler, Diane Long. "The Female Captivity Narrative: Blood, Water, and Orientalism." In *Interrogating Orientalism: Contextual Approaches and Pedagogical Practices*. Ed. Diane Long Hoeveler and Jeffrey Cass. Columbus: Ohio State University Press, 2006, 46-71.

———. *Gothic Feminism: The Professionalization of Gender from Charlotte Smith to the Brontës*. University Park: Pennsylvania State University Press, 1998.

———, and James D. Jenkins. "Where the Evidence Leads: Gothic Narratives and Legal Technologies." *European Romantic Review* 18 (2007), forthcoming.

Mellor, Anne. *Romanticism and Gender*. New York: Routledge, 1993.

Myrone, Martin. *Gothic Nightmares: Fuseli, Blake and the Romantic Imagination*. London: Tate Publishing, 2006, 166-67.

Newman, Gerald. *The Rise of English Nationalism: A Cultural History, 1740-1830*. New York: St. Martin's Press, 1997.

Sadleir, Michael. "The Northanger Novels: A Footnote to Jane Austen." *The English Association Pamphlet 68*. Oxford: Oxford University Press, 1927. Rpt. "All Horrid?: Jane Austen and the Gothic Romance." In *Things Past*. London: Constable, 1944, 167-200.

Stone, Lawrence. *The Family, Sex and Marriage in England 1500-1800*. New York: Harper and Row, 1977.

Summers, Montague. *A Gothic Bibliography*. London: Fortune Press, 1941.

Tompkins, J. M. S. *The Popular Novel in England, 1770-1800*. 1932; Rpt. Lincoln: University of Nebraska Press, 1961.

Varma, Devendra P. "Introduction" to Eliza Parsons, *The Mysterious Warning: A German Tale*. London: Folio Press, 1968.

Wollstonecraft, Mary. *A Vindication of the Rights of Woman*. In *Mary Wollstonecraft: Political Writings*. Ed. Janet Todd. Toronto: University of Toronto Press, 1993.

SUGGESTIONS FOR FURTHER READING

Blakey, Dorothy. *The Minerva Press, 1790-1820*. London: Bibliographical Society, 1939.

Colley, Linda. *Britons: Forging the Nation 1707-1837*. New Haven: Yale University Press, 1992.

Ellis, Markman. *The Politics of Sensibility: Race, Gender, and Commerce in the Sentimental Novel*. Cambridge: Cambridge University Press, 1996.

Frank, Frederick S. *The First Gothics: A Critical Guide to the English Gothic Novel*. New York: Garland, 1987, 271-72.

Grenby, M. O. *The Anti-Jacobin Novel: British Conservatism and the French Revolution*. Cambridge: Cambridge University Press, 2001.

Keane, Angela. *Women Writers and the English Nation in the 1790s: Romantic Belongings*. Cambridge: Cambridge University Press, 2000.

Neill, Natalie. "'the trash with which the press now groans': *Northanger Abbey* and the Gothic Best Sellers of the 1790s." In *The Eighteenth-Century Novel* 4 (2004), 163-92.

Stafford, William. *English Feminists and their Opponents in the 1790s: Unsex'd and Proper Females*. Manchester: Manchester University Press, 2002.

Thomson, Douglass H. and Frederick S. Frank. "Jane Austen and the Northanger Novelists." In *Gothic Writers: A Critical and Bibliographic Guide*. Ed. Douglass Thomson et al. Westport: Greenwood, 2002.

Todd, Janet. *The Sign of Angellica: Women, Writing, and Fiction, 1660-1800*. New York: Columbia University Press, 1989.

Varma, Devendra. *The Gothic Flame*. London: Barker, 1957.

A NOTE ON THE TEXT

The Valancourt Books edition of *Castle of Wolfenbach* is based on the first edition published by William Lane in 1793. A second edition followed in 1794, and the novel was reprinted several times during the nineteenth century, including an 1839 appearance in William Hazlitt's *Romanticist and Novelist's Library*. The most recent edition, published by the Folio Press in 1968 and edited by Devendra Varma, radically alters the novel's punctuation, apparently in an attempt to modernize it; this practice has not been followed for the present edition.

The first edition contains innumerable errors, both of punctuation (e.g., missing quotation marks, seemingly random and nonsensical commas) and of spelling (e.g., "desert" for "dessert", "meer" for "mere", and dozens of others). For the most part, these typographical errors have been silently corrected. Archaic spellings and punctuation have been retained, in order to preserve the flavor of the original, except where a minor change was necessary for clarity. Finally, it should be noted that Parsons spells the Countess of Marcellini's name in at least three different ways (Marcellini, Marsillini, Marsallini); all instances of this name have been regularized in this edition to Marcellini.

CASTLE OF WOLFENBACH;

A

GERMAN STORY.

IN TWO VOLUMES.

By Mrs. PARSONS,

AUTHOR OF
ERRORS OF EDUCATION, MISS MEREDITH, WOMAN AS
SHE SHOULD BE, AND INTRIGUES OF A MORNING.

LONDON:

PRINTED FOR WILLIAM LANE,
AT THE
Minerva Press,
LEADENHALL-STREET,
AND SOLD BY E. HARLOW, PALL-MALL.

M.DCC.XCIII.

Title page of the first edition (1793)

Castle of Wolfenbach

Volume I

CASTLE OF WOLFENBACH,

A GERMAN STORY.

THE clock from the old castle had just gone eight when the peaceful inhabitants of a neighbouring cottage, on the skirts of the wood, were about to seek that repose which labour had rendered necessary, and minds blessed with innocence and tranquillity assured them the enjoyment of. The evening was cold and tempestuous, the rain poured in torrents, and the distant thunders rolled with tremendous noise round the adjacent mountains, whilst the pale lightning added horrors to the scene.

Pierre was already in bed, and Jaqueline preparing to follow, when the trampling of horses was heard, and immediately a loud knocking at the door; they were both alarmed; Pierre listened, Jaqueline trembled; the knocking was repeated with more violence; the peasant threw on his humble garment, and, advancing to the door, demanded who was there? "Two travellers, (answered a gentle voice) overtaken by the storm; pray, friend, afford us shelter." "O! (cried Jaqueline) perhaps they may be robbers, and we shall be murdered." "Pho! simpleton, (said Pierre) what can they expect to rob us of." He opened the door, and discovered a man supporting a lady who appeared almost fainting. "Pray, friend, (said the man) permit this lady to enter your cottage, I fear she has suffered much from the storm." "Poor soul, I am sorry for her; enter and welcome," (cried Pierre.) Jaqueline placed her wooden arm-chair by the chimney, ran for some wood, and kindled a blaze in a moment, whilst Pierre put the horse into a little out-house which held their firing and his working implements, and returned with a portmantua to the lady. They had only some bread and milk to offer, but they made it warm, and prevailed on their guest to take some. The man, who appeared an attendant, did the same. The lady soon got her clothes dry, but she wanted rest, and they had no bed to offer. One single room answered all their purposes of life; their humble bed was on the floor, in a corner of it, but though mean it was whole and clean. Jaqueline entreated the lady to lie down; she refused for some time, but growing faint from exhausted spirits and fatigue, she was compelled to accept the offer; the others sat silently round the fire: but, alas! horror and affliction precluded sleep, and the fair traveller, after laying about two hours, returned again to the fire-side, weary and unrefreshed. "Is there any house near this?" (demanded she.) "No, madam, (replied Jaqueline) there is no house, but there is a fine old castle just by, where there is room enough, for only one old man and his wife live in it, and, Lord help us, I would not be in their place for all the fine things there." "Why so?" (said the lady.) "O! dear madam, why it is haunted; there are bloody floors, prison rooms, and scriptions, they say, on the windows, to make a body's hair stand on end." "And how far from your cottage is this castle?" "A little step, madam, farther up the wood." "And do you think we could obtain entrance there?" "O, Lord! yes, madam, and thank you too: why the poor old souls rejoice to see a body call there now and then; I go sometimes in the middle of the day, but I take good care to keep from the fine rooms and never to be out after dark." "I wish, (said the lady) It was possible to get there." Pierre instantly offered his service to conduct her as soon as it was light, and notwithstanding some very horrible stories recounted by Jaqueline, she determined to visit this proscribed place.

When the morning came, the inhabitants of the cottage set out for the castle. The lady was so much enfeebled, from fatigue and want of rest, that she was obliged to be placed on the horse, and they found it very difficult to lead him through the thickets. They at length espied a fine old building, with two wings, and a turret on the top, where a large clock stood, a high wall surrounded the house, a pair of great gates gave entrance into a spacious court, surrounded with flowering shrubs, which lay broken and neglected on the ground, intermixed with the weeds which were above a foot high in every part.

Whilst the lady's attendant lifted her from the horse, Pierre repaired to the kitchen door where the old couple lived, which stood in one of the wings, and knocking pretty loudly, the old woman opened it, and, with a look of astonishment, fixed her eyes on the lady and her servant. "Good neighbour, (said Pierre) here is a great gentlewoman cruel ill; she wants food and sleep, we have brought her here, she is not afeared of your ghosts, and so therefore you can give her a good bed, I suppose." "To be sure I can, (answered Bertha, which was the woman's name:) to be sure I can make a bed fit for the emperor, when the linen is aired: walk in, madam; you look very weak." Indeed the want of rest the preceding night had so much added to her former feeble state, that it was with difficulty they conveyed her into the kitchen. Bertha warmed a little wine, toasted a bit of bread, and leaving Jaqueline to attend the lady, she made a fire in a handsome bed-room that was in that wing, took some fine linen out of a chest and brought it down to air. "Dear, my lady, (cried she) make yourself easy, I'll take care of you, and if you ar'nt afeared, you will have rooms for a princess." Pierre and Jaqueline being about to return to their daily labour, found their kindness amply rewarded by the generosity of the stranger, who gave them money enough, they said, to serve them for six months. With a thousand blessings they retired, promising however to call daily on the lady whilst she staid at the castle, though their hearts misgave them that they should never see her more, from their apprehensions of the ghosts that inhabited the rooms above stairs. When the apartment was arranged, the lady was assisted by Bertha and laid comfortably to rest; she gave her some money to procure food and necessaries, and desired her servant might have a bed also. This the good woman promised, and, wishing her a good sleep, returned to the kitchen.

"God bless the poor lady, (said she) why she is as weak as a child; sure you must have come a great way from home." "Yes, (answered Albert, the servant's name), we have indeed, and my poor lady is worn down by sorrow and fatigue; I fear she must rest some time before she can pursue her journey." "Well, (said Bertha) she may stay as long as she likes here, no body will disturb her in the day time, I am sure." "And what will disturb her at night?" (asked Albert.) "O, my good friend, (answered she) no body will sleep in the rooms up stairs; the gentlefolks who were in it last could not rest, such strange noises, and groans, and screams, and such like terrible things are heard; then at t'other end of the house the rooms are never opened; they say bloody work has been carried on there." "How comes it, then, (said Albert) that you and your husband have courage to live here?" "Dear me, (replied she) why the ghosts never come down stairs, and I take care never to go up o' nights; so that if madam stays here I fear she must sleep by day, or else have a ground room, for they never comes down; they were some of your high gentry, I warrant, who never went into kitchens." Albert smiled at the idea, but, resuming his discourse, asked the woman to whom the castle belonged? "To a great Baron, (said she) but I forget his name." "And how long have you lived here?" "Many a long year, friend; we have a small matter allowed us to live upon, a good garden that gives us plenty of vegetables, for my husband, you must know, is a bit of a gardener, and works in it when he is able." "And where is he now? (said Albert.) "Gone to the village six leagues off to get a little meat, bread and wine." "What! does he walk?" "Lord help him, poor soul, he walk! no, bless your heart, he rides upon our faithful little ass, and takes care never to overload her, as we don't want much meat, thank God. But where will you like to sleep? (added she;) will you go up stairs, or shall I bring some bedding in the next room?" Albert hesitated, but, ashamed to have less courage than his mistress, asked if there was any room near the lady's? "Aye, sure, (answered Bertha) close to her there is one as good as hers." "Then I will sleep there," (said he.) His good hostess now nimbly as she could, bestirred herself to put his room in order, and was very careful not to disturb the lady. Albert was soon accommodated and retired to rest.

In the evening the lady came down into the kitchen, much refreshed, and expressed her thanks to the good woman for her kindness. "Heavens bless your sweet face, (cried Bertha) I am glad to my heart you be so well. Ah! as I live, here's my Joseph and the ass." She ran out into the court to acquaint her good man with what had befallen her in his absence. "As sure as you be alive, Joseph, she is some great lady under trouble, poor soul, for she does sigh so piteously, but she has given me plenty of money to get things for her, so you know it's nothing to us, if she likes to stay here, so much the better." "I hope, (said the old man) she is no bad body." "No, that she an't, I'll swear, (cried Bertha;) she looks as mild as the flowers in May." They had now unloaded their faithful ass, and entered the kitchen with their provender. Joseph was confounded at the appearance of the lady; he made his humble bow, but was very silent. Bertha prepared some eggs and fruit for her supper; she ate but little, and that little was to oblige the old couple; she then asked for a candle, and said she would retire to her room. Joseph and Bertha looked at each other with terror, both were silent; at length Joseph, with much hesitation of voice and manner, said, "I fear, madam, you will not be quiet there, it will be better, to my thinking, if a fire was made in one of the parlours and the bedding brought down." "There is no occasion for fire, (answered the lady) but merely to air the room; however I am not in any apprehension of sleeping in the room above, at least I will try it this night." It was with great reluctance the honest couple permitted her to retire; Bertha had not even the courage to accompany her, but Albert and Joseph offering to go, she ventured

up to make the bed, and her work finished, flew dow[n]
from great danger.

The men having withdrawn, the lady seated herself a[t]
table, and having opened her portmantua to take out som[e]
the ensuing day, she burst into tears on viewing the small qua[n]
necessaries she possessed; she cast a retrospection on her past ca[lami]
ties, they made her shudder; she looked forward to the future, all w[as]
dark and gloomy; she wrung her hands, "What will become of me,
unhappy as I am, where can I fly? who will receive a poor unfortunate,
without family or friends? The little money I have will be soon exhausted, and what is to be the fate of poor Albert, who has left all to follow
me!" Overcome with sorrow, she wept aloud. When, turning her eyes
to the window, she saw a light glide by from the opposite wing, which
her room fronted, and which Bertha had informed her was particularly haunted. At first she thought it was imagination; she arose and
placed her candle in the chimney; curiosity suspended sorrow—she
returned and seated herself at the window, and very soon after she
saw a faint glimmering light pass a second time; exceedingly surprised,
but not terrified, she continued in her situation: she saw nothing further. She at length determined to go to rest, but with an intention to
visit every part of the house the following day. She got into bed, but
could not sleep. About twelve o'clock she heard plainly a clanking of
chains, which was followed by two or three heavy groans; she started
up and listened, it was presently repeated, and seemed to die away by
gentle degrees; soon after she heard a violent noise, like two or three
doors clapping to with great force. Though unaccustomed to fear, she
could not help trembling. She felt some inclination to call Joseph, she
then recollected Albert was in the next room; she knocked at the wain-
scot and called Albert! No answer was made. She got out of bed, and
throwing on a loose gown, took her candle, and, opening the door of
the next apartment, went up to the bed; she saw he was buried under
the clothes. "Albert, (said she) do not be afraid, 'tis your mistress with a
light;" he then ventured to raise himself and though but little inclined
to mirth, she could not refrain from smiling at the fright he was in; the
drops of perspiration ran down his face, his eyes were starting, and he
was incapable of speaking for some time. "Pray, Albert, (said his lady)
"have you heard any particular noise?" "Noise," (repeated he) O Lord!
all the ghosts have been here together to frighten me." "Here—where,
(asked she) in this room?" "I believe so, (he replied;) in this or the next

score or two in chains, then there was
...am, leave the candle a minute at the
...s and get down into the kitchen and
...ell, but, Albert, (said she) I must stay
...e for fear than I have?" "No, madam,
...man, woman or child." "Then take
...candle, and, as I shall be in the next
...r open, you may either call to me
...ond time alarmed." It was with re-
...y desired the doors might remain

The lady retired to her room, for some time hesitating whether she should dress herself or go into bed, she at length threw herself down in her night gown, but could not sleep. Strange and various were her conjectures respecting the lights she had seen, and the unaccountable noises she had heard; she was not surprised that the weak minds of the old people should be terrified, or that Albert, who was likewise far advanced in years, above sixty, should shrink from alarms which had given her a momentary terror; but as she did not suffer her mind to dwell on the causes being supernatural, she conceived there must be some mystery which, on the following day, if her health permitted, she resolved, if possible, to explore. Towards morning she fell into a profound sleep, undisturbed by groans or noises of any sort.

Albert, who, by his terror and apprehensions of seeing those ghosts that had so greatly frightened him, was prevented from sleeping, got up the moment day appeared and crept down stairs, where he was soon after joined by Joseph. "How have you slept, my good friend?" (asked he.) "Slept! (replied the other;) "why, who could sleep, d'ye think, when chains were rattling, ghosts roaring and groaning, doors banging with violence enough to shake the foundation of the walls? Lord help me, I would not live in such a place—no, not to be master of the whole estate." "Aye, I knew how it would be, (said Joseph;) it's always the same business when any body comes here to sleep; we never hear any noise else." "Why, then your ghosts are very rude unsociable folks, (answered Albert) for strangers can do them no hurt, and there's room enough, methinks, in this great house for them to have their merriments, without coming to frighten honest travellers, that never desire to interrupt them." "I don't know how it is," replied Joseph, "but as to merriment, sure there can be none in groans and cries, and they do say that cruel wicked deeds have been done in this castle, and I suppose the poor souls can't lay quiet." "Dear me, (cried Albert) I wish my mistress may be well enough to go farther, though poor soul, she doesn't know where to go to, that's true." "Poor lady, that's bad indeed; has she no parents, nor husband, nor uncles, nor aunts, nor——" "Yes, yes, (said Albert, interrupting him) she has some relations, but what of that, better she had none, I believe for her—— O, here comes Bertha." On her entrance the good morrows and enquiries were repeated; Bertha expressed her sorrow for the lady, and immediately ascended the stairs to see if she was not frightened out of her wits by such a cruel disturbance.

She soon returned with the lady, and breakfast being quickly set before her, she endeavoured to eat, but her appetite was so indifferent as to cause great pain to the friendly Bertha.

Joseph mounted his favorite beast and repaired to the town, that he might procure necessaries for his family, superior to what he had bought the day before. After his departure, and that Albert was gone to look after his horse, the fair stranger demanded of Bertha if she could give her any account of the owners of the castle. "Why, madam, (answered she) the present lord of this estate is—aye, his name is Count Wolfenbach; he married a very handsome lady at Vienna, and brought her here; it was then a beautiful place, very unlike such as it be now; but howsomever they say he was very jealous, and behaved very ill to the poor lady, and locked her up, and there she was brought to bed, and the child was taken from her, and so she died, and 'twas said the child died, and so every body believes 'tis their ghosts that make such dismal noises in the castle, for soon after my Lord the Count went away, and Joseph, who worked under the gardener, was ordered to take care of the house; and I lived then under the cook, so we married: all the other servants were discharged, and so we have lived here ever since. My Lord came here once or twice, but the ghosts made such a noise he could not stay. Several gentry have slept here at times, but no body would stay a second night, and so we have all to ourselves by day, and the ghosts, or what they be, have got all the rooms by night and then they be quiet enough." "Pray, (interrogated the lady) can I walk through the rooms and examine the opposite wing?" "To be sure, madam, you can, if you be so bold, but neither I nor Joseph ever goes there, because that's the part where the poor Countess died." "How many years ago was it?" "Near eighteen, my Lady; for next Christmas we have been married so many years, and I was fifty-three and Joseph fifty-two when we came together; not very young, to be sure, what of that, we live very comfortable, only a little lonely or so." "Well, (said her guest) I shall be glad to walk through all the apartments." "I will attend you, madam, except to the other side, there I never goes."

After breakfast was over, the lady and Bertha walked up stairs; they went through several fine apartments, the furniture rich though old fashioned; one hung with family portraits she was particularly pleased with; two attracted her attention greatly, which Bertha told her, she had heard say, were the present Count and his late lady.

After going through the body of the house they came to the doors that led to the other wing: "Now, for goodness sake, dear madam, don't go no farther, for as sure as you are alive, here the ghosts live, for Joseph says he often sees lights and hears strange things." "My good friend, (replied the lady) you may return, but I certainly will look into those rooms." "O, pray good, your ladyship, don't go now." She persisted however in her determination, and on Bertha's leaving her she opened the door which led to a gallery, and a handsome stair-case, on the right hand she saw a suite of four rooms, all well furnished, two as bed rooms, one handsome sitting room, the other a library, well filled with books, in handsome cases; these two last rooms, she observed, exactly fronted the one on the opposite side, where she had slept. Having examined those apartments, she saw, on the other side of the gallery, two other doors; these, on trial, she found locked. She then returned and went down the stair-case; after the first landing place the windows were shut, and when she came to the bottom she entered a hall, in which were three doors; one she attempted to open, immediately a murmuring noise was heard, and the instant she opened the door, another at the end of the room was shut to with great violence. The lady for a moment stood suspended; she trembled, and deliberated whether she should return or not; but recovering resolution, she entered; a candle was burning on a table, the windows were closed up, there were books and implements for drawing on the table; this convinced her the inhabitants were alive, however, and going to the door, she said aloud, "Whoever resides in this apartment need not be under any apprehensions from the intrusion of an unfortunate woman, whom distress has driven to this castle, and only a melancholy kind of curiosity has induced her to explore a part of it proscribed by everyone."

She had scarcely uttered these words when the door opened, and a lady, attended by an elderly woman, appeared. Both started; but the visitor, in a confused manner, apologized for her intrusion. The other, taking her hand, placed her in a chair. "Perhaps, madam, (said she) this may prove the happiest day of my life, and I may rejoice that your curiosity and courage is superior to those terrors by which others have been intimidated." "At least, madam, you will do me the justice to believe (answered the lady) that I would not have been guilty of this intrusion, had I known these apartments were really inhabited, but be assured, madam, your secret is perfectly safe with me." "I do not doubt it, (replied the other;) your countenance is a letter of recommendation to every heart." She then ordered her attendant to bring some refreshments, which consisted of biscuits and fruits.

The woman being withdrawn, the lady of the house said, "However, madam, I may rejoice in seeing a female of your appearance, I cannot help lamenting that one so young should know sorrow, or be driven to seek an asylum in such a melancholy place as this castle." "I am indeed, madam, an object of pity, (replied the other) without friends, a home, or one acquaintance to sooth my sorrows. I have fled from oppression and infamy, unknowing where to direct my steps, or what will become of me." "Surely, (said the former lady) heaven directed your steps here, that we might communicate comfort to each other: griefs, when divided, become less poignant; I have known years of sorrow, yet I still support life in a feeble hope of one day being restored to happiness." "Alas! (replied the other) not one shadow of hope can I derive from either past or future prospects; and as I have intruded thus upon you, madam, it is but fit you should know who and what I am. I was born, as I have been told, at Fribourg, and lost both my parents in my infancy. My birth was noble, but my fortune very trifling. The first thing I can remember was a gentleman who I was taught to call uncle, an elderly woman his housekeeper, and a young girl attendant on me; we lived in the country, about three miles from any town or village. As I grew up masters were hired to attend me, and by their skill and my own attention, having nothing to divert my mind from my studies, I became tolerably accomplished at twelve years of age, when my masters were discharged. We received no company; a few gentlemen called now and then, but those I never saw. My uncle was exceedingly fond of me; his name was Mr. Weimar, mine Matilda Weimar. Our ancestors, he said, had been Counts, and persons of high rank and fortunes, but r and prodigality, they had been reduced to comparative poverty; ...fore it was fortunate for me he had never been married. I think I am naturally affectionate and grateful, yet I never felt any degree of either for my uncle; and, young as I was, have frequently taken myself to task when I found a repugnance to return his caresses. I devoted my whole time to my studies; my uncle, when I was about fifteen, having some property in France, was compelled, by the failure of a house, to go there in person; at first he talked of taking me with him, but changed his mind, and gave me in charge to his housekeeper and an old servant called Albert, with strict orders I should never go beyond the walks belonging to his castle. Nothing could exceed the tenderness of his behaviour at parting, and for the first time in my life I was affected; I returned his embraces and shed some tears. "Ah! Matilda, (said he) are you indeed sorry I should leave you?" "I am, indeed," (I replied.) "Then you shall go with me, (cried he, eagerly; but striking his forehead, he exclaimed,) No! that will not do; dear Matilda, my sweet niece, keep yourself retired, apply to your studies, I shall soon return, and, I hope, make you the happiest of women." I felt at that moment real gratitude and affection; I promised strictly to obey his commands, and by my endeavours to improve my mind, deserve his love and esteem. He quitted me with extreme reluctance, and for several days I found the want of his company and conversation, but by degrees I grew reconciled, and as Agatha and Albert were respectable and intelligent persons, for their stations in life, I made them both my friends and companions. This was really the happiest period of my life; I was capable of amusing myself with music and drawing, in the evenings I walked in the garden and adjoining wood with Agatha, returned with a good appetite, and slept quietly. My uncle remained in France near nine months, he constantly wrote to me, and I was punctual in my answers; at the end of that period he returned; I was overjoyed to see him, but the pleasure I felt and expressed fell very short of the rapture and transport with which he embraced and praised me; he dwelt on the improvement in my person with such delight, that I felt confused and uneasy; the attention which used to give me pleasure now was painful, and I repulsed his caresses involuntarily. He told me he had brought me a present of some books and drawings, both of which he knew would be acceptable to me; I acknowledged his kindness with an apparent gratitude, yet I was in reality but little thankful, though I could not account for the increasing coldness of my behaviour. After a hasty supper I retired to bed, notwithstanding his wishes to detain me, and after I was alone I began to reflect on my conduct, so cold and thankless, towards so kind an uncle, whose affection for me seemed greatly increased. I was displeased with my own reflections, and resolved to behave better to him the following day.

"The next morning I rose early; my uncle was not up, Agatha met me going into the garden. "My dear Miss, (said she) you were very shy and unkind to your uncle last night; the good man loves you dearly, and 'tis not your business to be shewing him such slights, I can tell you." Though conscious I was wrong I was amazed at the freedom of her observations, as she was not much in the room with us; I therefore made some trifling answer and pursued my walk.

"It was plain my uncle had taken notice of my coldness, and complained to her: I was mortified and vexed; after taking two or three turns I went into the house, and met my uncle in the breakfast room; I assumed the kindest manner possible in my salutations to him, and I saw he was highly gratified by it. He produced his books and drawings, the latter were very beautiful, but the attitudes and want of decent drapery confused and hurt me, for although I had never received any particular lessons on delicacy or modesty, yet there is that innate virtuous principle within us, that shrinks involuntarily from any thing tending to violate that sense of decency we are all, I believe, born with; I therefore could not examine them with the accuracy I wished, much less praise them, as I saw he expected. "Are they not exquisite pieces?" (demanded he.) "They are very fine drawings, I believe, Sir, but I think the subjects of them are exceptionable." "My dear girl, (he replied, laughing,) you know nothing of the world; whoever excepts against the subjects of drawings, or the attitudes of statues? 'tis the execution and proportions that attract our notice, and I assure you, my little prude, there is nothing objectionable in any point of view, in those drawings before you, nor in the books, which are now most in repute among the fashionable circles in France."

"Though my reason was not convinced I made no further scruples, but thanked him for his attention to my amusement, and, breakfast over, retired to my own apartment, having my presents carried there, that I might examine them at my leisure.

"From this time my uncle's behaviour was to me unaccountable, he was for ever seeking opportunities to caress me, his language was expressive of the utmost fondness, he praised my person in such glowing colours as sometimes filled me with confusion. In short, madam, not to tire you, within three months after his return I began to be extremely uneasy at freedoms I scarce knew how to repulse. One morning after dressing I went into the garden, a thing unusual with me at that hour, and going round a serpentine walk, which led to a summerhouse, I thought I heard voices there; I stopt at the back of it, which, as well as the front, had a door that opened into the garden, and plainly heard Agatha's voice, saying, "I tell you, Sir, there is no other way, send Albert off for a few days, or turn him off at once, for he loves Miss Matilda as if she were his own child, and therefore we must get rid of him; but you are so long settling your mind—get into her room at night when she's asleep, I'll take care nobody comes there, or tell her roundly at once you are not an uncle to her—I would not longer stand upon ceremony." "Well, Agatha, I'll take your advice, and dispatch Albert to-morrow, and the next night I will be happy." You may suppose, madam, I was scarcely able to support myself. Having heard thus far I tottered from the summer house, and got into the shrubbery, where I threw myself on the ground, and preserved myself from fainting by a copious flood of tears.

"Overwhelmed by my own reflections, without a friend or habitation to fly to for protection, uncertain whether this man was really my uncle or not, yet convinced he had the most diabolical designs against me, and that in his house I could not be safe: it is impossible to describe my feelings and distress; at length I arose and recollected what the horrid woman had said of Albert, it was my only resource. I walked from the garden towards the stables; most fortunately I met him coming from them. "Albert, (said I, hastily) I wish to speak with you, follow me into the park." The man looked surprised—"Me, Miss—I follow you?" "Yes, immediately," (I replied.) I walked quickly to the park, he came after me; when out of sight of the house I turned to him—"Albert, do you love me? are you willing to serve me?" "Aye, that I will, dear Miss, to the last drop of my blood." I then, without losing time, told him the plot designed against me, and what was determined with respect to himself. The good creature was struck dumb with surprise, but recovering himself, "By my soul, (cried he) I will save and serve you whilst I have breath, from such devils. My dear young lady be easy, I have a sister who lives at Lucerne, she will be proud to serve you; 'tis a long journey, but never fear, you can ride behind me, as you have often done in sport: I'll manage the business to-night, never fear—get up a little early in the morning and meet me here." We then concerted our whole plan, and I returned to the house with a lighter heart, and got to my apartment unobserved. I was soon after summoned to dinner; when I saw my uncle I turned faint, he flew to me with tenderness—"My dear Matilda, are you ill?" "Only a sick head-ach," (I replied, disengaging myself from him, and sitting down.) "I fear you have been reading too much." "Very likely, Sir; I shall be better by and bye," was my answer. I could eat but little, yet I tried to do it, and also to rally my spirits to avoid suspicion. When Albert was removing the cloth, "I have a great favour to ask your Honour." "What is it Albert?" (said my uncle.) "Why, Sir, I have got a sister married at a village near Lausanne, and the poor soul does so long to see me, that if you could spare me for a week, I should be mightily obliged to you?" "For a week!" (replied his master, pleasure dancing in his eyes) you may set off to-morrow and stay a fortnight, it cannot be less time, to give you any comfort with your friends." The poor fellow bowed his thanks and withdrew.

"I now exulted in our prospect of success in my deliverance: I grew more cheerful, my uncle was tender and affectionate; I bore his caresses without any repulses, but left the room soon as possible. I employed myself in packing up a few necessaries in a small portmantua, with what little valuables I had, and was tolerably supplied with money, as I thought, knowing little of the expences of a journey. I did not go to bed, and about four in the morning, when the whole house was buried in sleep, I took my portmantua, and with some difficulty carried it down stairs, opened the doors with the greatest precaution, and, to my no small joy, found Albert walking upon the green; he took my load from me, and, without speaking, led the way to the stables, fastened on the portmantua, and getting me behind him, we rode off as fast as possible. Previous to my quitting the room the preceding evening, I desired my uncle not to wait breakfast for me, as I believed I should scarcely rise sooner than ten, as I had not slept well the night before; I therefore thought we should have some hours start of any pursuit, and we proceeded on to Lucerne, the very opposite road from Lausanne, where Albert had asked permission to go to. After a tedious and painful journey we got safe to Lucerne. Alas! how great was our disappointment; this sister, on whose protection I relied, had been dead three weeks, and her little shop and stock given to a young woman who lived with her, and only a small legacy left to Albert. What now was to be done? The mistress of the house humanely offered me a bed for a night or two; vexation and fatigue compelled me to accept the offer: my poor fellow traveller was more affected than myself. We consulted what was next to be done; he then recollected he had a relation at Zurich, and proposed my going on there. He said it was a good city, and some way or other, doubtless, I might procure a living by my talents. Small as this hope was I had no alternative but to embrace it, and the next morning we pursued our journey; the day before yesterday was the second day of our travelling from Zurich. The storm came on just before our entrance into the wood, we took shelter for some time, but the trees getting thoroughly wet, and the night setting in, we rode through it, in the hope of meeting some friendly cottage; we were fortunate to our wishes, and by the inhabitants of that cottage we were conducted to this castle."

She then proceeded to relate the conversation she had heard, relative to its being haunted, with her terror of the preceding night, and determination to explore every apartment in the castle.

"I hope, madam, (added Matilda) the relation I have given, though tedious and little interesting to you, will apologize for my abrupt intrusion here." "Dearest madam, (answered the Lady of the Castle) can you think it possible I should be uninterested for a situation like yours? Young, new to the world, with uncommon attractions, without friends or protectors, surely misfortunes have taken an early hold in your destiny; but do not despair, my good young lady, Providence never forsakes the virtuous, but in its own good time will relieve us from every difficulty; an assurance of that truth has supported me under the bitterest calamities, and though I am at present dead to the world, I flatter myself I may be of some service to you, but do not think of quitting this castle yet; happy should I think myself if I could enjoy your society always, but 'tis a selfish wish and shall not be indulged; however, our confidence ought to be reciprocal, and you shall know, in part, the peculiar distresses which have driven me to this asylum, though my confidence must be limited from restrictions I dare not break through." "I fear, madam, (answered Matilda) however eager my curiosity and anxiety may be awakened by your uncommon situation, I must for the present postpone the gratification of it; my long absence will, I am sure, cause much trouble to my hospitable entertainers, and therefore 'tis time I should return." "Well then, (said the lady) when may I hope to see you again?" "After dinner, madam, I will attend you." "I shall think every minute an hour till then," (replied the lady.) They parted with mutual regret. Matilda carefully shut the doors, and returned to Bertha's apartments, with a lighter heart and a dawn of hope.

On her entrance into the kitchen the good creature clasped her hands and shouted for joy; "O good God be thanked, (said she) that I see you once again; my dear lady, where have you been and what have you seen?" "An excellent library of books, (replied Matilda.) "And did you see no ghosts, nor hear no noises?" "I saw no ghosts, but I certainly did hear noises." "Lord have mercy upon us! and so, had you courage to stay?" "Yes, I stayed to view the apartments, but I was a little frightened, I must confess." "O, dear heart, but I hope you won't go again." "Indeed I shall, (said Matilda) I intend to sit there very often, and shall borrow some books to bring home with me." "O, madam, don't be so hardy, who knows what mischief may come of it one day." "I have no fears, good Bertha; if we perform our duties towards God and man, Providence will always preserve us from evil." "Ah! Lord, madam, you talk so good; I am sure I never did hurt to any body, nor Joseph neither, and when no company comes here we be as quiet as lambs, and yet methinks I do wish for folks sometimes, because you know 'tis very lonely—but will you have your bed made below stairs to-night?" "No, (replied Matilda) I will sleep in the same room, I have no apprehensions at all now." Bertha wondered at the lady's courage, but said nothing.

Albert had before this requested to sleep below, for as they were ghosts of quality, who never condescended to visit kitchens, he thought himself perfectly safe, on the ground floor.

When dinner was over, Matilda said she should go to the library and fetch some books. Bertha looked quite woe begone, but was silent: not so Albert, who had been informed of the perilous adventure his young mistress had undergone in the morning; he besought her, with tears in his eyes, not to trust herself again in the haunted rooms. "If any harm betides you, madam, I shall be a poor miserable fellow for the short remnant of my days." "Be not uneasy, my friend Albert, no ghosts can hurt me; 'tis the living only I fear, not the dead; assure yourself I shall return in perfect safety."

Saying this she went up stairs, leaving Bertha and Albert under great consternation. "Well, the Lord love her, (said the former) she must be a pure good creature to have so much courage—I hope no harm will come on't." "I hope so too, (cried Albert, wiping his eyes.) She is the best sweetest tempered young lady that ever lived;—ah! I little thought to have seen such a day as this for her."

Whilst these two worthy creatures were expatiating upon her praise, Matilda pursued her way to the Lady of the Castle, who was expecting her with impatience, and warmly embraced her upon her entrance. "How mortifying the reflection, (said the lady, leading her visitant to a chair) that the unexpected happiness I enjoy must be purchased so dearly as by your peace of mind; what delight should I feel in your society, if distress and misfortune had not driven you here!" "Believe me, madam, (answered Matilda) your presence and conversation has greatly alleviated those sorrows which oppress my heart; and if my company should be productive of pleasure to you, I shall feel much less regret for the causes which compelled me to seek this castle as an asylum for an unhappy orphan, though but a temporary one only." "Ah! my dear young lady, (replied the other) you are but young in the school of affliction; you can look forward with hope, you can feel only for yourself, and, God forbid, you should ever know the sorrows of a wife and mother, who knows not but that she is childless and cut off for ever from those endearing ties." "O, madam, (cried Matilda, interrupting her) forgive me that I have revived such terrible images to your mind; let not my curiosity occasion such painful ideas, at least we will enjoy the present hour with mutual satisfaction, and defer your painful recital 'till another day." "Charming girl, (said the lady) I accept the delay you offer me, and am happy that I can assure you of an asylum whenever you grow tired of this castle. I have a sister in France, married to the Marquis de Melfort, she is one of the best of women; she is no stranger to my situation and has repeatedly wished me to come into the world and reside with her, but I have powerful reasons for refusing, though she is the dearest friend I have on earth, and I am certain will rejoice to offer you an accommodation in her house, and a place in her heart, as she has no children to engage her attention." Matilda made the warmest acknowledgements for this kind offer, but said, unaccustomed as she was to the busy world, she was apprehensive Paris would be the last place she ought to reside in, particularly as her uncle might go there, having property and friends in that city, and she might run the hazard of being discovered.

Whilst she was speaking, the lady's attendant entered with a letter, "Joseph has just brought this, my lady." "Joseph! (repeated Matilda, involuntarily.) "Yes, (said the lady, smiling) your friend Joseph is my friend also; this letter is from my sister—but bid our old friend step in." Joseph entered, but started back with surprise when he beheld Matilda seated quietly in the room,—"Good Lord! (cried he) how came young madam here?" "This lady's courage, you see, has penetrated through our secret, and now we have no occasion for any reserve before her, she will as carefully guard it from your wife as you do." "Lord! I am sure, (answered Joseph) it goes to my heart to keep any thing from poor Bertha, she is such a good creature, but women's tongues will blab sometimes, to be sure, and as I have sworn to your ladyship, God forbid I should break my oath, though often and often I have longed to tell my wife." "However, Joseph, (said the lady, gravely) I depend upon your honesty and oath." "You have nothing to fear, my lady, eighteen years practice has learnt me to hold my tongue; have you any further commands?" The lady replying in the negative, he made his bow and retired.

"That man is a faithful good creature, I owe my life to him; I know nothing of his wife, though I am told she is a worthy woman; but as a secret should never, if possible, be trusted to chance or accident, I made him swear not to reveal mine, without permission from me." Matilda exprest her satisfaction that the lady had such a faithful serv-ant, and taking a book from the table, requested she would open her letter.

This being complied with, she presently exclaimed, "Alas! my brother and sister are going within a month to England, perhaps to stay some time; yet why should I grieve at that, they cannot come to me." Then reading on, she again cried out, "My dear Miss Weimar, if you will accept of my sister's protection, it is now at your service: hear what she says, after expressing her regret that I cannot be of her party, 'I wish I could meet with some amiable female companion, to take the tour of England with me, there are so few of one's acquaintance that are desirable as intimate friends, that nothing can be more difficult than to obtain such a one as I am anxious to have: young ones we can-not meet with, and I cannot bear the idea of being plagued with the ridiculous fopperies of an old coquet; for I am not yet so much of a French woman as to think there is no difference in ages, and that a fine dressed and high coloured lady, though near to her grand climacteric,[1] shall be indulged in all the expectations of youth and beauty.'

"Now, my dear Miss, you are exactly the lady that will suit my sis-ter; it is not proper, at your age, that you should be buried here, other-

---

[1] Menopause.

wise it would be the greatest felicity in the world for me to enjoy your conversation." "I certainly, madam, (answered Matilda) should think myself most fortunate in attending the Marchioness, but indeed my finances are so slender, and the necessaries I have are so trifling that I am unable to take a journey of consequence. When I left my uncle's house I was so entirely ignorant of travelling expences, that I conceived I had plenty of money to last a considerable time, but I find myself much mistaken; my little stock is considerably diminished, and I must try, by my industry, soon to support poor Albert as well as myself." "I am happy, (returned the lady) that I can obviate some of your objections. I have a large store of linen I never can wear in this place; I have a good deal of money by me, for I do not spend half the income allowed me; you must—you shall do me the favour to accept my little assistance, as from a mother to her child, I will not be denied." "Your goodness, madam, (said Matilda) overpowers me, but, alas! poor Albert, I cannot forsake him." "Nor shall you, my dear young lady; a faithful servant like him is an acquisition to any family: my sister, I am persuaded, will rejoice to receive him; tell me, therefore, you accept of my proposal, and I will write instantly: we shall then know when it will be absolutely necessary you should join her, that I may not be too soon deprived of the pleasure I now enjoy. I shall leave it to yourself to acquaint her, or not, as you please, with your story, 'tis sufficient I recommend you as a friend of mine." Matilda could form no objection to this kind offer in her desperate circumstances; and whilst she amused herself with a book, the lady wrote her letter, and having read it previous to its delivery to Joseph, her young friend exprest her warmest acknowledgements for the favourable manner in which she was mentioned in it. This business settled, the lady took her into the next apartment, the windows of which were also closed. "This room, (said she) opens into the garden, where I walk occasionally of an evening, when not liable to observation. In these drawers, my dear Miss, there are plenty of necessaries, all at your service; to-morrow we will examine them." "I cannot find language, madam, to express my gratitude." "Do not attempt it, be assured your acceptance of my little assistance is a sufficient return for what you consider as an obligation. But pray tell me how you came to venture visiting these apartments, which are generally believed to be haunted?" "As I never had my mind occupied by any ideas of ghosts, (answered Matilda) and could not conceive any actions of my life had subjected me to the terror of supernatural visitations, I believed there must be some other cause for the appearance of lights which I traced in the windows above, and for the noise I heard in the night, though I confess the latter did terrify me; I resolved therefore to visit these rooms, although I was told in one of them there was blood on the floor and horrid inscriptions on the windows." "Your information was true, (answered the lady, with a sigh she could not suppress) "it is the room above which answers the description you have heard; another day, when I have related my melancholy story, you shall see it. I am much pleased with your courage, which proceeded from a right principle: when the mind is conscious of no evil actions, nor any deviations from rectitude, there is no cause for fear or apprehensions in a thinking sensible person, and I hope, my dear Miss Weimar, you will never want resolution on similar occasions; judge always for yourself, and never be guided by the opinions of weak minds." "You are very good, madam, (replied Matilda) in favouring me with your approbation; I shall think myself particularly fortunate if you will condescend to instruct me, for it is with shame I confess, more attention has been paid to external accomplishments than to the cultivation of my mind, or any information respecting those principles of virtue a young woman ought early to be acquainted with." "You are truly good and amiable, (said the lady;) born with sentiments of virtue, and natural understanding pointed out the right path to happiness, pursue it through life, ever remember it is better to suffer from the follies or vices of others than to feel self-condemnation from a sense of your own: the one, time and patience may subdue, or at least blunt the sharp edge that wounds you; but, for the other there is no consolation, self-reproach admits no healing balm, that can enable us to stem the torrent of oppression, or the evils which arise from our own misconduct. You will pardon the freedom you have invited, my good young lady; when you know my story, you will find I am qualified to speak on the subject from very painful lessons, which I pray heaven you may ever be a stranger to." She now took her hand and led her to the other room, where refreshments and pleasing conversation made the two hours Matilda passed there the most pleasing she had ever known. When she took leave they parted with regret, and proposed meeting at an early hour the following day; when the lady promised to relate the events that had compelled her to a seclusion from the world, and the motives which induced her to alarm every stranger that came to the Castle.

Matilda stept into the library, and selecting two or three books, returned to her friendly hostess, whose surprise and pleasure seemed equally gratified by seeing her in safety. Joseph came in soon after; he looked with increased respect and kindness, but was entirely silent as to their meeting in the lady's apartment.

When the hour of retiring came, Matilda repaired to her room with great cheerfulness, and when Albert, with tears, entreated her to sleep below, she replied, "You may, my good Albert, if you chuse; but I shall sleep perfectly quiet above stairs; be under no apprehensions for me, (added she, smiling) I am no longer a stranger, and have not the smallest apprehensions of being molested this night." She took up her candle and left them.

"Well, (cried Bertha) the Lord be good unto her, for sure she is the best and most courageous lady I ever saw in my life; I believe it would kill me if any harm was to happen to such a sweet creature."

All now retired to rest, and Albert thought himself quite safe on the ground floor from the quality ghosts.

In the morning they met with great satisfaction; every one eagerly demanded of Matilda if she had slept undisturbed; she assured them she had, and was greatly refreshed. This account pleased them all. Albert went out to assist Joseph in the garden; and his mistress was preparing to visit her friend, when Jaqueline made her appearance from the kitchen with Bertha. Matilda was extremely glad to see the good woman, enquired after Pierre, and thanked her for the good accommodations she had procured for her in the Castle. "Dear me, (said Jaqueline) you cannot think how glad I am to see you, my lady; I was a-coming yesterday, but I was busy washing, and, Lord help me, this morning before day I was a-frightened out of my wits, for I heard some horses galloping by the door, and I thought I heard this lady screaming most piteously; so, says I, dear heart, Pierre, I am afraid some mischief has happened to young madam, so I'll be sure to go to the Castle when I have hung out my clothes; so Pierre he went to fell wood, and I made all haste here, and glad to my heart I am to see you all safe."

Matilda thanked the friendly woman for her attention, and after a little chat left the two gossips together, and hastened to the lady, telling them she was going to sit in the library. She crossed the apartment and descended the stairs, saw the lady's room open, and walked in; no one was there, but a great appearance of disorder in the room, one of the stools thrown down, a candle on the floor, another burning on the table, and several things scattered about: she was surprised—she knocked, she called, she had no answer. Terrified beyond expression, she ventured into the other room, where the bed was; it was empty, but had the appearance of being laid on; a little cabinet, which stood on the drawers, was open and emptied of its contents. She returned; she went through the several rooms that were open, all were desolate; she once more went back to the ground floor. The candle was nearly extinguished, she took up and lighted the other, and, on looking round, she saw the door that opened from the bed room into the garden was ajar, and on trial it opened; she then readily conceived the lady must have been carried away through the garden, but by whom it was impossible to guess; robbers would never have incommoded themselves with females. She came in and was about to shut the garden door, when she thought the sound of footsteps reached her ears—she trembled and stopt, presently a door, the opposite side of the bed, opened, and Joseph appeared: she was overjoyed—he looked surprised; "O, Joseph, (cried she) what is become of your lady?" Astonished at the question, the poor fellow repeated her words, and added, "Good Lord, madam, has not your ladyship seen her?" "No, (replied she;) I have searched every room in vain, and found this garden door open." "O, she is carried off then, (cried he) and we are all undone—O, my dear, dear lady, you are betrayed at last." Tears burst from his aged eyes; Matilda sunk into a chair, overcome with sorrow, "But, (said she, when able to speak) how could any one enter, there is no door forced?" "Yes, madam, there is, (answered Joseph) I found the kitchen door burst off its hinges, and came in trembling for fear of what had happened." "From whence could any one come into the kitchen?" "Why, madam, there is a private passage underground, from the garden to the under apartments, which is unknown to every body, as I thought, but to the lady and myself; but it must be discovered by somebody, and we are all undone. Hasten, madam, out of this place, I will fasten up the doors and follow you." "Joseph, (said Matilda) can you meet me in the garden by and bye, I wish to speak with you." "Directly after dinner, madam, I will wait upon your ladyship; I will look about a little, I think no one will come here in the open day." Matilda retired, with trembling limbs and a beating heart, to her own apartment; here she ruminated on what had happened to her friend so recently gained, and so irrecoverably lost—"Alas! poor lady, (said she) who knows what evils she may have to encounter with; a stranger as I am to her story, I have no clue to

guide me who may have carried her off, or by whom the cruel action
was committed; doubtless it must have been her cries that alarmed
Jaqueline—What will become of me? How are all my flattering prospects vanished?" With these bitter reflections she passed the hours 'till
dinner time came; she then went down, but with a countenance so
altered, that Bertha started back and cried out, "O, for a certain young
madam has seen something and been frightened!" Albert looked with
anxious curiosity, "Be not uneasy, my good friends, (said she;) I assure
you neither ghosts nor noises have terrified me, but I am not very well;
after dinner perhaps I may be better." "Heaven send it," (cried Bertha.) Albert joined in the wish; and Matilda, affected by their kindness,
went into the parlour, where her dinner was served up, not in state
or profusion indeed, but good wild fowls, eggs, salads, and fruit. She
waited impatiently until she thought Joseph had nearly dined, and then
walked towards the garden; in a little time Joseph joined her, and walking before, conducted her to a distant part of it, where a small arbour
in a shrubbery appeared almost choaked with weeds; he led her into
it, she sat down—"Now, Joseph, for heaven's sake, tell me every thing
about the dear lady." "That I cannot do, (replied Joseph, shaking his
head;) my oath will not permit me; but underneath this stone (said he,
stamping his foot) is an underground passage, one end of which goes
to that part of the castle, and opens into a private place behind the
kitchen; the other end goes through to the end of the wood, I believe,
for I never had courage to go so far on, but this morning, when I went
down the passage, and came round, I found both doors forced off their
hinges below, and was much afraid to come up, where I found you,
madam: who it is that has been so wicked, I can only guess, and Lord
have mercy on the poor lady, I fear no good will come to her." "But
how come the garden door is open; could they convey her through that
into the road?" "Yes, (replied Joseph) that was the way, for after you
went up stairs I went into the garden, and the great gate, at the end,
was unbolted just at the end of the wood, and I do suppose they had
horses waiting there, or a carriage. The few jewels my poor lady had is
taken from her little chest, but there are no locks broke on the drawers,
and her pockets are left behind, on a stool, with everything in them;
'twas no robbers, my lady, I fear." "I fear so too, (answered Matilda,
with a deep sigh;) I dread that she is fallen into worse hands—" "Into
worse than I fear has got her, (said Joseph) she cannot be fallen—Lord
how I rejoiced she had got your ladyship with her." "Aye, Joseph (re-

sumed Matilda) I grieve for her and feel my own loss;—Do you know her sister the Marchioness?" "I saw her once after my lady was married; they say she is very happy—God help us, 'twas n't so here." "Your lady has wrote to the Marchioness relative to me; did not you take a letter yesterday?" "Yes, my lady, and if there be any answer to it I shall be sure to have it, and you may open it, you know, because the good lady never wrote to any one else." Poor Matilda knew not what to do; she was desirous of staying 'till this answer arrived. She was anxious to explore those apartments that were locked, and after some hesitation asked Joseph if he would meet her there to-morrow morning. "Aye, sure, that I will, (returned he) and as I left the lamps burning in the passage, if you like, I will go down this way with you now." "No, (said she) not now; I will meet you to-morrow in the library, and we may return this way, for I own I should like to see it, though 'tis plain the passage must be known."

They now separated, and Matilda found no possibility of gratifying her curiosity, Joseph's oath being against her, and she too much respected her friend to urge a violation of it on any grounds.

She returned to her apartment and amused herself for a short time with a book; but the agitation of her mind would not admit of entertainment; she threw it aside and called for Albert; he instantly attended her. "My good friend, (said she) I propose remaining here a week or ten days, perhaps not so long, to refresh myself; how far are we from Zurich?" "About a day and a half's journey, not much more." "Well then, Albert, we will wait a few days until I am more in health, unless you are very anxious to get there." "Me, my dear young lady, Lord bless you, I want to go only on your account, it's all one to me where I am, if you are safe." Matilda was pleased at his answer and exprest her gratitude for his kindness in such terms as brought tears into his eyes. "God bless you, madam, I'll go with you all the world over." He bowed and retired. "Good creature! (exclaimed Matilda) heaven has blest you with an honest feeling heart; how much superior are thy sentiments to those of better understanding and cultivated talents, when their minds are depraved by the indulgence of irregular passions!"

She sought to compose her spirits, and wait with patience for the expected letter, which she thought must determine her future destiny. She had recommended to Albert not to stir from the house, lest he might be seen by any one that knew him in passing the road, which caution she observed herself.

The following morning after breakfast she repaired to the library; ah! thought she, what transport, if I should find the dear lady returned! but no such happiness awaited her; she entered the apartments with a beating heart, and remained near ten minutes in the library before Joseph made his appearance. "Well, Joseph, (said she hastily, on his entering the room) how are things below stairs?" "All the same as they were yesterday, madam; the doors were fast, and everything as I left them." "I have a very great desire, (said she) to see that room where the inscriptions are, and which I find is locked up, can you open it?" "Yes, I can; the key is below, but if I may speak my mind, I think you had better not go." "Why so," (demanded she.) "Why, because, to my thinking, it's a dismal place, and will put me in mind of sad doings." "You make me more curious—pray indulge me, Joseph?" "Well, madam, I'll go with you, but 'tis sore against my mind." He went down, and soon returned with two keys, but with evident reluctance in his countenance; "I believe one of these is the key (said he;) there used to hang three upon the peg, the other is gone, or left in the closet door perhaps yet: I don't think my lady ever came up to open these rooms." Whilst he was talking he was trying the keys; neither of them would open the first door, the second he unlocked presently; they entered; it was a dressing room, handsomely furnished; they tried the door which opened into the other room, it was fastened on the inside. "This is very strange, (said Joseph;) I will go down again and see if I can find the other key, if you are not afraid to stay alone." "Not in the least," (said Matilda, who was examining the room very carefully.) The windows were very high and grated with bars of iron, the hangings were dark green damask, every thing was handsome, yet the grated windows made it appear gloomy.

Joseph now returned with a countenance of horror and dismay— "O, my lady, I can find no key, but looking about the kitchen, behind the door I found a large knife, all over blood." "Gracious heaven! (cried Matilda) what is it you tell me; I tremble with apprehension; let us force that door, at all events." "I intend it, (answered Joseph) and have brought a bar with me for the purpose." The door in the dressing-room being the slightest, after a good deal of labour, the old man burst it open. What a scene presented itself! a woman on the bed weltering in blood! Both uttered a cry of horror, and ran to the bed; it was the elderly attendant of the lady dead, by a wound in her throat.

The sight was too much for poor Matilda, she sunk fainting into a chair; Joseph was frightened out of his wits; he flew down as fast as possible, and returned with water, he bathed her face and hands and she revived.

"O, Joseph! (cried she) the lady—the dear lady! what is become of her in such bloody hands?" "The Lord only knows," (answered he looking with terror towards the closet.) Directed by his eye, Matilda arose and walked to the door; the key was in it; she unlocked it, and was about to enter, when casting her eyes on the floor, she saw it was all over stained with blood, dried into the floor—she started, and involuntarily retreated, but Joseph, who had looked round said, "You may enter, madam, nothing is here." With trembling steps she entered the closet, her heart beating with terror; it was a large light closet, with a very high window, grated like the other, hung with dark green stuff; two stools covered with the same, and a large wardrobe in it. On the floor was plainly mark'd the shape of a hand and fingers traced in blood, which seemed to have flowed in great quantities. "Good heavens! (cried she) some person was doubtless murdered here too." "Intended to have been murdered, (answered Joseph, wiping his eyes) but thank God she escaped then." He said no more. Matilda, extremely terrified, hastened out of the closet, when the poor creature on the bed met her eyes, "O, Joseph! (exclaimed she, turning with horror from the scene) what is to be done with this unfortunate woman?" "Dear, my lady, I can't tell; I have neither strength to dig a grave, nor can I carry her down." "It is plain, (said Matilda) the wretches who have carried off the lady, murdered the servant to prevent discovery." "I fear, (cried Joseph) my turn will be next—my mouth will be stopt from the same fear." "God forbid, (said Matilda;) but as I have now no hopes of finding the lady, and it will be dangerous to entrust another person with the secret, I think, Joseph, if we can find a small trunk or chest, to fill it with the linen and necessaries your lady offered me, and convey it to one of the rooms in the other wing; I will write a line and leave it on the table: yet, on second thought, it will be useless, should she escape, she can never think of coming here again: we will therefore lock and bolt up every door; you can take the keys of the places below to your own kitchen, and now and then come through the passage to see if all is safe." Poor Joseph, with a heavy heart, agreed to this.

They had now stayed some time, and thought it best to separate and meet again after dinner: they gladly left these horrid rooms, and returned by different ways to their own habitation.

When Matilda came to her apartment, the terror of her mind was unspeakable; all she had seen, all she had heard crowded upon her remembrance, and gave her the most horrible ideas. She could not think Joseph's fears unreasonable: if he was supposed to be in the secret, his life was not safe, and in his fate the whole family might be involved: "What can I—what ought I to do? (cried she, shedding a torrent of tears) no friend to advise me, no certainty of a place to receive me, if I go from hence, and a probability, that, if I stay, I may be murdered;—what a dreadful alternative is mine!" After giving free vent to her tears, she endeavoured to compose her mind, by addressing the Almighty Power to protect her.

Sweet are the consolations which religion affords! In all our difficulties and distresses, when supplicating the Supreme Being with fervor and a perfect reliance on his goodness, we feel a resignation and confidence, that enable us to support present evils, and look forward with hope to happier days. Such were the feelings of Matilda: she rose from her knees with serenity; she recovered resolution and firmness; "I will not despair, (said she) the Almighty will preserve a friendless orphan, unconscious of guilt, that relies on his protection." She dried up her tears, and met the family as usual.

When dinner was over, she returned to the library; Joseph soon joined her; they went down to the deserted parlour, Matilda could not help shuddering: Joseph found a trunk, the drawers were opened, and she took out such necessaries of every kind as she thought she must want, yet left plenty behind. In one drawer she found a purse, with a good deal of money in it; here she hesitated; the lady had told her she would supply her, yet she knew not to what amount: Joseph persuaded her to take the whole, "Be assured, madam, my dear lady will never return," cried he. After much hesitation and reluctance, she at length divided it, and then taking a pen and ink, she took an inventory of the clothes and money, with an acknowledgement to repay it when able, and locked it in the drawer with the purse.

Having packed up those few things she had selected, and requested Joseph would take it, by and bye, to a room near hers, she said, "I cannot be easy under the idea, that the poor woman above should lie there to decay; is there no way to place her in a decent manner?" After some pause Joseph said, "there is a large chest in the back-kitchen, with old trumpery in it, if I take them out, perhaps we might get the body there, but I fear I have not strength to bring it down." "Let us see the chest first, (replied Matilda) and then we will consider of the other." She followed him into the back-kitchen, saw the chest, and its contents were soon tumbled into one corner. "Now, Joseph, (said she) I will assist you to bring the body down." "You, my lady! (cried he, staring at her.) "Yes, (rejoined she;) let us go up." She led the way and he followed; having unlocked and entered the room she could not help shuddering; yet took more observation of the gloomy apartment than she had been enabled to do in the morning; and recollecting what she had heard about inscriptions; she got upon a chair, and from thence to a kind of window seat very high from the ground: standing on this she examined the window; it looked out towards a sort of battlement, which surrounded the back part of the castle, the north wind blew full upon it, the only prospects were the walls and distant mountains. On the window she saw several lines apparently cut with a diamond; in one place she read,

I am dumb, as solemn sorrow ought to be;
Could my griefs speak, my tale I'd tell to thee.

In another place these lines were written;

A wife, a mother—sweet endearing ties!
Torn from my arms, and heedless of my cries;
Here I am doomed to waste my wretched life,
No more a mother—a discarded wife.

And again, in another place,

Would you be happy, fly this hated room,
For here the lost Victoria meets her doom.

O sweet oblivion calm my tortur'd mind
To grief, to sorrow, to despair consigned.

Let gentle sleep my heavy eye-lids close,
Or friendly death, the cure for all our woes,
By one kind stroke, give lasting sure repose.

Several other lines, expressive of misery, though not of poetical talents, were written in different places, that proved the unhappy writer sought to amuse her painful ideas by her melancholy employment.

Poor Matilda concluded the wretched victim to some merciless man was sacrificed in that closet where the hand was deeply imprinted in blood on the floor; she viewed it with horror, and getting down from the window; as Joseph had wrapt the body in the counterpane which lay on one side; he tried to lift it, and found the weight less than he expected, "I can carry it myself, my lady," and crept out of the room with it. Matilda, shutting the door hastily, followed him. They deposited the unfortunate woman in the chest, which was fastened down, and without speaking a single word returned to the parlour: here Matilda burst into tears, her resolution and spirits began to fail; the scenes she had witnessed, added to her own distresses, were indeed sufficient to wound and terrify a stouter heart than this young creature's; little acquainted with the calamities of life, she had flown from approaching danger, without the least idea of the miseries she might encounter in her journey! Joseph sympathized in her sorrow, and waited without speaking 'till she grew more composed; "Come, dear lady, let us leave this sorrowful place; I will take some oil and trim the lamps, for I shall come here every day, though, God knows, with very little hope of ever seeing my dear mistress again." Matilda, opprest and languid, rose from her chair; he followed her with the box to the apartment next her's, and having deposited it, returned to lock up the doors and trim the lamps in the passage, assuring her he would call daily at the post to seek for letters, as all came directed to him.

She threw herself on the bed after his departure, and gave her mind up to the most melancholy reflections; "Good heavens! (cried she) what scenes of murder and atrocious crimes must have been perpetrated in this castle; how great is my curiosity to know more of the unhappy Victoria so recently the cause of joy and sorrow, and her unfortunate attendant, but their fate is enveloped in mystery and horror, what mine may be, heaven only knows."

When it grew near dark she went up stairs, but so altered by the agitations of her mind, that Bertha started and exclaimed, "Dear, my lady, are you ill." "I am not very well, (replied Matilda;) I shall take an early supper, and retire to bed." The poor women with great nimbleness prepared her supper, of which her guest ate but sparingly, and after sending for Albert, who appeared very sorrowful for her indisposition; she comforted him by an assurance of its being very trifling, and that she should be better after a night's rest; which was indeed verified; for having commended herself to the protection of the Father to the fatherless, she dropped into a soft slumber, and arose the following morning quite refreshed and composed.

For several days nothing particular occurred; her friends at the cottage called often to see her; Joseph visited the deserted apartments every day, all remained quiet; the uncertainty of the lady's fate gave them great disquietude, but there was no hope of obtaining any information of an event which seemed buried in obscurity.

One day when Joseph returned from town, he whispered the lady to go into the garden; she walked thither to it directly, he soon followed, and delivered to her the expected letter from the Marchioness; she made no scruple of opening it. After lamenting the unhappy situation of her sister, and expressing her wishes that she would quit her gloomy abode, she thanks her most cordially for her recommendation of the young lady, whose company will be highly acceptable to her, and assures her sister she will endeavour, by every kindness and attention in her power, to make the young lady's situation agreeable, and shall esteem her acceptance of their protection as a very particular favor. She admires her resolution in visiting the apartments in the castle, and is only sorry her sister cannot participate in the pleasures of society. She concludes with requesting the young lady may join them at Paris, soon as possible, within a fortnight; and assure herself that her old and faithful servant will be received and retained in the family with kindness and ease to himself.

This letter, so gratifying to the wishes of Matilda, was read with transport; she determined to set forwards on her journey within two or three days. Joseph undertook to procure her a carriage from the next town, and she intended leaving the horse for his use, and take Albert in the chaise with her. The next consideration was in what manner to account to the latter for her sudden intention of going to Paris, and his reception in the family of the Marquis: after some deliberation, she returned to the kitchen, and calling Albert aside, told him, by the most fortunate and unexpected intelligence she had heard of an asylum for herself and him, at Paris, in the house of a worthy family, where she hoped they should both meet rest and happiness; and that it was her design to proceed on her journey the third day from that. Albert stared with wonder, but never interrupted her 'till she stopt speaking, then, in a hesitating manner, "Paris is a long journey—I have no friends there; are you sure, madam?" "Yes, Albert, (said she) I am very sure we shall find friends there to receive us; I cannot explain everything to you now, some time hence perhaps you shall be informed of every thing." "God bless you, my dear young lady! (cried he) if you are satisfied I am sure I ought to be so, and will go with you when and wherever you please." She was affected by his love and confidence; she assured him, she never should forget the obligations she owed to him, and that his ease and tranquillity would ever be her first care. The old man hurried from her with tears in his eyes. Bertha was next informed of her intended departure, and was truly sorry, because, as she said, 'twas comfortable to have some kind body in that lonely place, and because the lady having plenty of money, they had a very good living now, which, to say truth, she was sorry to lose.

The day previous to her departure she sent for Pierre and Jaqueline: the honest couple were vexed to hear she was about to leave them. She gave them some money, and assured both families, whenever she had it in her power, she would remember their kindness, and reward it in a more ample manner than she now could do. They bestowed a thousand blessings on her, and declared she had made them rich for life.

After they had left her, Joseph acquainted Bertha that a chaise would be there early the next morning, and desired she might have breakfast ready for the lady.

Matilda had but little rest; her journey, the circumstance of such an awkward situation, as a self-introduction amongst entire strangers, to one so little accustomed to company as she was, gave her much pain; yet on the other hand, she ought to consider that in her unfriended, unprotected state, an asylum, such as was now offered to her, must be desirable and advantageous; and that as in this life we seldom meet with pleasure or happiness, without some alloy, she ought to be thankful for the good, and submit to temporary inconveniences without murmuring. She arose early; her heart was depressed when she reflected on the uncertain fate of the lady to whose kindness she was indebted for her present hopes and expectations: "Ah! (cried she) heaven bless you, dearest lady, wherever you are, and may Providence one day restore you to felicity and your friends." She quitted the apartment with a flood of tears, and coming, found the breakfast ready, and soon after a chaise at the gate; Joseph conveyed her portmantua and box to the carriage; Albert stared a little at the latter, but said nothing.

She shook hands with the worthy couple, tears running down their cheeks at parting with so gentle a lady, she having liberally rewarded their kindness, and previously concerted a correspondence with Joseph, if any thing new occurred at the castle, and receiving advice from him how to manage at the post-houses about carriages and horses.

A few days after her departure, Joseph went to the neighbouring town, to procure a few necessaries, and, proud of his present, went upon the horse, instead of his old friend the ass. Whilst he was there, a gentleman came up to him, and, viewing the beast very attentively, asked him if the horse was his. Joseph answered in the affirmative. "Will you sell it?" (demanded he.) "No, Sir, (replied the other) I cannot sell it." "How long have you had it?" "Some time, (said Joseph, roughly, and rode off, not liking the stranger's curiosity.) He was however followed at a distance, and had scarcely put the horse into the stable, and entered the kitchen, before a knocking at the door was heard, and Joseph saw the same gentleman who was so inquisitive, with another, who had the appearance of a servant, enter the room. "Do not be alarmed, (said the stranger) I want to ask you a few questions, which, if you answer truly, no harm shall happen to you, else you must look to the consequence; tell me from whom you had the horse I saw you ride, and how long it has been in your possession? At your peril answer me with truth." Before Joseph could recollect himself to answer this demand Bertha fell on her knees, "O, Sir, do not hurt my poor husband, and I will tell you all." "Be quiet, wife, (said Joseph) I will answer for myself. I had the horse from a man, a friend of mine." "What was his name?" "Sir, I humbly think that is no concern of your's." "Villain! (cried the gentleman) tell me this instant, or I will send you and your wife to prison, for the horse was stolen from me." "O, the Lord be gracious unto us, (exclaimed Bertha) the man's name was Albert, Sir; we are innocent, indeed we are."

"I believe it, (said the other, very mildly;) you look like an honest woman, and I will reward you handsomely, if you speak truth. William, take care of the man, I will go into another room with this good woman." "Bertha! (cried Joseph, the stranger led her away into the parlour, she crying and begging no harm might happen to Joseph.) He quieted her fears on that head, and then asked if Albert was in the house. "No, indeed, Sir, (answered she;) he went away four days ago, in a chaise with the young lady." "Ah! (cried he) that is the very thing I wished to know; and where are they gone, my friend?" "Alack, Sir, I believe they be gone to *Parish*, or some place like that." "The devil! (exclaimed he) to Paris. Well, and are they to return here?" "O, no, Sir, (returned Bertha;) no such good luck to us, for to be sure she was as generous as an empress."

He then returned to the kitchen, where Joseph sat very sullen; "I tell you what, friend, I believe you may be innocent; but the lady you have had here is my niece, who has eloped from my care, and seduced my servant to steal the horse you rode to-day, and go off with her; I am now in search of her, and if I can find her, and she will return, I shall receive her with kindness and joy, and forgive every thing; therefore, if you can tell me where she is, you will do her a great piece of service, I assure you; some wicked person has persuaded her to run away." "Sir, (said Joseph, firmly) I heard the lady say she was going to travel,—it was not my business to be impertinent and ask questions." "But you know where she is." "I do not, Sir, (answered he) I cannot tell where she is, nor the places she is going to travel through." "You know she is gone to Paris?" "Yes, Sir; but I heard her say she should not stay there, but travel further; and this is all I know. As to the horse, if you can prove it yours, give me a receipt, and you may take it." "No, my friend, (replied the gentleman) keep it for your use, but if you should ever hear from, or see Albert or the lady, and will let me know, I will give you a hundred crowns." "O, the goodness (cried Bertha) bless your honour, you shall surely know." "What say you," (said he, turning to Joseph.) "I say, Sir, money would not tempt me to do a wrong thing, but as you say it will be for the young lady's advantage, to do her service I will obey you."

The gentleman appeared satisfied, and writing his address, whilst he desired Joseph to get a little wine and water for him, he whispered to Bertha, "Get every thing you can out of your husband, and I will make your fortune; my man shall call again to-morrow."

Having drank his wine, he took a civil leave, and, giving Bertha two crowns, rode off.

"Lord! (cried she, when he was gone) what luck attends us! what a kind gentleman; how sorry I am he didn't come before the poor lady went away." "So am not I, (answered Joseph;) I don't like him at all; he has a smooth speech to be sure, but if he was good, neither madam nor Albert would have run away I dare say: however I shan't ride the horse any more, 'till I know to whom he does belong." Bertha tried every way to find if he knew where the lady was gone, but he evaded all her questions, and though he loved his old woman dearly, yet he knew she could not be entrusted with a secret; not that she would discover from ill-nature, but from a garrulity natural to old age, and a desire of oblig-ing any one who wanted information from her.

Joseph, in the early part of his life, had obtained a tolerable edu-cation, and had better expectations, but the wars had carried off his friends and little possessions; he was glad, therefore, in a humble state, to earn his bread, and be contented with the situation Providence had ordained for him; but his sentiments were above his condition, and he prized his word, and kept it when pledged with much more exactness than a fine gentleman does his honour, when given to a favourite lady, or a humble tradesman: Joseph therefore persevered in his integrity, but thought there would be no harm in writing what had passed that day to the young lady, and take her directions how to conduct himself, for he had a perfect reliance on her truth, and thought only ill treat-ment could have induced her to quit an uncle's house, without a friend to help her.

The following day the gentleman's servant made his appearance, but to little purpose, for though Joseph was in the garden, Bertha had gained no information; but she told all she did know of the lady's com-ing there, the ghosts disturbing her the first night, her subsequent courage, her kindness and sudden resolution to leave them, and that she heard her say something about going to travel to *Parish*, but she knew no more, and she was sure Joseph knew no more than she—how should he? he never spoke twenty words to the lady. He asked who was the owner of the castle, she told his name, and with a present of another crown he took leave. Bertha looked at the money, "Ah! (said she) what a pity now I can't tell where she is; a hundred of these would make one happy for life."

A very few days after this, the old couple were at dinner, when they heard the trampling of horses; they hastily opened the door, and beheld, to their great astonishment, a carriage with three attendants, and in the carriage Joseph saw his master, Count Wolfenbach: struck with wonder, he forgot to tender his services, but stood staring at him until he alighted. Being conducted into the parlour, one of the horse-men with him, "Friend Joseph, (said he) I have sold this estate, and next month another family will take possession of it." "Good Lord! (cried

Joseph) what will become of me and Bertha?" "Don't be uneasy, friend Joseph, I shall take care of you; I have another estate in Suabia, a fine house and gardens, in perfect order; Bertha and you shall have the care of it, with a servant under her to keep it clean, and a man under you to work in the gardens—what say you to that?" "I am much obliged to your Lordship, (answered the honest man;) 'tis rather late in life for me to travel, but I must obey your pleasure, and if you have not already got a man and woman there, I know a very industrious couple hard by, the only friends we have, who will be glad to go with us." "By all means, (said the Count, eagerly) but pray are you pretty quiet now; do the ghosts trouble you, as has been foolishly talked of?" "I am seldom disturbed, my Lord, (answered Joseph;) I never saw nor heard any ghosts." "I believe not, (said the Count;) the silly imagination of some people conjure up frightful fancies, and endeavor to impose them upon others as realities; but pray Joseph how soon can you leave this house? my man Peter will go with you to the other; you will find a much better habitation, and can take your friends with you." "In about a week, my Lord, I shall be ready." "Not sooner?" "I must speak to my friends; we must get our little domestic business put in order, and then we shall be fit to go comfortably, though 'tis a long journey for old folks, my Lord." "Nothing at all—nothing at all, (said his Lordship;) Peter will see you safe. We shall be with you next week—use all the dispatch you can, for I have alterations to make in the house, before I give it up."

The Count and his attendants mounted their horses and rode off, leaving Joseph in great perplexity. Bertha, ignorant of the events which caused his uneasiness, was well pleased to change her abode for a better one, and was in a violent hurry to call on Pierre and Jaqueline, but Joseph requested she would wait another day, 'till he had considered the matter. He well knew, that if the Count visited the other wing, he must be sensible that it had been lately inhabited. If he was innocent of his conjectures, and unconcerned in the late transactions he would judge unfavourably of Joseph; if, on the contrary, he had any hand in carrying off the lady and murdering her attendant, the removal of the body would convince him some person must have been there; his suspicions would naturally fall on himself, and perhaps he might be sacrificed also. These considerations greatly distressed Joseph; every way he saw perplexity and vexation, and was afraid to throw himself into the Count's power, though he saw no chance of avoiding it. He had been every day to the other apartments, except the preceding one, and found everything tranquil; but now that the Count was in the neighbourhood, he was afraid to go: yet he thought the only way to avoid suspicion, or impending evils, would be to replace the body on the bed, at all events.

Endeavouring to derive courage from necessity, he tremblingly ventured to the private passage, but, to his surprise and horror, the lamps were all extinguished; he knew they must have been put out, otherwise they would have lasted that day; he therefore hastily turned back, and regained the house. After a little deliberation he went up the stair-case, and opening every apartment very softly till he came to the door which led to the gallery of the other wing, he found it fastened on the other side. This circumstance confirmed his fears: he listened some time, and plainly heard voices, but could distinguish nothing; he then retreated with the same care, locking up all the doors on the outside, for whether it was the Count and his servant, or a set of banditti, he thought his situation equally dangerous.

Poor Joseph could not communicate his fears to Bertha, and therefore his uneasiness passed off for indisposition, but he had a sleepless night.

The next morning he went to the post town, and, to his great joy, received a letter from Matilda. She was safe at Paris; and the Marquis and his Lady, under the greatest apprehensions for their sister; convinced she would never return to the castle, should she be alive, and grateful to their old friend Joseph, offered him and his wife an asylum at their house, thinking they might one day or other be sacrificed to the Count's revenge.

Scarcely had he read this letter, when he saw Peter, the Count's servant, coming towards him; he had the paper still in his hand. "So, Joseph, you have been at the post, I see." "Yes, (answered he, with as much ease as he could assume;) I hear now and then from a sister of mine, who is in service at Paris: but is my Lord here in this town, Peter?" "Yes, (replied he) his Lordship is settling some business with his tenants." "Well, (said Joseph) next week we shall be ready to go, Peter." "Very well," (cried the other, with a smile) and they parted.

On Joseph's return to his house, he began to consider of his removal; he was sure he could not depend on the Count, but how to get away without his knowledge was the difficulty; after much deliberation, he took his resolution and going to Bertha, told her the Lady Matilda was in Paris, and had sent for them to live with her. She was out of her wits with joy: "O, (cried she) that will be a thousand times better than living in the Count's house; yes, yes, let's go, the sooner the better, say I." "But, (said Joseph) you must not say a word to the Count, or any body, for the world." She promised secrecy, and they began to contrive about taking away their little matters, and setting off in a day or two.

That night Joseph thought to get some rest, though his fears still remained, and kept him waking for some hours: about midnight he dropped asleep, but was soon awakened by a great smoke and a terrible smell of fire. He hastily got up, and opening the door, the flames burst in upon him; he ran to the bed and called Bertha to follow him; she jumped out, as he thought, for that purpose: he got into the court, and saw the other wing also on fire, and presently the building he came out of fell in. He called Bertha; alas! she was smothered in the ruins. The whole building was now in flames. He ran to the stable, got the horse, and riding through the wood as fast as possible, a contrary way from the town, he stopped not till he came to the foot of a mountain; with difficulty he crept off his horse, and threw himself on the ground. "Bertha! my dear Bertha, I have lost thee forever; I am now a poor forlorn creature, without a friend in the world: why did I fly,—why did I not perish in the fire with my wife? What a coward I am! O, that cursed Count, this is all his doings; I expected he would seek my death, but poor Bertha, she was unconscious of offence to the barbarian, yet she is gone, and I am left desolate who ought to have been the sufferer." Exhausted by grief and lassitude the wretched old man lay almost motionless for some hours, when Providence conducted a carriage that way, with a lady and gentleman in it, and two attendants on horseback. Seeing the horse grazing and an elderly man lying on the ground, the gentleman stopt the carriage, and sent a servant to him: he explained his situation in a brief manner, which when the domestic informed his master of, he ordered he should be brought and put into the carriage, and the horse led on by the servant to their seat.

We will now return to Matilda, who with her faithful Albert, arrived at Paris without meeting any accident. They soon found the Hotel de Melfort, and Matilda writing a short billet to the Marchioness, reposed herself a little after the fatigue of her journey.

In less than three hours the Marchioness arrived in her carriage, and entered the room with that delight in her countenance which plainly testified the pleasure she expected to receive in the company of her young friend; she flew towards her, and embraced her with a warmth that affected the grateful heart of Matilda to tears. "Welcome, a thousand times welcome, my dear Miss Weimar; the friend of my poor sister must be the friend of my heart! Charming girl! (said she, gazing on her) that countenance needs no recommendation; what do I not owe my Victoria." Matilda, in returning her caresses, involuntarily started and repeated, "Victoria!" "Yes, my love, that is my sister's name; you know her only as the unhappy Countess of Wolfenbach, I suppose: but let me see your faithful Albert, to whom I hear you are greatly indebted." "I am indeed madam, (replied Matilda) my whole life at present is and must be a state of obligation." "Dismiss that idea, my dear Miss Weimar, and feel that you have the power of obliging in your society those whose study it will be to convince you how grateful they are for the favour you confer on them." Matilda bowed and kissed the hand of the Marchioness, with an expression in her eyes that spoke volumes to the heart. Albert now entered the room; "My good friend, (said the Lady) I hope you are well; I wished to see you, to thank you for your services to this young lady." "I humbly thank your Ladyship, (cried Albert) but I have only done my duty, and when you know my mistress you will think so, for she deserves all the world should serve her." "I doubt it not, (replied the Lady) and after my first care to render your mistress happy, my second shall be to make the remainder of your days comfortable." Neither Matilda nor Albert could refrain from tears. "Come, come, (said the Marchioness) let us be gone; my carriage waits; the Marquis is impatient to see you, and I have a thousand questions to ask about my dear sister." Ah! thought Matilda, how shall I unfold the dismal tale—how must I wound a bosom so tender and affectionate! This reflection threw her into a melancholy reverie, as the carriage drove on. The Marchioness observed it, and taking her hand, "We are not strangers, my dear Miss Weimar; I have only been to meet my younger sister and introduce her to my husband, already prepared to love her." Matilda, overcome by a reception so kind, cried out, whilst sobs spoke the genuine feelings of her heart, "Dear madam, you oppress me with your generosity and goodness: O that I may be found, on further knowledge, to deserve your good opinion." "I am persuaded of it, (replied the other) and if you please, (added she, with a smile) here ends the chapter of favours, obligations, and such kind of stuff, as I have an utter aversion to."

By this time they were arrived at the hotel, and the Marchioness led her young friend to the saloon, where the Marquis sat expecting them. "Here, my Lord, permit me to introduce to you my younger sister; I bespeak your affection for her, and think you will find no difficulty in bestowing it." "You judge right, my beloved Charlotte: your sister claims a double share of my esteem from her own merit, legible in her countenance and your introduction." Having saluted and led her to a chair: "I am charmed, (added he) that our dear Victoria has procured us such a delightful companion; she must have sacrificed a great deal to give us pleasure, in losing your society." Matilda unable any longer to repress her feelings, burst into tears. Both were alarmed; the Marchioness, taking her hand, "Dear Miss Weimar, you have something on your spirits; tell me, pray tell me, did you leave my sister well? you have, I think, avoided mentioning her." "Ah! madam, (she replied) I am very unfortunate that my introduction to you must occasion pain and sorrow; yet I trust the dear lady will be the care of Providence, though alas! I know not where she is." "Not know where she is? (exclaimed the Marchioness) good heavens! has she then left the Castle?" Matilda then entered into a detail of every event that had happened at the Castle, the death of the attendant, and the absence of the Countess. Perceiving the agitation and distress of her auditors, she added, "I have little doubt of the poor Lady's safety, from a persuasion that if any ill was intended towards her, they would have destroyed her, as well as the servant." "You judge very properly, my dear Miss Weimar: be comforted, my Charlotte; your friend's observation is founded on truth and reason; I hope, ere long we shall hear from the injured sufferer, or else, (said he, raising his voice) by heavens! neither oaths nor promises shall prevent me from publicly calling on the Count to produce her." This threat alarmed his Lady, and suspended her grief. "Tell me, my sweet girl, are you in her confidence—do you know my sister's story?" "Indeed, madam, I do not; Joseph, whom I have mentioned, is the only one acquainted with her woes, and he is bound by oath not to reveal them without her leave; unfortunately I postponed a recital which otherwise might have been a clue to trace her now." "Dear unhappy sister! (cried the Marchioness) how severe has been your punishment! Another time, my beloved Miss Weimar, I will acquaint you with all I know relative to her situation: I trust heaven will protect her, and therefore I will not sadden your heart now, nor give you only sighs and tears for your reception, when we wish to make you cheerful and happy." With a deep sigh, which she endeavoured, though in vain, to repress, she conducted Matilda to the apartments appropriated for her, and embracing her, "You are dearer to me than ever; the child of misfortune, as you just now styled yourself, and the friend of my sister, has entire possession of my heart; love me but half as well as I feel inclined to do you, and I shall be very happy." Matilda replied in the most affectionate and grateful terms. The Marchioness insisted upon her taking a few hours rest, previous to their meeting at supper.

When she was alone she began to reflect on her situation; a recollection of past distresses impeded the satisfaction she must otherwise have felt for the fervent reception she had met with. An unhappy orphan, thought she, without a single claim on the world, from affinity or natural affection—a dependent on the bounty of friends, even for my daily subsistence, and of which I am liable to be deprived by a hundred accidents; is it possible any one can be more unfortunately circumstanced than myself? Yet, when I left my uncle's house, could I have hoped for such a protection as I am now under? O, I will not despair, heaven will preserve me, if I persevere in virtue and integrity; if I can acquit myself of wilful error, and dare appeal to the rectitude of my sentiments, when misfortunes and distresses befall me, I will kiss the rod of correction, and submit with resignation to the Almighty will.

Composed a little in her mind, she dropt asleep for above three hours, and then rose, refreshed and with recruited spirits. She was received by her good friends with the greatest and most flattering marks of kindness, and her grateful heart impelled her to return them by every attention in her power. The Marquis said, it was time, from Albert's age, that he should be laid up to rest; "his honesty and affection to Miss Weimar deserves reward, I shall therefore allow him something above the wages he has had, and only request he will superintend my stables, and see that they take proper care of my horses, but on no account to take an active part in the business." Matilda most gratefully acknowledged this kindness to her old friend, whose welfare was very near her heart. The Marchioness told her they had intended leaving Paris in about ten days, now, said she, "I shall feel great reluctance to quit France without obtaining some knowledge of my poor sister's destiny; but as you expect to hear from Joseph, I will still try to flatter myself he will give you some information concerning her." Matilda encouraged the hope as it appeared to compose her, but she thought it a very slender one.

Two days passed swiftly away. The Marchioness carried her young friend round the city, pointed out every place worth observation, or that could afford amusement. Matilda was in a new world: the polite and sensible conversation she now enjoyed was so different from everything of the kind to which she had been accustomed, that she was mortified at her own deficiencies, and most assiduously endeavoured to profit by the good sense and elegant manners of her protectoress.

The third day after her arrival the Marchioness was to have an assembly. Matilda requested that she might not appear, as the clothes she had were by no means suitable to such an occasion. "Indeed, my love, I cannot excuse you; that objection shall soon be done away" (said her friend.) And presently some elegant silks, laces, linen, &c. were produced for her acceptance. "These things are for my younger sister; she must not presume to refuse a small testimony of affection from her elder one." Before Matilda could reply several trades people came in, and the Marchioness gave orders everything must be ready that evening; which was promised. When they were alone she kissed the hand of her benefactress, "O, madam, in what a gracious manner do you confer favors, without wounding the feelings of the person obliged." "A truce, if you please, (said her friend) to your—Oh! and Ah! the favor, if any, is conferred on me by your acceptance; but once for all, I beg it may be understood, I acknowledge you as my sister by adoption; I have no children, therefore, in the rights of a sister, you have a claim to participate with me in everything; you must only bring yourself to submit to the commands of eldership, and let the words favor and obligation be blotted from your vocabulary." Saying this, she hastened from her, and left Matilda overwhelmed with grateful emotions. Before she had recovered Albert appeared, "Pardon me, madam, for coming up, but I longed to tell you what a blessed family we are got into; such kindness as I am treated with! such good servants, all doating on their Lord and Lady! O, it was a happy day when we entered the gates of Paris! I hope, my dear young lady, you think so too?" "I do indeed, my friend; I have a thousand obligations to this noble family; and 'tis not the least of them, that they have provided for you, to whom I shall always think myself indebted for every good I enjoy." Albert, overcome by this acknowledgement, hurried from her, tears of joy running down his cheeks.

In the evening Matilda's clothes were brought home: the servant, who was ordered particularly to wait on her, dressed her in the most fashionable style. When the Marchioness came into the room, she was charmed with her appearance. "My love," said she, "you will cause a variety of emotions this evening; I foresee an abundance of admiration and envy, when I introduce my lovely relation, for such you are remember; but there are two families I wish you to like; the Countess De Bouville and her daughter, and Madame De Nancy and her sister Mademoiselle De Bancre. You will receive a hundred professions of admiration and esteem from everyone, but these ladies will speak from their hearts, and I trust they will thank me for the acquisition of a friend for their select parties." "You leave me nothing to say, my dear madam, but a repetition of the same words, and the same feelings for your uncommon goodness; I will study to deserve your recommendation, and to render myself agreeable to the ladies, as the only proof I can give of my sensibility."

The Marchioness conducted her to the salon, and soon after a croud of ladies and gentlemen made their appearance; to whom she was severally introduced, and a buz of admiration, with a hundred audible compliments circulated through the room: at length two ladies addressed the Lady of the house with an affectionate freedom that told Matilda they were the persons she was bid to love; nor was she mistaken. "My dear Countess, (said the Marchioness) for this young lady I bespeak your friendship; not only because she is a relation of mine, but because I am persuaded Miss Weimar has merit of her own to recommend her to your esteem, and that of your charming daughter." "You could not have paid us a greater compliment, (answered the Countess saluting Matilda;) this young lady's mind is legible in her countenance. Adelaide, (said she, turning to her daughter) I present you an amiable companion, whose esteem you must endeavour to merit." She joined their hands. "You could not, my dear madam, (replied the young Lady) have given me a command more agreeable to my inclinations." "You do me great honour, ladies, (said Matilda) in your approbation. It must be my care to merit the distinction which I already perceive will be necessary to my happiness." The young ladies were indeed mutually struck with each other. Mademoiselle De Bouville was an only daughter, and, contrary to the general fashion in France, had been educated at home, under the eye of a respectable mother, who, though she submitted to the frivolities, the gaieties, and round of trifling amusements which engage the attention of that lively nation, yet found time to superintend and direct the education of her child, by which she avoided the stiff monastic air of a convent, and was equally unacquainted with the follies and vices which too generally prevail in those seminaries of education; for though they do not always incur general censure, yet it is extremely difficult to discriminate, as too often it is the punishment of profligacy to be confined in a cloyster; and what injury a person of that description may do amongst a number of young people, some with weak heads, and others with bad hearts, cannot be expressed nor thought of without horror.

Adelaide De Bouville had a very pleasing person, great sweetness of temper, and a cultivated understanding; she was near twenty, and had been for some time addressed by Monsieur De Clermont, son to the Marquis of that name, an amiable and accomplished young man; and it was expected by their friends the union would take place when the young Count De Bouville returned from his travels: Adelaide being particularly fond of her brother, made a point of waiting till she could have his presence at an affair on which her happiness must entirely depend. She was charmed with the introduction of Miss Weimar to her acquaintance, and sought, by the most polite attention, to obtain her esteem. Matilda was equally delighted with her companion, and they soon after had an additional charm to their party by the arrival of Madame De Nancy and Mademoiselle De Bancre; the latter was near two and twenty, very handsome, a great share of good humour, and a most enchanting vivacity; her sister being sacrificed very early in life to an elderly man, every way unworthy of her, except by his immense fortune; he used her extremely ill, always out of humour and suspicious: she suffered under his tyranny five or six years; he then died, and left her mistress of a large independence, the expenditure of which did her great honor. Her sister, who had witnessed her bad treatment from an unworthy husband, determined never to marry; they resided together, equally beloved and respected.

Matilda was charmed with her new acquaintance; a swarm of beaus surrounded them, but she thought their conversation, their fopperies, and fulsome compliments truly disgusting, on a comparison with the sensible and elegant manners of her newly-acquired female friends.

When the company separated Matilda received numerous invitations, everyone professing themselves delighted with the charming Miss Weimar; but those professions were not equally sincere. A Mademoiselle De Fontelle beheld her with envy and dislike: she was a young woman of family and large fortune, had been taken about two years from a convent, where she was placed on the death of her mother; and soon after that period her father also died suddenly, and left her solely to the care of an aunt, an old gay coquet, whom every body despised, yet every body visited, because she had large parties, elegant entertainments, and high play. Under the care, if it can be so called, of this ridiculous old woman, Mademoiselle De Fontelle had acquired all the follies and vanities incident to youth and beauty, when under no restrictions, no proper precepts or example. She detested handsome women, was desirous of engrossing universal admiration to herself, had a malignant heart, yet as far as a coquet's affections could be engaged, hers were devoted to the young Count De Bouville; but as her attractions were not powerful enough to detain him from pursuing his travels, she flirted with every one that came in her way, to the utmost extent that French manners and customs would allow among young persons, where there is certainly more reserve than in any other country (Spain excepted.) Therefore 'tis no uncommon thing for girls gladly to marry the man pointed out by the parents, if he is ever so old, ugly, or little known; the restraint laid upon them is so strict, and their conduct so narrowly observed, that to enjoy liberty they marry; from hence proceeds that levity for which the married ladies in France are so remarkable, and which has given rise to an almost general censure, which they do not always deserve: for those who have studied the characters and manners of the French ladies declare, there is more the semblance than reality of vice in them; and though many are profligate, like some of their neighbouring kingdom, who apparently carry more modesty and reserve in their outward deportments; yet there are very many amiable French women, who, under their national gaiety of heart and freedom of manners, are most truly respectable in every situation in life. But the old aunt of Mademoiselle De Fontelle was not one of these, nor had she instilled any such sentiments of respectability in her niece, consequently the young lady ventured to the utmost bounds custom or courtesy would allow: she no sooner saw Miss Weimar than she dreaded and hated her; being a stranger, beautiful and engaging, she obtained universal admiration; but when she observed the decided preference and selection of Mademoiselle De Bouville for her companion, she was outraged. The Count was soon expected home; he would doubtless be attracted by this hateful stranger—the idea was dreadful, and from that moment she was the declared enemy of Miss Weimar, though resolved to cultivate the most violent intimacy with her; consequently when the party broke up, she advanced and solicited the young lady's acquaintance, in the politest manner possible.

When the company had left the rooms Matilda thanked the Marchioness for the pleasure she had procured her, in the introduction to such charming young women as Mesdemoiselles De Bouville and De Bancre. "There was another lady, (said she) who paid me much attention, and invited my acquaintance." "Yes, (answered the Marchioness) Mademoiselle de Fontelle; but beware of her, my dear Matilda; she is far from being a desirable intimate—I neither like her nor her aunt, Madame Le Brun; but I know not how it is, one meets with them everywhere, and cannot avoid seeing them sometimes in public, but they are never of my private parties, therefore let common civility only pass between you."

The young lady promised to observe her advice, and they separated to their respective apartments.

On Matilda's table lay a letter, which the servant placed there, not to disturb her whilst in company. She hastily broke it open; it was from Joseph: he related the incident respecting the horse, mentioned the gentleman's enquiries, and described his person. It was her uncle. She was terrified and shocked beyond measure, she sunk into a chair, and burst into a flood of tears: "Good heavens! (said she) if he should trace me here: yet so many days before him, I think I may be safe; Bertha was not in the secret, and Joseph I can, I know, depend upon not to betray me." Under the most painful reflections, she retired to rest, but sleep forsook her pillow: the dread of falling again into the power of a man so abandoned gave her the most poignant affliction—"O, that we were in England (said she) I should then, I think, be safe from his pursuit."

She passed a restless night, and in the morning met her friends, with a pale countenance and uneasy mind.

"My dear child, (exclaimed the Marchioness) what is the matter, are you ill?" Matilda gave her Joseph's letter, and expressed her fears of being found in Paris by her uncle. Her friends requested she would compose her mind. The Marquis assured her of his protection. "You are not well enough, my love, to go out or see company this morning; we will retire to my dressing-room, and to amuse you from thinking of your own troubles, I will enter upon the story of my unfortunate sister, as far as I know of it, for great part is involved in mystery, and she has taken, she says, the most sacred oaths never to divulge the rest, without permission of another person. My father, Baron Stielberg, inherited from his ancestors a respectable name, a great share of family pride, and very small possessions, which by wars, and a struggle to keep up the family consequence, had been diminished greatly within the last fifty years. He had no son, a source of eternal regret to him, and two daughters, whom he determined should marry advantageously, or not at all. Our mother died when I was about ten, and my sister eight years of age. We were placed in a convent for six years, at the expiration of which time we were sent for home. Our father seemed satisfied with our improvements. We had the good fortune to please, and it was the fashion to admire us. In a few months after our return to the world the Marquis De Melfort, who was on his travels, stopt at Vienna; we met at an assembly, and a mutual approbation took place; he was introduced to my father; and, in short, not to be tedious, his addresses were allowed, for though my father would have preferred a German nobleman, yet the amiable character of the Marquis, his very large fortune, and an earnest desire to see me settled in his life time, prevailed on him to accede to the advantageous proposals made for me, and in a short time I became the happy wife of one of the best of men. We remained near six months at Vienna, but the Marquis beginning to express a wish of returning to Paris, having been absent above two years. I requested my father would permit my sister to accompany me; but to this he peremptorily objected. I took leave of my friends and my country with tears and reluctance. The dear Victoria was ready to expire—it was our first separation, and we had lived in the most perfect harmony with each other: she was my father's favourite and therefore he did not feel that grief on my leaving him, which might have been expected. I had a consolation—I accompanied a beloved husband, and was received by his friends with the most flattering attention. My sister and I constantly corresponded. In about eight months after my residence at Paris she wrote me, that at an assembly she had met with one of the most amiable men in the world, a Chevalier De Montreville, a gentleman of a noble family, but small fortune, secretary to the French ambassador. The manner in which she described this young man, convinced me she liked him: I was sorry for it, I knew he never would be countenanced by my father. She also added, that Count Wolfenbach was her very shadow—that she detested him, notwithstanding his immense fortune and prodigious stock of love. In my answer, I cautioned her against indulging a partiality for the Chevalier, as I well knew my father never would approve of it. A short time after I received a very melancholy letter. "Pity me, my dear sister, for I am miserable—I cannot deny my attachment to the most deserving of men: he has been rejected with contempt by my father, and yesterday I was commanded to receive Count Wolfenbach as my destined husband! I hate, I detest him—he is morose, savage, sneering, revengeful—Alas! what am I saying? this man may be my husband—O, my dear sister, death is far preferable to that situation.'

"These expressions filled me with extreme grief; my generous husband wrote my father immediately; he besought him not to sacrifice his child,—that if the want of fortune was his only objection to the Chevalier, he would gladly remove that deficiency, and he had both interest and inclination to procure him a handsome establishment: that from the affection he bore me and my sister, it was his earnest desire to see her happy, if at the expence of one-third of his fortune.

"To this letter we received no answer within the expected time. I grew very uneasy, I wrote again to my sister. It was more than a month before I received any return. I have it now in my pocket book": the Marchioness took it out, and read as follows.

COUNTESS OF WOLFENBACH,

TO

THE MARCHIONESS.

"*My dearest Sister,*

"JUST recovered from the jaws of death, the lost unhappy Victoria acknowledges the receipt of your kind letter: alas! the contents have almost broken a heart already exhausted by grief and despair. I have been a wife five weeks, near a month I was confined to my bed; but if I can, I will be methodical in the relation of what has befallen me. The letter your generous and respectable husband wrote, unfortunately was delivered by the servant in the same moment with one from the Chevalier. My father believed you acted in concert. Never shall I forget the fury of his countenance. "This insolent Frenchman wants to degrade me into a dependence on him, and marry my daughter to his beggarly countryman." "Ah! my father, (cried I) do not judge so unkindly of my excellent brother, his views are for our general happiness." "And that, (said he, interrupting me furiously) can be accomplished without his interference; the Count has a noble fortune, high birth, a title, and is a German—not another word, (added he, seeing me about to speak) not a single objection; on Monday next you become his wife—see that you obey without the least reluctance." Saying this, he left the room, and in a few minutes afterwards I fell senseless from my seat. How long I continued thus, I know not, but on my recovery I found myself on my bed, and Therese with me; she was bathing me with her tears. "Thank heaven, my dear young lady, you are alive still! O, what a dismal day for me to see you thus." I thanked the poor creature, her kindness was of service,—I shed a copious flood of tears. Soon after my father sent to know how I did, and to tell me I was expected in the library. I obeyed the summons with trembling steps. The odious Count, I must call him so, was with him. My father advanced, and rudely snatching my hand, "There, my Lord, I give her to you, your day shall be ours." "This day, this hour, (cried he, eagerly, kissing my hand,) do not delay my happiness." A sickness came over my heart—I sunk into a chair. "Victoria!" (cried my father, in an angry voice.) I endeavoured to reply, but burst into tears. "Foolish girl, (said he) receive the honour my Lord does you, in a manner more worthy of yourself and me." He left the room. The Count approached me with a malicious air, "Charming Victoria, am I so very hateful; has the Chevalier so many advantages over me, as to engross all your affection?" I started, but indignation rouzed my spirits,—"Whatever are his advantages, my lord, or whether he has any real superiority or not, for I make no invidious comparisons; yet if you suppose he is the object of my affections, surely I am unworthy the honour of being your wife; no man of spirit could bear a divided heart; but if he engrosses all, which I neither affirm nor deny, your Lordship will do well, both for your own sake and mine, to renounce all thoughts of me." "No, madam, (said he, in the highest rage) your father has given me your hand, and you shall be mine, let the consequence be what it may." He flung out of the room with a look of vengeance. You may conceive, I cannot describe my situation. In the evening my father told me the Chevalier was gone to Switzerland. From the hour my father rejected him, I gave him up to outward appearance: I wrote and conjured him, if he valued my peace, to think of me no more. His answer almost broke my heart, "but my commands were sacred, my peace all the good he sought for in this life." When I heard he had quitted Vienna a momentary pleasure seized hold of my heart; he would not be here when I was sacrificed to his rival, nor until I had left the city. Not to tire you, my dear sister, the Monday following I became a wife—spare me the repetition of the dreadful circumstances. The following day I was in a high fever and continued ill for a month; I received but little attention from the Count—there was more of resentment than tenderness in his manner when he came into my apartment, and involuntarily I used to shrink from his view. However, it pleased heaven to restore me to health. I am gaining strength daily, but as yet keep my own apartment;—to-morrow I have engaged to meet our father down stairs for dinner. Pray for me, advise me, dearest sister; depend upon my honour, I will deserve your love whatever becomes of me. Heavens bless you and my dear generous brother.

"Victoria Wolfenbach."

"You must suppose, my dear Miss Weimar, (said the Marchioness) that this letter made us extremely unhappy; I wrote, however, and, fearful the Count might have meanness enough to insist upon seeing her letters, I took little notice of her complaints, but congratulated her on the recovery of her health, desired she would pay attention to it, for the sake of her husband and friends; in short, it was an equivocal kind of a letter, and I thought could give no offence. After this I heard from her but seldom, and then there was an evident restraint in her style, which hurt me, but which I dared not take notice of. She had been married about eight months, when the Marquis received a letter from the Count, acquainting us that my father was dead, after only three days illness, giving an account of his effects, and inviting the Marquis over to see a proper division of them. I persuaded him to comply. He would not go without me, and I was not sorry for the opportunity offered me to see my sister. We got safe to Vienna. We met the Count and his lady, who had come from their country seat, about seven leagues from Vienna, for that purpose. We flew into each other's arms, with tears of mingled joy and sorrow. Alas! it was but the shadow of the once blooming Victoria. I surveyed her with surprise and distress: she took no notice, but introduced me to her husband; the cause of the alteration I observed was then explained. Never surely was there a man with a more ferocious countenance; he inspired me with horror the moment I examined him: I felt for my sister, but tried to receive his cold civilities with politeness for her sake. After dinner we were glad to leave the gentlemen to business, and retire to ourselves. "My dearest Victoria, (cried I, embracing her) tell me—tell me all: you are not happy, your fragile form too plainly speaks it." "I endeavor to be contented, (she replied:) my dear father thought happiness must be connected with splendour and riches, he sought to aggrandize his children; I respect the motive, however he has been deceived." "The Count, I must own, (said I) is a disagreeable object." "My dear Charlotte, (she cried) do not think so meanly of me, as to suppose his want of personal attractions weighs anything with me—I should despise myself in that case; neither is it now any preference for another: I have never seen or heard from the Chevalier since my marriage. I will strictly fulfil every duty I have sworn to observe, perhaps time may do much for me; it will either soften the severity of the Count's disposition, or habit will enable me to bear with less feeling, evils I cannot prevent. Ask me no questions, my dear sister, I am not at liberty to answer them; but if you regard my peace, meet my husband with good-humour and complaisance: and now tell me, (said she) of your comforts, your pleasures and mutual happiness—in your felicity I will find my own." I was drowned in tears, her manner was so solemn, so touching, so resigned, that my heart was wrung with sorrow, and I could not speak. "Dear Charlotte, (continued she, wiping my eyes) spare me those tears, I cannot bear them: remember what I have told you, be cheerful when you return to company, or I shall be the sufferer. I met you with tears of joy, 'tis long since they were shed for grief. Here (putting her hand to her heart), here my sorrows are buried, too deep for that relief——but I have done, dear sister let me enjoy pleasure now in your society." She attempted to smile, it was a smile of woe; I tried however to suppress my emotions, and to divert her attention; asked a few questions relative to our old acquaintance, and in about an hour we returned tolerably composed. The Count examined my looks; I approached him with smiles, chatted about our journey, and I observed his features grew relaxed, and he behaved with great civility. We continued at Vienna a fortnight; he never asked us to his seat. Victoria conducted herself like an angel; she was attentive to every word and wish of his; her deportment was grave but perfectly obliging, so that it appeared more a natural disposition than arising from any particular cause. When all our business was finished, the Count one morning took occasion to observe his presence was much wanted in the country; that he had lately purchased an estate in Switzerland, and should go there soon, consequently had many affairs which required his inspection. We took the hint, and finding I must part with my sister, I was very ready to leave Vienna. The day previous to our departure an old friend of my father's paid me a visit; after chatting some time, "My dear Marchioness, (said he) I sincerely lament the unhappy fate of your charming sister; she has certainly the worst husband in the world; she is shut up, denied all society; he is jealous, cruel, and revengeful: I am sorry to grieve you, but I tremble for her life—she cannot long support such wretchedness. The poor Chevalier, (added he) has been absent from hence ever since her marriage: I am told he is now daily expected; he will hear most afflictive news, for her happiness is the chief wish of his heart." I answered this worthy man, and told him my sister's reserve, as to her husband's treatment of her: he praised her prudence, and added, "your father had two motives in obliging her to marry the Count; he was disappointed in both, for he was no stranger to her situation before he died." "And what, Sir, was his other motive?" "An intention to marry a relation of the Count's, but she absolutely refused him, and married another two months ago. You know, I suppose, (added he) that the Count was a widower?" "No, Sir, I never heard that circumstance." "Why, it is a black story, as it is reported: 'tis said about three years ago he married a young lady, an orphan, of good family, but small fortune, at Bern, in Switzerland; that he treated her so ill as to cause her death, and left two children, who were put to nurse, afterwards taken from thence, without any one's knowing what became of them; however, your father told me the Count informed him they were both dead. Almost every person believes his wife and children came to an untimely end; but he is a man of such rank and large possessions, nobody chuses to say much. I hinted the affair to your father, but fortune and love was too powerful to be given up, he affected not to believe it; but after his own disappointment, he thought more of his daughter, and had he not been so suddenly cut off, I believe would have interfered; at least, I am sure, would have made some separate provision for her, independent of that bad man her husband."

"You may conceive, my dear Miss Weimar, how much I was shocked at this relation. I trembled for my Victoria, in the hands of such a monster, but alas! we could do nothing. I entreated my good friend to watch the Count narrowly, and to give me information, from time to time, concerning her, who I considered a victim to a villain.

"The following day we took a heart-breaking leave. The Marquis entreated the Count to pay us a visit. "In another year perhaps he might." My sister, dear unhappy creature, never shed a tear. "My Charlotte, my beloved sister, think no more of me, (said she, an hour before we parted;) my pilgrimage will be short; the hour which gives birth to an unfortunate being (I had forgot to tell you she was with child) will, in all probability, give me everlasting peace: fortunate if the dear infant accompanies me to the grave, if not, O, my sister, consider it as the only remains of the wretched Victoria, who has, does, and ever will love you to her last hour." I will not wound your heart, my dear Matilda, by any further recital of our conversation. When we parted, in presence of her husband, I could have struck a dagger to his heart. She embraced me with fervor, "Heavens bless you, my dear and happy sister! and you, my generous my noble brother, may you both live to enjoy years of uninterrupted happiness." "Doubtless they will, (said the Count, with a malicious smile;) surely you forget we are to meet again at Paris next year, and not taking leave for life." "True, (returned the Marquis;) I thank you for the remembrance, Sir,—a few months hence, my valued friends, I hope to see you at Paris." She tore herself from my arms, and I got into the carriage, more dead than alive. Not to enter into an unnecessary detail, we returned safe to Paris, and in a short time after I received a few lines from my sister, dated from their castle in Switzerland, telling me she was tolerably well, both in health and spirits, but hourly in expectation of an event which might affect both.

"Near three weeks after this letter we received two; one from the Count, informing the Marquis, that, to his inexpressible grief, he had lost both wife and child; the other from the medical gentleman who attended her, informing me of the same event, and that my sister, in her last moments, requested he would write to express her affection and wishes for my happiness with her departing breath.

"Though I had always apprehended this event, yet it caused me inexpressible misery; and there being no longer any ties to bind us to that detested Count, we never answered or took any further notice of him.

"About six weeks after the dreadful information we had received, a letter came to me, directed in an unknown hand; I opened it—judge what were my emotions in reading these words, deeply impressed upon my memory.

"Your sister lives, though dead to all the world but you; a solemn vow has passed her lips, never to disclose preceding events without permission—ask no questions, and you shall soon hear more, but more than one life depends upon your secresy.

VICTORIA."

"I flew to the Marquis with this billet; he was equally surprised and overjoyed, but naturally concluded we might have spies upon us, and that therefore we had better continue our mourning the usual time.

"It was upwards of a fortnight before I heard again, and I grew very impatient; at length I had another letter: this informed me she was confined, that she had reason to hope her child (a boy) was alive. Under that hope she lived, and, notwithstanding her confinement, was better in health than when I saw her last. I might write a few lines now and then, under cover to Joseph Kierman, in a vulgar disguised hand; that she perhaps might never see me more, and meet certain death if her secret was discovered.

"This letter, like the former, was in a different hand from hers. I answered it, and from that time, near eighteen years, we have corresponded about once in two months, never oftener, till our last epistles concerning you.

"The whole affair is certainly very strange: often has the Marquis vowed to apply either to the Count or courts of justice; but the letters we received were never written by her, we could adduce no actual proofs of his guilt, and she continually warned us to take no steps without her permission. Thus, in a most unaccountable manner we are prohibited from doing her justice, whilst all the world believes her dead: he lives chiefly at Vienna, a dissipated life; though from my friend I hear he is at times gloomy, and apparently unhappy: this gentleman however believes my sister and her child dead, nor dare I undeceive him.

"Thus, my dear Miss Weimar, you have before you all I know of this melancholy affair; what now is become of this hapless victim heaven only knows,—I cannot think of leaving Paris yet; the Marquis can scarcely be restrained from exerting himself, and, indeed, in a short time, if we gain no further information, I shall feel disposed to coincide with his wishes."

Matilda returned the Marchioness thanks for the trouble she had taken in giving this painful relation: she felt deeply for the poor suffering Countess, and could not help joining in the opinion that some step ought to be taken, if she was not heard of soon.

They both waited with impatience to have another letter from Joseph, as he promised to write again about the gentleman and his horse; and the Marquis and Marchioness requested Matilda to offer him and Bertha, in their name, an asylum at Paris, if they had any fears of remaining at the Castle.

Three or four days passed, and nothing new occurred. Mademoiselles De Bouville and De Bancre had frequently called on Miss Weimar, also Madame Le Brun and her niece.

On the fifth morning the first mentioned young lady entered the house, accompanied by a very elegant young man, whom she introduced to Matilda as her brother. The Marquis and his lady were rejoiced to see him and gave him the most cordial welcome.

Matilda was uncommonly struck by his appearance; she thought him, (and with justice) the most amiable man she had ever seen. The Count De Bouville was indeed deserving of approbation: he had all the elegance of French manners, without their frivolities, an excellent understanding, and a desire of improving it induced him to visit England, after his tour through Italy and Germany; he had gained knowledge from the different manners and customs of each nation, and returned a truly accomplished young man, with much good sense and polished manners, a strict integrity of heart, and the highest sense of duty and love for his mother and sister. He had always entertained great respect for the Marquis and Marchioness De Melfort, and that, added to his sister's warm eulogiums on Miss Weimar's perfections, brought him the morning after his return to make his compliments. He had never seen a young woman like Matilda; she was in truth the child of nature; for, though accomplished and well informed, having been bred up in obscurity, never visiting nor being visited, a stranger to young men, to flattery, or even the praises of a chamber-maid, with a most beautiful face, and elegant shape, and many natural if not acquired graces; she was unconscious of her perfections—she knew not the art of displaying them to advantage—she had no vanity to gratify—thought but humbly of herself, and received every mark of admiration and respect as favors to which she had no pretensions. A character so new to the world, which was easily understood in a short visit, from the frankness and naivete of her manners, could not fail of engaging the attention and esteem of the Count. Her person was charming; her conversation and unaffected sweetness insensibly gained upon the heart, and rendered it impossible to avoid bestowing that homage to which she made no claims. When the visit was over and an engagement made for the Melfort family to dine the following day at the Bouville's. Matilda, with her usual candour, warmly praised the young Count: her friends smiled, but coincided with her sentiments, and expatiated on his good qualities with all the warmth of friendship and esteem. They were yet on the same subject, when a servant entered and delivered a letter to Matilda. "From Joseph," (said she, looking at the address.) "O, pray open it," (cried the Marchioness.) She did so, and perusing it hastily to herself was struck with horror at the contents. He was now at the seat of Baron Wolmar, from whence he writes an account of all the proceedings at the Castle. He concludes with telling her the Baron and his niece have given him an asylum, but that the Count's story was still unknown; is desirous of receiving her commands, and bitterly regrets the loss of poor Bertha.

When she had looked it over, without a single comment she gave it to the Marchioness, but her looks prepared her friend for some dreadful intelligence. "Good heavens! (cried she) what a villain! every thing now is past a doubt—most certainly he has destroyed my sister, and by burning the castle, sought to make away with the person privy to his transactions."

When the Marquis had read it, "By all means, (said he) let Joseph be sent for immediately, he will prove a material witness, and I am determined, if no news arrives from her shortly, to enter a process against the Count, and oblige him to produce her."

A servant was ordered to set off the following morning to bring Joseph, and the Marquis wrote to thank the Baron for protecting him.

Various and melancholy were their conjectures relative to the Countess, whose strange fate they all deplored.

"I shall never forgive myself, (cried the Marquis) for not interfering in this business years ago. When I knew she was first confined, though we never understood so clearly the nature of that confinement till she wrote to us of the courage and resolution a young lady, driven by accident to the castle, had shewn, in exploring the way to her gloomy apartments. At the same time she was cautious in withholding any particular information as to the nature of her situation. Maria, her attendant, always wrote for her, nor was any name signed on either side."

"Every circumstance, (returned Matilda) convinces me her life is not in danger, for had that been determined on so many years would never have passed, and left her in possession of it." "I hope and wish your observation may be verified," (said the Marchioness.) "But pray, madam, (cried Matilda) what became of the poor Chevalier after her marriage and the subsequent report of her death?" "My friend at Vienna, (replied the Lady) informed me, he returned there soon after the Count carried my sister into Switzerland, and in a short time quitted the ambassador, and talked of visiting Asia, and remaining abroad some years; since which we have never heard of him, whether he is living or not."

Some company now broke in upon them; and an engagement in the evening prevented any particular conversation.

The following day they were to dine with the Countess De Bouville. Matilda, for the first time in her life, took some pains with her dress, and felt an anxiety about her appearance; yet, unconscious of her motives, she attributed them solely to a desire of pleasing the Marchioness. When they arrived at their hotel, the Count was ready to conduct and introduce them. The Countess received them with pleasure. "I know, (said she) my good friends, you rejoice with me on the return of my son. We are a family of love, (added she, turning to Matilda) therefore you must not be surprised to see us a little intoxicated with joy on meeting again after so long an absence." "Indeed, madam, such affectionate feelings do you great honour."

Adelaide was all transport, which was soon after rather checked by the introduction of the Marquis de Clermont and his son: the young men ran into each other's arms. "A thousand welcomes, my dear De Bouville, I impatiently longed to see you." "I believe it, (returned the other, with a smile;) you had powerful reasons, and I have shortened my stay in England considerably on your account." "Apropos, (said the Marquis;) how do you like England, my young friend?" "So well, Sir, (replied the Count) that I could be contented to pass my life there in the bosom of my friends. I consider the English as the happiest people under the sun: they are naturally brave, friendly, and benevolent; they enjoy the blessings of a mild and free government; their personal safety is secured by the laws; no man can be punished for an imaginary crime, they have fair trials, confront their accusers, can even object to a partial jury; in short, as far as human judgment admits can be deemed infallible. Very few, if any, suffer but for actual crimes, adduced from the clearest proofs. Their commerce extends all over the known world; their merchants are rich and respectable, the first nobility do not disdain an alliance with them, they are considered as the supporters of the kingdom: 'tis incredible to think of the liberal sums subscribed by these opulent, respectable, generous people, on any popular occasion, or private benefaction, without astonishment. The men of fashion are many of them admirable orators, great politicians, and perfectly acquainted with the government of different nations, as much as of their own. The young men, I believe, are the same everywhere—fond of pleasure, expence, and intrigue; but the rock on which they most generally split is that spirit of gambling which pervades through almost all ranks of people, dissipates fortunes, distresses families, hardens the heart, depraves the mind, and renders useless all the good qualities they receive from nature and education. There are very strict laws against play, but those laws only awe the middling or poorer kind of people, the great infringe them with impunity.

"But I beg pardon, (added the Count) for falling into the common mode of travellers, engrossing the attention of the company to myself." "I desire you will go on, (said the Marquis;) I am pleased with your observations." "And the ladies, dear brother, (cried Mademoiselle De Bouville) pray tell us something of the ladies." "I shall punish your curiosity, (replied he, smiling) by and bye. What I most admire in the English, is the great encouragement given to all manufactories, and to all useful discoveries; there ought not to be any poor, that is, I mean beggars, in England, such immense sums are raised for their support, such resources for industry, and so many hospitals for the sick and aged, that, if proper management was observed, none need complain of cold or hunger; yet in my life I never saw so many painful and disgusting objects as there are in the streets and environs of London. I admire the public buildings, the places of entertainment, and the performers at them; but sometimes, as will ever be the case, liberty degenerates into licentiousness, and the mob will rudely interrupt the performers, and carry their applause or censure in opposition to every effort of their betters: this certainly is an abuse of their freedom, but 'tis an evil they know not how to remedy in a land of liberty.

"As for the ladies, my dear sister." "Aye, brother, now for it;—I hate your English belles, they are such monopolizers when they make their appearance at Paris." "And yet, Adelaide, I assure you, it is not often you see the most beautiful of them here, doubtless there are very many charming women among the first circles of fashion, who may dispute the palm of beauty with any court in the known world; but generally speaking, the middling ranks of people are by far the handsomest of both sexes, and I account for it in this manner. In fashionable circles they keep very late hours, play deep, enter into every scheme for amusement and dissipation, without regard to their health or complexions; hence they injure one, and destroy the other: no artificial resources can give brilliancy to the eyes, or health and vivacity to the figure; acquired bloom can never deceive, and the natural beautiful complexions of the English ladies are so delicate and transparent, that art may disguise, but never can improve them. Their ill hours, and deforming their lovely faces by the anxiety of avarice, envy, and passion, when at their midnight orgies, adorning and watching the effects of chance in their favour, destroys their beauty many years before age would have lessened their attractions; for I must confess, (added he, smiling at his sister) the English women, take them all in all, are more fascinating than any other nation I ever saw." "And yet, (said she) you are returned heart-whole, brother?" "That is begging the question, my curious sister; but where there are so many charmers, men's eyes involuntarily wander, and must consider it almost an insult upon the rest to select one, when there are such equal pretensions."

"The English ladies are much obliged to you, Count, (said the Marquis de Melfort) and we shall soon have an opportunity of judging if your picture is over-charged, as we design visiting England within this month."

This declaration conveyed no pleasure to any of the party. The De Bouvilles were already so much prejudiced in favour of Miss Weimar, that they were hurt at the idea of parting: the Count particularly felt uneasy, though he could not express it upon so short an acquaintance.

Matilda was highly pleased with Monsieur De Clermont, her friend's lover; he was polite, sensible, and intelligent; the Marquis, his father, lively, chatty, and attentive to the ladies.

The dinner hours passed very agreeably, and they regretted that an assembly in the evening must break in upon their party.

The young folks had an hour to themselves: the Count paid Matilda the most marked attention; congratulated his sister on the acquisition of such a friend, and hoped some event, favourable to his wishes, might prevent their tour to England, though he acknowledged the hope a selfish one. After chatting on various subjects, the Count accidentally enquired of Matilda, if she liked Paris as well as she did Vienna? The question confused her, and she replied, with some hesitation, she had never seen Vienna. "I beg your pardon, madam, (said he) I understood you came from thence." "No, brother, Miss Weimar resided in Switzerland." "At Berne, madam?" (asked he.) "No, Sir, (answered she, still more confused) I chiefly resided in the country." The Count saw by her manner he had been guilty of some impropriety, though he hardly knew of what nature; he was therefore silent, and she recovered from her embarrassment.

In the evening the company began to assemble; amongst the rest that eternal gadabout Madame Le Brun, and her niece, Mademoiselle De Fontelle. The Count was obliged to pay his compliments, and receive their congratulations on his return; which done, he hastily returned to the side of Matilda.

The envious De Fontelle could not bear this; she made her way to them, took the hand of Matilda, called her her sweet friend, assured her they must be violently intimate, she was quite charmed with her; with a hundred such delusive compliments, as meant nothing, and to which the other only replied with a cold civility. All at once, turning quickly to her, "Bless me, Miss Weimar, I forgot to ask if you have a relation of your name now in Paris?" The roses forsook Matilda's cheek, she trembled, and could scarce stand; everyone observed her confusion; the Count caught her arm. "Bless me! (cried Mademoiselle De Fontelle) has my question disordered you; I only asked because I was in company yesterday with a gentleman of your name, just arrived from Germany."

This was enough for the unhappy girl—down she dropped, and had not the Count been attentive to her motions, and caught her in his arms, she must have fallen to the ground. Every body was alarmed, and crowded round her, the Marchioness particularly so; she was carried into another room, the Count still supporting her, and followed by his sister. It was some time before she returned to life. The first objects that struck her, was the Count holding her in his arms, the Marchioness on her knees, applying salts, and Mademoiselle De Bouville pressing her hand. "O, madam! (cried she, eagerly and trembling) he is come—he is come." "Compose yourself, my love, (said the Marchioness) no one is come that can hurt you." "Yes, yes, (answered she, hardly knowing what she said) 'tis he, he will carry me off, he will take me from you."

Her friend still endeavoured to sooth and calm her spirits. The Count and his sister were surprised; they saw there was some mystery, but forebore any enquiries.

It was some time before she was perfectly restored: they urged her to return to the company—she felt a repugnance, "I fear that Miss ——" "Fear nothing, madam, (interrupted the Count;) you have friends who will protect you with their lives." She looked at him with an expression of gratitude, but said nothing. She arose, and with feeble steps attended her friends into the saloon.

Mademoiselle De Fontelle officiously came to congratulate her return. The amiable De Bancre felt real concern, and expressed it with feeling, and without exaggeration.

Matilda, sensible of the kindness of her friends, and ashamed of the observation she had attracted, tried to acquire new spirits; but it was an endeavour only; her eyes were incessantly turned towards the door, she dreaded every moment she should see her uncle enter, and nothing could exceed her joy when the evening closed and they were seated in the Marquis's carriage.

"O, madam! O, Sir! 'tis assuredly my uncle—he will know where I am, and tear me from you." "Do not afflict yourself, my dear Miss Weimar, (answered the Marquis;) if it should be him, he shall prove his pretensions before he gets any footing here, much less take you from our protection."

Poor Matilda thanked him with a grateful heart, and retired to her bed, but not to sleep: her mind was greatly disturbed. "What a poor creature I am, (cried she;) no father, brother, or protector, not even the clothes I wear my own property; if this man, this uncle claims, who can dare detain me? What are the evils which may befall me—whatever becomes of me, I will not embroil my friends. Happy, happy Miss De Bouville! (said she) you have a mother, a brother to protect you! Such a brother! what an amiable man! O, I never knew my wretchedness 'till now, that I am humbled to the dust!" Under these melancholy impressions she passed the night, and when morning came was in a high fever.

The servant who came to attend her was alarmed at her indisposition, and flew to inform the Marchioness, who instantly went to her apartment. She found her very ill. A physician was sent for, who ordered her to be bled and kept very quiet. About noon the Marchioness left her asleep, and had scarcely entered the parlour, when she was informed a gentleman requested to speak with her; she ordered his admittance.

A middle aged man, of respectable appearance, politely entered the room. "I must apologize to your Ladyship for my intrusion, without sending in my name, which I now avow to be Weimar, and I am uncle, I may say father, to a young lady of that name now in your house. I fear, madam, you have been strangely imposed upon to afford her protection; it is painful to a person so nearly connected as I am to that unhappy girl." "I beg your pardon, Sir, for interrupting you, but I have no person under my roof that answers to your description; you are therefore, I presume, in an error as to the lady you allude to." "I believe not, madam, (answered he, rather haughtily;) I come here to demand my niece, Matilda Weimar, and through her to discover a servant with whom she went off, after robbing me." "Robbing you, Sir! take care what you say; you shall bring proofs of your assertions, and then we will answer you: at present Miss Weimar is safe in our protection, and you will find, Sir, she has powerful friends to guard her, and expose those who are her enemies." "'Tis well, madam, (replied he) you will hear from me in another manner." He bowed and quitted the house.

She was glad he did not see the Marquis, at the same time she felt they were in an awkward predicament.

Soon after the Count De Bouville and his sister called on her. "My dear madam, (said the latter) how does our charming young friend? we have been quite unhappy for her indisposition." "You are very obliging, my dear Adelaide; she well deserves your solicitude, and I am sorry to say she is really very ill this morning." "Ill! (cried the Count, eagerly;) O, madam, has she any advice—has she a physician?" "Yes, (replied the Marchioness;) I hope there is no danger,—her spirits are hurried and she is a little feverish."

The Count walked about the room. His sister said, "Will you pardon me, madam, if I tell you the strange reports we have heard this morning?" "I shall thank you for the communication," (replied the other.) "This morning early Mademoiselle De Fontelle called on us, 'O heavens!' said she, eagerly, 'no wonder Miss Weimar fainted last night; why she turns out to be an imposter, and a shocking creature.' 'Who, Miss Weimar, (cried my brother) impossible madam; go and circulate that envious tale somewhere else, there will be no credit given to it here.' 'You are very ready, Sir, to insult your friends, and take the part of strangers; but I assure you, (added she, haughtily) I have no cause to envy Miss Weimar, and should be extremely unhappy to be thought like her.' Seeing my brother smile contemptuously, 'Well, (said she) 'tis of little consequence to me if her uncle is come in search of her; if she ran away from his house with a servant, and jointly robbed him of his property, and now has contrived to impose herself upon the Marchioness for a different person; perhaps she may elope with one of her servants next, the thing is nothing to me, only people ought to be careful how they introduce improper persons into a circle, though they *are beauties* and objects of *envy*—envy indeed! I shall never forget the pretty idea.' She flung out of the room, leaving us almost petrified with astonishment. When my brother recovered, he said—" "What I say now, (cried the Count, interrupting her) that I will stake my life upon the honour and integrity of the young lady—that ingenuous countenance speaks a heart which never knew deception."

"You judge rightly, my dear Count, (said the Marchioness:) I have not time to explain things now, but be assured she is truth and virtue itself; the servant, a worthy and very old man, who knew her from her infancy, is now in my house; he fled with her to save her from dishonour, from the wretch who now pursues her." "Heaven and earth! (cried the Count) where is the miscreant, I will haunt him through the world for daring to asperse her character." "Softly, my good friend, (returned she, smiling) your interference will do no good; the Marquis and myself take upon us to do her justice; meantime you may pay him a visit, and your sister shall just step up and see my patient, provided she is very silent." "My best respects, Adelaide," (said he.) "O, doubtless, (returned the Marchioness) we shall make abundance of compliments and fine speeches, but it will be by dumb show, for I prohibit talking."

Being let blood, had checked the fever, and Matilda lay tolerably composed when her friends entered; she rejoiced to see them, and held out her hand. "Yes, (said the Marchioness) we can take hands, but you are only to tell us how you are." "Much better, my dearest, best——" "Enough, enough, (said the Lady) that's all we wanted to know, so now kiss and part—by and bye you may meet again. My brother, dear Miss Weimar, sends his best respects." "Very well that is sufficient." "Heaven bless you, my love, go to sleep and compose your mind."

The ladies returned to the parlour; the Marquis and Count were there, and expressed great joy to hear so favourable an account of Matilda's health. The Marquis entered into a little detail of her story, and strongly engaged the affection and compassion of the Count and his sister. "I tell you this in secret, (said the Marquis) remember it goes no farther; we have powerful reasons not to extend our confidence, nor withdraw our protection from a friendless orphan recommended to us by a valued relation." "I admire, I honour you, (cried the Count, with earnestness;) do not give her up to this pretended uncle: but how shall we silence calumny, how stop the tongue of that malignant girl? We must act as circumstances shall require; I will call at Madame Le Brun's myself, and assure them there is a mistake in the affair, and warn them not to speak ill of my protégée, for I will defend her with my life and fortune."

They now separated; Mademoiselle De Bouville promised to return in the evening, and the Marchioness went out to pay a few visits, and see if the scandal was extended among her acquaintance; to her great mortification she was told of it everywhere, some condoled with her on being so greatly imposed upon, others affected to resent such a creature should have the assurance to get herself introduced into company, but all agreed, "They saw what she was, nothing but a little pretender, who was a stranger to good breeding; no body was deceived but the Marchioness, for everyone could see art and duplicity in her face."

Thus she, who the preceding evening was the most delightful, most engaging, most elegant girl in the world, by one stroke of slander, was deprived of every perfection, and admiration turned into contempt; so prone is the world to believe ill, and so little dependence is there to be placed on the breath of praise.

The Marchioness was exceedingly exasperated; she defended her young friend with warmth;—she congratulated the ladies on their ingenuity, in finding every virtue and every vice, every charm and deformity in the same person, within the space of eight and forty hours. "Their candour and good nature was highly commendable (she said) and the compliments they paid her judgment were certainly very flattering."

In this ironical manner she treated the tittle-tattle of the envious and malicious; but, driving to Madame Le Brun's, she met her niece, just arrived before her, from circulating her scandalous tale: a malignant joy danced in her eyes, though she was a little confused when she saw the Marchioness. "I beg the favour of speaking to you, Mademoiselle, (said the Lady; and taking her seat) I find I am to thank you for presuming to propagate reports to the disadvantage of my relation:

you would do well to recollect, Mademoiselle, there is no character so truly despicable as the slanderer and tale bearer; you should also be well informed of the facts you relate, and of their origin in truth, before you asperse characters, or subject yourself to the mortification of being disappointed in your views, and of having the calumny retorted on yourself." "What views do you mean, madam,—what is it to me whether Miss Weimar is the runaway niece of Mr. Weimar, or not?" "Your views, (answered the Marchioness) are pretty evident; but permit me to observe the Count De Bouville's esteem will never be obtained at the expence of veracity and generosity, and it would have been more becoming a young lady of liberal sentiments, in at least a doubtful case, to have suspended her judgment, and have inclined to the good-natured side of the question; but I am now to inform you the whole tale you have, with so much avidity, related, is false; that Miss Weimar is as irreproachable as she is beautiful, and in a short time the Marquis will severely punish and expose those who dare assert any thing to the prejudice of that young lady: you will do well, Mademoiselle, to profit by the information." Saying this, she arose, with a look of contempt, and returned to her carriage.

When she met the Marquis at dinner she repeated what she had heard, and her behaviour in consequence. The Marquis applauded her proceedings.

"When I left you this morning, (said he) crossing the street St. Honore, I met Monsieur Du Versac, with another gentleman. "This is the Marquis De Melfort, (said he, and immediately added) permit me to introduce to your Lordship, Mr. Weimar; we were going to your hotel." "Has Mr. Weimar any business, Sir, with me?" "I have, Sir, (he replied, in a very calm tone of voice;) I had the pleasure to wait on the Marchioness, but there was a misunderstanding took place." "Suppose we step home to my house," (said Du Versac.) We agreed so to do. When seated, "Now, Sir, (addressing Mr. Weimar) I am prepared to hear whatever you please to say." He then began a long story of taking Matilda from her infancy, after the death of her father and mother; the tenderness he had treated her with, the education he had given her, his design of giving her his moderate fortune; mentioned a variety of circumstances to prove his affection, and her subsequent flight with Albert, taking a horse from his stable, and deceiving him with false pretences. As her uncle, he had a right to claim her: her behaviour to him made her undeserving protection, but duty to his deceased brother called upon him to protect his child; and he would therefore forgive the error she had been drawn into, and receive her as kindly as ever. When he stopt, I replied, "Sir, there is much plausibility, also, I believe, great truth in what you have related: you must not be offended if I also state facts exactly as Miss Weimar has related them to us." I repeated her story; when I came to the circumstance of the conversation between him and Agatha in the summer-house, he started and turned pale, but quickly recovered. I added, that meeting accidentally with a relation of mine, she was recommended to our house as an asylum, which it was my determination to afford her, and I should suppose no uncle of her's could object to her situation with the Marchioness, who was desirous of considering her as an adopted daughter. "I am no longer at a loss to account for her conduct, (replied he;) and so far from blaming, I must applaud her adherence to those ideas of virtue and propriety I had always inculcated in her mind; but she ought not to have taken up things lightly, nor have proceeded to such lengths upon hearing imperfectly a desultory conversation, which, if she had heard the whole, and its true meaning, she would have formed a very different judgment of; therefore, at the same time I applaud her discretion, I blame her precipitant decision: however, my Lord, I beg the favor of seeing my niece alone for an hour in your house, before I take any steps equally as disagreeable to myself as to her and your family." I told him I would consult Miss Weimar, without the least interference on my part, and transmit to him this evening her answer."

"This is indeed a very complex piece of business, (replied the Marchioness) but I really think she ought to see him, and I shall conceive it no breach of honor to be within hearing of their conversation; for although not a shadow of a doubt remains with me concerning her truth and innocence, yet I wish to have an investigation of the affair, that I may openly assert both, from a thorough conviction of it."

When dinner was over she went to Matilda's apartment. She was infinitely better, and proposed getting up in the evening. After a thousand expressions of kindness and assurances of protection, she mentioned the meeting between Mr. Weimar and the Marquis, related the conversation that took place, and his wish to see her.

Matilda clasped her hands, "Oh! I cannot, cannot see him! I could not be mistaken. His words,—his actions previous to the scene I overheard in the summer-house, leaves no doubts upon my mind; yet I ought not, I cannot involve my benefactors in trouble: instruct me, tell me, dearest madam, what I ought to do, and that I will do,—your opinion shall decide for me." "Why then, my dear Miss Weimar, I think you had best hear what he has to say." "Not alone, madam." "Mr. Weimar is desirous of being alone with you." "No, my dearest lady, that cannot be; let me entreat the favor of your supporting presence." "Since you are so desirous of it, (said the Marchioness) and think you can see him to-morrow, I will appoint him to attend you in the library, the closet adjoining having a very thin partition, I can distinctly hear your conversation, and he will then have no restraint on his words or behaviour."

This plan being adopted, a note was dispatched by the Marquis to Mr. Weimar, signifying that the young lady would be glad to see him the next day, at twelve, if her health would permit.

Poor Matilda dreaded the interview, and the power he might exert over her, yet it was a justice due to her character and friends, that she should confront him; she therefore endeavoured to reconcile herself to the meeting, though she knew it would be extremely painful to her.

Mademoiselle De Bouville paid her a visit in the evening: she was sitting up, and, from the quantity of blood taken from her in the morning, and the little hectic which the fever occasioned, she looked uncommonly delicate and beautiful. After saluting her in the most affectionate manner, she said, "I am charged with a thousand compliments from my brother; he has been extremely uneasy, but if he was to see you this evening, I think he would have but little cause for it;—without any flattery, my dear Miss Weimar, you look quite enchanting."

Matilda smiled, but it was not a smile of pleasure. Ah! thought she, if the Count, if Mademoiselle De Bouville knew me, for what I am, a poor dependant, without friends or family—I should have few pretensions to their notice.

Adelaide took notice of her dejection,—"Come, my sweet friend, recover your spirits. My brother will be anxious for my return; you must enable me to give a good report, if you are desirous he should have rest to-night." "If I am desirous, (replied poor Matilda;) is there anything I more sincerely wish than happiness to you and your amiable brother?" "Well then, (answered Adelaide) you must make haste to be well." "You are very obliging, (returned Matilda;) I am much better, and should be very ungrateful to my friends if I did not exert myself against trifling indispositions."

Adelaide surveyed her with admiration and compassion, her generosity felt an increase of affection from the knowledge of her misfortunes, though she was cautious not to drop a word that might give the other any suspicion that she was acquainted with them.

They parted at night with mutual reluctance, and Matilda endeavoured to compose her spirits for the dreaded interview that was to take place the following day.

When the Marchioness entered her apartment next morning she found her dressing, and much better, which gave her great satisfaction: she encouraged and applauded the resolution she had assumed; but when the time came, and the name of Mr. Weimar was brought in, she could scarcely keep from fainting. The Marchioness retired to the closet, and he entered; Matilda rose to receive him, he hastily advanced and embraced her. "My dearest child, I rejoice to see you, cruelly as you have used me, miserable as I have been from apprehensions of your safety, I am happy to see you under such respectable protection." He seated her and himself. "The Marquis De Melfort, (said he) has explained to me the cause of your absenting yourself from my house, therefore, I am neither surprised nor angry; but surely you acted precipitantly, and on very slight grounds, the conversation you only partially heard and little understood." "I heard enough, Sir, (said Matilda with some spirit) to inform me I was not in safety in a house with a woman of Agatha's principles." "You entirely mistook the affair, (interrupted he) but before I explain myself farther, tell me, Matilda, is there no gratitude, no affection due to the man who has supported you from childhood, who took you, a helpless infant, without a friend to protect you from every evil incident to deserted infancy? Did I not treat you, love you, as a blessing sent from heaven?"

Matilda was drowned in tears at this representation of her forlorn state; with a deep sigh she answered, "Yes, Sir, all this I acknowledge, and heaven can witness for me how grateful I was for your kindness, until my delicacy was alarmed by freedoms I thought improper from our near connexion."

"One question more, (said he;) should you have been offended at those freedoms (as you call very innocent attentions), had they been offered by a man who designed to make you his wife?"

Matilda started, "His wife! 'tis a strange question, but I answer, yes, Sir, I should; for confined as my knowledge of mankind was, nature and decency had taught me the impropriety of such behaviour."

"Perhaps," said he, "you carried your ideas of propriety too far; but doubtless you erred on the right side. But now, Matilda, I am going to disclose a secret, known only to Agatha, and which occasioned the conversation you misunderstood and misrepresented—I am not your uncle." "Good God! (cried Matilda) who, or what am I then?" "That, (replied he) is a question I cannot resolve, I wish for your ease I could do so; but what I do know, I will repeat. One day I was in the garden, when Agatha came running to me with a bundle in her arms, 'Lord, Sir, the strangest thing; I am sure I am as innocent as the babe itself, where it came from, or to whom it belongs, but Lord, Sir, here is a child sent you from God.' Very much surprised, I uncovered a cloth, and beheld the most beautiful infant I ever saw. I asked her how she came by it: this was her account; she heard a knocking at the door, and going to open it, saw a man at a distance, running very fast and a bundle at the gate; the man was soon out of sight; she took up the parcel, and found the child, wrapped in a dimity petticoat, and two or three cambrick handkerchiefs, but no cloaths, and apparently just born; a bit of paper was pinned to the petticoat, on which was wrote, with a pencil, 'Look on this child as committed to your care by the hand of Providence; be careful of it, and you will not repent it.' I was very much struck, (continued Mr. Weimar) by such an extraordinary circumstance, but resolved to do my duty: a nurse was provided in the house; I had it baptized and named it Matilda. I said it was my niece; having then no other servant but Agatha, and she being faithful to my wishes, as my niece the beloved adopted child was brought up, and had masters of every kind to instruct her. Years rolled away, no enquiry was ever made, and I began to see a thousand graces in this young creature, which insensibly warmed my heart, and taught it what it was to love, a lesson I had never learnt till then. When I returned from France my protégée was improved in beauty and stature; she knew little of men, and she was less known by them; I determined to acquaint her with the secret I have related, and to offer her my hand. I deliberated some time in what manner to disclose it, and was consulting with Agatha how to make the discovery when you overheard the conversation, mistook the purport of it, and in consequence of that mistake gave me inexpressible misery."

Here Mr. Weimar stopt. Matilda, who sat almost breathless and stupified, fetched a deep sigh, "Then I am an outcast, a forsaken orphan, without friends or protectors! Gracious heaven! the offspring of guilt perhaps, for who but guilty wretches would give up their child to strangers?" A friendly burst of tears relieved her beating heart.

"Take comfort, my dearest Matilda, permit me to offer you my hand, my heart, I will be your protector through life; I consent that you shall consult the Marquis and Marchioness; you shall make your own terms for Albert, whom I shall value for his fidelity to you. If I have mentioned you in Paris as my niece, it was to avoid disagreeable questions, and keep your secret. The marriage may be private or public, as you like, no one will dare interfere with my wife. Think of every thing; I will return to-morrow for your determination." He arose, he kissed her hand, and left her motionless in the chair.

The moment he quitted the room the Marchioness entered, and, embracing the warm statue, as she called her, "I have heard all, my dear Matilda, and am equally astonished with yourself: his tale is plausible, perhaps true. Whoever were your parents, I should suppose them dead, from their not making enquiries during so many years after their child. Some praise is doubtless due to Mr. Weimar, for his care of you; his first motives were certainly benevolent ones; whether he latterly intended you honourable, or not, cannot be known; he offers to marry you now, in the face of your friends; 'tis possible you might mistake the tenor of the conversation you overheard—at any rate he seems now ready to act with honour. All this I say for Mr. Weimar,—justice demands I should be impartial; now, on the other hand, if your heart is repugnant to his offers; if you cannot be reconciled in your own mind to the account he has given you; if the gratitude due to his care of you in early life is effaced from your heart by his subsequent conduct, and you cannot overcome the disgust it inspired, never think of accepting his hand, to render both wretched. I have adopted you, I love you as a child, and will protect you; in me you shall find the mother you have lost: fear not, therefore, my dearest Matilda, to decide as your heart and judgment shall direct; do nothing hastily, take this day and night to reflect and determine with your whole heart to-morrow. I shall, with your permission, inform the Marquis of this extraordinary story, and I am sure his affection for you will coincide with mine."

Whilst the Marchioness was speaking Matilda had time to recover herself from the astonishment she had been thrown into, and still more from the humiliating idea, that she was indeed a friendless orphan, and owed unbounded obligations to a man she had for some time past looked on with detestation.

When the Marchioness was silent the unhappy girl took her hand, and kissing it, with a flood of tears, "My dear, my generous benefactress, do you and the Marquis decide for me, I am incapable of judging for myself; I feel what I owe to Mr. Weimar's humanity—I honour him for his benevolence and charity to a poor deserted infant; he is a good master, and beloved, as I have heard, by his tenants; I may have erred, I may have condemned him wrongfully, yet my heart, my judgment is not on his side. Condescend, dear madam, to direct me; I will take this day and night to reflect on everything I have heard; have the goodness to inform me in the morning of your own and the Marquis's opinion, and I hope I shall act so as not to forfeit the friendship you have honoured me with."

The Marchioness embraced her with expressions of tenderness, and repaired to the Marquis, to whom she repeated the preceding conversation.

He was very much surprised and puzzled. "We cannot controvert any of the circumstances he has related, and his behaviour to her, from the moment she was thrown on his protection, deserves the greatest praise; one would scarcely believe a mind capable of such good actions could entertain designs so contrary to honour and the tenor of his former conduct; his offers now certainly prove his affection, but I own I should be sorry to see such a lovely young creature compelled to be sacrificed to a man older perhaps than her father: If there is a mystery in her birth, time yet may bring it to light; however she must determine for herself, but let it be free from the idea of necessity, for on our protection she may rely."

The Count De Bouville, anxious for Matilda's health, and the result of the expected conference, made the Marchioness an early visit; as he had been informed of the preceding circumstances, they made no scruple to relate every particular that had taken place that morning. The Count was very much shocked; he scarcely knew the nature of the sentiments he entertained for Matilda; 'tis true, he admired and esteemed her, from the little observations he had found an opportunity of making on her character, but he possessed too much good sense to be violently attached on so slender an acquaintance; yet he could still less bear the idea, that she should marry Mr. Weimar. A man of quality in France to marry an obscure young woman without even knowing the authors of her being, would, he knew, incur everlasting contempt; yet, were the Germans less proud? but then Mr. Weimar was an elderly man, accountable to no one, lived in the country, detached from the world, and could do as he pleased. In short, he saw insuperable difficulties attending an attachment to Matilda from himself, and the certainty of it gave him more pain than in prudence he ought to have indulged. He had forgot himself, his long reverie surprised his friends, the Marquis interrupted it by asking his sentiments on the story he had heard? He said it was impossible for him to form an opinion; the account, with respect to her birth, was uncommon, yet nevertheless it might be true, such things had happened, and were not impossible; but if Mr. Weimar was just in every particular, although he had a claim upon her gratitude, he could not see he had any to her person, contrary to her inclinations. The Marquis said, "Your sentiments exactly coincide with mine, therefore, the young lady must determine for herself; for my own part I have little doubt but her birth is noble; her person, her figure, the extraordinary natural understanding she possesses confirms my opinion that so many graces seldom belong to a mean birth or dishonest connexions." "There may be some truth in your observation, (said the Marchioness) but we have seen and heard of many instances where a noble soul has been inclosed within a vulgar body, and honour, fidelity, integrity, and attachment are seen in a thousand examples among people of the lowest class, though I grant not in common to be met with; but then every one has not had the cultivation nor accomplishments of Matilda." "Ah! (cried the Count) your remarks are undoubtedly very just; but there are so many natural graces in this lady, that I think with the Marquis, they never could spring from a mean or improper connexion." "I think so too, (replied she) but be that as it may, she shall always command our friendship and protection."

She had scarcely said this before a servant entered with a letter, she looked with surprise at the post-mark, and withdrew to the window, she had no sooner opened it and perused two or three lines, than she exclaimed, "Gracious Heaven! in England, O, my Lord, the Countess is safe in England?" The Count De Bouville instantly took leave, nor did they attempt to detain him, but engaged his return in the evening, with his mother and sister, if they were disengaged.

He had no sooner left the room, than she eagerly read the contents of her letter as follows:

"My dearest sister will, I know, rejoice when I tell her I have escaped from the worst of evils, perhaps from death, and am safe in the protection of a charming English Lady, Mrs. Courtney, at her villa about three miles from London. The uncertainty whether you have left France, or on your journey to England, prevents me from being more explicit; if you have not left France, write under cover to Mrs. Courtney, Harley-street, Cavendish-square. If this letter is sent after you, hasten to me, dearest sister,—O, what happiness I promise myself in embracing my dearest friends. I hope Miss Weimar is with you; the uncertainty has given me great concern. Do not delay an hour to satisfy your affectionate sister and friend.

"VICTORIA."

"Good God! I thank thee, (cried the Marchioness) this is blessed news indeed." "I rejoice with you, my dearest love, (said the Marquis) but pray communicate the news to your lovely protégée."

She hastened to Matilda; she was reclining on her arms, thrown across the table, and weeping bitterly. "My charming girl, do not give way to sorrow, heaven, in its own good time, will send you relief; here is an instance to prove it," (giving her the letter.) Poor Matilda raised her drooping head, and hastily looked it over, clasped her hand with joy, "O, my dearest madam, this is happiness indeed—let me not be so selfish to mourn on a day of joy like this." "Let this, my dear young friend, be a lesson to yourself, never despair; to misfortunes and contradictions to our best wishes, we are all liable, and all must expect; none are exempt from the calamities incident to human nature; to bear those inevitable evils with patience, to acquire resolution and fortitude under them, and to look forward with hope, that you may one day be delivered from them, will blunt the arrows of affliction, and enable you to support them with resignation."

"My beloved, my charming monitress, (cried Matilda) I will try to profit by your advice; the Countess and yourself shall be my great examples—dear lady, how kind to think of the poor Matilda; I wish I could see her, but alas!—" "No sighs, (said the Marchioness) you must and shall be cheerful this day; hope, my dear girl, and all may be well yet."

They descended to the parlour, and in the afternoon had the pleasure of hearing Joseph was just arrived with the servant. "Let him come in," (they all cried, as with one breath.) He entered; poor fellow, he fell on his knees and wept, it was difficult to say whether with joy or sorrow—he felt both; the sight of Miss Weimar remembered him of Bertha's dreadful fate, though he rejoiced to see her safe. The Marchioness and Matilda ran to raise him. "Welcome, my good Joseph, (said the former) you are come on a happy day." "My dear friend, (said the latter, pressing his hand) do not give way to grief; we have all our sorrows, but we have our pleasures too, and I have news for you, Joseph. Our good lady is alive, and safe from the power of her enemies." "Heaven be thanked, (said the old man, wiping his eyes) this is blessed news indeed; and to see you safe too, my dear young madam, makes me happy, though I can't forget poor Bertha: alas, your ladyship, she was a good and faithful wife; she knew nothing about my lady—poor soul, she kept no secrets from me." He seemed to feel a reproach for his secrecy.

"My honest friend, (said the Marquis) your kindness and fidelity to our dear sister deserves reward; in this house you may rest free from care the remainder of your days, and I will settle two hundred livres on you yearly besides."

Joseph again dropt on his knees, "God bless your honour! God bless the dear ladies!" And he hurried out of the room, tears of thankfulness running down his cheeks.

"Good creature! (cried Matilda, wiping her eyes) may the rest of your life be peaceful and happy."

They now again recurred to the subject of the Countess and her letter. The Marchioness expressed her wishes to set off with all possible expedition to England, and within ten days it was fixed they should depart. Matilda heard this determination with a sigh, which did not pass unobserved, though they forbore to notice it; they concluded however she should be left to herself until the next morning, that their opinions might not appear to influence her. For herself, the idea of her obscure birth was a severe mortification; she considered her friends De Bouville and De Bancre as so much her superiors, that she could no longer treat them with that easy familiarity she had been accustomed, though she little thought the former was acquainted with her whole story.

In the evening came the Countess of Bouville and her family, with Madame De Nancy and her sister. After the first compliments, "Bless me! (cried Mademoiselle De Bancre) what in the world, ladies, have you done to Mademoiselle De Fontelle; I met her this morning, and pleading an engagement here as a reason for refusing her invitation, she flew into a violent rage, accused the Marchioness of treating her with rudeness unpardonable; and for Miss Weimar, she lavished such a torrent of abuse on her, that had I not known her fixed aversion to all handsome women, and a small predilection in favor of a certain person, whose attentions she is fearful of losing, I should have been at a loss to account for her acrimony."

"If the lady has any dislike, or fears respecting me, (answered Matilda, with evident confusion) she does me great injustice; 'tis impossible I should ever injure her, or clash with any views she has formed." "There is no saying what her views may be, (said the Count) but I will venture to assert, there can be no divided opinion concerning the merits of Miss Weimar and Mademoiselle De Fontelle; and the jealousy of a mean mind, when conscious of its deficiencies, is natural enough." "Come, come, (said the Marchioness) no scandal, my good friends: we cannot be hurt by malice, any more than we can be gratified by undue praises at the expence of others."

The uncommon spirits of the Marquis and Marchioness attracted observation, as well as the dejection of Matilda, which she attributed to ill health. The Count and his sister sympathized with her, and the former was so agitated for the event of the following day, that he did not dare ask himself why he was so much interested.

Matilda rejoiced when the evening concluded and she could retire to herself: she was far from well; her anxiety in what manner she should answer Mr. Weimar distracted her mind; she felt the strongest repugnance to become his wife—she was sure she could not be happy with him; if she had wronged him, he never could, she thought, cordially forgive, nor should she ever look up to him with confidence. She passed a restless night, and arose ill and unrefreshed. She entreated her friends to be present; they at first objected, but she was so extremely unhappy at their refusal, that they at length consented to come in after his appearance, if she sent for them.

His name was at length announced, and he absolutely started at the alteration in her countenance. "The solemnity of your air, my charming Matilda, gives me great uneasiness; how great will be my transport to remove every cause of sorrow from your heart, and see cheerfulness restored to your features. Have you acquainted your friends here with my communications?" "I have, Sir, (replied she, endeavouring to collect some firmness) but they decline giving any opinion; have you any objection to their being present now?" He hesitated; "I see no necessity for it—but as you please." She then rung the bell, and requested the Marquis and his lady would do them the favor of their company. They entered, and after mutual compliments, and they were seated, Matilda addressed herself to Mr. Weimar. "At the time, Sir, when you permitted

me to believe I had the honour of being your niece, although sensible of
your kindness, and conscious of my obligations to you, for the care of
my infancy, I have often taken my heart to task, and upbraided its want
of gratitude; what must I accuse myself of now, when I am informed
that to your charity alone I am indebted for the advantages I possess. O,
Sir, never, never can I return what I owe you—least of all, by becoming
your wife; 'tis an honour I do not deserve—". "Pardon me for interrupting you, my dear Matilda: I disclaim the name of obligation; you owe
me no gratitude but for my affection; consider how many years you
have been the delight, the darling of my heart, and now, when my love
is stronger than ever, am I to be thrown off at once; have you no feeling
for the wretchedness you doom me to for the remainder of my life?"
"Oh! Sir, what can I say, (answered Matilda;) impressions once strongly
conceived are difficult to eradicate; the conversation I overheard is ever
present to my mind, and could I forget that, then my reverence for
my uncle would return, and I should shudder at the idea of a nearer
connexion. When I think of it, and indeed, Sir, I have endeavoured to
think of it, an unaccountable repugnance makes the idea horrible to
me; yet after all, if you persist in wishing me to become your wife, I do
not think myself at liberty absolutely to refuse, but I tell you candidly,
I never can love you, that though I will obey you, and do my duty, I
know I shall be miserable, and in that persuasion surely 'tis impossible
I can make you happy." "I am sensible, (said he) that my age is against
me, I cannot expect to be loved like a young fellow, but my unremitting
attentions to please will make me deserving your esteem." "Well, Sir,
(said Matilda, hastily) it is fit you should prefer your own happiness to
mine, I have no right to refuse, nor any way of discharging the obligations I owe you for the care of my early life, but by the sacrifice of the
maturer part of it."

Unable any longer to struggle with the grief and horror that opprest her, she burst into tears. Her friends felt for her, but were as yet
silent. Mr. Weimar took her hand and kissed it, "Cruel Matilda, is this
the return for all my tenderness; but I do not prefer my own happiness
to yours; consider, pardon me if I say, consider your situation; with all
the charms you possess, such is the cruel prejudice against those who
have neither friends nor family to protect and provide for them, that
in France you could not hope or expect any proper establishment."
"Hold, Sir, (said she, with indignation) do not insult me; I know what I
am, and since I am unworthy of an establishment in France, I never will

have one in Germany. No, Sir, you have now convinced me, if I cannot honour you I ought not to degrade you. I will retire to a convent: I will become a lay-sister, 'tis perhaps the line Providence intended for me; be that as it may, you have convinced me I ought not, nor I solemnly declare I never will be your wife." She spoke with a force and spirit as surprised them all. "Do not be rash, Matilda; I offer you a handsome fortune; you shall no longer be confined in the country, as my wife, you shall have a house at Berne, at Lausanne, or where you please; every pleasure shall attend you; the Marquis himself shall secure your future fortune: do not be offended for trifles, and what never was intended as an insult; trust to my love to create an interest in your heart." "No, Sir, (answered she) the die is cast; a little while since I thought, if you desired it, I ought to be your's; but if you can stoop to degrade yourself by a connexion with a friendless deserted orphan, I never will owe the obligation to any man, nor have the chance of being upbraided, that I belong to nobody. Pardon me, my good friends, the trouble I have given you, a few days hence I will hide myself for ever." She arose to leave the room. "Stop, madam, (said Mr. Weimar;) since nothing can prevail on you to accept my hand, at least permit me to tell you, you have no right to dispose of yourself without my permission; you were committed to my care, doubtless by your parents; you may one day be reclaimed; I am answerable for the trust reposed in me, and with me I shall insist upon your remaining till those to whom you belong appear to claim you."

Matilda sunk back in her chair, overwhelmed with horror; he looked furious with passion; the Marquis and his lady were perplexed and chagrined, at length the former said, "Without the smallest intent of contesting your rights, Sir, I have patiently attended to what has passed between this young lady and yourself; the Marchioness and I have been scrupulously exact not to give our opinion, much less advice on the subject; but now, since she has resolutely made up her mind, you certainly have too just a sense of what is owing to yourself, to persist in addressing her; taking that for granted, and that you think it improper she should become a Nun, I request it as a favor, that Miss Matilda may be permitted to spend a few months with us; should any person appear to claim her, I trust it will be no dishonour to have her found in my protection; and I pledge my honor she shall form no marriage or engagement under our care, but return to you as she now is." "My Lord, (returned Mr. Weimar) I must consider of this request, and she will do well to consider and repent her rash determination; if she does, I will receive her with open arms. I trust her to your honor, and shall to-morrow wait on you with my decided opinion." With a polite, but general bow, he left the room.

The Marchioness was supporting Matilda's head upon her shoulder. "Look up, my dear girl, be composed, he is gone." "Thank heaven! (said she) but my head is very bad, and with your leave I will lay down an hour or two." "Do so, my dear," (replied her friend;) and calling the servant to attend her, she was conducted to her apartment.

When she left the room the Marchioness said, "Mr. Weimar's conduct appears very strange, and unbecoming a man of his years; I know not what to think; had he not injudiciously mentioned her birth she would certainly have accepted his hand, though I own it would have given me pain had she done so."

"For my part, (answered the Marquis) I marked him well during the whole scene; that he is excessively fond of her, I believe, but I am not perfectly satisfied, although I know not what part to blame of his conduct; nevertheless she has now taken her resolution, and only force shall compel me to withdraw my protection from a friendless orphan, whose situation is really deplorable. If the circumstances he related of her birth are true, I have no doubt but one time or other a discovery will take place to her advantage; all I wish at present is, that she may accompany you to England." "Do you not think, (said the Marchioness) the Count De Bouville is very fond of her?" "I fear so, (replied he;) but you know Mr. Weimar's observations with respect to the obscurity of her birth are founded on truth, I would by no means encourage a dangerous intimacy between them, which might be productive of misery to both; 'tis for that reason I should wish her to leave Paris whilst the liking which I think mutual is in its infancy."

During the conversation of her generous friends, the unhappy Matilda gave herself up to extreme sorrow. If Mr. Weimar chose to exert his right over her, she saw no one to whom she could appeal for redress; but determined as she now was never to become his wife, she was sensible she had little chance of becoming the wife of any other man; to engage her benefactors in disputes and controversies with him was equally repugnant to her inclinations, and without his consent it would be in vain to think of accompanying her friends, as he might pursue her everywhere. She knew she had many obligations to him, but she could not return them in the way he was desirous of, which must make her miserable, and of course give no happiness to him. What then, (cried she, weeping) am I to do? there is no alternative but Mr. Weimar or a convent; the latter is my preferable choice, and if he persists to-morrow in exerting the authority he claims over me, I will fly to that for protection.

Having now made up her mind, she dropt asleep, but her slumbers were broken and disturbed; and in about three hours she returned to her friends, very little refreshed, but was much gratified by their peculiar tenderness and attention, and an increased respect in their manner proved they wished to restore her self-consequence, and make her at ease with herself.

This is true benevolence; 'tis the mode of conferring favours that either obliges or wounds a feeling heart. Many people are generous, but they forget how painful it is to ask favors, and think it quite sufficient if they give, let the manner of giving be ever so ungracious, and their superiority ever so ostentatiously displayed. Not so the Marquis and his lady—they endeavoured to persuade her, they were the persons obliged by her acceptance of their little civilities, and entered into all her concerns with the affection and anxiety of her nearest relatives.

Matilda's grateful heart overflowed; speech indeed was not lent her, but her tears, her expressive looks forcibly conveyed the language she could not utter.

In the meantime Mademoiselle De Fontelle was not idle; scarce a person the Marchioness was acquainted with, but knew she had taken a girl under her protection, who had robbed and run away from her uncle, with a young handsome footman; and during two days circulation of the story Miss Weimar was detected by her uncle in several low intrigues, which he kindly forgave, 'till quite abandoned and incorrigible, she had taken away all his gold and jewels, and came to Paris with this fellow, whom the Marchioness herself had taken into the house.

"Ciel, (cries one, shrugging her shoulders) a pretty story indeed; this is the discreet, the admirable Marchioness De Melfort, held up as a pattern to all the women in Paris." "Yes, I thought she was a wonder, (said another;) abundance of art, to be sure she has; for I'll answer for it, this intrigue with a footman is not the first by many; but, poor woman, her charms are in their wane now, so the man is a substitute for the master." "What, (cries a third) has the Marchioness herself an intrigue? Lord, didn't you hear that? why this girl is only a cover to her own amusements." "Well, (said a fourth) I saw both the other night at

Madame De Bouville's, and I am sure they are both ugly enough, not-withstanding the men made such a fuss about them."

'Twas thus the scandal of Mademoiselle's fabricating was increased and magnified among their generous and charitable acquaintance: like Sir Peter Teazle's wound, it was in all parts of his body, and by a va-riety of murderous weapons, when the poor man was unconscious of having received any himself, and could scarce obtain credit when he appeared in perfect health: so unwilling is the good-natured world to give up a story that is to the disadvantage of others. It was in vain the Countess De Bouville, her son and daughter, Madame De Nancy and her sister, attempted to stop the scandalous tales; like lightning it flew from house to house, and everyone who had no character to lose, and others of suspected reputation only rejoiced to level an amiable respectable woman with themselves.

The Count De Bouville was distracted; he flew from a set of envi-ous wretches to the Marquis De Melfort's; when he entered the room he met the eyes of the lovely dejected Matilda, with such an expression of grief and softness in them, that it pierced his heart: she blushed, and withdrew them, with a sigh she could not suppress. The Marquis had left the room, the Marchioness was holding her young friend's hand with an affectionate tender air.

After the usual compliments he enquired particularly after Mat-ilda's health; she could not trust her voice just then to speak. The Mar-chioness answered, "She is better, only a dejection on her spirits, which you must assist in removing: I was trying to persuade her to accom-pany me in a carriage to pay a few visits." The Count, alarmed at the intention, replied, "Paying visits might possibly be too fatiguing, but an airing would surely be of service." "Well then, (said the Marchion-ess, forgetful of her Lord's caution) you shall accompany us." The car-riage, which was in waiting, drawing up, he gladly escorted the two ladies to it, and took his seat very quietly opposite to Matilda, who had hitherto observed a profound silence. He contrived however to draw her into a little conversation, and was charmed with her good sense and sweetness of manners. The languor that pervaded her fine features, powerfully engaged the heart, and the Count could not help thinking how happy that man must be who was destined to possess so great a treasure! This reflection caused a sudden alteration in his countenance; he grew thoughtful and uneasy, when he was disturbed in his reverie by an exclamation from the Marchioness, "Good heavens! what insolence." "What's the matter, madam?" "Bless me, didn't you observe the two carriages that passed, in one was Madame Remini and her two daughters, in the other Madame Le Brun, her niece, and two others of my acquaintance. As the carriage passed, I bowed and kissed my hand; they one and all returned a slight bow, and laughed in each other's faces: upon my word I never saw such rudeness." The Count, who could too well account for this behaviour, was however very much vexed. "Dear madam, (said he) such impertinent women are scarce worth your notice, and only deserving contempt." "That's true, Count, (replied she) and henceforth I shall treat them as they deserve."

As neither of the parties were in high spirits, their airing was not a long one, and they returned to the house as the Marquis entered it.

After they were seated the Marchioness was expressing her wishes to be in England. "Does Miss Weimar accompany you?" (asked the Count.) "I hope so," (replied the Marchioness.) The Marquis giving the Count a glance, they retired to the library, where the conversation of the morning, between Mr. Weimar and Matilda, was repeated. The Count felt indignation, pity, and resentment; he was delighted with Matilda's spirit, yet most sincerely felt for her unhappy situation. "Good God, my dear Marquis, what is to be done for this amiable girl?" "I hope, (he replied) we shall prevail on him to leave her with us,—tomorrow will determine; but take it how he will, I have this day made several persons acquainted with his being the guardian of Matilda, and his offers of marriage in my presence: the circumstance of a young lady's flying from her guardian is nothing extraordinary, and will, I hope, do away the scandal that has been propagated at her expence." "You are very good, (returned the Count) and I am sure she merits the esteem of all the world." He took his leave under such a contrariety of sentiments, and so much real concern for the unfortunate Matilda, that when he returned to his sister she was quite alarmed, and asked a thousand questions relative to her friend. When he had explained every thing, the gentle Adelaide felt equal concern, and lamented that her troubles were of a kind that placed it out of the power of their friendship to afford her any consolation or relief.

Whilst they were expressing mutual regret, Mademoiselle De Fontelle was announced; she was received with a coldness that would have mortified any other person, but putting on a gay air, "Ah! Count, so soon returned from your party; I did not expect to find you here." "Perhaps, madam, had I known of your intended visit, I might have been elsewhere." "Very polite, upon my word, (said she, colouring deeply;) your brother, my dear Bouville, has acquired the English roughness of manners by his tour to that country." "I hope, madam, (replied he, significantly) I have acquired the sincerity of that nation, at least, to speak as I think; and as a proof of it, were you not my sister's guest, I should be free enough to say, I so much detest the fabricators of scandal, that I heartily rejoice when they are mortified by being obliged to hear the object of their envy is as much superior to them in every amiable quality of the mind, as she is in the beauty of her person, and that it will be her own fault only if she is not established in a more brilliant situation than her enemies can boast of."

With these words he left the room, with a look of scorn she could not support, but burst into tears. "Your brother has cruelly insulted me," (said she.) "I am sorry for it, and for the occasion," (answered Mademoiselle De Bouville;) but indeed you have been too unguarded in your reports to the disadvantage of Miss Weimar." "Name her not, (cried she) I hate her." "That may be, (returned the other) nevertheless I hold it my duty to do her justice." She then briefly mentioned Mr. Weimar was only her guardian, and that he was come after her to solicit her hand, the only thing for which she left him. His offers before the Marquis and his lady, and the very great justice he did her character were related. The malicious girl was ready to burst with spleen, but carried it off with an air. "Upon my word, (said she) Mr. Weimar was himself the person who first mentioned the affair to her disadvantage; and I suppose there is some point to carry, or some mystery in an affair where there are such contradictions, which I do not comprehend, and which, I dare say, will deceive nobody, though I would venture to swear, hardly any person will concern themselves about the Marchioness's little protégée, or whether the German is uncle or not to one whom no body knows." She arose, and desiring her respects to her *very polite* brother, flounced out of the room.

Neither her resentment nor absence was a subject of regret to Adelaide, who only visited her in compliance with the fashion of the times, which is to go every where with the rest of the world, and assist in forming a crowd, without knowing or caring for three-fourths of the company.

Meantime the remainder of the day was spent at the Marquis's in the most affectionate endeavours to console Matilda, and the warmest assurances of love and attention to her interests. They all anxiously expected the return of Mr. Weimar next morning, as the crisis on which her future destiny appeared to depend.

At the appointed hour Mr. Weimar sent in his name; her friends had persuaded Matilda to receive him alone, and send for them when she thought it necessary. She had tried all the morning to reconcile herself to his displeasure, but she was resolved to persevere in the resolution she had formed of retiring to a convent, if he made it necessary.

He entered the room with an air of kindness and complacency, took her hand and kissed it, "Let me flatter myself, dearest Matilda, (said he) that you are in better health and disposition than when I left you yesterday. I have passed many uneasy hours lately, indeed I may say truly, from the day you was committed to my care, every hour of my life has been spent in anxiety on your account." "Do not, Sir, (said she) for heaven's sake, do not crush me with the weight of obligations I owe you: a poor forlorn being, without family or friends, as you have justly told me, is entitled to no one's consideration; I am therefore beyond all possibility of return at present; indebted to you for every thing, for the life I enjoy, hard is the task upon me to refuse anything you request, but as this meeting is to decide once for all, pardon me if I say I cannot marry you, but this deference I owe to your fatherly care of me, I solemnly declare, that unless the authors of my being claim my first reverence, I never will encourage any man without your permission; this, Sir, is all I can, or ever will promise in your favour." "Ungrateful girl! (cried he, raising his voice) and is this all, this all you owe to a man who preserved your life, and bestowed his time and fortune to make you what you are?" "Oh! that I had died, (cried Matilda, in an agony) rather than to live and be thus upbraided for favours I never can return; but my mind tells me you will one day be repaid for all;—yes, I have a pre-sentiment I am no base-born unworthy offspring; one day, Sir, I may yet have the power to prove my sense of the obligations you reproach me with, and it will be the happiest moment of my life." She had spoken with such vehemence as precluded interruption; he was surprised; "You are warm, Matilda, (said he, very calmly.) "I cannot help it, Sir, you have made me desperate; I will seek peace and quietness in a convent. You will not permit me to accompany the Marchioness, (said she, softening, and tears running down her cheeks) and I think I owe you that respect not to go without your leave; therefore I have no other asylum but a convent to hope for." "Have I not a house, Matilda?" "Yes, Sir; I might have resided in my uncle's house, but I cannot, with propriety, in your's, when I have no such claim to boast of." She arose and rang the bell; "Desire the Marquis and his lady to favour me with their company." When the servant retired, "You are then determined, madam?" "I am, Sir." "Then so am I, and you may take the consequence." Her friends now entered; after they were seated Matilda spoke, "I took the liberty to request your presence, that you might be witness to my declaration for the last time, That I never will be the wife of Mr. Weimar, nor without his consent, unless commanded by my parents, (alas! how unlikely at present that hope) never to marry any other man. It would be the joy of my heart to have been permitted to accept the honor of the protection you have offered me, but as I fear that cannot be, I will retire into a convent, 'tis the only place of refuge for a poor unfortunate, friendless being, without family, friends, or even a name." She wept aloud, pronouncing those last words. The Marchioness sympathized with her, and addressing Mr. Weimar, "Come, Sir, (said she) let me prevail on you to accede to our request, we ask it as a favor; permit Miss Matilda to be in our care for six months; I engage my honor she shall return by that time free from every engagement." He made no answer.

"Shall I entreat the favor of a few words in private, Sir," said the Marquis. They arose and left the room. Within a short time they returned. Mr. Weimar, advancing to Matilda, "I have consented to oblige you, too ungrateful girl; I permit you to remain with the Marchioness, but conditionally, that you write me constantly every occurrence, nor presume to enter into any engagement without my acquiescence." "To these conditions, (cried she, her eyes sparkling with joy) I most cheerfully subscribe." He looked full of resentment at her, but taking a polite leave, declined an invitation to stay for dinner, and hastily withdrew.

The moment he left the room Matilda arose, and throwing her arms round the Marchioness, her grateful heart overflowing into tears, "Oh! my dearest, my generous protectress, how shall I ever return your goodness?" "By loving me, my precious girl, as affectionately as I do you," (answered she, embracing her.) Observing the Marquis seeming musing, "May I ask, my Lord, what occupies your thoughts?" "Yes, (replied he;) it is fit you should know; to be plain then, I don't like Mr. Weimar; I suspect he means to deceive us." "Good God, (cried Matilda, alarmed) how is that possible?" "Be it as it may, (answered the Marquis) we will guard against any sinister design; let our young friend retire this night to some place of safety." "You do not surely apprehend he will apply for a lettre de cachet?" (said the Marchioness.) "I should not be surprised at it," (returned he.) "Then, (said she) we will set off instantly on our journey; Louison and Antoine can attend us; Marianne shall take care of all our baggage here, and follow us, with Pierre, in a day or two, or come with you." "'Tis a hasty, and rather an inconvenient scheme, (said he) but I have no other to offer at present." "O, what trouble I occasion to my friends," (cried Matilda.) "Go to your apartment, set about packing, my dear girl; we must take a few necessaries with us, and set off immediately after dinner." She obeyed. The Marquis set about the arrangements for their journey, and promised to follow in four or five days.

Poor Joseph and Albert deplored their fate, in being too old to accompany the ladies, and were the only domestics left in the house, who knew to what place they were going.

Every thing being settled in a few hours, it was given out in the family, they were going into the country for a short time; even Marianne and Pierre knew no more for the present; and the ladies, attended by Louison and Antoine, set off, with all expedition: fortunately, Antoine had been in England once before, with a former master; he was therefore acquainted with the roads and accommodations, and consequently extremely useful.

The Marquis found the following day he had been right in his conjectures. Two men came to his hotel, armed with authority, to demand a lady commonly known by the name of Matilda Weimar, with a description of her person, then under the protection of the Marquis De Melfort. The Marquis was not at home; the men were informed the young lady was gone, with their mistress, into the country. They searched the house, and being disappointed, waited till the Marquis returned; he gave them the same information, and drew up a paper, signifying, that having taken the young lady under his protection, by the consent of Mr. Weimar, who called himself her guardian, she had accompanied the Marchioness on a visit to some friends; that he pledged his honor for her safety, also to answer any charges that could be brought against her. With this declaration the men departed and returned no more; but a person was observed to watch the house for some days after.

The Marquis made no secret to the Bouville family of the past transactions, and though they felt great regret for the loss of their friends, they acknowledged the event had justified their prudence in the steps they had taken.

The Count felt more than he dared express, yet tried to subdue his feelings, from a consciousness of their impropriety to be indulged. His sister was to be married the following week to Monsieur De Clermont, and her establishment engrossed much of his time and attention.

The Marquis very soon arranged all his affairs, and within five days after the ladies left Paris, he followed them.

The Marchioness and her friend pursued their route, arrived at Calais, and crossed over to Dover, without meeting a single accident; here they determined to rest, and wait for the Marquis. They were exceedingly fatigued with the expedition they had used, and were glad to sit down comfortably.

The Marchioness understood the English language perfectly well, and spoke enough to make herself comprehended in common matters; Antoine did the same, but as to Matilda and Louison, they knew not a single word 'till the Marchioness taught them to name a few necessary articles, and write down common words.

Much sooner than they expected, they had the pleasure of embracing the Marquis, and then learned the danger Matilda had escaped, and the duplicity of Mr. Weimar. She shuddered to think how near she had been to misery, and her affection and gratitude to the worthy pair, who protected her, was proportionably increased.

The following morning they left Dover, and by easy journies arrived at the Royal Hotel in Jermyn-street. A card was instantly sent off to Harley-street. The messenger returned, with a line only, from the Countess, that they should follow the bearer with all speed, and within ten minutes after the coach drew up. The Marquis hastened down to receive and conduct the ladies. The Countess was almost breathless with joy; she flew up stairs, and in a moment was in her sister's arms. Their mutual joy, their tears of affection and transport excited sympathy in everyone. The Countess, recovering, led her sister to Mrs. Courtney, "The two dearest friends I have on earth, (said she) love each other for my sake now, you have congenial hearts." She then warmly embraced Matilda. "This is the first day of my life, (cried she, putting her hand to her heart;) I have all that I love in the world about me, at least, all that I know," (added she, with a suppressed sigh.)

Matilda, whose grateful heart expanded with delight, to see all her friends happy, expressed her feelings with such a warmth of satisfaction as engaged all their affections. She was introduced also to Mrs. Courtney: and when the first tumults of joy were over, the Countess, taking that lady's hand, said, "Behold, my dear sister and brother, the preserver of Victoria's life; to her goodness I am indebted for all the happiness I now enjoy, a vast debt of gratitude, never to be repaid." "You neither do me nor yourself justice, (answered Mrs. Courtney;) if you do not think I am a thousand times overpaid for any little services, I have been so happy to render you, by the pleasure of your company, and the honor you have procured me, of knowing your respectable friends." They all gratefully bowed to this compliment, and then began to talk of their future residence. The Marquis wished to have a ready furnished house in the neighbourhood of Mrs. Courtney. She contended for the pleasure of accommodating them in hers; but this, for several reasons, they declined; and after a long and friendly contest it was decided a house should be procured for them in her neighbourhood, but that they should spend every other week at Mrs. Courtney's villa, and until a habitation was fixed on they would remain at the hotel, where they all supped together that evening.

"I know, (said the Countess) you must all be very anxious to understand by what means I obtained my present happy situation, and I am equally curious to know how my dear Miss Weimar conducted herself from the time we last met; but we will suspend curiosity for the present, nor cloud our happy meeting with a recital of painful events." "You are right, my dear Countess, (said Mrs. Courtney) we are now all happily met, and 'tis of little consequence by what means it came about at present."

They passed a most delightful evening, and parted with reluctance, after engaging to spend the following day in Harley-street, and Mrs. Courtney promising to search the neighbourhood for a house to accommodate them.

"What a charming woman is Mrs. Courtney," (said the Marchioness. "Ah! (cried Matilda) I wish I understood English. I should like to speak to that lady in her own language." "You shall learn it, my love, when we are settled; but as the lady speaks French remarkably well, you have no cause for regret."

They retired to rest, and the following morning had some trades people with them, who are always on the watch to attend foreigners at

the hotels. They purchased a few trifles, but chose to have Mrs. Courtney's judgment before they bought anything of consequence.

The Marquis, who had letters of credit on the house of Sir Tho-
mas Herries, attended by the master of the hotel, went out to get cash,
whilst the ladies attended to the business of the toilet, as they had engaged to be with their friends at a very early hour.

Soon after his return they drove to Harley-street, and were received with that affectionate cordiality, a thousand times more desirable than distant civility and respect: they met like old friends, with
congenial minds, to enjoy the pleasures of society. Mrs. Courtney told
them, she hoped she had already succeeded in her endeavours to procure a residence for them; "and, fortunately, (said she) only three doors
from hence; if you are inclined, we can now look at it." The proposal
was accepted. The house and furniture, which had been all new within
the twelvemonth, and belonged to Lord G——, who found it convenient to go abroad for his health; was now to be let for a year certain,
at 400l. per annum. They were extremely well pleased with the house,
and readily agreed to the terms. Within two or three days it would be
ready for their reception.

This being settled, they returned in high spirits, and spent a most
delightful day in a quiet family party.

The next day was appropriated to shopping and excursions round
the town; and indeed, except sleeping hours, they passed their time
solely together; Mrs. Courtney having shut her doors to all company
'till they were settled in their new abode: for the same reason the Marquis deferred sending all his letters of recommendation, or waiting on
the French Ambassador.

The fourth day after their arrival in England they took possession
of their house; and having been fortunate enough to obtain a respectable woman, who was perfectly conversant in the French language, as
housekeeper, they agreed to spend the following week in the country,
previous to their being publicly announced in town.

Nothing particular occurred until their arrival at Bellvue, Mrs.
Courtney's little paradise: they were quite delighted with its situation,
and charmed with its polite and friendly owner. The second morning
after their residence here, the Countess entered the Marchioness's
dressing-room, (Matilda was with her;) "Mrs. Courtney has just got
two or three neighbours with her; my presence not being necessary, I
have seized the opportunity, to make our respective communications:

I am sensible you must be very curious, but I wish to hear my dear Miss Weimar's story taken up from the visit she promised me, and I suppose intended paying me." Matilda very readily gave an account of every event at the castle. The Countess shuddered, and heaved a sigh to the fate of poor Margarite, but did not interrupt 'till she came to the letter received from Joseph, of the fire in the castle, Bertha's miserable fate and his escape. "Good heavens! (cried she) of what atrocious wickedness is that man capable! Poor wretch, what a long account has he one day to make—God grant him repentance!" Matilda proceeded, and related every circumstance until their safe arrival in London. The Countess embraced the lovely girl, who had betrayed a sense of mortification in recounting the particulars of her birth. "I thank my beloved sister, (said she) for the attention she paid to my request, and I am persuaded your charming society has amply recompensed her for the favor she did me." "You judge right, my dear Victoria; I am indeed the obliged person: but come, pray begin your narration, and take it up from the time you married that brute whose name you bear——" "But which I do not assume here, (answered the Countess;) I pass for a Madame Le Roche, and as we neither go to court nor attend any public galas, I have never been particularly introduced, and am known among my dear Mrs. Courtney's friends as a widow of some fashion, but small fortune, on a visit to her, and not very desirous of much company; therefore, you must get your lesson by heart against we return to town. Now, as to your request, you may possibly think I am too observant of my word towards an inhuman monster, when I declare that the sacred vows he drew from me still bind me to secrecy, as to what occasioned my being shut up in the Castle, and permitting the general belief of my death." "Good God! sister, (cried the Marchioness) vows forced upon you, under such circumstances, have no power to bind; and you have sufficiently proved your truth and honour, by preserving them so many years from your dearest friends;—I am sure our confessor will absolve you." "Maybe so, (replied Madame Le Roche) and on our return to town I will consult him, till when I shall take up my story from the day Matilda left me. Charmed that I was likely to procure an asylum for her, as I doubted not of your acceding to my request, I retired to bed at an early hour, but could not sleep; about midnight I thought I heard an uncommon noise at the outward doors; I listened, and, convinced it was not fancy, I called on Margarite; the noise had alarmed her, she ran to me in the same instant that we heard the door in the kitchen burst open, and the Count appeared with an ill-looking fellow. I was out of bed, and had thrown on a wrapping gown about me; I trembled from head to foot; he came up to me furiously; "Wretch, (cried he) you have broken your oath with me, and therefore mine is no longer binding—prepare to die." Despair had given me courage—I was no longer the poor weak creature he had entangled some years before; my spirits returned, "Strike, barbarian, and complete your crimes, I fear not death, it will free me from all the miseries you have heaped upon me; but I will not suffer under imputed guilt—I have broke no vows, I have kept the fatal oath you extorted from me in the hour of terror." "How dare you persist in falsehoods, (cried he;) you have had a woman here—you see and converse with Joseph daily; dare you deny those charges?" "I do not, (answered I) but still I have preserved my faith; the woman came here by accident, unawed by the terrors Joseph and I endeavoured to inspire, but she knew not who I was, nor anything relative to my situation, and goes from hence in a few days: as to Joseph, the poor fellow, when he brings my provisions, enters into a little chat with Margarite, and sometimes I speak to him, and where is the mighty crime? You must know your diabolical secret is too well kept, or I need not be here in your power." He paused a few minutes, then withdrew to the window, and spoke to the man in a low tone; they came again towards me, and I expected instant death, but they locked the doors, and stopping the mouth of poor Margarite, dragged her out of the room, still locking the door after them. The apprehensions I was under for that poor creature overcame the courage I assumed, and I swooned; how long I was deprived of my senses, I know not, but I recovered by cold water they threw in my face. "O, what have you done with my poor nurse?" "She is safe from betraying secrets, (replied he:) come, madam, put on your clothes, and I shall bestow you safely too." "If you design my death, (said I) let me die here." "Do as I command, (cried he, furiously) or I shall carry you off as you are." I threw on my clothes, as well as my terror would permit; meantime he broke the locks of my cabinet, although he could have had the keys, took out what valuables belonged to me; and then taking me between them, they led me through a long subterraneous passage, till we came out through a thicket to the skirts of the wood; it was but faint star light; I saw two horses fastened; I was immediately put upon one, though I made some resistance, expecting they intended carrying me into the thick part of the wood, and murder me there,—and I still think it was so designed. The man held me fast; we passed a small cottage, but all was quiet, and soon after entered another part of the wood, when suddenly the Count's horse fell and threw him over his head; he lay motionless; the man who held me rode up to him; he did not move. "I must see what hurt he has," (cried he;) and jumping off, left me on the horse; at the same instant I gave him a kick, and the animal set off full speed through the wood. I must inevitably have been killed, had it pursued its way through the thickets, but providentially he made towards the road, and being tired, slackened his pace. Unable any longer to support the fatigue; my head giddy, and dreadfully galled with the saddle, I slipped off on a small hillock, on one side, and lay quite exhausted, expecting every moment to be overtaken and murdered. I had been there but a few minutes before a carriage appeared, with two or three horsemen; I uttered a cry; the carriage stopt—a servant came up, "Who are you—what is the matter?" (said he.) I replied, feebly, "An unfortunate woman, escaped from being murdered, for God sake save me." The man went to the carriage, it drew up, the door was opened, and I was put in. The sudden joy added to the terror and fatigue I had gone through overpowered my senses, and I fainted; I was soon restored by the help of the lady's salts; I was able to look up, by my side sat the charming Mrs. Courtney, supporting me; opposite was a middle aged gentleman, and a young one about seventeen or eighteen; I tried to speak, and kissed her hand. "Be composed, dear lady, (said she) your spirits are already too much exhausted; (seeing me look with terror then on one side and then another) you fear being pursued, (she continued;) we shall stop very soon, but as the day appears the blinds shall be drawn up." This was accordingly done: 'tis needless to tell you our conversation. My heart expanded with gratitude to heaven for my deliverance. I was unable to give a satisfactory account of myself, only so far as related to my escape from the wood; I mentioned you, my sister, and your intended journey to England, and the uncertainty how soon you might depart, and therefore my wishes to join you. Mrs. Courtney told me she was immediately going there, and as I was apprehensive of being known, it would be much better to accompany her, and write my sister from England. Before I could reply to this obliging proposal, we stopt at the post-house, changed horses, and pursued our journey with rapidity 'till about noon, when we drew up to a very fine old castle, which I found belonged to a friend of theirs, and where they proposed passing the night. I was shocked at my appearance; my clothes thrown on in a hurry, discomposed by the flight of the horse, and not one article about me calculated for travelling. My amiable preserver requested I would make myself easy. "Fortunately, (said she) we are nearly of a size; I have another habit in my trunk, with which I can accommodate you, and my woman will soon make your appearance decent, and reconcile your feelings, which I see are much oppressed." The moment we alighted, "My friend has been ill, (said she) and is in dishabille, will you shew her an apartment, that she may alter her dress?" The lady's woman instantly attended me to an elegant room, whilst Mrs. Courtney's got the trunk opened and procured me necessaries. I was soon equipped; my charming friend came to conduct me to the company; I was received with kindness and attention by an elderly gentleman and lady, the owners of the castle, and passed a comfortable night. The next day we pursued our journey, though much pressed to stay, and arrived at Lausanne. I found the gentleman with us was uncle to Mrs. Courtney, and was come over to place his son at Lausanne, to finish his education; but having formerly resided some years in Switzerland, he had been paying a few visits to his friends, and was returning from one of them, when I was so fortunate to obtain their protection. We stayed a week at Lausanne. I kept very close in my apartment, in a constant dread of being discovered; I was heartily rejoiced when we pursued our journey, much more so when we arrived in England. Mrs. Courtney's kindness cannot be described; she treats me like her dearest sister, and her uncle, who lives not far from us in Cavendish-square, appears to make no difference between us; he is a nobleman, a widower, about forty; has an only son, and is one of the most amiable men I ever knew. Judge how much happiness is now my lot with such friends, and blessed with the company of my dearest relations. Sometimes, (continued she) I thought it possible the Count might have been killed by his fall; at other times, that he might be only senseless; in short, I had a hundred conjectures about him, but 'tis plain he was not much hurt, since he could return to the castle and contrive more mischief. Now, in this land of liberty should he ever appear to persecute me again, I shall make no scruple to open the whole scenes of wickedness he has been guilty of;—there is one corroding care that hangs about my heart, but of that hereafter." She arose in visible emotion, "Come let us take a ramble in the garden after my tedious narrative." They accompanied her.

"I think, my dear sister, (said the Marquis) 'tis a justice you owe yourself and friends to institute a process against this monster." "I shall think of it, (said she) but I have many objections; at present let us drop the subject." They acquiesced.

Mrs. Courtney joined them in the garden; "Lord bless me! (said she, laughing) how eager and persevering is curiosity; here I have had three ladies dying to see the French family with me; asking ten thousand questions about their dress and their persons, their fashions, and many other matters equally important. They made a most tedious visit, and as I discovered the motive, I was at length obliged to inform them my Parisian friends saw no company until they had been introduced in town: this effectually did the business,—they rose all together, made their congeés, and put an end to their tiresome enquiries."

A week was spent at Bellvue, in all the delights of love and friendship, in little excursions round the neighbourhood, and in viewing the delightful prospects the Surry hills afforded them.

Persons of good sense, like the present party, were never at a loss for rational amusement when at home, and on their return to the metropolis they separated with reluctance, though so near to each other.

Two days after their arrival the Marquis received a letter from the Count De Bouville, informing him of his sister's marriage, and that three days subsequent to an event which had given them so much joy, they had been exceedingly alarmed by the sudden illness of their respectable mother, who continued in a dangerous way, which was the reason Madame De Clermont had not written to Matilda, whose health they were extremely anxious to hear of. He further said, he had made some secret enquiries about Mr. Weimar, and learnt, that after remaining in Paris near a week, he had disappeared, but whether returned to Germany or not, they could not tell; that great prejudice was still entertained against Matilda, in consequence of which their family had declined seeing Madame Le Brun and her envious niece.

The Marquis communicated this letter to his friends, but as Matilda was ignorant of the scandal circulated at her expence, what related to Mademoiselle De Fontelle was omitted. She shuddered at the name of Mr. Weimar, and dreaded lest he might have pursued her to England. But this, the Marchioness said, was by no means to be apprehended, as it could answer no purpose.

The Marquis and his lady now prepared for their presentation at court, and had sent their friend's introductory letters to several persons of fashion.

On Thursday they were at the drawing room with the French Ambassador, and returned highly gratified with the politeness and affability of the king and queen, and equally charmed with the princesses. The following day they received abundance of visits from the nobility, both English and foreign, and very readily coincided with the sentiments of the Count De Bouville, as to the attention and charms of the English ladies.

They were now obliged to be in public, and both pay and receive a number of visits, consequently Matilda spent most of her time with Madame Le Roche and Mrs. Courtney; both ladies were extremely fond of her; they sometimes accompanied her to the play, and as she studied the language with care, she hoped in time to have her ears equally gratified with her eyes.

Lord Delby, Mrs. Courtney's uncle, was always of their parties, and his great partiality and admiration of Madame Le Roche was evident to the whole family; she was sometimes rallied about it; the subject gave her pain. "Compassion is the only claim I can have to his Lordship's notice, (said she, one day;) do not, my dear friends, suggest an idea which would make me very miserable." "I see not, (answered the Marquis) why you are to give up every pleasure in life, and compel yourself to refuse the blessings of love and friendship, through any dread of a villain who deserves the severest punishments; but I will send another person to talk with you to-morrow, for I really will not permit you to live in a situation so unworthy of yourself and friends."

The following day Doctor Demouriez, the Ambassador's Chaplain, called at Mrs. Courtney's, and had above three hours conversation with her. He returned to the Marquis. "I have heard a tale of horror, (said he;) and having subdued all your sister's scruples respecting her compulsatory vows, she has confessed every thing to me, and will this evening, she says, repeat each circumstance to you, after which we must consult what steps will be necessary to pursue."

They all anxiously expected the hour of meeting in the evening; and after they had dined, and retired to the drawing-room, the Marchioness eagerly claimed her sister's promise. "I will obey you, my dear sister, though you little think what it costs me to make such a painful relation.

"You well know the reluctance with which I married the Count, my subsequent illness and recovery. When my health was restored I began seriously to consider my situation, and the sacrament I had vowed to observe: I determined to do my duty; and if I could not love the Count, at least, to esteem and oblige him. I was then a stranger to his real disposition; I thought him severe and stern, but I soon found he was gloomy, suspicious, and revengeful. Whilst my father lived he observed some little decency towards me, but after his death, and you had quitted Vienna, my sufferings, from his causeless ill-humour, cannot be described. I was now far advanced in my pregnancy, an event I looked forward to as the end of all my troubles; for I had lost my spirits, my strength, and appetite. One day he went to Vienna, he returned at night in a most horrid temper. "Prepare yourself, (said he) for a journey to Switzerland, the day after to-morrow." "Good God, to Switzerland, in my situation?" "Yes, (he replied;) you can bear the journey very well, and Margarite, who is to be your nurse, shall attend you." "Indeed I am very unable to travel so far," (said I.) "I know better, (he replied;) but the reasons you have for declining, madam, make me the more anxious for it." "Well, Sir, I have no more to say, but to obey you." "You do well, madam; for anything you could urge will have no effect upon me." I was silent; I withdrew, and passed a wretched night. The next day poor Margarite and I were employed in packing our clothes and other necessaries, and the following day, soon as it was light, we set off on our journey. We at length arrived at the old Castle which Matilda has described to you. My blood chilled when I entered the gates. I was conducted to the right hand wing, which had then a door into the court, though it was afterwards bricked up. The furniture was handsome, but antique even then. "This, madam, is your apartment, and I think the Chevalier will have good luck to obtain entrance here." "Chevalier! what Chevalier? (repeated I.) "Your Chevalier, madam; don't suppose I was ignorant of his return to Vienna, and sauntering about my grounds." "I don't know, Sir, what you mean; there is no Chevalier belongs to me, nor do I know of any man sauntering, as you call it, in your grounds. My heart justifies me, that ever since I became your wife, I have strictly fulfilled the duties of that situation." "Your conscience, madam, is mighty convenient to your wishes, I don't doubt; but I am not to be duped by either. This is your habitation; the other parts of the house are not so good, but with them you need have no communications; they are occupied by the gardener." My bed room was the horrid one where Miss Weimar saw poor Margarite murdered, and very gloomy it was then, though without iron bars. I wept almost incessantly; my nurse was still more miserable, but she had been brought up from a child in the Count's family, and was obsequious to his will.

"I had been in the castle about three weeks, when, one evening, as I was sitting in my room, at the close of the day I heard a little noise at the window. I was startled, but recovering myself, I took a chair and got upon the window seat; I saw the figure of a man, I shrunk down; again the window rattled, I recovered and looked up; presently I distinctly perceived a man, who, with a diamond, was cutting a small strip out of a pane of glass; he accomplished his work, thrust a letter in, and disappeared behind the battlements in a moment; I secured the letter, with a beating heart, and on opening it, found it came from the Chevalier De Montreville. I was surprised and agitated; I perused this fatal letter; it was filled with the tenderest expressions of regret at my unhappy fate. His own misery he could have borne, he said, had I been happy; but to see the woman he adored treated so unworthily was more pain than he had philosophy to support; he entreated I would write a few lines, to tell him in what manner my husband behaved to me, and if there was a possibility of his doing me either service or pleasure. I shed floods of tears over this epistle: I found, though I had suppressed, I had not subdued my affection for him; yet what would it avail to encourage a correspondence I felt was improper: I hesitated,—I considered for some time whether I should write or not; at length I took up my pen. I acknowledged myself obliged for the interest he took in my happiness, but at the same time assured him any attentions of his never could do me service; on the contrary, I had reason to believe the Marquis was very jealous of him, and that possibly all his motions might be watched; I therefore besought him to return to Vienna, and leave me to my destiny. The following day, nearly at the same hour, I heard the noise at the window repeated; trembling for fear of interruption, I hastily got up, and slid my answer through, resolved at the same time to run no such risks, nor receive any more letters,—happy had it been could I have kept my resolution. The next evening I did not go to my room till accompanied by Margarite: I trembled every moment, lest the signal should be repeated, but I heard nothing. The next day I was peevish and dissatisfied; the Count gloomy and sullen. After dinner, as usual, he went out among the people he had at work in the wood: involuntarily I hastened to my apartment; I will own the truth, I wished, though

I dreaded hearing the signal. Towards the close of [...]
at the window were repeated: scarce knowing wh[...]
window-seat, and secured the letter: fancying I hea[...]
up stairs, I too hastily stept back on the chair, wl[...]
came with violence to the ground; at the same inst[...]
I had received a dreadful blow on the side of my he[...]
altogether deprive me of life, yet I was unable to speak. The Count ran
to me, he snatched the fatal paper from my hand, and then rang for
assistance; Margarite came up. With his help I was placed on the bed;
she bathed my head, gave me drops and water, and I was soon restored
to sense and misery. He ordered the nurse out of the room, and then
coming up to me, "Wretch! (cried he, furiously) behold a proof of thy
guilt and falsehood: I could sacrifice thee to my vengeance, but I will
have more exquisite satisfaction, and complete revenge, such as shall
strike thee with remorse and endless sorrow." I besought him to hear
me; I repeated what I have told you, and added it was the last I ever
intended to receive. He smiled with disdain, "Doubtless it was, and I
take upon me to say it will be the last you shall ever receive from him."
He never left me the whole evening, but used every cruel malicious
expression it was possible to conceive. I continued very ill and agitated
that night and the great part of the day. In the afternoon my persecutor
left me, but Margarite remained; I got up, and was under the most
dreadful apprehensions of what might happen; my eyes were continually turned to the window; I suffered the most agonizing terrors, when
in a moment they were realized beyond whatever I could conceive of
horror. A violent noise was heard on the stairs, like persons struggling,
and in a moment the door was burst open; the Count and his man appeared, dragging in the Chevalier, with his mouth bound, his hands
tied, and every mark of cruel treatment; I screamed, and clasped my
hands, but could not speak; he made several desperate efforts to free
himself—alas! to little purpose. Let me hasten over the dreadful catas-
trophe. "Now, (said the cruel Count) you have your minion where you
wished him to be, in your bed-chamber, nor shall he ever quit it alive."
I tried to speak, I threw myself on my knees, Spare, O spare! was all I
could say, and fell senseless, but I was soon recovered by the officious
Margarite, to still greater horror. "We have waited your recovery, (said
the barbarian;) I would not deprive you of so great a pleasure as seeing
your lover's last breath expire for you." He was then dragged into the
closet opposite to where I sat, and immediately repeated stabs were

...ith a short dagger, by the Count, through several parts of his ...; his blood flowed in torrents, and with groans he fell on his face ...d expired. Great God! (cried she) here the scene never will be absent from my remembrance. I sat like one petrified; I neither spoke, shrieked, or groaned, but with my eyes fixed on the closet I appeared insensible to every thing. The inhuman Count was not satisfied; he came and dragged me to the closet, and seated me by the side of the body, the blood flowing round me. "Now, (said he) clasp your beloved Chevalier—now despise the old and cross-looking Count, (words I had once said in his hearing, long before I was married) and now enjoy the company of him for whom you despised your husband." Saying this, he ordered Margarite and Peter to leave the room; and finding I was still unable to speak or move, he pushed me farther into the closet, locked the door, and left me. How long I continued in this state, I know not; I believe I swooned, for it was day-light when I found myself on the floor, my clothes covered with blood, and the unhappy murdered Chevalier dead before me. 'Tis impossible to describe the horror of that moment; I found myself seized with violent pains; I began to think the monster had poisoned me—the idea gave me pleasure, and I endeavoured to bear my pangs without a groan; nature however asserted its claims; I became so very ill, I could be silent no longer, I groaned, I cried aloud. Presently the door was unlocked,—the Count and Margarite appeared; they saw me in agonies; "I am dying, barbarian; you will be satisfied, you have murdered a worthy man who never injured you—you have killed an innocent wife." I could say no more. Margarite cried out, "My Lord, my dear mistress is in labour, for God's sake assist her to her apartment." He seemed to hesitate, but she urging her request, between them I was conveyed to the bed, and without any other assistance than her's delivered of a boy. When a little recovered, the Count entered the room, Peter with him. "I do not design to destroy you; no, you may live a life of horror, but dead to all the world; yet your infant shall be sacrificed." I screamed,—I cried for mercy to my child and instant death to me. He paused and I expected the welcome stroke at last. "On one condition your child may live." "Oh! name it, (I said;) any conditions." "Remember what you say: you shall join with these two persons, in taking a solemn oath, with the sacrament, that without my permission, you will never reveal the transactions of this night and day—never mention the Chevalier's name, nor ever presume to contradict the report I shall make of your death to the world."

I shuddered, but alas! there was no alternative; he fetched a prayer-book, and making the two poor creatures kneel, we all joined in the solemn oath, and received the sacrament from his polluted hands. Me-thinks at this moment I tremble at the impiety of that horrid wretch. My child was delivered to me; Peter was ordered to assist Margarite in making a fire and getting necessaries for me. How I survived such hor-rors is astonishing! The curtains were drawn, and that night the body was removed, but where it was carried to, heaven only knows, for Mar-garite never was informed. A coffin and every necessary for a funeral was bespoke and brought home. It was given out I had died in child-bed, and therefore in decency my own women only could attend me. A figure or bundle, wrapt in a sheet, was placed in the coffin (Margarite used to think it was the Chevalier's body) and the whole ceremony took place without any one's presuming to doubt the truth. Judge what must have been my feelings, and what an excellent constitution I must have had, to bear such dreadful scenes without dying of distraction. In a few days I was removed to another room, and, as I heard, the fatal closet was cleaned out by Peter; the rooms locked up, and orders given no one should enter them. The Count never appeared before me until I was up, and able to walk about the room; one morning he entered, just as I had done breakfast. I forgot to tell you I had no sustenance for my poor babe, consequently it was brought up by hand. The dear in-fant was laying on my lap; I started with surprise and terror. "Come, madam, (said he, with a look that made me tremble) come and view your former apartment." "Good God! (I cried) why must I return there?" "'Tis my pleasure," (answered he;) then bidding Margarite take the child, he ordered me to follow him. I tottered across the gallery, and on entering the room saw the windows barricaded with iron bars, the pictures and toilet taken away, and the whole appearance gloomy to excess. "This is once more your bed-chamber; no more Chevaliers, (said he, with horrid grin) can convey letters here—here you are to re-side forever." "Oh! kill me! (I cried) rather than shut me up here—death is far more desirable." "That is the reason I chuse you shall live, to re-pent every hour of your life the wrongs you have done me: and now hear me—your child you will see no more." At these words, overcome with the unexpected shock, I dropped senseless on the floor; I was soon recalled to life. "Your oath, (I cried;) O, spare my child!" "I do not mean to hurt its life; I will have it properly taken care of, but the indulgence is too great for you to enjoy. I here swear, that as long as you remain confined in this castle, and observe your oath, never to reveal the Chevalier's murder, nor undeceive the world respecting your fate, so long your boy's life is safe; I will take care of him, and one day or other, there is a possibility you may see him again; but if you ever escape from hence, or divulge these particulars, without my permission, instant death awaits you both, for I shall have a constant spy." To these conditions, dreadful as they were, I was compelled to subscribe. Margarite was ordered into confinement with me, for he found she was my friend. That night the child was conveyed away: dear and precious boy! alas, heaven only knows whether I shall ever see him more; unconscious he has a mother, if he lives, we may remain strangers to each other! We were locked in, and for three days the Count himself brought our scanty fare; the fourth, he entered with Joseph, who was the under gardener. I was startled to see a stranger,—he appeared equally shocked at seeing me. "Here you both are, remember your oath, madam, for on it more than one life depends. And you, (said he, turning to Joseph) tremble, if you dare break your solemn vow, never to let any person know this woman is alive, never to suffer her to pass from these apartments, without my permission, to hold no conversation with her, but when you bring her food, and in fine, to obey every command of mine and not her's." "I will obey your Lordship," (cried the man, trembling.) "'Tis well, then you will preserve her life, and gain my favor. No strangers must be permitted to remain here, should chance or inclination engage any one to visit this castle. Remember this side of it must never be seen, 'tis haunted—do you understand me?" "I do, my Lord, (answered Joseph) and I promise you, these apartments shall never be looked into." "On that depends her existence and your's.' They now quitted my room, and left me scarcely able to breathe. The following day the Count and Peter left the castle. Every other day Joseph came with necessaries, and Margarite was permitted to go down, accompanied by Joseph, to carry up and down water and other conveniences. In this state I lived two years, if living it could be called, having no other consolation than now and then hearing from my sister; for I had so far gained upon Joseph to permit Margarite's letters, after shewing them to him, to pass under cover to him, and as he found I carefully preserved my secret from others, the poor fellow granted me that indulgence. At the expiration of two years, the Count unexpectedly made his appearance. I shrunk from his sight; he viewed me some time with great emotion; "I am satisfied with your conduct, (said he) and am come to extend my indulgence to you." "O, my child!" (I cried out.) "No, (answered he) that cannot be granted; but you shall have permission to live in the rooms below, and if you swear to enter the garden only at night, the door into it shall be opened." I joyfully agreed to this, and was once more led to the rooms below. Peter was still with him; a bed was brought from another room, and placed in a small parlour, also one for Margarite. The apartments above were again locked up. I tried to soften the Count; he sometimes appeared moved and affected, then again stern and cruel; he stayed near a week—the day he left the Castle he came to visit me. "Once more I leave you, but as there is some danger that strangers may come here, I charge you, by every thing that is sacred, by your child's life and your own, should any person sleep in this castle, that you go to the gallery or next apartments, rattle a chain I shall leave for that purpose, groan, and make such kind of noises as may appal those who come here, and drive them hence, under an idea of the Castle's being haunted: I have already sworn Joseph, do you promise the same." "Ah! Sir, (cried I) why all these oaths, why all these persecutions, which must give you a world of pains, to punish an innocent woman?" "Because, (said he, furiously) because I prefer revenge to my own quiet; because I will be feared, and make your destiny hang on my pleasure." I could say no more, I wept bitterly, but nothing could soften his heart; he made me renew my vows, still threatening the life of my child, if I failed—he told me it was well, and carefully attended. I was compelled to acquiesce with his request, or rather command, and he once more left me. He regularly came once in two years, for some time, but latterly it was above four years since I had seen him, till the fatal night he carried me off. 'Tis plain he was well informed of every thing, and knew of Matilda's being at the Castle.

"I dragged on a wretched existence, in a daily hope, that from his own words, "There might be a possibility I should see my child again;" and that time might soften his heart, or death deprive him of all power over me. Margarite, who at first hardly brooked her confinement, grew more reconciled, and awed by the dreadful oaths we had taken, we submitted to what we could not prevent, being always in terror of being watched, and that nothing in the Castle passed unnoticed. This was our situation when Matilda came. Joseph came to me late in the evening, the day she arrived at the castle, acquainting me with the circumstance, and in consequence of our vows we were obliged to conform to our orders,—he to give hints of what might happen, and myself and Margarite try to frighten her from thence—you know the consequence. Had Joseph been at home, probably she would hardly have obtained permission to sleep in the Castle, but Bertha knew nothing of me, and was prevented by her fears from ever venturing through the apartments. The rest you know. I intended to have placed a confidence in Matilda, as far as being brought to the Castle, but beyond that I dared not violate my oath. At your request, my dear brother, I consulted our good Dr. Demouriez, and he absolved me from my vows, which were compulsory, and made under such horrid circumstances; I have therefore complied with your wishes, and now pray tell me what I can do, or what I ought to do? I cannot disclose to the world what I have related, without bringing the Count to condign punishment, for the death of the unfortunate and ever-lamented Chevalier, and perhaps may irritate him never to inform me whether my child exists or not—Alas! every way I turn is replete with difficulties and horror."

Here the Countess stopt, leaving her auditors overcome with astonishment and terror.

"Good heavens! (said the Marquis) I never could have supposed it possible a man should carry jealousy and revenge to such frightful guilty lengths, and the whole story appears incredible and almost impossible, that he should proceed so far, trust so many with his secret, and that you should remain such a number of years a victim to his diabolical passions, when there was always open to you the means for escaping and appealing to your friends."

"Consider, my good brother, (said she) the difficulties, the oaths I had taken never to leave the castle without his permission, the fate of my child, the certainty that every step I took was known, otherwise I could have offered Matilda an asylum with me, but he assured me I was constantly watched, and therefore any attempts I might make to free myself, would, too probably, accelerate the events I dreaded, and my life (as I doubt not was intended, when he carried me to the wood) would have been the sacrifice. If you look back, you will observe his cunning: when he afterwards came to the Castle and saw Joseph, he did not mention my name, and to be sure expected that he would have told him of my being carried away by some banditti, as he doubtless intended Joseph should believe, but the old man being silent, he supposed he was suspected as the author of the outrage, and therefore determined to put that witness out of the way——"

"What a villain! (cried Mrs. Courtney) and what a wretched life that man must have endured, with such fears of detection, and conscious of such complicated wickedness."

"It is ever the fate of villany, (said the Marchioness) to plunge deeper into vice, and suffer tenfold the miseries they inflict, from the apprehensions of a discovery, which they know seldom fails at some time or other to overtake them, and Providence has so ordered it, that we generally see the very means they take to hide their crimes from a knowledge of the world, are productive of such events as lead to their detection. I sincerely lament the fate of the poor Chevalier——"

"Ah! sister, (cried the Countess) never shall I cease reproaching myself on that account; had I with firmness refused to receive his second letter, and avoided going to that room alone, perhaps his life, and all my subsequent miseries would have been spared: I failed in the duty I owed my husband and myself, in permitting a clandestine correspondence, although I did not intend to continue it; and one false step, you see, brought on irreparable evils and eternal remorse!"

"I will not pretend, my dear Victoria, (answered the Marchioness) to exculpate you as entirely free from blame, but if we consider the ill-treatment you received from the Count, previous to the Chevalier's attempts to see you, and the sudden surprise of the moment, when the first letter was conveyed to you, doubtless some allowance ought to be made in your favor; and had you positively refused to receive a second, you would, 'tis possible, have escaped much bitter reflection; but the worst that can be said of you, in my opinion, is, that in your difficult and unpleasant situation, it was an error in judgment, for I am well assured in you there was no depravity of heart."

The poor Countess was drowned in tears. "Be comforted, my dearest sister, (said the Marquis, kissing her hand, whilst the ladies tenderly embraced her) you are, thank heaven, and that good lady, restored to your friends; I will consult Dr. Demouriez, as to our future proceedings, for I will do nothing rashly, and for your sake, would avoid dragging your husband's crimes into public view."

END OF VOLUME ONE

Castle of Wolfenbach

Volume II

CASTLE OF WOLFENBACH,

A GERMAN STORY.

THE ladies proposed an airing, to divert the Countess from dwelling on past events, and Matilda from apprehensions of future ones. The carriage was ordered, and they drove as far as Hampstead. The evening was uncommonly beautiful, and when they returned, the moon, which was in its meridian, shone with all its splendour. Just as the carriage stopped in Harley-street, Matilda, who sat next the door, saw two gentlemen pass slowly and look into the coach; she plainly perceived one of them was Mr. Weimar: she met his eyes, and he turned his hastily from her; she gave a faint shriek, and hid her head behind Mrs. Courtney. Her friends were alarmed, but hastened her into the house; she ran into the dining-parlour, and, in inconceivable terror, cried out, "He is come—he is come!" "Who, who?" (exclaimed the Countess.) "Mr. Weimar, (answered she;) did you not see him?" "No, (replied the Marchioness) and I hope your fears deceived you." "Too sure they did not, (said Matilda) and I am convinced also that he knew me." "Fear nothing, (said Mrs. Courtney;) you are in the power of your friends; he must prove his right to you before he can take you from us: here are no lettres de cachet, the laws will protect you from injury; compose your-self, therefore, my dear girl—in England no violence can be offered to you in any shape."

This kind and seasonable assurance calmed the terrors of the trembling Matilda; but when she retired to rest, and reflected on her cruel destiny, she shed floods of tears, and passed a sleepless night.

The following day was appointed for their return to Mrs. Court-ney's villa, to spend a week or two, previous to the preparations for the birth-day, after which the whole party, with Lord Delby, proposed going to Scarborough.

The Countess and Matilda bore evident marks in their features and pale looks, of the uneasy state of their minds; their amiable friends sought to raise their spirits, and they felt too much gratitude to their kindness not to make the effort, though their smiles were clouded with sorrow.

They had a pleasant excursion to Mrs. Courtney's house, and its delightful situation, with the cheerful hospitality of its charming owner, could not fail of making those happy who had the honor of her friendship.

The Countess, who was known in public only as Madame Le Roche, and by which name her friends always called her in company, found in the sympathy of Matilda more consolation than the conversation of strangers or any amusements could afford her; they generally contrived to steal from company and ramble in the gardens, relating past sorrows, and mutually endeavoring to inspire each other with hopes of happier days, though despairing of any to themselves.

A few days after they had been in the country, the Marquis received another packet from the Count De Bouville, enclosing a letter from Madame de Clermont, to Matilda. They learnt, with much sorrow, that the Countess died three days after the Count's first letter; that their affliction had been very great, and preyed much on the spirits of her affectionate daughter, in consequence of which she had been advised to visit Aix, and from thence to the Spa; their departure was fixed for the end of that week—Madame De Nancy and her amiable sister De Bancre were going with them. Madame De Clermont requested the correspondence of Matilda, and charged her to take great care of her brother. This charge Matilda did not comprehend, until the Marquis congratulated the party on the agreeable addition they might daily expect from the company of the Count De Bouville, who had written to him, that his sister having a party of her own going to Aix, he had no inclination to visit that place, and therefore should gratify his wishes, by returning to England for a few months, and hoped to enjoy additional satisfaction by the pleasures of their society.

Every one appeared gratified by this information, except Matilda. She felt her heart flutter at his name; she was convinced he was more interesting to her than any other man, and that in her circumstances she ought not to indulge a preference which never could be returned. Ah! thought she, where is the sorrows that can equal mine? Scarce a wretch that breathes but has some connexion, some relation to own them and sympathise in their troubles, I alone am destitute of family, or fortune; I can carry only disgrace to the arms of a husband, and am therefore an outcast—a being without any natural ties, and must

despair of procuring any other protection but what charity and benevolence affords me! She felt the full force of these melancholy reflections, and it threw such a sad impression on her features that everyone
was touched with compassion, though they knew not the cause, and
sought by kindness and attention to render her more cheerful.

Within three days after this letter, which had occasioned so much
pleasure and pain to different parties, the Marquis, by a note, was informed of the Count's arrival in London. Mrs. Courtney entreated
the honor of his company, and Lord Delby offered to accompany the
Marquis and escort him to their friends. This offer was too obliging
to be declined; they set off that evening, and the following morning
returned with the Count.

Matilda spent the intermediate time in laying down rules for her
behaviour. She still suffered under the apprehensions that Mr. Weimar
had pursued, and would occasion more trouble to her; she therefore
resolved to avail herself of that fear, keep as much in her apartment as
possible, and avoid mixing in all the little pleasurable parties where the
Count might make one.

The company received the Count with the politest attention. His
amiable person, his polished manners, and enchanting vivacity, could
not fail of engaging the esteem of everyone who had taste and dis-
cernment. After he had been introduced to the lady of the mansion,
to the Marchioness, and to Madame Le Roche, whom he knew not, he
advanced to Matilda; she trembled; he took her hand, and bowing on
it, "I am charged, (said he) with a thousand expressions of kindness and
friendship from my sister and Mademoiselle De Bancre, to the charming Miss Matilda; but you must take them upon trust now, and permit
me to express my own happiness in seeing my lovely friend well, and
situated in the midst of a society so delightful as this." She attempted
to speak, her voice, her powers failed her; "Your Lordship does me
honor," was all she could utter. The conversation became general and
sprightly, but she had no share in it; the day appeared uncommonly
long, and she rejoiced when night came, that she could escape to her
apartment and enjoy her own reflections.

The Count, who had observed her emotions, her silence and melancholy air, felt himself much concerned for the unfortunate girl; he
thought her more lovely, more interesting than ever: the soft melancholy which pervaded her fine features could not fail of touching a
susceptible heart; and the Count soon found the tender interest he had

formerly taken in Matilda's misfortunes, revive with more solicitude than ever. He seized an opportunity the following morning, to enquire some particulars respecting the cause of her distress. The Marquis told him of her alarm on seeing a gentleman she believed to be, and possibly, said he, might be, Mr. Weimar. "I am really, (added he) unhappy about this charming young woman; we all love her exceedingly; beauty is her least merit; she has every amiable quality, joined to an excellent understanding, that can adorn a human being; I could not love my own child better; but she has too much sensibility to be happy—she feels her dependent and unprotected state too keenly,—it preys upon her mind and injures her health. Consulting with the Marchioness on this subject last night, I intend this day to write, and order a deed to be drawn, agreeable to our design of making her independent, at the same time, I wish not to burthen her feelings with too high a sense of obligation, by settling any very large sum on her: four hundred a year, English money, paid her quarterly, will enable her to live genteelly, should she ever wish to separate from us, and will be a handsome provision for pocket expences, if she does us the favor of continuing under our protection."

"Will you permit me, (said the Count, eagerly) to add another two hundred to her income?" "Indeed I will not, (replied the Marquis;) I think myself as much the guardian of Matilda's honor and delicacy as of her person: no young man shall boast any claims upon her, nor shall she be humbled by receiving favors, which, if known, might subject her to censure—say no more, my dear Count, (added he, observing he was about to reply) the Marchioness will not have her protegée under any obligations but to herself." "Shall I be sincere with you, Marquis?" (demanded the Count.) "Doubtless, my Lord, you may, and assure yourself of my secresy, if necessary." "Well then, (resumed the Count) I confess to you, that with the Marchioness's protegée, as you call her, I should be the happiest of men: I feel, and acknowledge, that she has more than beauty—she has a soul; she has those virtues, those amiable qualities, which must render any man happy: but, my dear Marquis, her birth—the scandalous stories promulgated of her in Paris: ah! what can do away these objections which rise hourly before me, and bar me from happiness and Matilda?" "Since you do me the honor of your confidence, my Lord, 'tis my duty to be candid and explicit. That I entertain the highest opinion of Matilda, is most certain—that I think whoever the man is, who is honored with her hand, will be a happy one, I also acknowledge; but, my Lord, family and society have great claims upon us; we ought not to injure the one, nor disregard the other. Could you bear to see your wife treated with contempt, as one whom nobody knew, as one who had no claims to distinction, but what your very great friends might allow her? Could you support the idea, that she whose genuine merit might entitle her to the first society, should be refused admittance among such, as in real worth she very far surpassed? No; I know you would feel such a degradation most painfully; and, though young men, in the moment of passion, think they could sacrifice everything to the object of it; yet, believe me, passion is but short-lived, and though your wife may yet retain your love and esteem, you will regret the loss of society—you will feel the insults offered to your wife, and you will both be unhappy."

"Ah! my dear Marquis, (cried the Count) say no more. How happy are Englishmen! free from all those false prejudices, they can confer honor on whom they please, and the want of noble birth is no degradation where merit and character deserve esteem; but we are the victims to false notions, and from thence originates all that levity and vice for which we are censured by other nations." He walked away with a melancholy air: the Marquis felt for him, but national honor was in his opinion of more consequence than the gratification of a private individual, how great soever the merit of the object.

The Count walked into the garden, his arms folded, his mind distrest, unknowing what he should, what he ought to do. Turning into a small alcove, he beheld Matilda, her head reclining on one hand, whilst with the other she dried the tears which fell on her face: they both started; she rose from her seat; he advanced, prevented her going and seated himself by her. Both were silent for a moment, at length Matilda, making a second effort to rise, exclaimed in a faint voice, "Bless me! I dare say I have made the family wait breakfast," and attempted to pass him. "Stay, Miss Weimar, I beseech you; tell me why I behold you a prey to sorrow and grief?" "Because, Sir, (said she, withdrawing her hand) I am the child of sorrow; I never knew another parent; poor, forlorn, proscribed and dependant, I never can belong to any one." She snatched her hand, which he endeavoured to retain, from him, and flew like lightning towards the house; the Count followed, full of admiration and grief. He entered the breakfast room; every one was seated, and rallied him on his passion for morning rambles: his natural vivacity returned, and he tried to make himself agreeable and pleasant.

They had scarce finished breakfast when the Marquis received a letter from the French Ambassador, requesting he might see him in town immediately, on an important affair. The Marquis was surprised, but gave orders for his horses to be ready. The Countess trembled, Matilda was terrified; each thought herself concerned, and when the Marquis quitted the house, retired together.

"Ah! (cried the Countess) the Count has discovered me!" "No, no, madam, (replied Matilda) 'tis I am discovered and shall be torn from you." Both burst into tears, equally for herself and friend.

The Marchioness, who saw him depart, now entered the room; "As I supposed, (said he) you retired to frighten each other, but that I shall not allow, so ladies, if you please, throw on your cloaks; I have made up two parties this morning for an airing: in my coach goes Lord Delby, the Count, my sister, and Miss Matilda; I accompany Mrs. Courtney, in her chariot;—so pray hasten directly, the carriages wait."

She withdrew on saying these words, and left them no power to frame excuses, and consequently they were obliged to follow, though with aching hearts.

They were disposed of according to the Marchioness's arrangements, but for some minutes after the carriage proceeded all were silent. Lord Delby first spoke, and regretted the party did not seem to accord with the wishes of the ladies, if he might judge from their averted looks. "Indeed, my Lord, (replied the Countess) you do me particular injustice; I entertain the highest respect for every person here; to your Lordship I owe obligations never to be forgotten; I infinitely esteem the Count, as a friend, and this young lady I love with the affection of a sister. I have been a little agitated by the sudden departure of the Marquis, and my uneasiness has communicated itself to my friend; we beg your pardon, and will endeavor to be better company." After this the conversation became more general and amusing.

The Marquis proceeded to town, and instantly waited on the Ambassador. "I am sorry, my dear Lord, (said his Excellency) to have broken in upon your retirement, and must mention the visit I received yesterday as my apology. A German gentleman, who sent in his name as Mr. Weimar, requested permission to wait on me; he was consequently admitted: he entered upon a long story of an orphan he had preserved from perishing, of a paper fastened to the child, deputing him the guardian of it 'till claimed by its parents; and in short, that despairing, from the number of years past, that those parents had any existence, he resolved to marry the young lady, that he might provide for her without injury to her reputation; that, from what motives he knew not, she had been induced to fly from his house, seducing a servant of his to go with her; and she was now detained from him by you, notwithstanding he had a lettre de cachet, which he produced, commanding you to give her up; consequently, by virtue of that order, he requested I would compel you to deliver the young lady to his care. Now, my dear Marquis, I am prepared to hear you on the subject, for it is a delicate affair, and I am convinced you would be sorry it should be noised abroad." "No otherwise, Sir, (replied the Marquis) than as it might wound the young lady's delicacy to be publicly talked of. I am obliged to your Excellency for your communications, and must trespass on your patience to elucidate the affair properly." He then recapitulated the whole of Matilda's story, concealing everything relative to the Countess at that time; and having deduced it down to the present period, he besought his Excellency to protect an amiable young woman, under the most unfortunate circumstances.

"I am really (he replied) much interested for her, and perfectly disposed to comply with your wishes, but the whole affair is replete with so many extraordinary circumstances, that I think we had best consult the German Ambassador before anything can be determined on."

The carriage was ordered, and his Excellency took the Marquis with him. They most fortunately found the German Minister at home, and after some deliberation it was settled Matilda should remain under the protection of the Marquis for one year, he to be answerable for her; during that interval advertisements should be sent to the different kingdoms, in quest of her parents; and if in the course of one twelvemonth no such persons appeared, Mr. Weimar was the natural protector of the young lady, but could not oblige her to marry him—neither could he prevent her retiring to a convent, though she might be accountable to him for her choice of such a retirement.

The Marquis was obliged to be contented with this decision, and returning with the Ambassador, he said, "I shall in all probability have to trouble you again soon, on a still more extraordinary affair, and relative to one more dear and nearer to me than this young lady." "Upon my word, Marquis, (replied the Minister, smiling) you are quite a knight-errant, to protect distressed damsels." "A very honourable employment, (answered the other, in the same tone;) but though these are not the days of romance, yet I have met with such extraordinary incidents lately as carry much the face of the wonderful stories we have heard of former times: but as the development of this business will be attended with serious consequences, I must consider a few days before I make the discovery." "Very well, (said his Excellency;) you have excited my curiosity, and, if I am not too old to join in a Quixote-like expedition, behold me ready to assist in the defence of the fair." The Marquis smiled, thanked him, and declining an invitation to dine at his house, got into his own carriage, and drove back with all speed, rightly conceiving every one would entertain uneasy conjectures.

The party were but just returned from a long morning's drive when the Marquis arrived; every one met him with anxiety in their looks—he accosted them with a smiling countenance; "A truce to interrogatories at present, (said he) I have good news for all, but I am really faint for want of refreshment; order something for me, and then I shall give an account of my proceedings."

Every one flew to the bells, and in a moment he had chocolate, jellies, wine, and biscuits set before him.

"Ah! (said he, laughing) nothing like giving a little spur to curiosity, I see; this is an excellent lesson for me how to be well served."

When he had taken his repast, which he maliciously prolonged 'till the Marchioness in a pet rang the bell, and declared he should eat no more, the things taken away, and the servants withdrawn. "Now listen, ladies, and thank me for having procured, in the person of our gallant Ambassador, a Don Quixote, ready to fight in your defence." He then, in a more serious tone, repeated the particulars which have been already related.

Poor Matilda felt but a gleam of satisfaction; "A twelvemonth," (cried she.) "A twelvemonth," (repeated Mrs. Courtney;) "why, do you consider, my dear girl, how many strange events may happen in that time?" "Yes, (answered she, sighing) I consider and hope death will free me from his power long before that period expires."

The Count de Bouville rose and left the room to conceal his emotions.

"I will not forgive you, my dear child, (said the Marchioness) if you indulge such desponding ideas; depend upon it happier days await you—trust in Providence, and rejoice you are now free from anxiety:

equally under the protection of the ambassadors and the Marquis, Mr. Weimar will not dare to molest you."

The ladies all congratulated Matilda; and, the Marchioness taking her hand, "Come with me into the garden, I must chide you, but I will not do it publicly, though you deserve it." She led her to a little temple, at one end of the garden, and when seated she said to the still silent Matilda, "You do not consider the advantages we have gained." "O, my dear madam, (cried the other, interrupting her) how sensible I am of that kind *we* have gained!" "Well, well, (resumed the Marchioness) hear me out. We can now take public methods to enquire, if there yet exists a being who has any claim to you, without fear of Mr. Weimar; a twelvemonth may make great alterations in his sentiments; should it appear you have no particular relations, he has no legal claim upon you, but from his expenditure for your maintenance and clothes—let him bring in his bill, he shall be paid to the uttermost farthing; you are my adopted child; consider yourself as such, and dare not refuse that trifle for your future expences;—if you utter any ohs! or ahs! if you ever talk of obligations, I will never pardon you: to be cheerful and happy is the only return you can make or I accept." She then placed the deed mentioned by the Marquis, with a fifty pound note, upon the lap of the astonished Matilda, and hastened away to the house.

It was some moments before she recovered herself enough to examine the papers. The contents overwhelmed her with gratitude; she burst into a flood of tears, the papers in her hand, when unexpectedly the Count stood before her. "Good heavens! (he cried) what means this distress, these tears?" "O, my Lord, (answered she) they are tears of sensibility and gratitude." "I rejoice to hear it, (replied the Count) heaven forbid they should ever flow from any other cause." He seated himself by her, she dried her eyes, and put the papers in her pocket. "I congratulate you, madam, (resumed he) on the happy turn in your affairs, which the Marquis has informed me of." "You know me then for an unhappy deserted orphan?" (said she, blushing and mortified.) "I know you, (replied he, eagerly) for the most amiable of your sex; no adventitious advantages of birth or fortune can add to those claims your own merit gives you to universal esteem." "Ah, my Lord, (said she) to generous spirits like your's and this family's, misfortunes are a recommendation to kindness and attention, but with the generality of mankind I have not to learn it must be otherwise. Stranger as I am to the manners and customs of the world, I am sensible birth and fortune have superior advantages, and that without them, though with liberal minds we may obtain compassion, we can never hope for consideration or respect." "Pardon me, madam, (replied the Count) if I presume to say you judge erroneously; she who with merit, with good sense, delicacy, and refined sentiments can command respect, is a thousand times superior to those whose inferiority of mind disgraces a rank which the other would ennoble." "You are very kind, Sir, (said Matilda, rising, and unable to support a conversation which she feared might grow too interesting for her peace:) you are truly friendly, in endeavouring to reconcile me to myself; and I have no way of deserving your favorable judgment, but by constantly remembering what I am, that I may at least preserve my humility." She courtesied and walked fast towards the house, and to the apartment of the Countess. That lady was alone, her head resting on her hand, and seemed buried in thought. Matilda would have withdrawn, the other entreated her return; "Come in, my dear girl, (said she) my own thoughts are the worst company you could leave me in at present." "I come to tell you, my dear madam, (cried her young friend) that my heart is bursting with gratitude: the Marchioness will not hear me, but I must have vent for my feelings, or I shall be opprest to death." She burst into tears. "My dear April girl, (said the Countess) no more of those showers,—you have too much sensibility; I know what you want to tell me, therefore spare yourself the trouble, and let me acquaint you, that I am indebted to my generous brother, for a settlement of treble the value of what he has given you, yet I make no fuss about the matter." "But, dear madam, (cried Matilda) sure there is great difference in our situations, you have a natural claim—" "A natural claim (repeated the Countess;) the best claim to a generous mind, is being unfortunate with merit that deserves a better fate. I think little of those favours which are bestowed from claims of affinity only; since family pride, the censure of the world, and many causes, may unlock a heart to support their own consequence in their connexions, but the truly benificent mind looks upon every child of sorrow as their relation, and entitled to their assistance; but when beauty and virtue suffer, from whatsoever cause, believe me, dear Matilda, they receive a superior gratification that have the power of relieving sorrows, than the receiver can in accepting the favors." "I believe, my dear madam, (replied Matilda, her heart warmed by the idea) I believe you are right; for if there is a human being I could envy, it would be the one who can raise the desponding heart to hope and peace." "With that conviction, (resumed the Countess) feel as if you conferred a favor, without the oppressive notion of having received one; and now pray listen to me. My brother and sister hourly importune me to prosecute the Count: you know my objections,—God only knows whether I have a child living or not—the doubt gives me a thousand pangs; as to the murder of the poor Chevalier, Peter only was a witness beside myself, and he is a creature of the Count's; then to accuse one's husband, what an indelible reproach! I never can submit to it: tell me, advise me, dear girl, what I must do?" "Impossible madam, (replied she;) I am incompetent to advise,—your own good sense, and the opinion of your friends, are more capable of it than one so little conversant in the world as I am." "Well, (resumed the Countess) I will be guided by Lord Delby and Mrs. Courtney; my own relations are too warmly interested in my favor to give an impartial opinion:—but pray, my dear, what do you think of our Count, is not he a charming youth?"

A question so mal-a-propos, when poor Matilda's heart bore testimony to his merit, threw her into the greatest confusion, she was unable to speak.

The Countess observed her emotion, but was too delicate to notice it; she therefore added, "'Tis a needless question; I see your sentiments correspond with mine; but your spirits are low, child—in truth mine are not high, so let us seek for better company." She arose, and taking Matilda's passive hand, led her to the drawing room, where the company was assembled.

Matilda could not see her benefactors without being visibly affected, which the Marchioness observing, "Come, ladies, (said she) give me your votes, I am collecting them for a party to Windsor to-morrow." "O, doubtless you may command ours, (replied the Countess;) novelty has always its charms for us females." "Very well, (said the Marquis) then it's a settled business."

The excursion to Windsor, and several other places, in the fortnight they staid at Mrs. Courtney's jumbled the Count and Matilda so frequently together, and he had so many opportunities of admiring her strong understanding and polished manners, that his affection was insensibly engaged beyond all power of resistance, and he determined to brave the censures of the world, and marry her, if he could obtain her heart. From the moment this resolution took place, he treated her with that insinuating tenderness in his voice and manners, which seldom fails of communicating the infection to a susceptible mind. Ma-

tilda's feelings alarmed her; she was conscious of the impropriety of
indulging them, and felt the necessity of avoiding the Count as much
as possible. He quickly observed the alteration in her behaviour, and
was determined to come to an immediate explanation; justly conceiving nothing could be more wounding to a delicate mind than suspense
under such circumstances.

She so carefully shunned him, that it was not easy to find her
alone; but the morning, when it was intended to return in the evening
to London, chance afforded him an opportunity. The Marchioness,
Matilda, and the Count were in the garden; the Marquis came to them
and requested to speak a few words to his Lady. She disengaged her
arm from her companion, and went with him to the house. Matilda
turned with an intention to follow; the Count took her hand, "Let me
entreat you, madam, to pursue your walk; I wish to speak a few words,
on an affair of consequence, that will not detain you long from your
friends." She trembled, and without speaking, suffered him to conduct
her to an alcove at the bottom of the garden. They were both seated
for a minute before he could assume courage to speak, at length, "I
believe from the first hour I had the happiness of being introduced
to you, my admiration was very visible, but it was that admiration
which a beautiful person naturally inspires,—I knew not then it was
your least perfection. Your story, which the Marquis related, convinced
me you had every virtue which should adorn your sex, joined with a
courage and perseverance, through difficulties which might do honor
even to our's. Since I have been admitted a visitor in this house, I have
been confirmed in the exalted opinion I entertained of your superiority to most women, and under this conviction I may justly fear you
will condemn my presumption, in offering myself and fortune to your
disposal." "How, my Lord, (cried Matilda, recovering from her confusion, and interrupting him) do you consider who and what I am?" "Yes,
madam, (replied he) I have already told you, I think you one of the
most perfect of your sex, and as to any other consideration 'tis beneath
my notice: if you will deign to accept of me, it shall be the study of
my life to make you amends for the injustice of fortune, who blindly
bestows her favors on the unworthy." "You will pardon me, my Lord,
(said she) for interrupting you a second time, but I cannot suffer you
to proceed in error; I entreat you, therefore, to hear me with patience,
and believe that the sentiments I express are the genuine feelings of my
heart, from which no persuasions, no temptations shall ever make me

depart. I acknowledge, with a grateful mind, the honor you offer me is far beyond any expectations I can ever form in life, and such as affords me both pride and pleasure, that I am not deemed unworthy your esteem. At the same time, although you can generously resolve to forego the respect you owe to yourself and family, my duty to myself obliges me to remember it: without family and connexions, without even a name—perhaps the offspring of poor, or still worse, of infamous parents, brought up and supported by charity; shall I intrude myself into a noble family, contaminate its lustre, reflect indelible disgrace on the author of my undeserved elevation, and live despised and reproached, as the artful creature who had taken advantage of your generosity and compassion? No, my Lord, permit me to say on such terms I never would condescend to be the wife of a prince. I shrink at my own littleness; I am in a state of obligation for my support, but I never will incur my own contempt, by deserving it from others. My mind is indeed, I hope, superior to my situation: I will preserve a rectitude of principles under every evil that may befal me; those principles impel me to avow, with the greatest solemnity in the face of heaven, that under the disgraceful circumstances in which my fate seems enveloped, I never will be yours." "Hold, hold, madam, (cried the Count, endeavouring to interrupt her) great God! what have you vowed!" "What duty to myself and you required of me, (said she;) and now, my Lord, let this subject never be renewed. If it can afford you any consolation, (added she, softened by the disorder and distress of his appearance) be assured, my Lord, that as I never can be yours, I never will be another's; and if my happiness is as dear to you as your's will ever be to me, you will from this moment cease to think of me but as an unfortunate girl, deprived of all power to return obligations, and therefore with too much pride and spirit to receive them, but from this worthy family, where I conceive it no disgrace to hold myself dependent."

As she ended these words she rose. "Stop one moment, madam, (exclaimed the Count;) unless you would drive me to madness, afford me one gleam of hope, distant as it may be: your cruel vow precludes me from bliss, yet tell me, too lovely Matilda, that you do not hate me, that if——"

"Ah! Sir, (said she, involuntarily) hate you! Heaven is my witness, that did my birth and rank equal yours, it would be my glory to accept your hand; but as there exists not a possibility of that, I beseech you to spare me and yourself unnecessary pain; from this instant determine to avoid me, and I will esteem you as the most exalted of men."

Without giving him time to reply, she darted like lightning towards the house, leaving him overwhelmed with admiration, grief, and despair.

"What are the advantages of birth and rank, (cried he) which this sweet girl does not possess? A dignity of sentiment, a rectitude of heart;—how greatly superior to that wretch Fontelle, whose malicious stories have so much injured her reputation, and whose birth and fortune only render her the more despicable; as mine must be to me of no value, when considered as bars to happiness and Matilda."

He walked slowly to the house and met the Marquis. "Dear Count, (said he) what have you done or said to my amiable protegée; I met her running up stairs, out of breath, and tears trembling in her eyes?" The Count, without the least reserve, repeated the preceding conversation. "And did you really make such an offer, (cried he) and did she refuse it?" "'Tis very true," (replied the Count.) "Why then, (said the Marquis) you are two of the noblest creatures under heaven; that you, my worthy friend, should step beyond the prejudices of your country— that you should resolve to brave the censure, the malevolent whispers and contemptuous neglect of your equals, and support the insolent derision of your inferiors, in favour of a young woman under such peculiarly distressing circumstances, excites my wonder and admiration: but I scarce know any words that can do justice to my sentiments, when I reflect that this very young woman, without friends or fortune, from a sense of rectitude, and a loftiness of sentiment which would do honor to the highest rank, could peremptorily refuse a situation and prospects so brilliant—do violence to her own heart, and prefer a dependence her soul is much superior to, rather than incur self-reproach for your degradation. Indeed, my Lord, I know not any language sufficiently expressive of my feelings: you must admire her more than ever." "Doubt not, (answered the Count, in a melancholy tone) of my more than admiration—my adoration; but, alas! she is inflexible—she has sworn never to be mine—she has charged me to see her, to think of her, no more." "Do her justice, my Lord, and obey her; prove your esteem for such an extraordinary exertion of virtue and prudence, imitate an example so deserving praise, and be assured the trial, however severe at present, will afford you satisfaction hereafter, in subduing love, though your highest esteem she has a right to challenge." "Say no more, Marquis, (cried the Count;) I must cease to think of her before I can cease to love, for this day has riveted my chains more firmly than ever. I will not however be an inmate of your house; though I cannot relinquish the charms of her society altogether, yet I promise you I will indulge in no more dangerous tête-à-têtes, but I must see her sometimes." "Ah! Count, (said the Marquis, shaking his head.) "Trust my honour and discretion, (replied he, to his significant looks;) you may, for that angelic girl will never put them to the proof."

They proceeded to the house, and the carriages drawing up, the party was collected together. Matilda contrived to accompany the Marquis, his Lady, and Mrs. Courtney. The two latter kept up a sprightly conversation with the Marquis, and but once or twice broke in upon her reveries; yet she appeared easy and cheerful; in truth, the delight of being dear to the amiable Count, and a consciousness of having performed her duty, gave that peace and serenity to her mind which never fails of communicating itself to the countenance.

On their arrival in Harley-street the party separated, and the Count was compelled to accept an invitation from Lord Delby, to reside with him. "The Marquis, (said his Lordship) has his family party, but I am alone, and therefore you will do me particular honor and pleasure in complying with my wishes."

As the Count could not reside with the Marquis, this was certainly the next best situation, for his Lordship was himself too fond of the "family party" to be long absent from them; he therefore gladly accompanied him to Cavendish-square.

They had been now near a fortnight in town, enjoying its variety of amusements, and preparing for their journey to Scarborough, which was now to take place in four days. The birth-day being arrived, the Marquis, his Lady and the Count proposed paying their compliments at court, with Lord Delby: the Count had been previously presented. The Countess (still known even by the Count only as Madame Le Roche), Mrs. Courtney, and Matilda, contented themselves with attending the ball at night, in the Lord Chamberlain's box. They were accordingly accommodated with an excellent situation, and were extremely charmed with the beauty and splendor of the British court.

Matilda's eyes were so intently fixed on the Royal Family, she had scarce thought of looking round her, until some audible whispers in French reached her ear; turning her head quickly, her eyes met those of Mademoiselle De Fontelle. A stranger to the malice of that young lady, she bowed with a smile, being rather too distant to speak; the lady gave her a look of contempt, and speaking low to the person next her; before Matilda could recover from her surprise and confusion, she observed three or four persons look full at her, with scorn and disdain strongly marked in their features. Shocked beyond measure at this to her unaccountable behaviour, she turned sick and faint, was obliged to have recourse to her salts, and heard a laughing whisper on one side of her, whilst the Countess on the other was eagerly enquiring the cause of her illness. Her salts, and natural dignity of mind soon enabled her to recover. She evaded the curiosity of her friend, by complaining of the heat, and declaring herself better. She then turned her head towards Fontelle and her companions; she viewed them with a steady air of the highest contempt and indifference, 'till even the eyes of that malicious girl fell under her's, and she was evidently confused. Matilda then returned to the amusements below her, and, though her mind was not easy, she appeared to enjoy uncommon satisfaction.

When the Royal Family had withdrawn, and they were about to quit their seats, they perceived Lord Delby and the Count making way to assist them in getting out. The latter had no eyes but for Matilda, 'till a sudden exclamation, and his name, caught his ear in the moment he had presented his hand to her; quickly turning, he saw Mademoiselle De Fontelle and her aunt Madame Le Brun. Surprised and vexed, he darted at them a look of scorn, and with an air of the highest respect and attention, assisted Matilda into the room, joined her friends, and they were safely conveyed through the crowd to their carriage,—Lord Delby and himself following in their's.

When they alighted in Harley-street, Matilda, who had suppressed her feelings in the ball room, and had been likewise deeply affected by the Count's attentions, scarcely entered the drawing room before she fainted: everyone was alarmed, but the Count was distracted; his behaviour discovered the secrets of his heart to all the company, and when she recovered, she saw him on his knees, holding one of her hands, whilst his air of distraction was but too expressive of his feelings; she withdrew her hand, and he arose; she apologized to the company, and imputed her disorder to the heat of the room, and the sudden chill she felt in getting out of the carriage. Her friends, glad to see her recovered, enquired no further, but the Count drew the Marquis out of the room, and in much agitation, cried out, "That persecuting fiend, in a female form, is the cause of her illness." "Who do you mean?" (demanded the Marquis.) "Who should I mean, (answered he, warmly) but that malicious Fontelle; I saw her not far from Matilda, and I dare say she insulted her; but, by heavens! if she propagates her infamous falsehoods here, she shall repent it, however she may trust to my honor."

The Marquis was a little surprised at this sally, but without appearing to observe it, said, "You know, Count, we shall leave town three days hence, and consequently be out of her malice. I wonder what brought her to England." "Spite and envy (replied he;) but does the amiable girl know how much Mademoiselle De Fontelle is her enemy?" "No certainly (answered the Marquis;) you do not suppose we would wound her feelings by repeating the disagreeable reports spread among our acquaintance at Paris." "I am glad of it, (said the Count) yet I cannot but think the other affronted her." "We shall know to-morrow, but let us return and eat our supper now."

They went down to the supper room, and were much pleased in beholding Matilda cheerful and perfectly well.

When the company separated, and she was retired to her apartment, she gave way to her own reflections; she could no otherwise account for the impertinence of Mademoiselle De Fontelle, but by supposing she was acquainted with her birth; "Ah! (said she) I doubt not but Mr. Weimar published it at Paris, from motives of revenge, and she, who as a relation to the Marchioness received a thousand civilities, is now despised as an imposter; an orphan, and a dependent on charity; nay, even my benefactors may suffer in the opinion of their friends for introducing me! Good heavens! (cried she) why should I continue in the world—why assume a character and appearance I have no pretensions to? What blameable pride, what meanness, in accepting gifts which draw upon me contempt and derision—I will no longer support it."

Tormented all night by the distress of her situation, she arose unrefreshed, pale, feeble and agitated.

The Marchioness, alarmed at her appearance, insisted upon sending for a physician; the Marquis was going to pull the bell. "Stay, my dear friends, (cried she) I beseech you; 'tis my mind, not my body, that is disordered, and you only have the power to heal it." "Speak your wishes, my dear child, (said the Marchioness;) be assured, if in our power, you may command the grant of them." "On that promise, my dearest benefactress, your poor Matilda founds her hopes of peace."

She then repeated the affronts of the preceding evening, and her own conjectures upon it. "I am humbled, my dearest madam, as all false pretenders ought to be, (added she:) I can no longer support the up-braidings of my heart; a false pride, a despicable vanity induced me to lay hold of your sentiments in my favour, which, after the discovery of my original meanness, I ought to have blushed at your condescension, and sought some humble situation, or retired to a convent, where, unknowing and unknown, I might have pursued the lowly path Providence seems to have pointed out for me. I have been punished for my presumption and duplicity—it has made me look into myself; doubtless, out of this family, everyone beholds me with the scorn and contempt I have justly incurred from Mademoiselle De Fontelle, and all who know my doubtful origin. O, my beloved friends, (cried she, wringing her hands, tears running down her cheeks) save me from future insults, save me from self-reproach! complete your generosity and goodness, and let me retire to a convent. My poor endeavours to amuse you as a companion are no longer necessary; the Countess is restored to you, and I have only been a source of vexation and trouble ever since the hour you first condescended to receive me;—a convent is the only asylum I ought to wish for, and there only I can find rest." Here she stopt, overwhelmed with the most painful emotions.

The Marquis was affected, the Marchioness drowned in tears. "My dear, but too susceptible girl, (said she, when able to speak) why will you thus unnecessarily torment yourself; what is Fontelle and her opinions to us? We are going to Scarborough; you have friends who will protect you from every insult,—who will treat you with increased respect, from a conviction that your mind is superior to all the advantages which birth and fortune has given to Mademoiselle De Fontelle, or a thousand such: besides, depend upon my assertions,—you sprung not from humble or dishonest parents,—the virtues you possess are hereditary ones, doubt it not, my dear Matilda; if nobleness of birth can add any lustre to qualities like your's, you will one day possess that advantage."

'Tis impossible to express the agitations of Matilda on hearing such kind and consoling sentiments; but her resolution to retire from the world was unconquerable; she found her heart too tenderly attached to the Count—she knew the impossibility that she should ever be his; she was convinced her story was known, her friends had not attempted to deny it; in whatever public place she might visit, it was very possible to meet persons who had heard it, and she might be exposed to similar insults, which her spirit could not brook.

The Marquis and his lady made use of persuasions, arguments, and even reproaches, but she had so much resolution and fortitude, when once she had formed a design, approved by her judgment, as could not be easily shaken; and though her heart was wounded with sorrow, and her mind impressed with grief in being obliged to resist the kindness of her friends, yet she still persevered.

"Well, Matilda, (said the Marchioness, in a reproachful tone) since you are inflexible to our wishes, I must insist upon your going with me to Mrs. Courtney's: what will she, what will my sister think, but that I have treated you ill, and you can no longer remain with one you have ceased to love."

"Kill me not, (cried she, in an agony) with such reproaches; let me fly to the Countess and disclose my reasons—ah! surely she will do more justice to my heart: oh! madam, that you could see it—that you could read the love, the admiration and respect indelibly imprinted there, with your image, never, never to be erased whilst it beats within my bosom."

Overcome with these sensations, she wept aloud; the Marchioness embraced and soothed her.

The carriage was ordered, and they drove to Mrs. Courtney's, the Marquis setting them down, and going on to Lord Delby's.

It is needless to repeat what passed at Mrs. Courtney's, since it was only a repetition of every argument and persuasion which her protectors had before used in vain. Nothing could shake her resolution; and all the favour they could obtain, was to permit Louison and Antoine to accompany her to Boulogne, and remain in a convent there, 'till her friends returned to France, and the twelvemonth expired Mr. Weimar had allowed her to remain under the care of the Marquis.

Whilst every countenance spoke pity, grief, and admiration, the gentlemen suddenly entered the room, the Count with an air of wildness and distress. The moment Matilda saw him she trembled violently, and could with difficulty keep her seat. "Ah! madam, (said he) what is it I hear—is it possible you mean to abandon your friends, to distress the most affectionate hearts in the world, to give up society, and, from romantic notions, bury yourself in a convent? Hear me thus publicly, (cried he, throwing himself at her feet, with a frantic look) hear me avow myself your lover, your protector, and if you will condescend to accept of me, your husband; yes, that is the enviable distinction I aspire to; plead for me, my friends,—soften the obdurate heart that would consign me to everlasting misery. Oh! Matilda, cruel, unfeeling girl, has a proud and unrelenting spirit subdued every tender and compassionate sentiment,—has neither love nor friendship any claims upon your heart?" His emotions were violent.

The ladies, 'till now strangers to his sentiments, sat mute with wonder.

Matilda had covered her face with her handkerchief; when he stopt she withdrew it; it was wet with tears: he snatched it from her trembling hand, kissed it, and thrust it into his bosom. "I beseech you, Sir, to rise, (said she, when able to speak) this posture is unbecoming of yourself and me. The resolution I have formed is such as my reason approves, and my particular circumstances call upon me to adopt; I ought to have done it long ago, and blush at my own folly in delaying it." "But, good God! madam, (interrupted the Count) can the ridiculous behaviour, or unjust prejudices of one worthless woman weigh against the affections, the esteem of so many respectable friends? What have we done to deserve being rendered miserable through her envy and malice?" "Could the warmest love, gratitude and respect, which I owe to everyone here, (answered she;) could the arguments of the most condescending kindness, deeply imprinted here (putting her hand to her heart) could these avail to alter my purpose, I might not be able to withstand your persuasions; but, my Lord, when I have had fortitude sufficient to deny those who are dearer to me than life, you cannot be offended, that 'tis impossible for me to oblige you; and here, in the presence of those who have been witnesses to the honors you have offered me, I release you from every vow, every obligation your too ardent love has conferred on me, and from this hour beseech you to think of me as a friend, zealous for your honor and happiness, for your fame, and the respect you owe to your family; but equally jealous of every duty I owe myself, and therefore determined to see you no more." She rose quickly from her chair, and ran into Mrs. Courtney's dressing-room, giving way to a violent burst of tears. The astonished Count, who had not the power to prevent her departure, threw himself into a chair without speaking. The Countess had followed Matilda.

"This is really (said Mrs. Courtney) the most extraordinary young woman I ever met with; I wonder not at your attachment, my dear Count, but after this public declaration, you have nothing to hope for:

imitate her example of fortitude and self-denial, and suffer not your mind to be depressed, when it is necessary you should exert man's boasted superiority of reason and firmness." The Count replied not.

The Marchioness looked with a little surprise at Mrs. Courtney, who she thought appeared less affected than she ought for her young friend.

Lord Delby was warm in her praise, and offered to be her escort to Boulogne, as he thought it highly improper she should be accompanied by servants only.

This offer was thankfully accepted by the Marchioness. "She has absolutely prohibited the Marquis and myself, (said she) but I hope will make no objections to the honor you intend her."

The Count, making a slight apology, withdrew, and every one joined in pitying the necessity for a separation of two persons so worthy of each other. "Was fortune the only obstacle her delicacy could raise, (said the Marquis) there are those who would rejoice to remove it; but when we consider the particular disadvantages of her situation—the disgrace and insults which would attend the Count, from her want of birth, however great her merit: unjust as I know those prejudices are, yet I confess it would have given me pain, had she acted otherwise. I applaud, I admire, I love her more than ever, but I do not wish to see her the Count's wife, unless those bars could be removed, which now appear next to an impossibility." "No! (cried the Marchioness, briskly) no! I will not believe merit like Matilda's is born to wither in the shade; I will hope to see her one day in a conspicuous point of view, that may reflect honor on all who are connected with her, either by blood or friendship."

"You are romantic, my dear madam, (said Mrs. Courtney, with a smile;) but suppose we go to your young favorite, and see how the poor thing does after her heroics."

This was said with so little feeling, that the Marchioness was surprised; and a sudden idea darting into the mind of the Marquis, he could not suppress a smile, whilst Lord Delby looked offended with his sister's light manner of speaking.

Under these different impressions they entered the dressing-room, and found poor Matilda reclining her head on the Countess, and both weeping. "Fie, fie, my good friend, (said Mrs. Courtney) is this the way to comfort the young lady for the sacrifices she has made to honor and principle?" "I adore your sensibility, madam, (cried Lord Delby, hastily;) in my opinion, who ever loves Miss Matilda does honor to their own heart."

Both ladies bowed to his lordship, though unable to speak; but endeavouring to recover themselves, the Countess said, "This dear obstinate girl proposes setting off the day after to-morrow." "Well, and if she is so determined, what hinders us from all taking a trip to Dover, previous to our Scarborough journey?" (said Lord Delby.) Every one agreed to the proposal, after which they sought to amuse their minds, by talking on different subjects.

The Countess and Mrs. Courtney accompanied the Marchioness home to dinner, but Lord Delby excused himself, that he might attend to the Count. On his return to Cavendish-square he was informed his guest was in the library. He found him writing, and would have retired; the Count requested he would sit down: the conversation naturally turned on the recent occurrences in Harley-street. "Don't think meanly of me, my dear Lord, (said the Count) if I cannot help gratifying a little malice and revenge; I have just finished a few lines to Mademoiselle De Fontelle; I will, at least, make her remember she is in my power, and tremble every moment, lest I should put my threats in execution; I will plant a thorn in her bosom, if she is capable of feeling, though, alas! I can never draw the one from my breast she has been the cause of transfixing there for life! I shall send to the Ambassador's, to procure her address, as doubtless from old acquaintance Madame Le Brun has been to pay her respects to his lady, and that is the only clue at present, I have to find her."

When Lord Delby acquainted him the day was fixed for Matilda's departure, and their intended jaunt with her, "Ah! (said he) how hard, that the person most interested in that event should be precluded from being a witness of it, though I know I could not stand the shock." "If my sister does not accompany us, which I rather doubt, as one coach cannot hold them, and I intend going on horseback, there being no necessity for great expedition, I shall consign her to your care, my dear Count, in our absence." "If Mrs. Courtney will accept the attendance of such a spiritless being as myself, (answered he) I shall be honoured by permission to wait upon her."

Not to dwell on the melancholy circumstances of parting, when nothing new or particular occurred, 'tis sufficient to say both parties were overwhelmed with grief, and Matilda submitted, with much reluctance, to Lord Delby's going in the packet with her; but her friends all protesting, if she refused, every one would go, she was obliged to acquiesce; and embracing the two ladies a thousand times, with streaming eyes, she tore herself from them and embarked.

The wind was fair; they reached Boulogne in seven hours; and whilst they partook of some refreshment at the hotel, Louison and Antoine walked to the Ursuline Convent, in the high town, and having acquainted the porteress with their errand, found, to their great mortification, they took no ladies in chamber, or high pensioners. They were directed to the Annunciate Convent, and there soon procured admission, and accommodations for Matilda, and Louison, who gladly attended her, thinking it would be only for a short time, 'till her lady came from England.

Within a few hours Matilda was received and settled. She took leave of Lord Delby with tears of gratitude. "Ah! (said he, much moved) not one word of remembrance to my worthy guest?" "Yes, Sir, (said she, raising her voice) tell him I admire, I esteem him—that his happiness is the first wish of my heart. Take care, my dear Lord, of the worthy Count; teach him to forget me, and if ever he should be united to an amiable woman, deserving and possessing his affection, I will then boldly claim his esteem—'till then we must be for ever separated."

She entered the gates, unable to say more, and when they were shut upon her, Lord Delby, overcome with pity and admiration, returned to the hotel; that same evening re-embarked for Dover, and joined his friends before nine the next morning.

Spiritless and unhappy, they arrived in Harley-street the following evening, and sending a messenger to Mrs. Courtney, that lady shortly after entered the house, the Count with her; she cheerful and lively, he looking pale and dejected. She enquired, with an air of indifference, the particulars of their journey, but seemed little interested in it; not so the Count, he asked a thousand questions. "I have a message to you from the amiable Matilda," (said Lord Delby.) "For me, (said the Count, eagerly;) O! why have you delayed it?" His Lordship repeated her last words. "Sweet angelic girl! (cried he) is my happiness dear to her! but why should I doubt it? she is truth and goodness itself; my esteem, my love, must ever be hers, for no other woman shall ever possess that heart she condescended to prize, and never will I marry, if Matilda cannot be my wife." "Lord bless me! (exclaimed Mrs. Courtney) let's have no more dismals; I declare these last five days have vapoured me to death: I hope our journey to Scarborough will teem with more pleasant incidents than yours to Dover seems to have produced." "I am sure so, (answered the Count;) the world does not abound with characters like Matilda's to lament."

No more was said; supper was announced, and more general conversation introduced during the remainder of the evening, though every one appeared absent and uneasy.

After the company had left them the Marchioness took notice of Mrs. Courtney's behaviour. "Surely she has taken some pique against Matilda," (said she.) "Yes, (replied the Marquis) the pique natural to a jealous woman." "Jealous!" (repeated the Marchioness) why, surely you do not think she is fond of the Count." "Indeed, but I do, (replied he;) nay, I am certain of it, from many observations I lately made on her conduct." "Bless me! (returned she) why Mrs. Courtney is seven or eight and thirty, the Count only two and twenty." "That's true, (said he, smiling) but, my love, ladies have various ways of concealing their age, and the depredations of time; besides, vanity never forsakes them; and to do Mrs. Courtney justice, she is an agreeable woman." "Yes, and a sensible woman, (returned she;) I never can suppose her guilty of such a weakness; I rather think her prejudiced against Matilda, by some falsehoods or other." "Very well, (replied the Marquis) be it so: I am always more gratified by your favorable opinion of your own sex, than a readiness to condemn them; the one shews a generous mind, free from guile itself—the other, a malignant spirit, desirous of acquiring merit from the deficiencies of others." "But, pray, (said the Marchioness) how will you account to Mr. Weimar for the retirement of Matilda, should he hear of it, and apply to you?" "By the simplest truth, (replied he) except what relates to Bouville. He must thank himself for all the stories Mademoiselle De Fontelle has repeated to her disadvantage, and from whence originated her sudden determination. She is now safe; the letter I procured from the Ambassador, addressed to any convent, at least, the superior of it, will always protect her, since mine is the only claim she is subject to."

Tranquillised by this, the Marchioness recommended her young friend to the care of Providence, and retired to rest with a virtuous heart, and an easy mind, which could not fail of producing quiet and refreshing slumbers.

The Count, Lord Delby, and Mrs. Courtney, were not equally happy. The former, more sensible every hour of Matilda's worth, cursed the pride of birth, which stood between him and happiness, and determined to live only for her. Lord Delby had been many years a widower; he had only one son, whom he carried to Switzerland at the time the Countess so fortunately obtained his protection: he was then extremely struck with her appearance; beauty in distress has a thousand claims upon a susceptible mind; but the Countess had good sense, sweetness of temper, and delicacy of manners to recommend her; and though the first bloom of beauty was worn off, she had sufficient charms both of mind and body to procure for her the admiration of any man. Lord Delby conceived a very warm affection for her, though he knew it was entirely hopeless, unless death should rid her of her persecutor; he was therefore condemned to silence on a subject nearest his heart, and felt the restraint very painfully. Mrs. Courtney, from the first moment she beheld the Count, was charmed with his person and manners. She had been a widow four years: when about three and twenty, at the request of her father, Lord Delby, and the temptations of a very capital fortune, superb carriages, fine jewels, and those other avenues to the heart of a young and fashionable female, she gave her hand to Mr. Courtney, who was struck with her person, and thinking it right to have an heir to his immense possessions, suspended for a time the delights of Newmarket, and his favorite sprightly, to attend the laws of Hymen; but in a very few weeks his former propensity returned; his young bride was forsaken for the pleasures of the turf, Newmarket, its jockies, its tumultuous pursuits, deep bets, and jovial companions, engrossed all his time and attention. His lady, happily for her, was not doatingly fond of her husband; she was possessed of every appendage proper for a female in fashionable life, and outshone two-thirds of her acquaintance in jewels, plate, carriages, and dress; she was therefore extremely easy about the absence of her husband, and whilst he neither contracted her expences, nor deprived her of the amusements she liked, she was perfectly disposed to shew him the same complaisance. This very modish pair lived some years together, without feeling either pleasure or pain, from their different engagements. Mr. Courtney was at first much disappointed by not having an heir, but time reconciled him to an event he could not remove; and having determined to make a distant relation, who was to inherit his estate, take his name by Act of Parliament, he ceased giving himself any further concern about the matter. They had been married upwards of ten years, when unfortunately taking cold after very hard riding, a violent fever terminated his life in six days, and his disconsolate widow was left to undergo all the forms and ceremonies of deep mourning, and to wear odious black for three months. This state of mortification being rubbed through, she found herself mistress of all her former finery, and a very noble jointure, to live as she pleased. Mrs. Courtney was good-natured, not from principle but constitution; she hated trouble of any sort, therefore bore any thing, rather than have the fatigue of being out of humour; she was polite and friendly, where she had no temptation to be otherwise; in short, she had many negative virtues, without any active ones. Such was Mrs. Courtney, when she appeared in this book first. All men were indifferent alike, 'till she saw the engaging Count; a few interviews decided her fate; she found she loved to excess, and hated Matilda in proportion; she discovered his partiality in her favor long before it was publicly known, and sought to recommend herself to his notice, by paying attention to his favorite; but finding all her endeavours ineffectual, she began to dislike the innocent object of her jealousy, and was casting about in her mind how to get rid of her, when Matilda unexpectedly declared her intention of going into a convent. The Count's subsequent behaviour, his public declaration and protestations, were mortifying circumstances, 'tis true, but she depended upon time, absence, and her own endeavours, to conquer a passion he could not but look upon as hopeless. The Countess, so many years secluded from the world, at first felt only the warmest gratitude to Mrs. Courtney and her brother for their generous protection; but the polite attention, the mark'd kindness of Lord Delby, inspired her with the most perfect esteem for him,—and though, from the melancholy circumstances which attended her early prepossession, her heart was dead to love, she yet experienced all that partiality in his Lordship's favor which her heart was capable of feeling.

Such was the state and sentiments of the party, now about to set off for Scarborough. The day previous to which, after a consultation between the Marquis, his Lady, and the Countess, on the entrance of the Count, to pay his morning compliments, the Marquis led him to the Countess, "My dear friend, you have hitherto known this lady only as Madame Le Roche, the name she bears in England; I now introduce you to her as our dearest sister, the Countess of Wolfenbach, whose death you have heard us often lament."

The Count started with surprise; "Good heavens! (said he, after saluting her) how is this possible?"

The Marquis gave him a brief recital of her confinement, and promised him the particulars another day. "I could no longer keep our secret from you, but she must still retain her former name until the whole affair is brought forward. The Ambassador was made acquainted with it yesterday; he will take some private steps, at first, if possible, to do us justice; and when we return to London for the winter, we shall use decisive measures; meantime, I have written to a friend, as has likewise my sister, to procure Joseph's testimony, as far as his knowledge extends, lest, as he is old, we should lose a witness of some consequence."

The Count entered warmly into the business; his life and fortune was at the service of his friends: they embraced and thanked him.

The following day they left town, after writing the most affectionate letters to their beloved Matilda, whose absence they most sincerely regretted.

Matilda, on her first residence in the convent, found it replete with many inconveniences she did not expect. For the first week she cried incessantly, and poor Louison, not happier, continually pressed her to return. "Ah, mon Dieu! (cried she) if my good master and lady, if the dear charming Count de Bouville knew how miserable you are, they would fly to bring you out again. Ah! the good Count, the morning before we came away, gave me ten English guineas; the tears were in his eyes; "Take care of your charming mistress, Louison, (said he) and I will always be your friend:"—Dear, dear gentleman! O, that he was but here!"

This little anecdote, which one might have supposed would have added to Matilda's grief, proved a most salutary remedy for it: she instantly dried her eyes. "Amiable, generous man! (said she) shall I repine, that I have devoted myself to retirement to preserve a mind like his from repentance and self-reproach, and from the disdain of those low-minded people incapable of the nobleness of heart which would prompt him to forget his own dignity to raise a friendless orphan. No; I will at least prove deserving of his esteem by my own self-denial; I will support every inconvenience, every trial with resignation—happy, if, in sacrificing the trifling amusements the world affords, I can promote his peace, and secure his future happiness."

Fortified by these generous sentiments, she no longer wept or sighed; she sought consolation in the practice of her religious duties, which strengthened her mind and composed her spirits: she found in

the uniform observance of piety, charity, and compassion towards the
sick and unfortunate, that peace which the world could not give, and
that serenity of mind which no recollection of misfortunes could deprive her of.

She became the admiration of the whole community; every one
was desirous of her favor, but Matilda, blessed with uncommon pen-
etration, and capable of the nicest discrimination, was at no loss to
distinguish the selfish and fulsome attentions of the officious, from the
approbation of the worthy and humble few who looked on her with
eyes of kindness, but never intruded; from these few, to whom she
payed particular civility, her heart selected mother St. Magdalene; she
was about eight and twenty, and had been a nun nearly ten years; she
was one of those very elegant forms you cannot behold without admiration; her face was more expressive than beautiful, yet more engaging
than a lifeless set of features without animation, however perfect or
blooming, could possibly be; she was pious without ostentation, kind
and affectionate to her sisterhood, and courteous, without design or
meanness, to the pensioners.

This charming woman soon attracted the notice of Matilda,—she
sought her company and conversation—she received her attentions
with particular complacency.

Mother Magdalene was sensible of her civilities—she plainly comprehended the value of them, but from peculiar notions of delicacy,
and to avoid giving umbrage to the sisterhood, she rather repressed
than encouraged her particular kindness. Matilda, however, would not
be repulsed, and Magdalene was at length compelled to be her "Dear
Mother."

They were frequently together, and by her example Matilda was
encouraged to the perseverance in every moral and religious duty.

Letters from her two friends, the Marchioness and Countess, were
the only things she permitted to break in upon them, and those letters
were a continual stimulation to a sense of gratitude and generosity,
which she found herself called upon to exert.

Whilst Matilda had thus happily reconciled her mind to her situation, her friends were enjoying the amusements that Scarborough afforded.

The Count was always the attendant on Mrs. Courtney; and
though his passion was as fervent as ever, and his regrets as powerful
for the loss of Matilda, he could not be always in company with an ami-

able woman, who paid him such particular attention, without being gratified by it, and sometimes shewing those little marks of gallantry which all women expect.

The Count, though he had a more than common share of solidity and stability, with the most refined understanding and integrity of heart, yet he was still a Frenchman—still possessed a natural gaiety of heart, the greatest politeness and attention to the fair sex, and sometimes fell into the hyperbolical compliments so natural to his countrymen, when addressing the ladies. Mrs. Courtney, too ready to believe every thing to be as she wished, gave him every encouragement, and contrived frequently to draw him into situations and expressions which were rather equivocal, but by which he meant nothing, though the lady thought otherwise.

They had been near three weeks at Scarborough; the ladies had heard twice from Matilda, but as she requested her name might never be mentioned to the Count, but from necessity, they only answered his eager enquiries by saying she was well, and appeared to be much pleased with her situation. He saw there was a reserve in their manner, and justly supposed it owing to her restrictions: he did justice to her greatness of mind, which only served to increase his love and regrets.

One morning Mrs. Courtney, entering the Marchioness's dressing-room, flung herself into a chair, "Bless me! (said she) what shall I do with your friend, the Count? he has drawn me into a pretty scrape,—I never intended marrying again, but he is so pressing, so irresistible—" "Who, (cried the Marchioness, surprised) the Count? he pressing?" "Why, yes, (answered she;) surely you must have observed his particular devoirs for some time past." "Not I, upon my honor (answered the Marchioness;) I never supposed his attentions to you wore the face of particularity." "Then you can have observed nothing, (said she, peevishly.) Pray, what think you, my dear madam?" (turning to the Countess.) "Upon my word, I am equally surprised (replied she;) but if you can settle the matter agreeably between yourselves, I shall certainly rejoice at it, because I am very sure Matilda will keep her resolution, in refusing his addresses."

Those last words, which were spoken undesignedly, piqued Mrs. Courtney a good deal. "I do not think 'tis of much consequence, (said she, haughtily) whether she keeps her resolution or not;—I believe by this time he is very sensible of the impropriety of his offer——but I forget, I appointed him to meet me at a friend's, in the next street,—bon jour, ladies," (said she, with a forced gaiety, and ran out of the room, leaving them looking at each other with astonishment.)

"Can this be Mrs. Courtney? (cried the Countess) my God, what a change!" "But is there, can there, be any truth, (said the Marchioness) in the Count's attentions?" "Heaven knows, (said she) but if it is so, I shall never depend upon man again."

Some company coming in, prevented further conversation; but at dinner, when they all met, the ladies observed the Count appeared to be thoughtful and uneasy, Mrs. Courtney gay and lively, Lord Delby rather attentive to both; in short, it was the first dinner in which the party seemed collected within themselves, and forgot their friends, except Mrs. Courtney, who behaved with remarkable politeness and sweetness to all.

When the ladies retired to the drawing-room the Count addressed the Marquis in the following manner. "I believe, my dear Sir, you are sufficiently acquainted with me, to know that I am equally incapable of a dishonourable thought or action to any one, much less towards a lady for whom I entertain the highest respect, and the sister of my hospitable entertainer." "For heaven's sake, (cried the Marquis) what is all this,—who dares accuse you?" "A misapprehension only, I hope, (said the Count, in a calm tone) not an accusation. Both you and all our friends are perfectly acquainted with my attachment to the amiable Matilda,—an attachment (added he, raising his voice) that will be as lasting as my life, for I never shall love any other woman: but unhappily, the respect and attentions I have paid to the merits of Mrs. Courtney, have been misconceived; I have been upbraided with seeking to gain her affections, and with having given colour to suppose mine were also devoted to her: the highest respect, nay, even admiration of her many amiable qualities, I have undoubtedly expressed, but not one word beyond what friendship would warrant, from a man who made no scruple to own his love for another, though perhaps that other never can be his. My heart, my honor, does not reproach me with the least duplicity or mean design. Can you, my dear Marquis, from the whole tenor of my conduct, suppose I could be a trifling coxcomb, much less a deliberate villain, for I must hold any man as such who could seek to gain the affections of an amiable woman, to gratify his vanity only?" "I am equally surprised and concerned (said the Marquis) that such misapprehensions should have taken place—" "And I (interrupted Lord Delby) equally displeased and mortified, at being made a party in the business; but there is no accounting for the vanity of women, and how very readily they entertain ideas they wish to indulge. I am very sorry, Count, I have been drawn into this foolish affair, for I observed at first it was very unaccountable, that a man should make his court to one woman, and avowedly profess his admiration of another; I shall, however, talk to my sister, and I beg the subject may drop and go no further." "I feel myself extremely at a loss how to behave (said the Count;) I think I had better leave Scarborough." "By no means, (said his Lordship, hastily;) behave as usual to Mrs. Courtney in public, but avoid tête-à-têtes;—if she is wise, she will herself approve this method, to escape observation."

The Count reluctantly submitted, knowing after what had passed, he must appear very awkward in his civilities, which had been so misconceived.

They attended the ladies in the drawing-room, and it being proposed to go to the theatre, the Count, as usual, offered his hand to Mrs. Courtney, though with a look of confusion and reserve; she accepted it with a polite and tender air.

Lord Delby, not knowing she had exposed herself to the ladies, requested the Marquis would not mention the affair to them.

The evening passed off very well, and at supper they were more cheerful and talkative than usual. The following day, however, Mrs. Courtney appeared with a new face; she looked pensive and unhappy, complained of a pain in her breast, ate little, sighed frequently, and in short, engaged that particular attention we naturally pay to those we love, and see indisposed. The Count looked the image of despair; he addressed her one moment, with an air of tenderness, the next he studiously seemed to avoid her; his behaviour was unequal, confused, and evidently perplexed.

Things continued in this state for some days,—Mrs. Courtney more melancholy, the Count more distressed; when one day, as they were at table, the Marquis received an express from London. Every one was alarmed; it came from the German Ambassador, requesting the Marquis would instantly come to town, the Count of Wolfenbach being there dangerously ill, and desirous of making all possible reparation to the Countess.

This news suspended all the new schemes. The Countess could scarcely be kept alive; she was apprehensive of some fresh plots, and dreaded the idea of being again within his power. "Fear not, madam, (cried Lord Delby;) the monster shall never see you without your friends to protect you." "Besides, sister, (urged the Marchioness) the Ambassador is himself a pledge of your safety, and tells us he is dangerously ill,—perhaps the poor wretch cannot die in peace without your pardon." "O, my God! (said she, starting up) let me go this instant!—alas! he has need of forgiveness; his crimes are great, yet if they were the consequence of his love for me, 'tis my duty to speak peace and pardon; grant heaven! (cried she, lifting up her hands) I may not come too late! I will set off this very hour." "Be composed, my dear sister, (said the Marquis) we will go this evening; the Marchioness and I will attend you." "And I," (exclaimed the Count.) "We will all accompany you," (said Lord Delby.) "Ah! my Lord, (answered the Countess) why should I so suddenly call you from the amusements of this place: you proposed staying three months, we have only been here a little better than one." "Wherever my friends are, (replied Lord Delby) is to me the desirable place; I have no local attachments without their presence; and I dare answer for my sister, she has no objections, as I think the air of Scarborough has been of little use to her health." "You judge very right, my Lord, I shall certainly accompany our friends, (said she, in a languid tone, adding) their happiness must constitute mine."

The Count, who took every thing literally which betrayed generosity of sentiment, could not help saying, "'Tis impossible to doubt Mrs. Courtney's concurrence in every scheme productive of pleasure to those she honors with her esteem." This compliment made her eyes dance with pleasure.

Their women were called and desired to set about packing immediately. Every thing was hurried on, and at five the next morning they were all on their return to London.

About a week previous to this Matilda received a letter from an unknown hand, and without a name, signifying that the Count De Bouville was paying his addresses to Mrs. Courtney; that he was extremely fond of her, but that she hesitated on account of his vows to Matilda, which made him very unhappy.

She read this letter with composure,—she felt some pangs at her heart, she tried to overcome them: "Why should I be uneasy, (said she) have not I wished the Count might make a suitable alliance?—did I not release him from his vows? Alas! I have neither claims nor expectations,—let him marry, I can then renounce the world, and settle here for life,—when lost to him I have only this asylum to bury myself in for ever." The tears would flow, but she quickly dried them. "From whence this sorrow, (said she again) had I any hopes? O, no! all is despair and bitterness on my side, but I will rejoice in the happiness of the amiable Count, whatever befalls myself."

Within three days after this, she received a letter from Mrs. Courtney; these were the contents:

"*My dear Miss Matilda,*

"Honor, sentiment, and generosity impel me to address you; I am well acquainted with the nobleness of your heart, and can confide in its integrity. You have refused the Count De Bouville, publicly refused him: was there a shadow of hope you ever could be his, I would have been silent; but as I deem that impossible, I trust to your generosity and fortitude when I tell you, he has for some time past paid his addresses to me, with the warm approbation of all our friends. I at first made objections on your account; he pleaded, you had publicly rejected him; and, as I did not feel satisfied, he offered to write you, and procure his release: but knowing men have great duplicity, when they wish to carry a point, I declined his offer and chose to write myself; and I conjure you, my dear Matilda, to believe I will not consent to what he calls his happiness, without your permission. If you have any hopes or expectations; if you think his love may ever return to you, and that different situations may give a countenance to his addresses, and admit of your claims upon him, depend upon it I will dismiss him, however unhappy he may be; for I would not wound your peace, by acceding to his wishes, be the consequence what it may. Your friends, who are mine also, choose to be entirely silent on the subject; nor will they take notice of it, until settled between you and me. Look on me as your friend, dear Matilda,—be explicit—do not consider the Count or myself; speak your wishes, your hopes, and be assured that your felicity is my first wish, whatever it may cost me.

"I am my dear Matilda's sincere friend

"And obedient servant,

"MARIA COURTNEY."

Prepared as Matilda had been, by the anonymous letter, to expect such intelligence, no words can express her feelings at receiving this letter; overcome with grief, she retired to her apartment and gave loose to the painful emotions that oppressed her. After a little time she grew more composed: "Is a heart like his worth regretting? (cried she.) Could he, if his love had been founded on esteem, so soon have offered his addresses to another? O, no! it was only a transient affection, not imprinted on the heart, but vanished with my person: how fortunate then our hands were not joined; how miserable should I have found myself, if united for life to so fickle a disposition."

Whilst this impression was strong upon her, she took up her pen and wrote the following answer:

"*Dear madam,*

"Accept, I beseech you, my warmest acknowledgements for your very friendly and obliging letter: your candid communications and consideration for my peace, I feel in the most sensible manner; but I beg leave to assure you, madam, neither my happiness nor peace depend now upon the Count De Bouville. I shall always think myself obliged for the affection he offered me, but as it is impossible we should ever meet on those terms, I hope reason has entirely subdued an improper sentiment, and if we ever should meet again, which is not likely, we shall behold each other with the indifference of common acquaintances. I am exceedingly happy here, and, if at the expiration of the twelvemonth Mr. Weimar allowed me, my friends will accede to my wishes, and permit my stay in this convent, I trust I shall be happy for the remainder of my life.

"I hope this will prove satisfactory to your very friendly offers respecting the Count, who has my sincerest wishes for his happiness, with any other woman but her who is, my dear madam,

"Your much obliged humble servant,

"MATILDA."

After she had sealed and sent off this letter her spirits grew more tranquillised; she tried to conquer her feelings, and consider only the fickleness of men's dispositions. "Yet why should I upbraid him, (thought she;) he has a family, a name to support, and ought to marry: Mrs. Courtney is amiable, has a large independent fortune, respectable friends, and a noble origin to boast of;—what am I in a comparative view with her? Ah! (cried she, bursting into tears) the retrospection humbles and subdues both my pride and regret: what have I to do but to submit to the lowly state I am placed in, and bless at a distance those generous spirits that have enabled me to procure such an asylum as this."

Mother Magdalene entered as she was wiping the tears from her cheeks; taking her hand affectionately between hers, "My dear young lady, why those tears? spare me the pain of seeing you unhappy; remember this is but a short and transitory life; our pilgrimage through it is painful, no doubt thorns are strewed in our paths, sorrows planted in our bosoms; but if planted and strewed by others, where is the sting to afflict our own hearts? Believe me, dear lady, reason can subdue every affliction but what arises from a condemnation within; with a self-approving conscience we can look forward with hope; and if turbulent and ungracious spirits are too powerful for us to contend with here, we can trust to our Heavenly Father, that our sufferings and patience will meet with a recompence hereafter, far superior to the brightest expectations that can be formed in this life." "My dear friend and comforter, (said Matilda, kissing her hand) be you my monitress if I grieve for temporal evils; yet, alas! my misfortunes are not common ones." "You think so (answered Mother Magdalene;) we are all apt to magnify our own troubles, and think them superior to what others feel; but, my dear child, you are yet a novice in affliction; when you know more of the world you will know also that there are varieties of misery which assail the human frame,—and 'tis our own feelings that constitute great part of our distress."

Matilda sighed, and after a little pause, "That I may not appear impatient, nor grieved at trifles, I will unbosom myself to you, and perhaps from you obtain that consolation I have hitherto sought in vain."

She then related every part of her story, except the name of the Countess and situation of the Castle.

Her gentle friend sympathized with her, and confessed, for so young a woman, her trials were very great. "But still, my dear lady, (said she) I bid you hope; you have a Father and Protector, trust in him, and you will one day assuredly be happy. Another time you shall know my sad story, and will then confess, of the two, I have been most wretched; and, though I cannot entirely exclude a painful remembrance sometimes, yet I am now comparatively happy,—my troubles no longer exist, and religion has restored peace to my mind. Adieu, my dear child,—take hope to your bosom and compose your spirit." "Yes, (cried Matilda) I will at least try to conquer one cause of my distress, and in destroying this fatal letter of Mrs. Courtney's, lose all remembrance of the Count: surely after having so solemnly renounced him, I have no right either to complain of him or grieve for myself,—'tis an unpardonable folly, for every way he is dead to me." She threw the letter into the fire and walked into the garden.

In the evening she received another visit from her good mother, who was much pleased to see her so tranquil. Matilda reminded her of her promise to relate her history.

"My story, my dear child, is not a long one, but replete with many melancholy circumstances. My father was a merchant at Dunkirk; he married a very amiable woman, and had a numerous family—five girls and four boys; few people lived more respectable than they did, but they were not rich; a large family, liberal minds, and hearts always disposed to relieve the wants of others, precluded affluence, though they had a decent competence. The failure of a very capital house in England, with whom my father was materially connected, obliged him to go over, without loss of time; he embarked from Dunkirk. Alas! my dear child, we saw him no more! A storm overtook them, as 'tis supposed, and all on board perished, for the packet was never but once seen or heard of after. When this dreadful news arrived, my mother was weeping over a letter just received from a friend in London, with the intelligence, that the house which had failed could not pay a shilling in the pound, and from some particular connexions between them and my father, all his effects would be seized, and he was likewise declared, or included in the bankruptcy. One of those unhappy gossiping persons, fond of telling everything, without considering the consequences, called upon my mother, as she was in an agony over the contents of this letter; "Ah! my dear madam, (cried she) I see you have received the fatal news?" "Yes, (answered my mother, wringing her hands) we are all undone for ever!" "But who, (said she again) could write you about it, for only the boat that is just come in saw the packet go down." "What packet?" (cried my mother, starting.) "Why the packet your good husband was in."

"She heard no more, but fell senseless on the floor. I had been out upon business, and entered the room just as this officious news-monger and the servants were trying to raise and recover my wretched parent. A stranger to all the circumstances, I was frightened to death almost, and teased everyone to know what had happened; no one answered. It was some time before she was brought to life. With a look of horror I shall never forget, she cried, "Hermine, you have no longer a father, a friend, nor a home!" "Great God! (I exclaimed) what is all this?" "'Tis misery in extreme, (said she, still with a fixed look and a dry eye;) your father is drowned, and I hourly expect everything to be seized. Well, (cried she, rather wildly) let it be complete! Ruin should not come by degrees." Two or three of the younger children came into the room; the moment she saw them she gave a violent shriek and fell into convulsions. Scarce in my senses, I flew about the house, and by my screams drew several persons to me. We got my mother up to her apartment, a physician was sent for, but it was many hours before she was restored; she lay three days at the point of death, the fourth the fever abated, and hopes were entertained of her life. This day a person came and took possession of the house and all our effects. By the interposition of a friend we were allowed to remain in it ten days. Judge, my dear young friend, what must have been my situation; a father dead, a mother scarcely alive, our whole property seized,—eight children younger than myself, I only fifteen, and all unprovided for—obliged to be the comforter, the supporter of all.

"Out of the numerous set of acquaintances we had, two only appeared as friends in our distress; one an old gentleman of small fortune, the other a young merchant, who had for some months paid particular attention to me, young as I was. These two persons interested themselves a good deal for us. My mother grew better, but her nerves were so shattered that a kind of partial palsy took effect upon her speech, she spoke thick and scarcely intelligible; a sort of convulsive cry succeeded every attempt to talk; in short, her situation was most truly deplorable. Within a few days we were removed to the house of the old gentleman, without any one thing we could call our own, but clothes. This good and worthy man placed out my sisters in a convent, put my brothers to school, raised a subscription for their support, his own fortune being insufficient to maintain us all, and in fine, did everything a father and friend could do, for the whole family. Not one of my mother's former gay acquaintance ever concerned themselves about her; she was poor and afflicted with sickness, "they could not bear to see a woman they esteemed in so miserable a situation, and therefore were obliged to give her up." Oh! my dear lady, of all the worldly evils that can befall us, surely there is nothing so painful to support as the ingratitude and contumely of those who once thought themselves honoured in your acquaintance: meer butterflies of the day! they bask in the sunshine of your prosperity, but when night shuts in and sorrows assail you, they fly elsewhere in search of those sweets you can no longer afford them, and despise what they once coveted and admired. Young, at that time, almost a stranger to mankind, I felt indignation and astonishment when I met any of our former friends—friends! let me not profane the name of friendship! I mean intimates and companions; my civilities were repressed with scorn; my appearance glanced over with a look of contempt, and "poor souls, they are supported by charity, I pity them to my heart," said aloud in my hearing, with features expressive of every thing but pity.

"I will not dwell on things so common as ingratitude and hardness of heart; stings which you, my young friend, have never yet experienced,—heaven grant you never may, for 'tis a bitter cup to taste of. We lived in the manner I have described for near eight months, my poor mother so ill and helpless I could not leave her. The young gentleman I have mentioned payed me the same attention, and scrupled not to acquaint our good friend, it was his design, in a short time, to make me his wife. "If you do, (said he, one day) you shall have a father's blessing with her when I die; whilst I live I will support the children: but Hermine is a good girl—she who can, at her time of life, give herself up to the care of a sick parent, and find delight in her duty, will make a good wife."

"One morning, when the old gentleman was in my mother's room, he was suddenly seized with an apoplexy and dropt senseless from his chair: my screams soon brought assistance—a surgeon was sent for;—alas! he was gone for ever. My mother was, in consequence of her fright, taken in a shivering fit, which in a few moments turned to a stroke of the palsy, and deprived her entirely of speech and the use of her limbs on the left side. That I preserved my senses at such a time, was wonderful. I sent for my lover, in an agony no words can describe; the news flew through the town, and two or three of our late friend's relations hastened to the house; they were rich and wanted nothing, however they began to assume an air of authority, when my lover interfered, told them he was convinced there was a will, and that I was the appointed heir. This enraged them greatly; the will was eagerly called for, and by all parties earnestly sought for: alas! no such thing was to be found. The unfeeling women ordered me to remove my mother and my trumpery the following morning. My lover was almost beside himself with vexation and disappointment: I was stupid with sorrow; I hung over my almost lifeless parent, without speaking, and unable to shed a tear. After some time, those women quitting the room, leaving orders with a woman servant to watch me, that I took nothing but my own, and to take care I quitted their house next day. When they were gone, this poor woman in circumstances, but rich (oh! how much richer than her employers!) in goodness of heart, approached the bed, and, gently raising me, she gave me some drops and water that rouzed me from the stupor which had seized upon my faculties, when, looking round the room for my departed friend, and then on my helpless parent, I burst into a flood of tears. "Thank God! (said the good creature) that you can weep: don't be unhappy, my dear Miss, Providence will provide for you: I have a sister, who lives in a very humble style indeed, and keeps a little shop; her husband was formerly an under clerk to your father; he loves the whole family dearly, and I dare say, if you will condescend to stay under their mean roof 'till you are better suited, they will wait upon you with joy." "Ah! where is Mr. ——?" meaning my lover. "I know not, madam, (answered she) but I think he followed the ladies." "Good heavens! (I cried) could he leave me under such a complication of horrid circumstances; this is bitterness indeed, if deserted by him,—but it cannot be,—he is doubtless gone to fetch a physician." In this vain hope I passed several hours, no lover, no physician appeared; I was in a state of distraction: the servant sent for her sister and brother; they came, and offered me their services with a heartiness which spoke their sincerity. I was incapable of determining; I sent to my lover, "he was particularly engaged, but would see me some time to-morrow." "O, let me begone! (cried I, in a frenzy) I will take my dear mother in my arms—we will die together." With difficulty they separated me from her: the dear saint was sensible, though incapable of speaking; her eyes told me all she felt—O! the expression in them can never be forgotten,—what a night was that! In the morning my dear mother was put into a kind of litter, and we were conveyed to the humble dwelling of this charitable pair. She was laid in a decent bed and dropt asleep: I was kneeling at the side of it when the door opened, and the man who called himself my lover appeared before me. I felt undescribeable emotions; he took my hand, and placing me in a chair, still unable to speak, he said, "I came to you, my love, the first moment of leisure; last night I was engaged; but you shall not stay in this poor place, I will take a decent lodging for you and your mother, and will be answerable for all expences; I will daily be your visitor, and I hope in a little time you will recover your spirits." At first my heart bounded with joy at his kindness; then again I thought there was something wrong, though I hardly knew what; at last, "I think, (replied I) that I ought not to put you to such great expences, nor would it be proper you should maintain me, unless—" There I stopt. "Unless what?" (said he, earnestly.) "Unless I had a claim to your protection," (said I, blushing.) "I will be very sincere with you, my dear Hermine: had your old friend performed his promise, and left you his fortune, though but a small one, I would have married you; but I am young, and only entering into life; a wife without a fortune, a mother in such a situation, and a family of young relations would soon ruin me, and of course you: I must prove my love another way; an old rich widow has been recommended to me; I will marry her; I shall then be enabled to support you all in affluence, and have no ill consequences to dread. What say you, my dearest Hermine, may I hope your sentiments concur with mine?" You will wonder, my dear child, at my patience and silence during this proposal; in truth I wondered at myself; heaven, no doubt, supported me, and gave me, at that trying moment, superior resolution. "Of my opinion, Sir, and of the sentiments you have avowed, you must collect my thoughts, when I tell you, that so far from living a life of obligation with such a man, were you this moment possessed of millions, and would offer to marry me, I would prefer poverty and want—I would starve, with this dear insulted woman, before I could condescend to marry a man of such infamous principles!—Leave me, Sir, forever; presume not to enter the habitation of virtuous poverty, and blush at your own littleness, when you enjoy the house of wealth and magnificence." He attempted to speak. "I hear you no longer, Sir; you are more mean and contemptible in my eyes than the poorest reptile that crawls upon the earth." I stampt with my foot, and Mrs. Bouté came up. I never saw a countenance so expressive of wonder and disappointment when she entered. "I am sorry to say, madam, you do not know your best friends; but should your mind alter upon consideration, you know where to find me, and I shall be always happy to attend your commands." I gave him no answer, but a look of contempt, and he left the room.

"The spirit and indignation which had supported me through this scene, now subsided; I shed a flood of tears. I saw no one being to whom I could look up with any hope or prospect of comfort. Mrs. Bouté, who sympathized with me, said, "Ah! madam, if Madame De Raikfort, if Madame De Creponiere were acquainted with your sorrows, I am sure you would find friends; they always assist the unfortunate, and particularly persons like you, born to higher expectations." I took my resolution immediately; I wrote to both, describing my past and present situation. From the latter lady I received an almost immediate visit: she condoled with me; she entered into my concerns with a kindness and delicacy peculiar to herself, as I then thought; I knew not that the principles of charity and benevolence were the same in every well informed mind and good heart. I received the same kind attentions from the other family: Madame De Raikfort sent me every comfort and convenience I could want for my poor mother. In short, to those good ladies I was indebted for my chief support during her existence. A fortnight, exactly, from the death of our good old friend, she expired. There was no apparent alteration till within a few hours of her death; and she went off without a sigh or groan. Though the shock was dreadful, yet I had so long expected it, and in her melancholy situation it was rather to be wished for, that I found myself, though grieved at my irreparable loss, yet rejoiced that she escaped from the evils of this life, to awake in a blessed immortality. The benevolent ladies I have mentioned, did not forsake me; they paid the last sad duties to my parent; they undertook to educate and place my younger brothers and sisters to get their living decently; they asked what were my views and wishes? I frankly answered, "To be a nun." Had I any choice of a convent? I named this; a young lady, a friend of my juvenile days, previous to my misfortunes, had professed here. The ladies told me I should enter upon my noviciate, but on no terms to be persuaded to assume the veil; it was by no means their wish; and the first summons from me they would take me out and provide for me in the world: that they rather complied with my wishes than their own inclinations—which would be more gratified in my residence with them. I thanked my generous benefactresses, but persisted in my desire of quitting the world. The day before I intended leaving Dunkirk, I received a letter from my quondam[1] lover, expressing regret for his behaviour, and an unequivocal offer of marriage. I put his letter under a cover, with these lines: "The man who presumes to insult the feelings of a virtuous female, and when he fails in his purpose, condescends to solicit pardon, and offers to raise that ill-treated woman to a level with himself, lowers her more by such an offer, than the bitterest poverty can inflict: but the person to whom this letter is addressed is fortunately beyond the reach of

---

[1] Former.

insult or indigence; she therefore rejects the proposal with her whole heart, and with the highest contempt."

"Having seen my brothers and sisters safe under the protection of those worthy ladies, and received from them every pecuniary assistance I could want, with letters of warm recommendation I arrived here; and here, in a short time, recovered tranquillity and ease: leaving nothing in the world to regret, I studied the duties of my situation, and, at the expiration of the time allowed to consider, I gave my decided choice of a monastic life, and took the veil. I hear often from my generous friends. Two of my sisters are well married; the rest of my family have every prospect of success.

"Now, my dear young lady, I have related my history, tell me candidly, have your troubles ever equalled mine?"

"Oh! no, (cried Matilda;) I am ashamed of my own impatience and inquietude. Good heavens! if such are the evils to be expected in life; if misfortunes are so frequent, ingratitude and malignancy so prevalent, men so abandoned, and the good and benevolent allotted so small a share in the proportion of the world, the only asylum for the unfortunate is a convent." "Not always, (answered Mother Magdalene;) there are situations and difficulties in life from which even the unfortunate may extract hope and comfort: your's is such: 'tis possible you have parents still living, who may one day fold you to their bosoms; 'tis likewise not impossible you may one day be united to the man you prefer. In short, your situation is not hopeless like mine: I saw the downfall of every expectation I could form, and had no one hope or engagement to the world; you have many: you have no right to dispose of your future destiny, whilst there is the least probable chance you may be reclaimed. Reside here as a boarder, my dear child; but under your doubtful circumstances, never take the veil, for the mind should be entirely disengaged from all worldly hopes, before it can renounce it properly."

From this day Matilda grew entirely resigned; she derived wisdom and comfort from her good mother's conversation, nor suffered anticipation of evils to disturb her serenity.

The Scarborough party were now arrived in London. The Marquis immediately waited on the Ambassador. His Excellency told him the Count Wolfenbach was alive, but past all hopes of recovery. "He knows you are hourly expected, and is anxious to see you."

The Marquis, taking his address in Dover-street, hastened thither, and sent up his name. He waited some time for the servant's return, at length he was desired to walk up, and on entering the room, scarce could he trace any recollection of the object in the bed before him. It was some years since he had seen the Count; he was not then young; but age, anxiety, and conscious guilt, with the disorder that now oppressed him, had indeed greatly altered him. When the Marquis drew near, he was for a moment silent; then, addressing him, "I am told, my Lord, you requested my presence." "I did, (replied the Count.) Pray, is your sister with you?" "Not in the house (answered the Marquis) but she is in town, and will soon attend, if it is your wish to see her." "Yes, (said the Count) let her come; I can tell my story but once, 'tis fit she should be present."

The Marquis instantly dispatched a messenger for his wife and sister. In the interim the Count desired to be informed in what manner the Countess effected her escape through the wood and got to England. The Marquis recounted every particular. "There was a fate in it, no doubt (said the Count;) Providence intervened, to prevent me from the commission of the crime I intended, and preserved her life."

Word was brought up that the Countess and Marchioness were below. They were desired to enter. When they came into the room the Countess involuntarily shrunk back. "Approach, madam, do not fear; the discovery is now made, and in a very short time I shall have nothing to hope for, nor you anything to dread." The Countess advanced, trembling, and seated herself by the bed. "I now (said he) entreat your forgiveness of all the wrongs my cruel jealousy heaped upon you; say, speak, can you pardon me? tell me that, before I begin my narrative, lest I should be cut off ere I have finished." "I do indeed (replied the Countess;) I pardon you from my soul, and may the God of mercy pardon you likewise." "I am satisfied, (said he) and now attend to my confessions.——I was well aware, before I married, of the affection subsisting between Victoria and the Chevalier; I was not blind to the difference in our persons and ages, and hated him in proportion to the advantages in his favor. I was resolved to carry my point, to gratify both passions; her father seconded my wishes, and she became mine. From that hour I never knew a peaceful moment. I doated on her to distraction; jealousy kept pace with love. Her conduct gave me no right to complain; yet she loved me not, and I feared the Chevalier was the object of her partiality and regret. My temper, naturally impetuous and furious, grew daily worse; for what hell can give torments equal to what a jealous man feels? One day I had been at Vienna, and was informed of the Chevalier's return: desperate and alarmed, I came home. In the Park I met Peter. He had lived some years with me; was blindly devoted to my service, and had been employed by me to watch the Countess. He told me a gentleman had been walking round the park, examining the house, and on his going to him, and enquiring who he wanted, he only asked if the Count and Countess of Wolfenbach were there; and Peter answering, yes, he walked hastily away. This information was a dagger to my soul: I resolved to carry her to my castle in Switzerland, secretly. I pursued my design. I had been there but a short time before I heard a man, disguised, had been about the grounds, who made off when any person came near him; I concluded 'twas the Chevalier, and resolved to have him watched, determined he should die; at the same time that I thought it impossible he should come at the Countess in her apartment. One day going to her room, I heard a sudden noise, found her on the floor, with a paper in her hand, and saw a figure glance from the window. I was struck with rage and astonishment. After confining and upbraiding her, as she may inform you, I closeted Peter, and by promises of present reward and future prospects, he took a solemn oath to assist in my revenge, and to be secret. We took our stand the following night by the wall, and saw him advance to climb up the battlements; we sallied out, knocked him down, bound and gagged him, and, determined to have complete revenge, we dragged him to the Countess's apartment." "Spare the repetition of what passed there (cried she;) it was a scene of horror; repeat only what were your transactions out of my sight." "You shall be obeyed (answered he.) It was in vain she protested innocence, I gave no credit. My first intention was to murder both; and when I locked her in the closet with the dead body, I hoped terror and fright would have done my business. In the morning we heard her groans; we entered; the sight of her agonies for a moment disarmed my rage, and I consented Margarite should assist her. After she was delivered, and the curtains fastened, Peter and myself took the body and carried it to one end of the subterraneous passage, dug a hole in the earth, on one side, and threw it in. I now grew irresolute with respect to my wife's death; my revenge cooled, but I knew it was impossible but she must hate and detest me. One day I went to her, uncertain whether to destroy her and the child or not, to prevent a discovery. She knows what followed. I felt a thousand soft emotions at the sight of the child, and both loved and hated her to madness. I resolved at last to confine her for life, and to preserve the child. Joseph, the under gardener, the only man who lived in the castle, I was obliged to confide in. I told him my wife had been detected in an intrigue, and I had intended to murder her, but she recovered of her wounds, and now I should only confine her for life. I swore him to secrecy, and vowed, if ever he betrayed her place of residence, or life, to any one, I would murder both. The poor fellow swore faithfully to obey me. The rest she can inform you."

"But my child! my child!" (cried the Countess, eagerly.) "Is alive, and an officer now in the Emperor's service." "Great God! I thank thee! (said she, falling on her knees;) and in this posture, when I return thanks to my Heavenly Father for his preservation, I also forgive and bless you, for the care of my child; may every evil deed be forgiven, and may you enjoy peace in your last moments, and everlasting happiness hereafter!"

The hard heart of the Count was softened into tears by the warmth of her expressions: he held out his hand; she kissed it, in token of peace. "May your prayers be heard (said he;) but I have more vices yet to confess. I took the child to Vienna, brought it up as the son of a friend, very privately. At a certain age he was placed in the military school, and about six months ago I procured for him a commission. But to return. Once in two years I generally visited the Castle. Her resignation and obedience to my orders sometimes moved me in her favor, and every visit my heart grew more and more softened; yet I dared not liberate her, her death had been so universally believed for many years; how could I account for my conduct, or her appearance, without incurring suspicions against myself? Distracted in my mind, I neither enjoyed peace nor rest;—alas! there is neither for the wicked, however we may disguise our crimes to the world—however we meet with respect and approbation from mankind, the man conscious of his wickedness, with doubt and terror gnawing at his heart, is the most miserable of human beings: we may swear to secrecy, we may silence every thing but conscience—there is the sting that forever wounds—there the monitor no bribes can suppress. Life became a burthen to me, yet I feared to die; I feared daily a discovery of my crimes; I resolved to forbear my visits, but to send Peter every six months to gain intelligence and see all was safe. On his return from his last errand of that kind he informed me, that, calling at a woodcutter's cottage near the Castle, who knew him not, from a curiosity to hear if they were acquainted with Joseph (of whose fidelity he was always doubtful) the woman told him a story of a young lady's coming there, being recommended to the Castle; and that she had so much courage as to go to the haunted rooms, (for I had taken care to have it supposed that wing was haunted) and that very day was there several hours. Alarmed at this intelligence, Peter flew to me, then on a visit about seven leagues from the Castle, frightened out of his senses. After a little consultation we resolved to go in the night, break open the doors, if locked, and murder both Victoria and Marga- rite, and after that fall upon some method to silence the young lady and Joseph in the same manner. We succeeded in our attempt: we dis- patched Margarite, and came down to do the same by her mistress, but Providence, who counteracts the designs of wicked men, and turns those very measures we take to secure ourselves to our destruction, suggested to me to take her into the wood and destroy her, that Joseph, if he came in the morning, might think it was a gang of banditti who had carried them off; for which reason, I thought my being concerned would never be suspected. This foolish concerted scheme we pursued; the Countess remembers I was thrown from my horse, and she took that opportunity to escape. When I recovered my senses I found I had some bruises on my head and shoulder. I looked round, "Where, where is the Countess?" "Ah! (cried Peter) I fear we are undone; the horse flew away with her as I alighted, and your horse also ran off." "Villain! (I cried) find her this moment, or I will murder you." "'Tis impossible to pursue her on foot; 'tis most likely she may be dashed to pieces in the wood; meantime, Sir, creep, if possible, to the town, have some assist- ance; I will borrow another horse and make all possible search." I had no alternative; distracted with pain and horror, I got with difficulty to the town, and was put to bed very ill. Peter rode off immediately; he was wanting a day and a night: I suffered a thousand tortures: I began to think he had betrayed me. 'Tis the curse attendant on villains always to be suspicious of each other: for what vows or ties can bind a man you know would commit the most atrocious crimes for money. In my conjectures, however, I wronged Peter; he returned. He had searched the wood, and every part of the adjacent neighbourhood, without gaining any intelligence, but that two or three persons had seen a horse saddled, galloping furiously in the wood: he had called at the cottage— nothing had transpired there. In short, we began to hope, as our only security, that she was killed somewhere in the road, and the body carried away by passengers. In a few days I got well, determined to visit the Castle, and either destroy Joseph, or decoy him away to some remote place. In short, my schemes were so many and unsettled by fear that I fixed on no positive plan. We arrived at the Castle; we saw no appearance of any lady; but Peter, taking an opportunity to speak to Bertha, was informed there had been a lady, but she had left them three or four days. This was another stroke: the lady, we knew, had seen the Countess; she might betray the secret, where could she be gone, or who was she? Peter enquired again, Bertha knew only that she talked of going to Paris. We were now distracted; the sword seemed suspended over our heads, and we every moment feared detection. That night we met in the Countess's apartments and searched thoroughly; in a drawer we found a purse with some money, and a paper signed Matilda, giving an account of sundry articles taken from the drawers. This convinced us we had reasons for our apprehensions: the death of Joseph would rid us of one witness—I secretly determined to destroy another. We went to the town the following morning—I procured from the different medical persons some laudanum. We agreed the best way would be to get Joseph and his wife to my other castle, and destroy them there, where they were unknown. I deceived Peter by this foolish scheme, having taken a different resolution. I told him we would return that night to the Castle, take the remaining valuables, money, &c., which should all be his, previous to our departure. He joyfully consented. I took an opportunity to give him the opium in the evening; by the time we got to the apartment he grew very heavy, and during his search among the drawers, dropt down in a heavy sleep; I put him upon the bed, fastened every window and door, set fire to the curtains and counterpane, and went out, locking the door after me; I then hastily proceeded to the wood house which joined Joseph's kitchen, and soon had that in a blaze; bringing some dry stubble, I lighted it against the door and window shutters, and seeing the whole take fire in both wings, I went to the stable, took my own horse, which was there fastened up, ready saddled, as we left them, and riding off to the town, went to the inn I had been ill at, and waited patiently for news. Within a few hours I was called up: my Castle was discovered by some wood-cutters to be in flames, and before assistance could be procured was entirely destroyed. I pretended great vexation and distress; rode to the spot; it was a dreadful sight; my soul shuddered—I was in agony. The people imputed it to a different cause. I asked, had nobody seen

Joseph nor his wife. No, was the general answer, and the fire imputed to their carelessness. Some of the neighbouring gentlemen rode over; everyone condoled with me, and offered me accommodations; I returned with the gentleman to whom I had first been on a visit. When retired to my apartment, a retrospection of all my crimes forced themselves on my remembrance. I tried to sleep, alas! there was no sleep befriended me; ten thousand horrid images swam before my sight; I threw myself out of bed; it was moonlight; my room commanded a view of the distant wood, I shrunk at the sight—there lies my wretched wife! then the Chevalier, Joseph, Bertha, and Peter, all seemed to walk before me;—great God! what were my sufferings that night, never to be effaced from my memory. When daylight came, I went down stairs to the garden; here I first thought of destroying myself—my boy shot across my mind—I took my resolution at once. I set off that day for Vienna. On my arrival I sent for Frederic, and after some preparation acknowledged him as my son, acquainted him his mother died in childbed, and I had particular reasons, immaterial to him, for not owning him sooner; I made my will, secured my whole fortune to him, by proper testimonials, that I acknowledged him my son, and then resolved to retire from the world, repent of my sins, and try to make my peace with heaven. All Vienna was astonished at my resolution; my son sought every argument to divert me from my purpose,—his tenderness, goodness, and virtue were daggers to my heart; I fell very ill, and earnestly prayed for the hour of death; heaven thought fit to spare me, that I might receive some comfort before the fatal hour arrived. I began to get better, though weak and declining, when, to my inexpressible surprise, I received a letter from our Minister in England, with a brief account of the Countess, the deposition of the Marquis, and requesting I would acknowledge the lady, and not permit such black transactions to appear before the public as the Countess said she had the power of disclosing. At first I thought this letter was all illusion; but when I considered the possibility of her escape from death, and the application of the Marquis to the Ambassador, I was convinced the whole was founded on truth. What a mountain was taken from my bosom! I wrote immediately, I would follow the letter. In three days my strength mended greatly, yet I was obliged to take very easy journies, and by the time I arrived in England fatigue had quite exhausted me. His Excellency sent off an express to you. I now thank heaven that both you and Joseph are alive, and adore the ways of Providence, who ex-

tracts good out of evil, and made the very crimes I intended to perpe-
trate the means of deliverance to you both. The death of the unfortunate Chevalier I bitterly repent, and can only observe here, that when
a man gives himself up to unrestrained passions of what nature soever,
one vicious indulgence leads to another, crimes succeed each other,
and to veil one, and avoid discoveries, we are drawn insensibly to the
commission of such detestable actions as once we most abhorred the
idea of: for, although my temper was not good, and my passions always
violent, had not love and jealousy urged me to desperation, and deprived me of reason, my soul would have shrunk at the thoughts of
murders, which grew at last necessary for my preservation."

Here the Count stopped, exhausted and fatigued; indeed he had
made several pauses in his relation, from weakness, and it was very visible he had not many days to live.

The Countess could not restrain her tears. "Ah! (said she) I have
been the unhappy cause of all—" "Do not reproach yourself, (cried he,
hastily;) I am now convinced of your innocence; indeed I long believed
it, even when I designed your death the second time; only innocence
could have supported you to bear my cruelties, and your horrid confinement with resignation: I knew too well the terrors of guilt; for let
not the unhappy wretch, who forgets his duties towards God and man,
who gives himself up to the indulgence of his passions, and wrongs
the innocent, think, if he escapes detection, he can be happy: alas! remorse and sorrow will one day assail him; he will find he cannot hide
his crimes from himself, and his own conscience will prove his bitterest
punishment."

The Countess, extremely rejoiced to find him so sensible of his
guilt, said everything in her power to ease and calm his mind.

After he had a little recovered, he turned to the Marquis. "I sent for
you, my Lord, not only to hear my confession, but to direct me in what
manner I must do my wife justice; if it be your pleasure, I will repeat
my story, or at least assent to a drawn up confession before witnesses."
"By no means, (answered the Marquis;) it will be perfectly sufficient if
one part of the story, nearly what relates to her confinement, so as to
authenticate her person, is related."

After some consultation the Marquis attended the German Minister. A paper was drawn up, signifying the jealousy of the Count, without naming any particular object, in consequence of which he shut
up his lady in the Castle, after her delivery, and gave out a report of

her death; that he had brought up her son, now an officer, who was lately acquainted with his real birth, and to whom his estates were secured: that the lady, after many years confinement, had found means to escape to her brother and sister, with whom she resided. The Count having accidentally heard of her residence, was come to England, with a view to obtain her pardon and do her justice; that he acknowledged her innocence in the strongest terms, and desired, in case of his death, she might enjoy every advantage settled on her, when married to him, in the fullest extent.

This paper was signed in presence of the Ambassador, his Chaplain, and all the friends of the Countess,—Lord Delby among the rest.

Not a word was said relative to the Chevalier, Margarite, or Peter: the former had been so many years given up as dead by his relations, though they never guessed in what manner he died, that it would have been the height of cruelty to have awakened sorrow so long dormant, had it even been necessary, but as no such occasion appeared to demand an investigation, every thing relative to him and the other victims was buried in oblivion.

The Count survived nearly a week after their arrival in town, and then expired with more resignation and composure than could have been hoped for. Two days previous to his death he wrote to his son a few lines, referring him to the testimony he had given the Countess, and requesting he would, by his duty and tenderness, atone for the cruelties of his father; bid him remember the awful lesson placed before him, and restrain those passions, the indulgence of which had brought sorrow and shame on his guilty parent, whom, nevertheless, he had the comfort to tell him was a truly penitent one.

The Marquis, taking upon him to direct every thing for preserving the body, and having it carried into Germany within a fortnight, a few days after the necessary orders were completed, told the Countess he thought it highly proper she should go in person to make her claim. She, who was impatient to see and embrace her son, received the proposition with joy. The Marchioness, Lord Delby and Mrs. Courtney accepted an invitation to accompany her with pleasure. The former had written to Matilda the late unexpected and agreeable turn in the affairs of the Countess, and again pressed her return to them. The latter, Mrs. Courtney, still persevered in her soft melancholy, her tender looks, and attentions to the Count, who, when he found the party fixed for Vienna, excused himself from attending them, but promised, if the

Marquis and his family did not return to France before Christmas, he would join them early in the spring.

This declaration was a thunderbolt to Mrs. Courtney. She seized an opportunity of speaking to him alone. "How, my Lord, (cried she) is it possible you can think of separating yourself from your friends,— will you not go to Germany?" "It is not in my power, madam," (answered he.) "Say rather not your inclination, (said she, warmly:) you pique yourself on speaking truth, you know." "I wish to do so always, (replied he) but the ladies will not always permit me." "I beg your pardon, Sir, for contradicting you; I, at least, gave you credit for truth and sincerity, when you unpardonably sought to gain those affections you have since cruelly trifled with." "Such a charge from Mrs. Courtney, (said he) has too much severity in it, not to call for a serious answer; I therefore protest, madam, I never sought—I never wished to gain the affections of any woman but Matilda: my love for her is no secret to my friends,—I glory in it. For you, madam, I entertained the highest respect; I thought it my duty to shew you every possible attention a man of politeness was bound to offer to an amiable woman; more I never intended—I never could be thought to intend, with a heart avowedly devoted to another." "And do you call this politeness? (cried she, highly enraged.) I must tell you, Sir, you have (if you please to call it so) trifled too much with my peace, by your gallantry; and was I not completely revenged by the entire indifference of your idol, I should resent it in a very different manner. There, Sir, (tossing Matilda's letter to him) there see how much you are beloved or regretted by an insensible paltry girl." The Count had caught up the letter, and in his eagerness to read, scarcely heard her last words. He devoured every line with his eager eyes; and when he came to the conclusion, "happier with another woman." "O, Matilda! never, never! You may indeed forget me; mine is a common character, but there are few like yours in the world." Then looking at it again, and turning to Mrs. Courtney, who looked full of fury and malice, "May I be permitted to ask, madam, on what occasion you wrote this young lady, and of what nature those offers of service were, made in my name by you." Mrs. Courtney blushed, and was in the highest confusion. "Shall I interpret your looks, madam?" (asked he again.) "No, Sir, I can speak their language myself. I wrote to know her sentiments, at the time you were amusing yourself at the expence of my folly, as I had too much honor to give you encouragement, if she had any hopes of you." "So then, (said he, in a rage) she believes

I was paying my addresses to you, madam." (She smiled contemptuously.) "No wonder she renounces me; if such ideas took possession of her mind, she must think me the most contemptible of men." "And of what signification are her thoughts to you? are there not insuperable difficulties to a connexion with her?" (asked she.) "Not on my side, madam; this hour, this instant, I would receive her hand with gratitude and transport; her dignity of sentiment, her true greatness of mind are the bars to my happiness." "Well, but if there are bars——" "I beg pardon for interrupting you, madam; I know what you would say; and it is far from my design to be rude to any lady, but you must permit me to declare, I am resolved to wait weeks, months, or years, to have a chance for the removal of those impediments; and if I do not succeed at last, in all probability I shall never marry at all." As he ended this speech he withdrew, with a respectful, but reserved air. "Heavens! (said she, peevishly) is this the gallant, polite Frenchman! I see 'tis all over; I can make nothing of him, and I will gratify his vanity no longer; on the contrary, treat him with levity and contempt." Pride stepped in to her aid, and produced that change of sentiment which reason, honor, and good sense had failed to do: so true is the poet's observation,

"Pride saves men oft, and women too, from falling."

She determined, however, not to accompany her friends; being so lately returned from the Continent, she had no inclination to revisit it, without a powerful inducement, such as she had no chance of.

The Count's motives for refusing were of a similar nature.

The Marchioness had heard from Matilda. She declined being of their party, and entreated to remain in the Convent 'till that lady returned to France. She wrote a letter of congratulation to her dear Countess, on the great change in her situation, but gave, what she thought, very satisfactory reasons for not going into Germany. Lord Delby, however, could not resist his desire of attending the Countess, though so recently returned from thence. He entreated the Count to accept his house, but he had previously accepted a similar offer from the Marquis.

In a few days the party separated: the Marquis, his Lady, the Countess, and Lord Delby for Germany: the Count, to avoid attendance on Mrs. Courtney, went to Bath, and that lady soon after accompanied a party of friends to Tunbridge.

From the time that Mr. Weimar had agreed, before the Ambassador, to permit Matilda's residence twelve months with the Marquis, her friends had sent advertisements to all the different courts in Europe describing the particular circumstances attending her birth, without mentioning names. No intelligence arrived, nor enquiries had yet been made on the subject, though they still entertained hopes of one day meeting with success. As to the young lady herself, she had none; resigned to her misfortunes, her only wish was to remain in the convent, free from the persecutions, and exempt from the temptations, of the world. She heard of her friend's unexpected restoration to her family and fortune with real delight; and no mention being made of the Count or Mrs. Courtney, in the letter she received from the Marchioness, she concluded they were either married, or soon to be; and though a few sighs would follow the idea, she supported herself with fortitude and resolution.

She was one day sitting in her apartment, and ruminating on past events, when the superior of the convent came in, and with a look of regret, "Ah! madam, (said she) I am grieved to be the messenger of ill news to you, and sorrow to the whole community." "Bless me! (cried Matilda) what is the matter?" "Alas! my dear child, I have received an order from the king to deliver you to a Mr. Weimar, and another gentleman, waiting to receive you."

The unhappy girl repeated faintly the name of Weimar, and fell back, almost senseless in her chair. The good mother ran to her assistance; she soon recovered. "Oh! madam, (said she) save me, keep me here; I wish to be a nun—I will not go into the world again." "Would it were possible for me to protect you (answered she, shrugging her shoulders) but we have no power to retain you from the king's order; you must go, we dare not keep you."

At this moment entered St. Magdalene, all in tears.

"Well, madam, (said Matilda, endeavouring to collect fortitude from despair) have the goodness to inform the gentlemen I will presently wait on them." The superior appeared rather unwilling to leave her with her favourite, but however she withdrew.

Her good mother advised her instantly to write a few lines to the Marquis, and likewise to the Countess at Vienna. "Give me the first letter, (said she) I will endeavour to have it conveyed; take the chance of leaving the other at some inn on the road: but make haste, for we have no time."

Poor Matilda, more dead than alive, soon executed her task, and the other assisting in packing, she was just ready when a messenger came to hasten her. With a resolution that astonished her friend, she followed the persons who came for her trunks, and went down to take leave of the community. Every one was affected, for she was generally beloved; but when she kissed the hand of her good mother, both burst into a flood of tears. "Farewell, my dear, my amiable friend, (said she;) farewell, my good mother: if my wishes are gratified, and I have ever any power over my own actions, I will return to reside with you for ever." "To the protection of heaven I leave you (said mother Magdalene;) persevere in virtue and goodness, trust in God, and doubt not of being the object of his care; for he is a Father to the fatherless, and will never forsake the virtuous."

With streaming eyes Matilda followed her conductor. The porteress opened the gates; there stood Mr. Weimar and his friend. He seemed at first to shrink from her view; but recovering himself, advanced and took her hand. "Well, ungrateful run-away, (said he) you are once more in the custody of your true and natural protector." She made no answer, nor any resistance; she was placed in the carriage between them. Mr. Weimar was hurt at her silence, "You are sullen, you are ungrateful, Matilda." "No, Sir, I am neither: I am grateful for past benefits, and if I do not speak, 'tis because my sincerity or sentiments cannot be pleasing." "You are mistaken (said he;) I wish you to speak with sincerity; to tell me why you forsook the friend of your youth,—the man who offered to make you his by every holy tie, to fly with an acquaintance of a day, and who, after all his professions, at last placed you in a convent?" "It was my own voluntary choice, Sir, and very distressing to my friends, that I persisted in choosing a retirement from the world. To the first part of your question 'tis not necessary for me to answer: you know my motives for quitting your house, and for the subsequent offer of your hand, if you really were sincere, I must confess I think circumstances more than inclination prompted you to it. How you mean to dispose of me, or by what right you assume to yourself to be master of my destiny, I know not; but of this you may be assured, no force shall prevail upon me to act contrary to my own inclinations and judgment; and since I am not your niece, you have no legal authority over me."

Weimar looked confounded at her spirit, the other stared with surprise; all were mute for some time, at length he said, "You have taken up unjust prejudices, Matilda; but you will find I am still your best friend." "Then (replied she) I shall truly rejoice, for it is grievous to me to think ill of any one, much more of him, whom, for many years, I was accustomed to think my nearest relation and protector. If you are sincere, permit me to write to the Marchioness that I am in your care, to dispel the anxiety she will naturally feel on my account." "We will think of that (said he) when we are settled."

This evasion proved to her, she had not much favour to expect.

She was entirely ignorant of the road they took; she knew it was different from the Paris route, and had no opportunity of asking a single question, much less of dropping her letter, as the chaise being their own, they sat in it whilst they procured horses at the different post-houses, and at night stopt at a miserable hut, where they got only a few eggs and a little milk; no beds were to be had, and they were obliged to remain four hours in the chaise, until they could enter the next town. The distress of mind, with fatigue and want of rest, over-powered Matilda; as they were changing horses, she fainted. Weimar was frightened; he had her taken out of the carriage, laid upon a bed, and every method used to restore her. It was a long time before she recovered, and then she was so weak and exhausted that he was at a loss how to get her on. Some wine and toasted bread was given to her, and he quitted the room a moment to order refreshments into the chaise: she seized the opportunity; taking the letter and a louis d'or out of her pocket, "If you have charity (said she) let that letter be sent to the post." The woman, surprised, took the letter and money, and go-ing to speak, Matilda heard his footsteps; she put her finger to her lips; the other understood, and thrust both into her bosom. Joy and hope gave her spirits, and when he told her she must pursue her journey, she arose with difficulty, but without speaking, and was rather carried than walked to the chaise. When they drove off she recollected she had forgot to ask the name of the town; she put the question to him. "Faith I have forgot," was his answer. She said no more.

The two gentlemen talked of indifferent matters, which afforded her no information; she therefore resigned herself to her own contem-plations until they arrived at a sea-port town.

She was astonished when he told her they were to embark on board a vessel. "Where are you going to carry me to," (said she, trembling.) "To Germany, doubtless," (replied he.) "By water?" "Yes, by water: but ask no questions, Matilda; I am once more your uncle during this voyage, to preserve your character." "And do you think, Sir, (said she, assuming courage under a palpitating heart) do you think I will give a sanction to your falsehoods, and permit myself to be made a slave of?" "You will find, (answered he) you can have no voice to alter my determinations; but I will now make you a fair proposal. If you will consent to marry me, I will, in this very town, receive your hand, and without scruple then carry you to join your friends: if you refuse, I will not part with you, but where I propose carrying you, shall be entire master of your destiny. The old story is propagated by my servant, that you are my niece, and I am saving you from a shameful marriage with a footman." "Good God! (cried she) is my character thus traduced? And do you suppose such methods will oblige me to become your wife? No! Sir; I will die first." "Very well, (answered he, calmly) you have had your choice—I shall pursue mine."

Presently they were informed the vessel was ready. She was lifted out of the chaise, and notwithstanding her resistance, and cries for help, she was carried on board and down to the room below.

"You are now safe in my possession," said he. "I am sorry you made force necessary; but you must be convinced 'tis now in vain to contend with me." Matilda sat stupidly gazing at him; but the vessel beginning to move, she turned very sick: without any female on board to assist her, she was compelled to let him place her on the bed; and then requesting to be alone, he retired, and left her to her own very painful reflections.

All hope of assistance from the Marquis was now at an end; she knew not the place of her destination; she saw no probability of escaping from Mr. Weimar; yet she felt an unconquerable repugnance to become his wife—a man capable of such duplicity and cruelty; "O, no! (cried she, weeping) sooner will I plunge into a watery grave than unite myself for life to a man I must hate and despise." She continued extremely sick and ill. They had been two days at sea when she was alarmed by an uncommon noise over her head; voices very loud, and everything in much agitation: soon after she heard the firing of guns, and Mr. Weimar entered with an air of distraction. "I am undone, (cried he) unfortunate girl; you have been my ruin and your own, but I will prevent both." He instantly drew a large case knife, stabbed her and then himself. At the same instant a number of strange men burst into the cabin, Weimar's friend with them. The Turks, (for they were taken by a Barbary Corsair) highly enraged with the bloody scene before them, were about to dispatch Weimar, who lay on the floor, when Matilda faintly cried, "Spare him, spare him." One of them who understood French, stopped their hands: he ordered him to be taken care of, and approached Matilda, who, growing faint with loss of blood, could with difficulty say, "My arm." The clothes being stript off, it was found the wound was indeed through her arm, which being laid across her breast, received the blow which he was in too much confusion to direct as he intended. The humane Turk soon staunched the blood; and having with him necessaries for dressing wounds, he sent on board his own ship for them, and a person who could apply them. He requested the lady to make herself easy, no insult should be offered to her person. Meantime Weimar was carried on board the Turkish vessel, and carefully guarded. His wound was a dangerous one, and the person who dressed it gave but little hopes of his life; it continued however in a fluctuating state 'till their arrival at Tunis.

Matilda was out of all danger, but a prey to the most dismal apprehensions of what might befall her.

On their arrival she was taken on shore to the captain's house, where a very amiable woman received her with complacency, though they could not understand each other. Weimar was likewise brought on shore; and his situation growing more desperate, he requested to know if there was any hopes of his recovery, and being answered in the negative, the poor wretch, after many apparent convulsive struggles, asked if there was any French or German priest in the city? and being informed there was none, he requested to see Matilda, in presence of the captain and his friend, but that friend had been carried to a country house, to work in the gardens; the captain and lady however attended him. When he saw her he groaned most bitterly, nor could she behold the man to whom she had owed so many obligations in her juvenile days, reduced to a situation so wretched, without being inexpressibly shocked. He saw her emotions, and keenly felt how little he deserved them. "Matilda, (he cried) I shall soon be past the power of persecuting you myself, but when I think where and in whose hands I leave you, I suffer torments worse than death can inflict." "Let not the situation of the lady grieve you, (said the generous Turk;) though I pursue an employment I am weary of, I never injure women; if she has friends, they may recover her." "O, Matilda! (said the dying man) I will not deceive you, your death would to me have been the greatest comfort; I cannot bear the idea another should possess you. Swear to me, (added

he, eagerly) that you will become a nun—that you will take the veil."
She was terrified by his vehemence; and though she both wished and
designed it, hesitated. The captain said, "How dare you, so near death,
compel an oath foreign to her heart; no such vow shall pass in my hearing, be your affinity to her what it may." "No, Mr. Weimar, (answered
she) I will not swear, though it is at present my intention so to do."
"Then I am dumb (said he;) I will not be the victim to procure happiness for others."

It was in vain Matilda and the Captain urged him to speak, he was
resolutely silent. The Turk whispered her to withdraw; she obeyed;
and in about half an hour was desired to return. "I am conquered (said
Mr. Weimar;) this man, this generous enemy has prevailed. Prepare
to hear a story will pierce you to the heart. I am your uncle, but not a
German, nor is my name Weimar." "O, tell me, (cried Matilda) have I
a father, have I a mother living?" "Not a father (answered he, sighing)
perhaps a mother you may have, but I have not heard for many years."
She clasped her hands and burst into tears. "O, tell me—tell me all, for
I am prepared to hear a tale of horror." "Horror, indeed! (repeated he)
but I will confess all. Your father, the Count Berniti—" "My father a
Count!" (cried she, in an accent of joy.) "Yes; but do not interrupt me.
Your father was a Neapolitan nobleman, I was his younger brother; he
had every good and amiable quality that could dignify human nature.
From my earliest remembrance, I hated him; his virtue procured him
the love of our parents and the esteem of our friends; I was envious,
malicious, crafty, and dissipated. My parents saw my early propensity
to wickedness, but entirely taken up with their darling boy, I must say
that they neglected to eradicate those seeds of vice in my nature, which
an early and proper attention might have done; but given up to the care
of profligate servants, never received but with frowns and scorn; my
learning, my dress, my company, all left to myself, and treated in general as a disgrace to the family: I soon grew hardened in wickedness,
and hated my relations in proportion to their neglect of me. Parents
would do well to consider this lesson: unjust, or even deserved parti-
alities, visibly bestowed on one child, whilst others are neglected, too
generally creates hatred to that child, and a carelessness in performing
their duties, which they see are little attended to. It lays a foundation
for much future misery in the family; creates every vice which envy
and malice can give birth to, and the darling object is generally the
victim. But here I will do my brother justice; the only kindness I ever

received was from him, and often with tears he has supplicated favours for me, which was the only ones that ever met with a refusal, all others he could command. I grew at last so desperate that I formed an association with the most abandoned youth of the city, and was universally despised. About this time my father died, leaving his whole fortune to my brother, except a very trifling pittance, weekly, to me. This disgrace affected me beyond all bounds of patience. My brother sent for me; with a heart bursting with rage, I went. The moment I appeared, he rose and embraced me, with tears. "My dear brother, (said he) I have now the power to make your life more comfortable; evil-minded persons set my father against you, nor could I ever remove the prejudice: henceforth we are brothers, more than ever; use this house as your own; give up your idle acquaintance—I will introduce you to the good and worthy, and those only shall be my friends that are my brother's also." A reception so unexpected for a few moments warmed my heart to virtue, but the impression soon wore off; I accepted his offer, nevertheless, and for some time endeavoured to keep within bounds, and to be as private in my vices as possible. I found it easy to deceive my brother; whilst I preserved a semblance of goodness before him, no suspicion entered his breast. I had so long accustomed myself to behold him with hatred and envy, that every proof of his kindness, which carried with it an obligation, I could not support; rendered him more hateful in my eyes, because I knew it was undeserved. One morning the Count asked what I thought of the Count Morlini's daughter? (at that time esteemed the most beautiful woman in Naples, and whom I had long looked at with desiring eyes.) I spoke my opinion freely. "I am glad (returned my brother) your sentiments correspond with mine; she is good as well as beautiful, and I hope in a short time will become my wife." This was a dagger to my heart: I knew she never could be mine, and therefore had suppressed my wishes, but the idea of her being my brother's wife threw me into a rage little short of madness; I hastened from him to vent my passion alone. Every plan which malice could suggest, I thought on, to prevent the marriage, but my plots proved abortive, and the union took place. The day previous to the marriage, my noble brother presented me with a deed, which secured a handsome annuity to me for life; assuring me his house was still my home—his country seat the same, but he chose to make me independent. From that day I was truly miserable: I adored the Countess, I hated my brother. She treated me with sweetness and civility, which increased my passion. In short, I grew so fond of her, that I neglected my old associates, and lived almost at home for ever. The deluded pair were delighted with my reformation, and behaved with redoubled kindness. Here I must pause (said Mr. Weimar) for I am much fatigued."

Matilda, whose eager curiosity could ill support any interruption of the narrative, hastened to give him a cordial, and some drops to recruit his spirits.

"Before I proceed any further (said Mr. Weimar) 'tis fit an instrument should be drawn and signed by me and proper witnesses, proving that I acknowledge Matilda to be the only child and heiress to the late Count Berniti's estates, which I have unjustly withheld; let this be done, lest the hand of death should cut me off, as I every hour expect."

The generous captain lost no time in procuring the instrument to be drawn and properly attested. Matilda withdrew meantime to reflect on what she had already heard, and in trembling expectation of what was to follow. A painful thought obtruded itself. "Ah! had I known, (cried she) some time ago, that my birth was noble, happiness might have been my portion—it is now too late!" She was soon recalled to the sick room; and everything being settled as the unhappy repentant Weimar desired, he lay a short time composed and then resumed his narrative.

"For some months I lived in the house, a torment to myself, and concerting schemes to ruin the happiness of others. The Countess advanced in her pregnancy: my brother was overjoyed—I affected to be the same. There was at this time a young woman in the city whom I had seduced and who was likewise with child; I knew I could bring her to any terms I pleased; I laid my plan accordingly: she went to live near my brother's country house, and passed for a young widow, greatly distressed. We contrived my sister should hear of her; the consequence was, as we expected, she was sent for, and told a plausible tale; was relieved, and engaged as a nurse for the Countess's child. She was brought to bed three weeks before that lady, of a girl. The Countess was delivered of Matilda. Agatha, for it was she, Matilda, whom you well remember, attended her and received the child. As soon as the Countess could be moved with safety, we all went to the house in the country. It was close to the sea, and at the back a beautiful wood, where my brother frequently amused himself by having little vistas cut. It was in this place I designed to execute the horrid plan I had long concerted. I had privately procured a disguise, which lay concealed at one part of the wood. I knew he generally walked in the evening, and proceeded accordingly. Taking a horse one morning, I pretended to go into the city: I did so; and returned about the hour I supposed my brother in the wood: I fastened my horse at the entrance of it, changed my dress, put a mask on my face, and crept on towards the lower part; I distinguished him through trees—let me hasten from the remembrance!—I suddenly came upon him, and by repeated stabs, laid him dead at my feet." Matilda uttered a cry of horror. "I do not wonder at your emotion, (said he) since at this moment I tremble at my own crimes! I rifled his pockets of every thing valuable, to make it believed he had been dispatched by robbers. I returned and dug a hole at a distant part, where my horse was, hid the clothes, mounted the beast, returned to the public road, and came on horseback to the door; previous to which I had thrown his watch and money into the sea. I had executed a few little commissions for my sister, in the city, and appeared before her in good spirits, with the trifles she had sent for. We waited for my brother's return, at the usual time, to supper; the hour elapsed—she grew alarmed. I made light of her fears for some time; at length I joined in her apprehensions, and calling the two men servants, proposed to search for him. She thankfully accepted the offer. We went to the wood, calling on him aloud, and for some time I pursued a contrary path to the one I knew he laid in; at last we came to the dreadful spot, where we all stood aghast; I made most moving lamentations. We found he had been robbed and murdered. The poor fellows took up the body, and we proceeded to the house. I bid them go the back way, whilst I prepared my sister. Villain, and hardened as I was in wickedness, I trembled at this talk, and the agitations of my mind, on entering her room, told the dreadful tale for me. "O, heavens! (cried she) what is become of the Count? He is dead! he is dead!" she repeated, as I was silent to the question. I drew out my handkerchief, and turned from her. She gave two or three heavy groans and fell to the ground."

Poor Matilda again gave way to the most lively emotions of grief Weimar seemed much affected, and was some moments before he could proceed.

"I will not dwell on a scene so horrid. An express was sent into the city, search made for the murderer, but no traces appeared that could lead to a discovery. My sister continued very ill for many days, and my brother was universally regretted. My melancholy was observed by every one, and kindly noticed by the Countess, who desired I would act for her without reserve: this proof of her confidence gave me great credit, and not one suspicion, I believe, ever glanced on me. It was my first intention to have destroyed the child, but the deed I had done filled my mind with such horror, I could not imbrue my hands a second time in blood. I was some time unresolved in what manner to act. The Countess still kept her bed, in a very languid state. One morning, going to Agatha's room, I found her in tears; her child had died that night, in convulsions; it was in the cradle, and the features much distorted. A thought darted instantly into my head, to change the children: I proposed it to Agatha, and promised her great rewards; she readily agreed to every thing I proposed; the dresses were changed in a moment, and the children being only six weeks old, had been little seen. I left the room. Soon after, a servant came to the Countess's apartment, (where I then was, to pay my morning respects, a custom I always observed) and requested me to step out on business. "O, Sir! (cried she) we are all undone—the poor nurse is frantic—the sweet child, the young Countess, is dead! expired an hour ago, in convulsions, whilst poor Agatha thought it in a sweet sleep." I pretended to be most exceedingly shocked; exclaimed against the nurse, sent for a physician—would have the body examined, I did so; I ran to Agatha's apartment, the other end of the house, abused her for her carelessness; she, who was really grieved for the loss of her own child, shed torrents of tears. The physician came; he examined the child; he said, it was really sudden convulsions had carried it off and no fault in the nurse, the disorder being common among infants. This satisfied every one; nobody troubled themselves about Agatha's child. I sent off to the Count Morlini's, who had left us the day before, intending to return the following one. He came immediately; I detained the physician. The Count made very minute enquiries, and was, or appeared to be contented with the physician's deposition. "Alas! my Lord, (cried I) who shall break this melancholy accident to the Countess? I cannot, I dare not do it. Unhappy lady! (I exclaimed) how great are your sorrows! my own share in them is lost, when I consider your's." The Count shook my hand in a friendly manner, but spoke not. He went from me to his daughter; I retired to my own apartment. I was now my brother's heir to his title and estates; every thing promised to give me an undisputed right; and I enjoyed, by anticipation, the pleasures which fortune and rank would bestow." Here Mr. Weimar stopt. "I cannot proceed now—I am fatigued and exhausted." He was quite faint, and they were obliged to give him a respite for the present, and administer cordials. He promised to proceed and finish his story in the evening. Matilda withdrew, overwhelmed with grief, horror, and a painful curiosity for the subsequent events which might have befallen her unhappy mother. Some time after she was in her apartment, the captain came in. "The surgeon (said he) has just examined Mr. Weimar's wound, and makes a much better report of it than in the morning. This last dressing has abated the inflammation, and the fever is not so violent." "If his repentance is sincere, heaven grant he may recover," (said she.)

In the evening, at Mr. Weimar's request, Matilda and the captain went to his apartment: he appeared much more easy and composed. After recollecting himself a little, he went on as follows.

"The Count took upon him to acquaint the Countess with the loss of the child; but notwithstanding all his precautions, it had a dreadful effect upon her. She was for some weeks deprived of reason, and when recovered, the disorder turned to a settled melancholy nothing could remove. Having some relations at Florence, the Count proposed taking her there to change the scene. What had been secured to her by marriage, was of course hers. From an affected generosity, I presented her with the house and furniture in the city; and under a pretence I could no longer stay where such melancholy accidents had taken place, and having no relations living, I disposed of my estates, and said I should travel into Turkey and Egypt, without assuming any title. In truth, I was ever in fear some unforeseen events might bring my evil deeds to light: for 'tis the fate of villainy never to be secure; and the constant apprehension of detection embitters every hour of their lives who once plunge into guilt. I had persuaded Agatha, with the child, to embark on board a French vessel, bound to Dieppe, and there wait for me; having engaged the captain to take care of her, though I secretly wished the waves might swallow them up; at the same time I had not resolution to destroy them. After the vessel sailed, I set off from Naples, glad to escape from a place I could not behold without shuddering. Whether any suspicions were entertained of me, I know not; for I kept up no correspondence there. I travelled into France, and arrived at Dieppe, where I found Agatha and the infant. I had a great inclination to settle in Switzerland, and determined to go through the country, and find a habitation. Leaving the woman at Dieppe, I went first to Paris, invested great part of my property there, in the name of Weimar; and from thence I went through Germany and Switzerland. Between Lausanne and Lucerne, I heard of an estate to be sold. I saw and liked it; the purchase was soon made, and every thing quickly settled. I sent for Agatha: she came part of the way by water, the rest, to Lausanne, by land; there I met her, and conducted her to my house. We now resumed our former intimacy, but she had no more children. I endeavoured, by my care of Matilda, to atone for the crimes I had been guilty of, in destroying her father, and robbing her of her fortune—a fortune I was afraid to enjoy, and a rank I dared not assume, always apprehensive my villainy would be discovered. I kept but little company. Agatha, who was my housekeeper, and directed every thing, many times I was tempted to destroy, but fear preserved her life. As Matilda grew up, I became passionately fond of her; my love increased with her years, and I determined to possess her. Agatha had too much cunning not to perceive my inclination; and having long ceased having any particular attachment to me, she blindly fell in with my desires, and encouraged me to proceed. The conversation you overheard, Matilda, was such as you apprehended; she persuaded me to say I was not your uncle, and the story I told you in Paris, was the one we had fabricated to deceive you. I did not at first intend marrying; I had an aversion to that tie, and therefore a different plan was proposed, which, overhearing, drove you from my house. 'Tis needless to tell you what ensued on discovering you had left me: I resolved to find you, if possible, and traced you to Paris. I thought to have deceived the Marquis; he was too cunning for me: but I obtained knowledge of your being in England through the means of Mademoiselle De Fontelle; a servant of her's having met the Marchioness and you at Calais. I still followed you. You know the concession I made to the Ambassador, which I never intended to observe, having intelligence the Count De Bouville was your lover. I had every step watched, and no sooner found you were at a convent than I repaired to Paris, told my own story, and obtained an order for your delivery. I found letters at Paris, from my steward, informing me of the death of Agatha, almost suddenly. This was a most agreeable piece of news; there was now no one living that could accuse me. Blind, infatuated mortals! we forget there is an all-seeing eye, that sooner or later brings us to justice, when most we think ourselves secure! I went to Brest, I hired a vessel to carry me to Venice, determined to reside there with you. With the order in my pocket, and a person who had attended me, more like a confidential friend than a servant, I came to Boulogne, and obtained your delivery to me. The rest you know. It was my intention to have married you, unless you rejected me—in that case you must take the consequence. When I saw the Turkish vessel I gave all up for lost; and when they boarded us, expecting you would be sacrificed to their desires, and myself made a slave, I resolved to prevent both: Providence preserved you—what I have suffered, and the near prospect of death, determined me to confess all my crimes—crimes that have embittered every hour of my life, and which have led me into a thousand inconsistencies, from fears and terrors, only created by guilt. Thus it is with the wicked; early plunged into vice, they proceed from one bad action to another; afraid to look back, unable to repent, they go on to fill up the measure of their crimes, 'till their best concerted schemes prove their ruin. Had not the hand of death overtaken me, this confession never would have been made; yet even at this moment I adore Matilda. Pardon me, dear unhappy girl, the evils I have caused you; let me die forgiven by you, and join in supplicating that mercy I have so little room to hope for, but from Divine goodness to the truly penitent."

Matilda assured him of her forgiveness, and implored heaven's mercy on him. "But tell me, Sir, (said she) did you never hear of my mother?" "Only once, and by accident, eight years ago; she was then at Naples, with her family." "Grant heaven! (said Matilda) she may be there still; O, what happiness, if I should ever embrace a mother!" Tears stopt her utterance; her uncle was affected. "O, Matilda! leave me; I cannot bear your tears, they reproach me too deeply; and I have much to repent of before I leave you for ever."

She quitted the room, oppressed with the most painful sensations: the tragical end of her father, the melancholy situation of her mother, the crimes of her uncle, and her own present distressed and forlorn state, altogether gave her unutterable pangs: yet a gleam of joy darted through the gloom that pervaded her fate—she was of noble birth; no unlawful offspring, no child of poverty: then she thought of the Count—"Ah!" cried she, "he is now the husband of Mrs. Courtney; in all probability I shall never see him more." A sigh followed the reflection, which she strove to place on another score.

She was soon after joined by the captain. "The surgeon came in as you left the room, madam; and notwithstanding the sick man's agitation in telling his story, he says, he is undoubtedly better, and he begins to entertain hopes, if no change happens for the worse." "I am glad to hear it, (replied she) may he live to repent." "Meantime, madam, (said he) if you wish to write your friends, I will take care your letters shall be conveyed by the quickest dispatch possible."

She accepted his generous offer, and retired to write the Marchioness and Countess what had befallen her; but recollecting that she could not wish to be in France until she had visited Naples, she left her letters unfinished, to consult the captain the following morning. She retired to rest, but the agitations of her mind precluded sleep: alternate joy and sorrow, hopes and fears, created such different ideas, that she passed the night without closing her eyes, and arose, at break of day, resolved to write and address a letter to her grandfather with her story. "If he lives, (said she) he will be overjoyed; if not, if I have no such relation, no dear mother alive, some one of the family will doubtless write and inform me."

When the captain came to breakfast, she imparted her different thoughts to him. She had no way of paying court to his amiable wife, but by kissing her hand, whilst the other pressed her's to her bosom, with tender affection, her husband having related the lady's story to her.

The Captain, after some deliberation, said, "I told you once, madam, the employment I am, or rather was engaged in, by no means suited me. I was not originally accustomed to this kind of life; my wife's father always was; he persuaded me to follow it. I sailed with him three years; we made a good deal of money. He died six months ago. This last voyage was the first I ever made for myself. I am disgusted at the service, and mean to quit it: my wife wishes me to do so; she is a good woman; we have enough; I do not want a plurality of wives—I am content with her. My mother was an English woman—I imbibe her sentiments. I have not disposed of my vessel; I will take you to Naples, or even to France, if you wish it, under neutral colours, which I can procure. This will be better than engaging your friends to come here. I have no enemy but the Russians to fear, and those I can provide against." "You are very kind, Sir, (said she;) I really am at a loss how to proceed, and will consult Mr. Weimar," (she could not reconcile herself to call him uncle). She did so: he approved of the Captain's advice, but thought she had best write her friends of her safety and situation, also of her intention to go to Naples, from whence they might expect to hear her decisive plan; previous to which the Captain could write to some persons to know if any of her relations were living. This being agreed upon as the best methods to be taken, Matilda resigned herself to patience 'till answers could be obtained, which must necessarily take up some time.

We must now return to the Countess and her friends, who arrived at Vienna without meeting any accident.

Their first step was to deliver the German Minister's letters to the English Ambassador; his Excellency having sent dispatches to his own court of this extraordinary affair.

The Countess found but little difficulty in being acknowledged, and put in possession of her rights. Her story engrossed the public attention at Vienna, and she received a thousand visits and congratulations from every person of distinction. Though abundantly gratified by their civilities, she was too anxious to see her son for her mind to be at ease. A messenger had been sent to his quarters by the Marquis, with leave from the Emperor for his return, and preparing him, by degrees, for the agreeable surprise of finding some near and dear relations. The youth had been apprised of his father's death, but not having read the Count's letter, was a stranger to all the circumstances relative to it. He made no difficulty of obeying the order and set off for his father's seat directly.

One day, when every heart beat high with expectation, a travelling carriage was seen driving through the park. "My son, my son! (cried the Countess starting up.) The Marquis ran out to meet him. In a moment a tall elegant youth, about sixteen, entered the room, with looks of eager expectation. The Countess flew towards him, threw her arms round him; attempted to speak, but overpowered by tender emotions 'till then a stranger to her breast, she fainted in his arms. The young gentleman, alarmed, and equally agitated, assisted, in silence, to convey her to a seat; and whilst the Marchioness was busy in her endeavours to restore her sister, he kissed her hand eagerly and cried to the Marquis, "Tell me, Sir, who is this dear lady?" "It is—— (said the other, with a little pause) she is your mother, Sir." "Mother! (repeated he, dropping on his knees) Great God! have I a mother? my own mother!" "Yes, (replied the Marquis) she is indeed your parent, for very many years believed to be dead."

Young Frederic was now in a state very little better than the Countess: surprise, joy, the soft emotions that at once assailed him, rendered him speechless and immoveable.

It was some time before they were both sufficiently recovered to be sensible of their felicity. The Countess embraced him with tears of expressive tenderness; he, on his knees, kissing her hands with ardour. "My mother! my dear mother!" was all he could utter for a long time. The Marchioness at length separated them. "My dear Frederic, (said she) you have other duties to pay, besides your present delightful one—I claim you as my nephew; this gentleman is my husband, consequently your uncle." He flew and embraced both. "Gracious heaven! (cried he) what happiness. A few months ago I supposed myself without family or friends, dependent on the Count's bounty; then I was agreeably surprised with being acknowledged as his son, then suddenly separated, and only ten days since informed of his death—again I was an orphan, and knew not what claims I could or ought to make; but now this unexpected tide of joy and happiness—to find a mother! O, the blessed sound! to find a mother, uncle, aunt, all dear and honoured relations! Great God, I adore thy bounty, make me deserving of thy favours." He again threw himself at the feet of the Countess, who had hung with rapture on his words, and now embraced him with the highest delight.

After this tumult of pleasure was a little subsided, he eagerly enquired the particulars of her story; which the Marquis repeated, as had been agreed upon, glossing over the Count's crimes, as much as possibly could be done, to exculpate the Countess. No mention was made of the Chevalier's death; but the youth heard sufficient to comprehend his mother had been cruelly used, and his features bore testimony of his emotions. "Dearest madam, (cried he) how great have been your sufferings! henceforth it shall be the study of my life to make you forget them in your future happiness."

Lord Delby, who had been rambling in the park, now entered the room. Young Frederic was introduced to him, and the foregoing scene slightly described by the Marchioness. "I am glad, (said his Lordship) I was not present; for though I adore sensibility, such a meeting would have been too much for me."

Growing more rational together, his relations were delighted with the young officer. "It must be confessed, (said the Marquis) the Count paid particular attention to Frederic's education." "Yes, my Lord, (answered the youth) it would have been my fault, if I had not profited by the instructions I received; but I thought my debt of gratitude so great for such uncommon kindness from a stranger, on whom I had no claims, that I strove to exert my small abilities, and by diligence and application, evince my sense of his favours, as the only return in my power." "The deception, as far as related to you, (said the Marchioness) proved a happy one; it laid the foundation for virtue, humility, and gratitude, which perhaps happier circumstances and legal claims might never have called forth. Thus sometimes good springs out of evil."

The following day, when the happy party was assembled, and projecting pleasurable schemes, the Marquis received the letter, which the good Mother Magdalene had found means to send off from Matilda. He started, with an exclamation of surprise. All were eager to know the contents. "Prepare yourselves for some regret, on account of your young friend," (said he.) "What! Matilda?" (cried both in a breath.) "Yes, I am sorry to tell you she is again in her uncle's power; he has again claimed her as his niece." He then read the letter, and all were equally grieved at the unfortunate destiny of this deserving young woman.

Frederic, with the warm enthusiasm of youth, cried out, "Is there no clue to trace them?—I will myself pursue them." "Alas! my son, (answered the Countess) 'tis impossible to say where he may have carried her to; but let us hope, as she found means to send this letter, she will find an opportunity to write again; at all events, she has a protector, to whose care we must trust her, until we can obtain further intelligence."

This letter threw a damp on the general joy.

Her story was repeated to Frederic, whose ardour was again raised to deliver the unhappy girl from her persecutor.

The Marquis, who was that day writing to the Count the happy event of their journey, and meeting with his nephew, could not resist throwing in a postscript. "My dear Bouville, (added he) we are thrown into the greatest consternation, by a letter from Matilda. She is again in the power of that villain, Weimar; who, contrary to his engagements has procured an order from the king, and carried her off, we know not where. We wait with impatience to hear further."

This letter from the Marquis found the Count De Bouville at Bath; where he vainly sought amusement, to remove the anguish which preyed upon his mind, arising from the impossibility of ever calling Matilda his. He viewed the gay females of fashion, with birth, beauty, and accomplishments to boast of, with perfect indifference. Ah! thought he, where is the modest retiring sweetness of Matilda? Where those unaffected charms—those natural graces of her deportment? Never shall I meet with a woman that I can admire or love, after knowing that lovely girl, whose very virtues preclude my happiness. He was in one of these reveries when the letter from the Marquis was delivered to him. The happiness of his friends gave him infinite delight; but how changed were his emotions on reading the postscript: his rage exceeded all bounds; he determined to leave Bath instantly. "I will hunt the villain through the world (cried he;) I will find her, if she is on earth, and no power shall ever take her from me again. O, Matilda! too scrupulous girl, you have undone us both, and ruined my peace for ever." He called his servants, and ordered the necessary arrangements for leaving Bath that night. He went out to call on some friends he had formed an engagement with, and to whom he thought more than a card was due. Crossing the parade, he saw, coming towards him, Madame Le Brun, Mademoiselle De Fontelle, and Mrs. Courtney, who had arrived from Tunbridge together the preceding evening. Nothing could have happened more unfortunate than this meeting. His temper irritated before, at the sight of the two ladies together, both of whom he considered as enemies to Matilda, his passion increased beyond the bounds of politeness to restrain. "I congratulate you, ladies, on an intimacy, minds like yours naturally create. For you, madam, (turning to Mademoiselle De Fontelle, who was pale with fear, observing his violence) you were never an object of my esteem, and long since of my aversion and contempt: your diabolical falsehoods have deprived me of happiness for ever; but vengeance will one day overtake you—I promise you it shall, (said he, in a voice that made her tremble and unable to go on.) For you, madam, (turning to Mrs. Courtney) I have still some respect: you have many good qualities; but your malice and dislike of an unoffending and excellent young woman, is inexcusable, and very evidently pursued, by attaching yourself to one you know all your and her friends despise; malice only is the cement of your intimacy. Take my advice, madam,—break it off, and entitle yourself to the respect and esteem of those who are the friends of yourself and Lord Delby."

He was going to leave them, but Mrs. Courtney, struck by his manner and words, still partial to him, cried out, "Stop, my Lord,—tell me how long you remain in Bath?" "This night I leave it, (said he) and a day or two hence I shall quit England." "For heaven's sake! (cried she) let me see you for five minutes, an hour hence;—do not deny me, 'tis the last favour I will ever ask." Seeing he hesitated, "At No. 11, on the South Parade—I will expect you."

She hastily followed her companions, who had gladly removed a few paces from them, and left the Count irresolute, whether he should oblige her or not: but recollecting the civilities he had received at her house and Lord Delby's, he thought gratitude and honour required his obedience.

He called on his friends, and at the appointed hour attended Mrs. Courtney. When introduced, she was alone, and very melancholy, but rose to receive him with evident pleasure. "I thank you for this visit, (said she) which I scarcely dared flatter myself with receiving, from your abrupt behaviour to me this morning." "You saw me, madam, very much ruffled; and the company I saw you in was not calculated to put me in better humour. You will pardon me, if I behaved any way rudely; but I really have too much respect for Mrs. Courtney, to whose hospitality and kindness I am under so many obligations, to see her in company with a dissolute woman whose want of chastity is perhaps her least crime; she is unprincipled, in every respect, with a base and malignant heart." "Good God! Count, (cried Mrs. Courtney) I did not know Mademoiselle De Fontelle was charged with any other faults than a dislike to Matilda." "That of itself, (replied he) would to me be a sufficient proof of a bad mind; for only those who dislike virtue and goodness can be enemies to her: but independent of that, Fontelle is a profligate young woman, and by no means a fit companion for a lady of your respectability, though, being unknown, she may be received into company. I hope, madam, you will deem this an apology for my abrupt behaviour; and now favour me with your commands." "Commands! (repeated she) dear Count, are you obliged to leave Bath so very soon?" "I am, madam; and I will frankly tell you the cause." He repeated the Marquis's letter. "The amiable Matilda ever was, and ever will be dear to me; tho' her superior greatness of mind will not permit her to accept my hand, I neither can nor will marry any other woman; nor shall she, if I can help it, be subject to the power of any man on earth." "But, (said she) without knowledge even of the road they travelled, how can you pursue them?" "It matters not, (answered he) I will not rest till I do obtain information." "This is really a Quixote expedition (said she;) travelling the world through to deliver distressed damsels." "It may appear so, (replied he, gravely) but don't let me think Mrs. Courtney possessed of so little feeling, as to be indifferent about the fate of an amiable girl who esteemed and respected her. But have you any commands for me, madam,—I am really hurried at present?"

"Well, Sir, (answered she) if you are determined to go, I must own I wish to preserve your esteem, at least, and therefore I promise you I will profit by your advice, and give up the French ladies." "You will entitle yourself to respect, madam, by so doing. Every French woman is not a Marchioness De Melfort, nor, I hope, a Mademoiselle De Fontelle; but 'tis necessary ladies should discriminate in their acquaintance." Then rising and kissing her hand, "Accept, madam, my grateful thanks for the favours you have honored me with. If I ever return to England, I shall again pay my respects to you, if you will permit me; and, if I am ever happily settled in France, I shall think myself highly honoured by a visit from Mrs. Courtney, and her worthy uncle, Lord Delby." Mrs. Courtney's pride forsook her at this polite address, she burst into tears, "Adieu, my dear Count; may happiness attend you, though you leave me a prey to regret and sorrow." He hastened from her with some emotion. That woman, thought he, has many amiable qualities, but she wants steadiness and respect for herself: an imbecility of mind makes her resign herself up to her passions, from the want of resolution or fortitude to subdue them; she has naturally a good and generous heart, but she is easily led aside by others more artful than herself. He thought however he had done his duty by warning her against Mademoiselle De Fontelle; and returned to his lodging with satisfaction to himself.

Every thing being ready, the Count quitted Bath that night; slept a few hours on the road, and arrived in town the next day.

He pursued his route to Dover, and from thence to Boulogne. He went to the convent, to gain intelligence; the porteress very readily answered his questions, but that afforded him not the least clue to guide his search, as she knew nothing of the road taken. She told him that Matilda had left money to convey Louison to Paris, who had been gone upwards of a fortnight.

Although the Count scarcely supposed Weimar would carry her to his own house, yet he determined to go there. He wrote the Marquis, and proposed being at Vienna, should he prove unsuccessful in Switzerland.

It would be tedious to follow the Count thro' his journey. He made all possible enquiries through the different towns, without obtaining any information. He arrived at Mr. Weimar's; they had not heard from him since he left England. Disappointed and mortified, he went from Switzerland to Vienna, and from thence to the villa of the Countess.

He was received with transport. The Countess eagerly exclaimed, "She is found, we have a letter—O, such good news!"

The Count had hardly patience to go through the ceremony of introduction, before he begged to know the good news!

The Marchioness had two days before received the letter Matilda had written from Tunis—she gave it him to read.

Matilda had briefly given an account of her voyage and arrival at Tunis, the civilities of the captain, and dangerous state of Mr. Weimar. She mentioned that she had reason to suppose she was descended from a noble family, in Naples; that a short time would relieve her doubts; and, at any rate, she would write again, if not join them, in a very little while.

Lovers, who are ever industrious to torment themselves, would perhaps, like the Count, have conjured up a thousand fears to distract their minds. "Is this all your good news? (cried he) alas! I see little to depend upon here; "she has hopes" she belongs to some noble family,—a scheme of that villain Weimar's to keep her easy 'till he recovers; besides, what dependence can be placed on a corsair? Ah! if these are all your hopes of safety, they are small indeed." "Upon my word, Count, (said the Marchioness) you are very cruel, to destroy the pleasing illusion we entertained of her safety; for my own part, I see no cause to doubt the kindness of the Captain, who, 'tis plain, must have permitted her to write; and for the other, he can have no power, in his circumstances, whether ill or well." "I hope, madam, (replied the Count) your conjectures are founded on truth and reason,—I shall rejoice to find my fears are groundless; but, be that as it may, I am determined to go immediately to Tunis." "You are right, my dear Sir, (cried the young Count, Frederic;) could I disengage my mind from superior duties, I would, with pleasure, accompany you." "Ah! the knight errantry of youthful folks! (said the Marquis, smiling) but I assure you, my good friend, we are all here equally interested in the fate of Matilda, and equally desirous of promoting any plan conducive to her safety." "I am sure of it, (answered the Count) and therefore hope you will not take it ill, if I leave you to-morrow, for I am resolved to go to Tunis, if a vessel can be hired."

They saw it was in vain to oppose his resolution, and were therefore silent.

He was delighted with the warmth of the young Count, and praised his spirit in the most lively terms.

He took leave of them the following morning, to pursue his plan, with the earnest good wishes of the whole family.

Meantime everything succeeded at Tunis to Matilda's wishes. Mr. Weimar daily grew better. At first his recovery seemed rather a matter of regret to him; but when she assured him of her entire forgiveness, that she never would betray the secret of her father's death, and that the restitution of her estates would sufficiently prove his penitence for the intended wrong done to her, he grew more reconciled, and by degrees, her sensible and pious observations wrought such a change in him, that he determined, when he got well, the Captain giving him his liberty, he would enter into a monastery for the rest of his days. Matilda encouraged him in the design.

The Captain, who was present at many of their conversations, said, one night, that his dislike to the cruel business he had been engaged in was considerably strengthened by Matilda's dissertations on virtue and vice; he was resolved never to make another voyage; and, though he could not but think the faith of Mahomet the true faith, yet, for her sake, he would always respect Christians; because the two best women he knew, exclusive of his wife, were both Europeans and Christians.

Matilda impatiently expected an answer from Naples. The Captain at last received one. The good Count Morlini had been dead three years; the Countess, his daughter, was alive, though in a languid state of health, and was gone, with another family to Nice, to stay two or three months.

This intelligence was delightful to Matilda: she was anxious to set off as soon as possible.

Mr. Weimar was now well enough to bear the voyage. He made a deed of gift to his niece, of all he possessed; having greatly improved the original fortune, from a fear of exciting too much notice and enquiry if he had lived otherwise; and told her, his intention was to enter into the order of poverty, as the proper retribution for his inordinate desire of wealth, which had induced him to commit such horrid crimes. She would have persuaded him to have chosen an order of less severity; but nothing could alter his resolutions.

The Captain having hastened his preparations, the day was appointed for sailing.

Matilda could not take leave of the Captain's amiable wife without feeling a very sincere regret; for, though they did not understand each other's language, yet the expression of the heart was comprehended by both, and engaged mutual esteem and tenderness.

The friend, or rather confidant of Mr. Weimar, was sent for from the country, his liberty given him, and Matilda, at her uncle's request, promised to pay him the sum agreed upon in France, for his assistance to carry her off.

They set sail with a prosperous gale, but with hearts very differently agitated.

Much about the same time the Count De Bouville had taken leave of his friends; and having hired a vessel at the first sea-port, he proceeded on his voyage to Tunis, and, without any accident or interruption, safely arrived there six days after Matilda had left it. He was soon on shore, procured an interpreter, and hastened to the Captain's house. His heart beat fast with hope, fear, and expectation; but who can describe his emotions when informed of their departure for Nice. He asked a thousand questions—could scarcely be persuaded but some sinister design was again practised against her, and it was with much difficulty he at length grew more reconciled and satisfied with the account he received.

He had nothing now to do but to follow her to Nice; but as water and some provisions were wanting for the vessel, he was obliged to bridle in his impatience, and remain there three or four days, which were ages in his calculation.

Matilda, meantime, safely arrived at Nice. Mr. Weimar instantly left the place, promising to write his niece, under cover to the Marquis De Melfort, soon as he was settled in a monastery.

The Captain conducted Matilda to a hotel, and they consulted how to act. It must be confessed her situation was a very distressing one; no female companion, no one to introduce her, she might be supposed an impostor, notwithstanding the testimony of Mr. Weimar, signed before the Captain. In short, they found themselves at a loss how to proceed. The first step was to know if the Countess Berniti was there; of this they were soon informed she was, accompanied by the Count and Countess Marcellini. After much deliberation the Captain proposed waiting on the Count, telling him a lady just arrived from Tunis, requested the favour of seeing him, to enquire after some very particular friends and relations she had at Naples. This scheme was adopted and put into execution. The Count was surprised at the message, but curiosity carried him immediately to the hotel, and he was introduced

to Matilda. He was extremely struck with her figure and appearance.
She trembled, and for some moments was incapable of speaking; but
endeavouring to collect fortitude from necessity she thus addressed
him, "The liberty I have taken in requesting the honour of seeing your
Lordship here requires many apologies, but I am in a very singular and
distressing situation. Will your Lordship permit me to ask you how
long you have known the Countess Berniti?" The Count started at the
question. "Almost from a child, madam; we were brought up in an intimacy from our youth." "You knew her unfortunate husband then, and
his brother, (said she) and possibly may recollect it was supposed the
infant daughter of the Countess died in convulsions?" "Supposed! (repeated he) good God! What can you mean, madam?" "To recall to your
mind, Sir, those circumstances, on the developing of which my future
happiness depends. I see your surprise, my Lord, and to elucidate my
meaning, I must entreat the favour of you to peruse these papers, the
confession of a dying man, once brother to the late Count Berniti."
The Count took the papers with the most eager curiosity.

Matilda, affected with hopes, doubts, and fears, could not suppress
her tears: on this important moment her fate seemed suspended.

The Count made two or three exclamations, but when he came to
the murder of his friend, he smote his breast, "Unparalleled wickedness and ingratitude!" (cried he.) Hastily proceeding in the narrative,
he no sooner came to the exchange of the children, than throwing
his eyes on Matilda, "My heart, and your striking resemblance to the
charming Countess, tell me, you are her child."

"I am! I am!" (replied Matilda, weeping, and strongly agitated) if
she will vouchsafe to own me!" He folded her to his bosom, "Own
you! O, what transport to recover such a daughter! Compose yourself, my dear young lady; I am little less affected than you are,—but let
me finish this interesting confession of a miserable wretch." He went
through the whole without any further interruption.

At the conclusion, the Captain related the events at Tunis, and the
result of their enquiries at Naples, which had brought them to Nice.

"Doubt not, my dear lady, but all your troubles are over: behold
the hand of Providence in every event; had not your wretched uncle
taken you from France; had you not fallen into the power, perhaps
of the only man who would have treated his captives with honor and
compassion, unknown in general to people of his profession,—forgive
me, Sir, the observation; (the Captain bowed) had not the dread of

death and everlasting punishments terrified the guilty wretch; had not all these singular events happened, through Divine permission, you might, to this hour, have been ignorant of your birth, and my amiable friend deprived of the joy and transport that await her in your arms."

The Count again warmly embraced her. He paid a thousand polite compliments to the Captain; and though he regretted leaving them, he was anxious to consult his lady in what manner to convey this delightful intelligence to the Countess.

When he returned to his lady she saw he was greatly agitated, and knowing the message he had received, was very curious to hear the result of his visit. She fortunately happened to be alone; he therefore related the whole story, read the papers, and spoke in raptures of Matilda's person, and engaging manners. Nothing could equal the astonishment of the Lady Marcellini. She anticipated the joy of her friend, yet was at a loss how to inform her of an event so entirely unexpected. They knew it must recall to her mind the horrid circumstances of her husband's murder, which neither time nor reason had ever reconciled her to support with any fortitude. "Yet, (said the Count) to recover such a child; to have a hold, a connexion in life so desirable and so unlooked for, must surely greatly overbalance the affliction of a painful remembrance, at least weakened, though not subdued."

They went to the apartment of the Countess. She was at her toilet. Her woman, being dismissed, "Well Count, (asked she) have you seen the lady from Tunis,—is she a Turkish woman?" "No, madam, she was brought up in Germany; she is a charming young creature, and you may be proud of the compliment (added he, smiling) when I assure you she very strongly resembles your ladyship." "You are very polite, my good friend, (answered she, in the same tone) but I am neither young nor handsome, and you say this lady is both;—but, pray, is she acquainted with any of our friends?" "Yes, but by name only; she has no personal knowledge of any one in Naples; she was very particular in her enquiries after you." "Of me! (said the Countess, surprised;) how could she know anything of me?" "You remember the Chevalier N——, who went abroad so many years since?" "Ah! (said she, with a sigh) I do indeed remember him; is he alive,—does this lady belong to him?" "He is not living, (answered the Count, for Matilda permitted him to suppose he was dead, without asserting it;) this young lady was in some degree related to him, but I think more nearly so to your ladyship." "Heavens! my dear Count, you surprise me! I know not of

any female relation I can possibly have." "She is certainly a near relation, however, (replied the Count) and you must prepare yourself for
a most agreeable surprise, as I am convinced you will love her dearly."
"Indeed, my good Count, (exclaimed the Countess) you have given me
violent emotions; my heart palpitates, and my whole frame trembles;
for God's sake, do not keep me in suspense—who can this lady be?"
"Before we answer you, my dear friend, (said the Count's Lady) let
me persuade you to take a few drops, in water, the agreeable flutter of
your spirits will require them." "All this preparation terrifies me; I will
take any thing, but pray be explicit at once." "Then, my dear lady, bear
the joyful recital I am about to give you with resolution."

He took up the story, at a French vessel, captured by the Corsair,
and a gentleman on board, attempting to destroy himself and a lady,
described the subsequent events, and then began the narrative. When
in his address to Matilda, he said, "The Count Berniti was your father,"
the Countess started from her chair, "Gracious God! what do I hear;
but no,—I can have no interest in it." She was silent. He proceeded,
whilst she hung her head, drowned in tears at the mention of her
husband whose death he slightly passed over, 'till he came to the circumstance of the children. She gave a shriek, and throwing her arms
around her friend, "If this is true, great God! if this is true, I may yet
have a child. O! say, (cried she looking wildly at him) tell me at once,
have I a child?" "You have, (said the Count, approaching her) you have
a daughter, my dear Countess, whom heaven has preserved to bless the
remainder of your days." "'Tis too much, too much, (said she, putting
her hand to her bosom and instantly fainted in the arms of her friend.)
Having drops and water at hand, she was soon recovered; and after a
few sighs, that removed the oppression from her heart, she said, "Tell
me, if it is the illusion of my senses only, or if indeed I have a child?"
"No, my dear lady, you are not deceived—we have told you truth."
"Then, where is she? (cried the Countess, eagerly) let me see her—I
die with impatience!" "Recover your spirits (answered the Count;) collect your fortitude, and I will immediately fetch her to your arms." "O,
hasten! hasten!" (cried she, dissolving in tears, which they were glad to
see.) And the Count, with joy, flew to the hotel, where poor Matilda
waited in all the agonies of suspense. "The discovery is made, my dear
young lady; your mother is impatient to receive and bless you."

This intelligence, though so anxiously wished for, gave her inexpressible agitations; she got up and sat down two or three times,

without speaking, or being able to move; and at length, with trembling knees, was conveyed to the carriage, the Captain, at the request of the Count, accompanying them. When arrived at the house, and conducted to a room, she had a glass of wine to raise her spirits, whilst the Count announced her arrival. In a few minutes he returned, and took her hand. The Captain wished not to be present at the first interview. With a tremor through her whole frame she gave her hand; the door opened; she saw a lady, at the top of the room, who appeared to be in tears. Matilda saw no more, she sprung from the Count, threw herself on her knees before her, and without uttering one word, sunk into insensibility. The friends hastened to her relief. The Countess sat stupid, gazing wildly on her, without moving. When Matilda's senses were a little restored she looked up, she exclaimed, "My mother! O, have I a mother?" That word recalled the Countess to sense and feeling; she clasped her in her arms, "Blessed! blessed sound! (she cried) my child, my dearest daughter! heaven be thanked." She dropped on her knees and lifted her hands and eyes to heaven, then again embraced her child, whose soft and tender emotions were too powerful to admit of speech, nor is it possible to describe the tumultuous joy of both for many minutes. The unhappy widow, the childless parent, dead to every hope of comfort, to embrace a child, adorned with every grace, to feel those delightful sensations to which her breast had been a stranger, and which mothers only can conceive,—a blessing so great, so unexpected, no language can describe. What then must be the feelings of Matilda after suffering such a variety of sorrows, to find herself in the arms of a parent? O, sweet and undefinable emotions! when reciprocal between a mother and a child! who can speak the rapture of each tender bosom, when parental and filial love unites!

After the first transports were a little abated, the Captain was introduced. The Countess welcomed him as the preserver of her child. He was struck with the perfect resemblance between the mother and daughter, and extremely gratified by the affectionate attention of every one present.

In the evening Matilda promised to relate the particulars of her whole story, and the following day to write to her friends.

The Count now pursued his voyage to Nice, still doubtful of Matilda's safety, and the sincerity of Mr. Weimar's repentance.

The wind was not favourable to his impatience, and the passage was a tedious one; at last, however, he was landed at Nice, and, after many enquiries, learnt there was a Turkish vessel on the point of sailing. He flew to the ship; the Captain was on board; without reserve the Count acquainted him with his errand, and search after Matilda.

"Indeed, Sir, (said the Captain) I pity you; 'tis peculiarly unfortunate, that they have quitted Nice three days, on their way to Vienna."

The poor Count was struck dumb with vexation and disappointment; the Captain, however, related to him the whole story, as he recollected, in Matilda's narrative, he was mentioned as a particular friend. "When, (added he) the Countess was acquainted with the extent of her daughter's obligations to the ladies in Germany, she instantly proposed going to Vienna, which being correspondent to Matilda's wishes, their friends consented to accompany them, and the happy party set off three days ago. Me, (said the Captain) they have rewarded with unbounded generosity much beyond my wishes or deserts; I shall now return to live in the bosom of my family and give up the sea for ever."

The Count applauded his resolution; and taking a ring from his finger, of value, "Wear this, my dear Sir, as a testimony of my esteem for the friend of Matilda, and remember, that in the Count de Bouville you will ever find one, upon any future occasion."

The Captain could not refuse so polite a compliment, though he was already amply gratified for the services he had done.

Thus we see a just and generous action scarcely ever fails of being properly recompensed.

The Count had now nothing to do but follow his mistress. He remembered Mrs. Courtney telling him he was going on a Quixote expedition. What would she say now, thought he, how exult at my disappointed knight-errantry? Then, when he thought of the discovery of Matilda's birth, "Ah! (said he) should I no longer be dear to her, of what use is my pursuit? she will now be introduced to the great world, and my pretensions may be distanced by a thousand pretenders of more merit and superior fortune! Nevertheless, I will not give her up until from herself I receive my doom." Accordingly the following morning, a little recovered from his fatigue, he set off for Vienna.

Meantime the Countess, her daughter, the Count and Countess Marcellini, with their attendants, were safely arrived at Vienna, from whence Matilda wrote to her beloved friends and earnestly requested the favour of seeing them.

'Tis impossible to describe the transports which her letter occasioned. They lost no time in setting off, and that very same evening their names were announced, Lord Delby and the young Count restraining their impatience 'till the following day.

The mutual joy, congratulations, and expressions of obligation which took place on their meeting may be easier conceived than described. The Countess Berniti was never weary of pouring forth her acknowledgements to the friends and preservers of her child, whilst they, on the other hand, could not help admiring the wonderful chain of events which had gradually led the way to such a happy discovery, both for her and the Countess of Wolfenbach.

"To-morrow, (said the Marquis) we shall beg leave to introduce our friend Lord Delby, and the young Count, my sister's son. I assure you, (said he, addressing Matilda) when we first heard of your being forced from the convent, our young Frederic, though only sixteen years old, had the gallantry to offer himself as your champion to pursue and deliver you." "Can I wonder at his generosity and heroism, my dear Sir, (answered she) born of such a mother, and possessing doubtless the virtues of his family? No; I am already prepossessed in his favor; I know he must resemble my charming Countess."

She forebore speaking of Lord Delby, that she might not be obliged to ask for the Countess, his sister, as she concluded the marriage must have taken place long ago.

They spent a most delightful evening together, and engaged to accompany the Countess of Wolfenbach to her seat, in three days from the present; that lady next day sending orders to prepare for the reception of her noble guests.

Matilda longed to see young Frederic, and her ideas of him were all confirmed when she beheld him: his elegant form and polished manners, in some measure, reconciled her to his late father, for having done his son so much justice in his education. Every one was charmed with him; and Lord Delby was received with all the respect due to his rank and merit.

As both the Countess Berniti and her daughter were silent respecting the Count, the others were equally cautious not to name him, lest they might say more than Matilda chose to have known; and there being no opportunities for private conversation, the Marchioness earnestly wished to be in the country that they might enjoy a few uninterrupted tête-à-têtes.

At the appointed time they all quitted Vienna, and arrived at the Countess's villa.

They were just seated at the dinner table when the Count De Bouville's name was announced. The Marchioness gave a cry of joy; the knife and fork dropped from Matilda's hand, and it was with difficulty she kept her seat when he entered the room.

The Marquis introduced him to the strangers as his particular friend: as they had never heard his name mentioned, they received him with the politeness due to that recommendation only: but when he advanced to Matilda she changed colour, and trembled so violently as to attract her mother's observation, although she was too attentive just then to speak, for the Count's agitations were visibly greater than her's; he bowed upon her hand and said a few words, but they were not intelligible. The Marquis hurried him through the rest of the company, and then placed him between Lord Delby and himself, saying, "Now, if you please, let us have our dinner; I put a negative to all compliments and questions for this hour to come—'tis plain we are all very glad to see each other."

In consequence of this seasonable order the conversation became general, and the Count and Matilda had time to recover themselves. She wondered indeed no one asked for his lady, nor that she appeared to be of the party. He cannot help being a little confused, thought she, and did not expect to find me here, I suppose: well, I must try to exert my fortitude, and, amidst so many blessings, I ought not to repine that one is withheld from my possession. Occupied by these reflections, she ate very little, nor attended to the conversation.

The Countess, her mother, who had been an attentive observer both of the Count and her daughter, said, "My love, Matilda, you eat nothing." She almost started, but replied, "I beg your pardon, madam, I am doing extremely well."

Bouville, who had been at no loss to discover Matilda's mother, as well from the likeness as the tender looks of the latter, now paid that lady particular attention.

When the dinner and servants were removed, the Marchioness complained of a trifling head-ach, and said she would go for a few minutes into the air. "Will you step out with me, Matilda?" "With pleasure, my dear madam," (answered she, rising quickly from her chair, and glad to escape.)

The two friends walked to the garden. "My dear Matilda, (cried the Marchioness) "I could rein in my impatience no longer; I was eager to congratulate you on the arrival of the Count, and on your happiness, in having now all your friends about you." "You are ever good and kind to me, my dear madam. I have indeed met with so many great and undeserved blessings, that my heart bounds in gratitude to heaven for its goodness towards one who, a short time since, thought herself the most unhappy of her sex." "You will remember, my dear, (said the Marchioness) it was my constant lesson to you, never to despair. Providence has now brought you out of all your troubles; a reliance on its justice and mercy, and an humble and grateful heart for the blessings you enjoy, will henceforth make your happiness permanent. But, my dear Matilda, I can perceive your confidence in your charming mother has not been quite unreserved; I plainly see she is a stranger even to the name of the Count De Bouville; how comes that to be the case?" "As all possibility of any connexion between the Count and myself was at an end, I conceived there would be an indelicacy in mentioning his former offers to my mother; yet perhaps I was wrong, and ought to have done justice to the sentiments he then honoured me with, as they proved his generosity and nobleness of mind. If I have been wrong, (said she, with a sigh) 'tis not too late to repair the fault, though it can be of no consequence to him now." "Your words astonish me, (cried the Marchioness;) what has the Count De Bouville done to have forfeited your esteem?" "Nothing, madam, (replied she, confused;) he has done nothing to lessen his merit or virtues in my estimation." "I think indeed, (resumed her friend) you must be strangely altered. If it should be so, for I thought you always an enthusiast in gratitude, and surely the man who made you an unreserved offer of his hand, and though rejected, still preserved his affection through many temptations—who has traversed lands and seas in search of you." "Of me, madam! (exclaimed Matilda, surprised;) pardon my interruption, but did you say the Count had been in search of me?" "Doubtless I did, (replied her friend;) can that surprise you; could you suppose we did not inform him, you were in the power of Weimar? or that he knowing it, would not range through the world to find you? I am sorry you do him so little justice, Matilda, for certainly he is entitled to your warmest gratitude, if your heart no longer speaks in his favor." Astonishment overpowered the senses of Matilda for a moment. "He is not then married to Mrs. Courtney?"

(said she, faintly.) "To Mrs. Courtney! good God! no; how came you to entertain such a ridiculous idea?"

Joy, transport, and unexpected relief from the painful thoughts she long had entertained were now too powerful for her feelings: with difficulty she tottered to a seat, and leaning her head on her friend's shoulder, burst into a flood of tears, which preserved her from fainting.

"My dear Matilda, (cried the Marchioness) I now clearly comprehend the whole; but, at the same time that I give you joy of your doubts being removed, I could beat you for presuming to wrong my amiable friend by entertaining them; see that you excuse yourself well, or depend upon my displeasure."

Matilda, after taking some time to recover her spirits, mentioned the anonymous letter; also, nearly as she could recollect, the contents of Mrs. Courtney's, written to her whilst she was in the convent; she repeated her answer. "After which (added Matilda) your journey taking place, when you kindly sent to invite me of your party, the Count was not mentioned; I therefore naturally concluded he was married, and remained with his lady, and that, from considerate motives you declined giving me the information." "How industrious some spirits are to torment themselves, (exclaimed the Marchioness) yet I own you had some little cause for your conclusions; but I am most inconceivably surprised Mrs. Courtney should have taken such a step; that she was very partial to him, I believe, and might wish for a return from him, is also very probable, but I am convinced the Count never did make, nor ever thought of making the smallest pretensions to her favour, any more than common politeness required; and so, my little credulous, jealous friend, I desire you will return to the company, make the Count one of your best courtesies, and pay him the highest attention, otherwise I will certainly put him out of the pain that now oppresses him, by telling the whole story."

Matilda, who felt her heart uncommonly light, readily promised to behave very well, and requested the Marchioness would take an opportunity to acquaint her mother with the Count's generosity and affection for her.

This being agreed on, the ladies returned to the dessert, with so much satisfaction in their countenances as excited the attention of their friends.

"I do not ask after the head-ach, (said the Marquis, smiling) a tête-à-tête seems to have driven it away." "You are right, (answered his lady, in the same tone;) "it sometimes cures both the head and the heart; but come, give us some fruit, it must be confessed you have done pretty well in our absence."

The Countess Berniti was delighted to see her daughter look cheerful; and as the Count De Bouville had engaged her in conversation, Matilda joined in it now and then with great complaisance towards him, which elevated his spirits to the highest pitch; and everything relative to her being full in his mind, he observed what an uncommon generous Turk the Captain of the corsair was.

"Why, do you know him, my Lord?" (asked the Countess.)

He was struck mute; Matilda hung her head, evidently confused.

"Ah! Count, Count, (said the Marquis) when men get tipsy, whether with wine or joy, out pops all their secrets; but I see you are dumb—I will answer for you. Yes, madam, (added he, addressing the Countess) I believe the Count does know the Captain, for he has been taken a prisoner too." "Indeed! (cried she) what, at the same time my daughter was?" "I will not take upon me to say, (answered he, smiling archly at Matilda) that it was exactly at the same time, but I believe it was pretty nearly so."

The Marchioness and her sister could not help laughing at this equivoque, which added to the confusion of Matilda.

"Come, come, (cried the Countess, her friend) none of your pleasantry, my Lord; the Count shall tell his own story to the ladies another time, and I will assist him where he fails to do himself justice."

The Count bowed; "You are very good to me, madam; I am only afraid I shall have occasion for troubling you and the Marchioness to prove your partiality for me, at the expence of your judgment." "Very well, Count, (said the Marquis) I am thrown out, I see. Faith, you are in the right; a young handsome fellow seldom fails of engaging the ladies, whilst no such dust is thrown in our eyes, to blind our judgment, or obtain a partial testimony." "Be quiet, Marquis, (said his sister;) you are really malicious."

The company arose soon after, and going into the garden, divided into little parties. The Marchioness and the two Countesses went towards an alcove; the lady of the house, with Matilda, the Count, Lord Delby and Frederic took another path; the Marquis and Count Marcellini strolled into a different one.

Matilda now took an opportunity to atone for the omission she had been guilty of, by asking Lord Delby after Mrs. Courtney and his

son. Meantime the Marchioness explained to the Countess the sentiments of the Count De Bouville; his early affection for Matilda, his
repeated offers of marriage, and her noble refusal openly grounded
on the uncertainty of her birth, since she did not deny a preferable
esteem for him. She also repeated his long and tedious searches after
her, as far as she knew of them, and concluded with observing, his
rank and fortune, elevated as both were, fell far short of his merit and
amiable disposition. When she had finished, "I own to you, madam,
(said the Countess) your relation has broke in upon my favourite plan.
I hoped to have carried my daughter to Naples, and to have seen her
married and settled there for life. Ah! (said she) to what purpose did I
find her, if we are to be separated again?" "But where is the necessity
for a separation? (said the Countess Marcellini) cannot you alternately
visit each other every year?" "No, (replied she;) when she marries there
will be many things to prevent it. Indeed, (added she, in tears) good and
amiable as the Count is, I wish Matilda had never known him." "Possibly, madam, (answered the Marchioness, very gravely) she might then
never have seen the convent, never have been carried off, and you still
ignorant you had such a daughter living, whose generous self-denial
deserves some praise, as the Count's disinterested and uncommon passion is entitled to some consideration: but I beg your ladyship's pardon;
I have only done my duty in making this communication; the Lady
Matilda will doubtless conform herself to your wishes."

The Countess struck with her words and manner of speaking
them, caught her hand, and kissing it, "Pardon me, dearest madam,
(said she) if I have appeared petulant and ungrateful, my heart is not
so, but consider how natural it is for a mother, just in possession of a
treasure so long and painfully regretted as entirely lost, to be jealous
of a superior attachment, and unhappy at the idea of parting from an
object so entwined about her heart." "It is natural, my dear madam,
(answered the Marchioness) and if I did not hope some method might
be found out to obviate the objection, I believe the Count would have
little chance of succeeding with——" "Your and my Matilda, (said the
Countess, eagerly.) That 'Lady Matilda' struck me to the heart." "She is
indeed mine, (replied the Marchioness) my adopted child; and had the
want of fortune only prevented her union with the Count, we offered
largely to remove it; but her objections proceeded from an elevation of
soul, a greatness of mind, that would not disgrace the man she married, whilst the Count thought she would dignify any rank, and honour

any man to whom she gave her hand." "Amiable, good young people! (said the Lady Marcellini.) O! my dear Countess, they ought not be separated." "Nor shall they, (answered she) if I find their affection is still mutual: I will have a private conversation with Matilda to-morrow, and you, madam, shall immediately know the result."

They now walked towards the house, and were soon joined by the rest of their party.

Notwithstanding every one wished to appear pleasing, the evening was not a gay one. The Countess Berniti seemed collected within herself; Matilda was confused and apprehensive; the Count De Bouville distracted with doubts, drew unfavourable omens from the looks of the mother and daughter, and therefore was very silent. They separated at an early hour, and sought in sleep a forgetfulness of care.

The following morning, the Countess and Matilda being alone in their dressing-room, the former said, "How comes it, my dear child, that, in relating your story to me, you never mentioned the particular obligations you owed to the Count De Bouville, for his generous offers?" "Because, madam, (answered Matilda, blushing) I thought it would appear to give myself a consequence I did not wish to arrogate, for merely doing my duty in declining them. Another reason was, I had been misled into a belief, that the Count had married an English lady, a sister of Lord Delby's; and therefore supposing he never could be anything to me, I judged it of no consequence, for the present, at least, to say any thing about him." "You have answered with candour and sincerity, (said the Countess) and I expect the same to the following question: Do you love the Count De Bouville?" "If, madam, (replied she, hesitating a little) to prefer him to any other man I ever saw; if to confess that I think him deserving of the highest esteem from everyone he honours with his acquaintance; if this is to be called love, I must answer in the affirmative." "You are not quite so ready and explicit in this answer, (said the Countess, with a smile) nevertheless I believe your sentiments in his favour are pretty decisive; and if my conjectures are right, what part am I to act, and how be expected to give a sanction to your union, which, in all probability will part us for ever." "Never, my dear mother, (answered she, in a firm tone) never; no power on earth shall part us again: how great soever my affection for the Count may be, be assured my duty, my love for you will greatly over-balance it; and if the alternative must be to part with one, behold me ready to give him up, without the least degree of hesitation." "Now, my dear

Matilda, (said the Countess, extremely moved by the firmness of her voice, and the expression in her eyes) now you have found the way to subdue me at once: you shall make no such sacrifices for me, my child; and I will think of some method to reconcile your duty and inclination to my wishes." Matilda kissed her mother's hand with the warmest affection, and some of their friends coming into the room precluded further conversation. She went in search of the Marchioness. She was told that lady was in the garden, and thither she repaired, when, coming to an alcove, she saw her seated in earnest conversation with the Count De Bouville. She would have turned back, but the Count ran, caught her hand, and led her to the Marchioness. "I am rejoiced to see you, (said she) my dear child; do, pray, take this troublesome young man off my hands, for I declare he has been making downright love to me." "Who, I?" (said the Count.) "Yes, (answered she) you know you have—as a proxy; and, as I am quite tired of being only a substitute, I leave Matilda to supply my place for the present." She got up and walked away, Matilda being too much confused to have the resolution to prevent her.

The Count seized this moment to know his doom. He besought her attention for a few moments; briefly ran over the affair between Mrs. Courtney and him, as a mere bagatelle, without wounding the lady's consequence. His distress and pursuit of her through France, Switzerland, Germany, from thence to Tunis and back again. He described the fervency of his love and the tortures of suspence; called upon her in the tenderest manner, to remember the time when she had said, "If her rank and fortune equalled his, she would, with pleasure, give him her hand." "And now, madam, (added he) that hour so much wished for by you, though of little consequence in my estimation, when thrown into the scale with unequalled merit and dignity of mind; that hour is arrived, deign, my beloved Matilda, to tell me, if I still can boast a share in your esteem; tell me, if I may presume to hope, that, however changed your situation, your heart, faithful to your other friends, has not withdrawn itself from him who lives only for you, and depends on you for happiness or misery in extreme?"

Matilda endeavoured to assume a composure she did not feel, for after the conversation with her mother she thought she was not at liberty to act for herself. Being silent a few moments she replied, "Believe me, Sir, my heart is still unchanged, still the same grateful and affectionate sentiments predominate in my mind: the Count De Bouville

possesses my esteem, if possible, more than ever, for my obligations
to him are increased; but—I have a mother; no longer mistress of my
own destiny, she must determine for me. I will not scruple to confess,
that it will be to me the happiest moment of my life, if my duty and
affection to her coincide with your wishes."

The Count, transported with joy, kissed her hand in expressive
silence, whilst Matilda rose from her seat and hurried to the house,
rejoiced that this interview was over. She returned to her mother's
apartment. The ladies were with her. The Marchioness smiled a little
maliciously at her, but observing she looked rather agitated, she asked,
"What is become of the gentlemen this morning? have you seen the
Marquis and his friends, my love?" "No, madam, (replied she) I suppose
they are rambling in the grounds."

Just then the Marquis entered. "Ah! ladies, (said he) I am happy
to see you together: I have undertaken to bring a cause before your
tribunal to-day, against one of your coterie, and I expect an impartial
judgment. What say you, ladies, dare you promise to be just and sincere?" "Your impertinent question is so affronting to us, (replied the
Countess) that I think we ought to decline hearing your cause." "Conscience, conscience, my dear sister, (cried he, smiling) nevertheless,
I will open my brief. A gentleman of rank, fortune, and unquestion-
able merit (here Matilda trembled) has, for some time, entertained the
warmest affection and respect for an amiable woman. When first he
knew and admired her she was in a situation that precluded hope, he
was therefore condemned to silence; that situation is changed; he has
no obstacles to combat but the lady's over-strained delicacy: she owns
a preferable esteem, but—she cannot approve of a second marriage."
Here all eyes were glanced at the Countess, who was confused. Matilda
began to respire. "Tell me, ladies, (resumed the Marquis, ingenuously)
should so futile an objection preclude her from making a worthy man
happy, gratifying her own partiality in his favour, and giving a dear and
valuable additional relation to her friends? You see I put the case simply
and plainly. Will you, madam (addressing the Countess Berniti) have
the goodness to speak first?" "I am not an advocate, Sir, (she answered)
for second marriages; on the contrary, I think there are but very few
cases that can justify them. If a woman is left with a family she is anxious to provide for, and has an eligible offer, that will enable her to do
so, duty to them should make her accept it; gratitude to the generous
man, should render her a good and affectionate wife. If a woman has

had a bad husband, who has used her ill, and unworthy of her merit, I conceive she owes no respect to his memory, but may, without any imputation whatever, reward the affection of a deserving object, and find her own happiness in so doing." The Countess Marcellini said, "My sentiments exactly correspond with my amiable friend's." "And mine, also, (cried the Marchioness) only I must be permitted to add, that if a woman so situated declines the offer, from over-delicacy, which is no delicacy at all, and by so doing renders a worthy man wretched, and refines away her own happiness at the same time, I think her quite inexcusable, and deserving reproach from her friends." "Thank you, my love, (said the Marquis;) and now, sister, your opinion, if you please." "Mine, (answered she, in some confusion) you are no stranger to, otherwise whence this appeal? but to convince you I am neither obstinate nor perverse, but open to conviction and the advice of my best friends, I will frankly subscribe to the opinion and judgment of these ladies." "Now, (said the Marquis) you have redeemed my love and esteem. I will not apply to our sweet Matilda here; she is unqualified at present to judge; and I fear her trial is not far off from an accusation something similar, though not on account of a second marriage; however I shall now rejoice my client with intelligence, that he has gained his cause." He bowed with a smiling air, and left the room.

"My dear sister, (said the Marchioness) accept my congratulations: Lord Delby is a most worthy nobleman, and offers to reside in whatever country you please; wherever you are will be his home."

The ladies all congratulated the Countess.

"I own, (said she) I have a very preferable regard for Lord Delby, and am, in all probability, indebted to him for my life and present happiness: it shall henceforth be my study to return those obligations."

This matter being settled, the ladies retired to dress; and, after a little hesitation in her voice, Matilda informed her mother of the preceding conversation between herself and the Count. "I have referred him to you, madam, and I beg previously to observe, I will implicitly, and without a murmur, abide by your decision. I never will be separated from you; and if my union with the Count must be attended with so great a sacrifice, no consideration whatever shall induce me to marry him. I have already shewn I can resign him when I think it my duty to do so." "You are an extraordinary good girl, (answered the Countess) but I will make no promises; when I have heard the Count, I shall be the better able to determine what I ought to do."

This day a cheerfulness pervaded through the whole party. Young Frederic, extremely attached to Lord Delby, was delighted with the prospect of a nearer connexion. He was charmed with the Count De Bouville; but his young heart felt a little degree of envy when he considered him as the favoured lover of Matilda, whom he admired so exceedingly, that his extreme youth only prevented him from being a formidable rival.

In the evening, when they took their usual walk, the Count requested the honour of a quarter of an hour's conversation with the Countess Berniti, and they retired to an alcove.

Matilda, who was leaning on the Lady Marcellini's arm, trembled so exceedingly, that she pressed her hand, and said, "Fear nothing, my good girl, and hope every thing." This a little re-assured her, and they pursued their walk.

The Marquis suddenly joined them, and observing her companion engaged in chat, drew her gently aside, "There is a letter for you, under my cover, and I suspect, from Weimar." They walked aside, and Matilda, hastily opening it, found it was really from him. He had entered among the Carthusians, at Paris. He pathetically laments all his past crimes, and acknowledges the justice and mercy of God: calls upon her to forgive and pray for him; cautions her against the allurements of the world, and takes an everlasting leave of her; meaning, from the hour he receives one line from her, to inform him that she has recovered a mother, and is happy in her present prospects, to shut up his correspondence and connexion with the world for ever.

This letter affected Matilda greatly; she remembered the care he had taken of her youth, though she shuddered when she considered him as the murderer of her father. "Unhappy man, (cried she) may God afford him penitence and peace in this life, and endless happiness in the world to come!" She promised the Marquis to write an answer the following morning, and he undertook to enclose it.

She joined her friends; but the letter had given so melancholy a turn to her thoughts, that every one took notice of her dejection; and judging it to arise from another cause, everyone was anxious to dispel it, and raise her spirits.

At supper they all met. Matilda glanced her eyes once towards the Count, and observed joy seemed to animate his whole frame; from thence she derived hope that he was not very displeasing to her mother.

When they retired for the night, the Countess was silent; Matilda of course asked no questions.

The next morning the Countess held a long conversation with her two Neapolitan friends; at the conclusion of which, the Count and her daughter was sent for. They attended, both visibly agitated. After they were seated, the Countess addressed herself to her child: "My dear Matilda, the Count has done you the honour to express a warm attachment to you, and has requested me to authorize his addresses, without which permission you have refused to listen to him. I expect you to answer me with sincerity; will my consent, my sanction to his addresses meet your wishes? or, can you renounce him, and follow me to Naples, if I desire it?" "Certainly I will, madam, there, or anywhere you command; at the same time, I should make a very poor return for the obligations I owe the Count De Bouville, if I hesitated to own, that had his addresses been favoured with the approbation of my mother, I could have preferred him to all men living; but no preference whatever shall militate against the superior obligations I am under to a parent." "Come to my arms, my dear children, (cried the Countess, extending them) I know not which is most dear to me."

They threw themselves at her feet: she blessed them with tears of joy and joined their hands. Both were speechless, but language was not necessary to prove their mutual transports. She raised them, and presented them to her friends, "Love my children, (said she) I think they deserve it."

When a little recovered from their joy, and seated by her, "Now listen to me, (said the Countess;) I will not repeat the conversation I had with the Count last evening, 'tis sufficient to say his offers were beyond my hopes or expectations: he frankly of himself requested my daughter and self should never be separated, for he would settle in Naples. That intention of his did away the only objection I could make. I consented to his wishes, but reserved to myself the pleasure of telling Matilda so. Last night, when I came to reflect on the sacrifice the Count was about to make, of his country, his friends, the injury his fortune must sustain, and the uncommon affection he manifested for my daughter, in paying me so great a compliment, I felt myself little in my own eyes for my acceptance of his generous offer. Dissatisfied and uneasy I said nothing to you, my love, of our conversation. This morning I consulted my friends; they were equally struck with myself at the Count's attention to my happiness; their opinion coincided with my

own—that it became my character not to accept such a resignation."
"My dear mother!" (exclaimed Matilda.) "Patience, my love; those generous friends, I presume to flatter myself, decided against their own inclinations. In one word, they approved that I should renounce Naples;
that your country, (turning to the Count) should be my country; and
that the satisfaction of entertaining the friends of my youth, who offer
to pay me a triennial visit, should be the only favour I ought to ask, or
you consistently can grant. Yes, my dear children, (added she) I will accompany you to France, and end my days under your roof."

Never was delight equal to what the Count felt at this unexpected
turn in his favour; for it could not be supposed he could renounce his
country and friends without a pang; on the contrary, only his superior
love for Matilda, and respect for the feelings of her mother, could have
induced him to offer so great a sacrifice. He thanked her, in transports
of joy. He embraced the Count and Countess. "Complete your goodness, (cried he) and add to my obligations, by making this your first
visit,—go with us to France, and let there be no drawback on my happiness."

The Countess and Matilda, urging the same request, they consented to spend three months with them.

"Now, young folks, (said the Countess, smiling) you may take a
walk and congratulate each other, conscious that you deserve the happiness that awaits you, from nobleness of mind, and a generous self-
denial, which preferred the satisfaction of others to your own gratification."

The Count availed himself of this permission, and led Matilda to
the garden, whilst the delighted mother sent for the rest of the family
and repeated the preceding scene.

Pleasure shone on every face—all were equally happy; and even
Frederic, with a repressed sigh, said, "They were deserving of each
other."

Within a week from that day the Countess of Wolfenbach gave
her hand to Lord Delby at Vienna, after a mutual agreement, that they
should divide their time equally between Germany and England, with
sometimes a visit to their friends in Paris, which was promised, on all
sides, should be reciprocal.

The Count De Bouville wrote to his sister, Madame De Clermont,
who was returned to Paris, with restored health, on the happy turn of
his affairs, and requested she would make every magnificent prepara-

tion for the reception of his guests, the Count and Countess Marcellini; the Countess Berniti and Matilda accompanying the Marchioness until proper arrangements should take place for their marriage, which all were desirous should be publicly performed at Paris, to confute the odium Mademoiselle De Fontelle had thrown upon Matilda's character.

Lord Delby and his lady had written to Mrs. Courtney, of the different events which had taken place, and requested a visit from her to Germany; the Marchioness and Matilda wrote also, and entreated the same favour.

These letters a little discomposed her at first; but as she had given up all hopes of the Count, and was not of a disposition to fret herself long on any subject, being naturally of an easy temper, she answered their letters with perfect good-humour, congratulated them on the happiness before them, and promised to visit all parties the following spring.

The parting of the friends from the Countess and Lord Delby was very painful: they were strongly entreated to accompany them, but Frederic having only another month's leave of absence to remain with his mother, the time was too short to admit of his going to Paris, and the Countess could not be persuaded to leave him; they were therefore obliged to be contented with the assurance of an early visit to the Count De Bouville in the spring, when they would come to meet Mrs. Courtney.

The Paris travellers, though much affected by taking leave, as they proceeded on their journey, recovered their spirits, and arrived without meeting any accident at Paris.

Madame De Clermont, her husband, Madame De Nancy, and Mademoiselle De Bancre waited to receive them. Great was the joy of all parties: a thousand embraces and felicitations passed between the Count's sister, Mademoiselle De Bancre and Matilda; and when the latter called to her remembrance the difference of her feelings now, and when before she had felt herself humbled by their caresses, as passing upon them in a false light, she bent herself, with a grateful adoration, to the Divine Being, who had protected her, and by such unforeseen, and apparently, untoward accidents, brought her to such unexpected happiness.

The Count Marcellini waited on the Neapolitan Minister, who came and paid his compliments to the ladies, congratulating the Countess on the recovery of such a daughter, and requesting he might have the honor of introducing them at court.

Three days after the Marchioness gave a superb entertainment: all the foreign ministers were invited, an extensive circle of friends, and among the rest, Madame Le Brun and her niece, who were just returned from England. Conscious as they were of their ill conduct, they had not the resolution to refuse being present at an entertainment where all the great world was invited, and appeared with much effrontery. When they entered, the Marchioness led them to the Countess Berniti, "The Countess Berniti, ladies, mother to the Lady Matilda, whom you had the honour of seeing with me a few months ago, as my relation." They bowed, paid their compliments, in a confused manner, and hurried on; but the Marchioness had not done with them; she observed the Imperial and Neapolitan Ambassadors were conversing with Matilda; they rather shrunk back; "Nay, ladies, (said she) you must pay your respects to the queen of the day." Mademoiselle felt extremely confused, yet resolved to put a good face on the matter; she assumed a gay and affectionate air as she advanced. The Marchioness having introduced Madame Le Brun, "And now, (said she, to Fontelle) let me present you to Lady Matilda Berniti, one of the first families in Naples, as his Excellency can bear witness; and to your Ladyship I beg leave to say, this is Mademoiselle De Fontelle, the envious traducer of your character; the despicable young woman, who, incapable of practising virtue, from the depravity of her own mind, naturally hates the good and exalted characters of those who entitle themselves to the respect and admiration of the world, and who now meets with that contempt and mortification worthless and censorious characters like her's deserve."

The struggles of Fontelle, to free her hand from the Marchioness, and the elevated voice of that lady had drawn a large circle round her. "Go, Mademoiselle, (added she) leave the presence of those you can never see without self-accusation; and may your example teach others how cautious they ought to be in judging of persons and appearances from the malignancy of their own hearts. Candour and good nature (said she, smiling) will give beauty to the most indifferent faces, whilst envy and malice will render the most beautiful persons truly contemptible."

Matilda, who had not expected this denouement, was extremely confused, and felt for the mortified Fontelle, but the numbers who crowded round her, and expressed their satisfaction, though it in some degree abated her regret, induced her to think there was little dependence on the applauses of the multitude: these very people, thought she, a few months ago encouraged the persons they now reprobate; let me not be vain of respect which only circumstances create!

Matilda thought justly; since every day's experience must convince her, fortuitous circumstance will engage the shew of esteem and respect, which the next moment of misfortune will as assuredly deprive us of, among those who are not capable of discriminating, and attach themselves only to persons gifted by fortune, and are incapable of giving merit, if in obscurity, the praise it deserves.

The two ladies having left the room, boiling with rage and indignation, and leaving a useful lesson to the envious and ill-natured, harmony was restored; everyone exerted themselves for the entertainment of others, and everyone agreed it was the most delightful evening they had ever spent; though many of them called on Mademoiselle De Fontelle the following morning, expressed their sorrow for the ill treatment she suffered, and assured her it was the most horrid entertainment; the Lady Matilda, the idol of the evening, the most vain, impertinent, conceited creature they had ever seen.

Such is the progress of envy, such the hatred of virtue, in bad minds, and such you meet with in all public circles.

In less than a fortnight after their arrival in Paris, the Count De Bouville, who had been indefatigable in his endeavours to hasten all the elegant arrangements he had projected for the reception of his bride, had the pleasure of seeing everything in proper order, and by the approbation of all their joint relations and friends, received the hand and heart of his Matilda, who all acknowledged was the only one deserving the entire affection of the accomplished and respectable Count De Bouville.

Thus, after a variety of strange and melancholy incidents, Matilda received the reward of her steadiness, fortitude, and virtuous self-denial. A consciousness of performing her several duties ensured her happiness; and when she wrote her beloved Mother St. Magdalene the happy conclusion of her adventures, "From you, (said she) I learned resignation, and a dependence on that Being who never forsakes the virtuous; from you I learned never to despair; to your precepts and prevention I am indebted for not taking the veil; and I trust, called into an elevated situation, I shall ever remember the unfortunate have claims upon the hearts of those whom God has blessed with affluence; and that, through your means, reserved to experience every blessing of life, I shall feel it my duty, by active virtues, to extend, to the utmost of my abilities, those blessings to others less fortunate than myself."

FINIS.